The Dead Tracks

Tim Weaver

W F HOWES LTD

This large print edition published in 2014 by
W F Howes Ltd
Unit 4, Rearsby Business Park, Gaddesby Lane,
Rearsby, Leicester LE7 4YH

1 3 5 7 9 10 8 6 4 2

First published in the United Kingdom in 2011
by Penguin Group

A CIP catalogue record for this book is available
from the British Library

ISBN 978 1 47126 757 4

Typeset by Palimpsest Book Production Limited,
Falkirk, Stirlingshire
Printed and bound by
www.printondemand-worldwide.com of Peterborough, England

This book is made entirely of chain-of-custody materials

For Mum and Dad

'All faces shall gather blackness . . .'

Joel i2:6

PART I

CHAPTER 1

We met in a restaurant on the Thames called Boneacres. They were sitting in a booth at the back. Rain was running down the windows and both of them were staring out at a queue of people waiting in line for the Eye. The woman looked up first. Caroline Carver. She'd been crying. The whites of her eyes were stained red, and some of her make-up had run. She was slim and well dressed, in her mid forties, but didn't wear it well: there were lines in her face – thick and dark like oil paint – that looked as if they'd been carved with a scalpel, and though she smiled as I approached, it wasn't warm. She'd been past warm. Most of the parents I dealt with were like that. The longer their kids were missing, the colder their lives became.

She slid out from the booth and we both shook hands, then she made way for her husband. James Carver. He was huge; a bear of a man. He didn't get up, just reached across the table and swallowed my hand in his. I knew a little about them already, mostly from Caroline's initial phone call a couple of days before. She'd told me they lived in an old church – converted into a four-bedroom home – from which he ran his building firm, a business he'd built up over fifteen years. Judging by the property's two-million-pound price tag, the name brands they were sporting and some of his celebrity clients, it was keeping them pretty comfortable.

He smiled at me, more genuine than his wife, and gestured to the other side of the booth. I slid in. The menu was open. The restaurant had been their suggestion, and when I looked at the prices, I was glad they were paying.

'Thanks for coming,' Carver said.

I nodded. 'It seems like a nice place.'

Both of them looked around, as if they hadn't thought about it before. Carver smiled. Caroline's eyes snapped back to the menu.

'We used to come in here before we were married,' he said. 'Back when it was a steak and seafood place.' His wife glanced at him, and he reached over and took her hand. 'Caroline tells me you used to be a journalist.'

'Once upon a time.'

'Must have been interesting.'

'Yeah, it was fun.'

He glanced at my left hand. Two of my finger-nails were sunken and cracked, a blob of white scarring prominent in the centre where the veneer would never grow back.

'Those your battle scars?' he asked.

I glanced at the nails. 'No. They got added more recently.'

'So why did you give it all up?'

I looked at him, then across to Caroline. 'My wife was dying.'

A real conversation stopper. They shifted uncomfortably. Caroline turned her gaze back to the table, then picked up her menu. He cleared his throat. Before the silence got too long, Carver reached into his jacket and brought out a photograph. Something moved in his eyes, a sadness, and then he turned it around and placed it in front of me.

'That's Megan,' he said.

When Caroline had originally called, I gave her directions to the office – but she said she wanted to meet somewhere neutral, as if coming to see me was confirmation her daughter was gone for good. After we'd arranged a time and a place, she told me a little about Megan: a good girl, part of a close family, no boyfriends, no reason to leave.

She'd been gone nearly seven months.

Two hundred thousand people go missing in the UK each year – thirty thousand in London alone – but the most powerful media story of them all is the young white female from a middle-class, two-parent family. When Megan first disappeared, there was a lot of media coverage: locally, nationally, some of it even playing out abroad. It ran for weeks, one headline after the next, every TV channel in the country reporting from outside the gates of her home. There was a name for cases

5

like hers that unravelled in the full glare of the camera lens: MWWS.

Missing White Woman Syndrome.

In the photograph they'd handed me, Megan was sitting with her mum on a beach. The sand was white, flecked with small stones and twigs and falling away to a sapphire sea. Behind Caroline and Megan, playing, was a small boy, probably four years old. He was half turned to the camera, his eyes looking into the hole he was digging.

Carver pointed at the boy. 'That's our son. Leigh.' He looked at me and could see what I was thinking: there was a thirteen-year age gap between their kids. 'I guess you could say . . .' He glanced at his wife. 'Leigh was a very pleasant surprise.'

'How old is the photograph?'

'About eight months.'

'Just before she disappeared?'

'Yes, our last holiday together, in Florida.'

Megan was very much her father's daughter. She had the same face, right down to identical creases next to the eyes, and was built like him too. Big, but not fat. She was an attractive seventeen-year-old girl: long blonde hair, beautifully kept, and olive skin that had browned appealingly in the sun.

'Tell me what happened the day she went missing.'

Both of them nodded but made no move to start. They knew this was where it began; the pain of scooping up memories, of going over old ground, of talking about their daughter in the past tense.

6

I got out a pad and a pen as a gentle nudge. Carver turned to his wife, but she gestured for him to tell the story.

'I'm not sure there's a lot to it,' he said finally. His voice was unsteady at first, but he began to find more rhythm. 'We dropped Meg off at school, and when we went to pick her up again later, she didn't come back out.'

'Did she seem okay when you dropped her off that morning?'

'Yes.'

'Nothing was up?'

He shook his head. 'No.'

'Megan didn't have a boyfriend at the time, is that right?'

'That's right,' Caroline said sharply.

Carver looked at his wife, then squeezed her hand. 'Not one that she told us about. That doesn't mean there wasn't one.'

'Did she have any boyfriends before then?'

'A couple,' Caroline said, 'but nothing serious.'

'Did you meet them?'

'Briefly. But she used to say that when she finally brought a boy home for longer than a few minutes, we'd know it was the real thing.' She attempted a smile. 'Hopefully we'll still get to see that day.'

I paused for a moment while Carver shifted up the booth and slid his arm around his wife. He looked into her eyes, and back to me.

'She never expressed a need to travel or leave London?' I asked.

Carver shook his head. 'Not unless you count university.'

'What about her friends – have you spoken to them?'

'Not personally. The police did that in the weeks after she disappeared.'

'No one knew anything?'

'No.'

I picked up the pen. 'I'll take the names and addresses of her closest friends, anyway. It'll be worth seeing them a second time.'

Caroline reached down to her handbag, opened it and brought out a green address book, small enough to slip into a jacket pocket. She handed it to me.

'All the addresses you need will be in there, including her school,' she said. 'That's Meg's book. She used to call it her Book of Life. Names, numbers, notes.'

I nodded my thanks and took it from her. 'What sort of stage would you say you're at with the police?'

'We're not really *at* a stage. We speak to them once a fortnight.' Carver stopped, shrugged. He glanced at his wife. 'To start with we made a lot of headway in a short space of time. The police told us they had some good leads. I guess we got our hopes up.'

'Did they tell you what leads they had?'

'No. It was difficult for them at the beginning.' He paused. 'We put out that reward for information,

8

so they had to field a *lot* of calls. Jamie Hart told us he didn't want to give us false hope, so he said he and his team would sort through the calls and collate the paperwork and then come back to us.'

'Jamie Hart was heading up the investigation?'

'Right.'

The waiter arrived to take our orders as I wrote Hart's name on my pad. I'd heard of him: once during my paper days when he'd led a task force trying to find a serial rapist; and once in a *Times* news story I'd pulled out of the archives on a previous case.

'So, did Hart get back to you?' I asked after the waiter was gone.

Carver rocked his head from side to side. The answer was no but he was trying to be diplomatic. 'Not in the way we would have hoped.'

'How do you mean?'

'At the beginning, they were calling us every day, asking us questions, coming to the house and taking things away. Then, a couple of months into the investigation, it all ground to a halt. The calls stopped coming as often. Officers stopped coming to the house. Now all we hear is that there's nothing new to report.' His mouth flattened. A flicker of pain. 'They would tell us if there was something worth knowing, wouldn't they?'

'They should do.'

He paused for a moment, his hand moving to his drink.

'What was the date of Megan's disappearance?'

'Monday 3 April,' Carver said.

It was now 19 October. One hundred and ninety-nine days and they hadn't heard a thing. The police tended not to get interested for forty-eight hours after a disappearance, but in my experience the first couple of days were crucial in missing persons. The longer you left it, the more you were playing with percentages. Sometimes you found the person five days, or a week, or two weeks after they vanished. But most of the time, if they didn't resurface in the first forty-eight hours it was either because they'd disappeared for good and didn't want to come home again – or their body was waiting to be found.

'When was the last time anyone saw her?'

'The afternoon of the third,' Carver said. 'She went to her first class after lunch, but didn't make the next one. She was supposed to meet her friend Kaitlin at their lockers because they both did Biology. But Megan never arrived.'

'Biology was the last lesson of the day?'

'Yes.'

'Does the school have CCTV?'

'Yes – but very limited coverage. Jamie told us they checked all the cameras, but none of them revealed anything.'

'Have you told him you've come to me?'

Carver shook his head. 'No.'

It was better that way. The best approach was going to be cold-calling Hart. The police, understandably,

didn't like outsiders stepping on their toes –
especially on active cases – and if they picked up
my scent, they'd close ranks and circle the wagons
before I even got near.

'So what's the next stage?' Carver asked.

'At a time that's convenient for you, I'd like
to come and speak to you at the house; have a
look around Megan's bedroom. I don't expect to
find anything significant, but it's something I like
to do.'

They nodded. Neither of them spoke.

'After that, I'll start working my way through
this,' I said, placing a hand on her Book of Life.
'The police have had a look at this presumably?'

'Yes,' Carver said.

'Did they find anything?'

He shrugged. 'They gave it back to us.'

Which meant no. A moment later, the waiter
returned with our meals.

'Do you think there's a chance she's alive?'
Caroline asked after he was gone.

We both looked at her, Carver turning in his
seat, shifting his bulk, as if he was surprised and
disappointed by the question. Maybe she'd never
asked it before. Or maybe he didn't want to know
the answer.

I looked at her, then at him, then back to her.

'There's always a chance.'

'Yes,' she replied. 'But do you think she's alive?'

I looked down at my meal, a lobster broken into
pieces, not wanting my eyes to betray me. But I

had to look at her eventually. And when I did, she must have seen the answer, because she slowly nodded, then started to cry.

Outside, James Carver shook my hand and we watched his wife slowly wander off along Victoria Embankment, the Houses of Parliament framed behind her. Boats moved on the Thames, the water dark and grey. Autumn was finally clawing its way out of hibernation after a warm, muggy summer.

'I don't know what you want to do about money,' he said.

'Let's talk tomorrow.'

He nodded. 'I'll be around, but Caroline might not be – she's got some work at a school in South Hackney.'

'That's fine. I'll catch up with her when she's free.'

I watched Carver head after his wife. When he got to her, he reached for her hand. She responded, but coolly, her fingers hard and rigid. When he spoke, she just shrugged and continued walking. They headed down to Westminster Pier and, as they crossed the road towards the tube station, she looked back over her shoulder at me. For a second I could see the truth: that something had remained hidden in our conversation; a trace of a secret, buried out of her husband's sight.

I just had to find out what.

★　★　★

The day had started to darken by five-thirty. I stopped in at the office on the way back from the restaurant. I'd left some notes in there, including some I'd made that morning on Megan Carver. By the time I got home, at just gone seven, the house was black. I hadn't set the alarm, so when I got in the sensors beeped gently as I moved around: first in the kitchen, then in the living room, then in the main bedroom at the end of the hall. I dumped my stuff, showered, and then spent a moment on the edge of the bed, looking at some photographs of Derryn and me.

One, right at the bottom of the pile, was of the two of us at the entrance to Imperial Beach in San Diego, back when I'd been seconded to the US to cover the 2004 elections. I was pulling her into the crook of my arm, sunglasses covering my eyes, dark hair wet from the surf. In the wetsuit I looked broad, well built and lean, every inch of my six-two. Next to me, Derryn seemed smaller than she really was, as if relying on me to keep her protected from something off camera. I liked the photo. It made me remember what it felt like to be the person she needed.

I put the pictures back into my bedside cabinet and got dressed, looking around the room at the things of hers that still remained. We'd bought the house when we still had plans to start a family, but as the ink was drying on the contracts, we found out she had breast cancer. Everything seemed to go fast after that. She battled on for two years, but our time together was short.

Some days I can handle the lack of time, can simply appreciate every moment we had together and be grateful for it. But some days all I feel inside is anger for what happened to her – and for the way I was left alone. On those days I find a way to push that feeling down and suppress it. Because, in the work I do, there are people who come at you through the chinks in your armour.

And people who feed on that weakness.

CHAPTER 2

The Carvers' house was an old Saxon church in Dartmouth Park, overlooking Hampstead Heath. There were three stained-glass windows at the front, and a half-oval oak door that tapered to a point at the top. It was a beautiful building. Vines crawled up the steel-grey brickwork, the roof a mass of dark tile and yellow moss. Two potted firs stood either side of the door. The whole place was set behind imposing gate-posts and an attractive gravel drive that curved around to a back garden. There was an intercom on one of the posts outside, but James Carver had already left the gate ajar, anticipating my arrival.

The gravel was a useful alarm call. Carver looked up as I moved through the gates, half bent over a bucket of water, washing down the back of a black Range Rover Sport with tinted windows and spotless steel rims. In the double garage behind him was a Ford pick-up with building supplies in the bed and a gleaming red Suzuki motorbike.

'David,' he said, dropping a sponge into the bucket. We shook hands. 'I like the car.'

I nodded at the Range Rover, soapsuds sliding down its bumper. He glanced back at it, but didn't say anything. I figured he was trying to play down the fact that his supercharged five-litre all-terrain vehicle was worth more than some people's houses. Or maybe he genuinely didn't care any more. Money didn't mean a lot when it couldn't buy back the only thing that mattered to you.

He ushered me through the front door.

Inside it was huge. Oak floorboards and thick carpets. A living room that led into a diner that led into a kitchen. The kitchen was open plan, steel and glass, the walls painted cream. Above, the ceiling soared up into an ornate cove, and there was a balcony that ran across three sides of the interior wall, with a staircase up to it. Off the balcony, I could make out two bedrooms and a bathroom.

'You designed this?'

He nodded. 'Well, the balcony portion of it. The church has been here a lot longer than any of us.'

'It's beautiful.'

'Thank you. We've been very fortunate.' A pause. The significance of what he'd said hit home. 'In some ways, anyway.'

I followed him across to the kitchen.

'You want some coffee?'

'Black would be great.'

He removed two mugs from a cupboard. 'I don't know what you want to do,' he said, filling both. 'Megan's room is upstairs. You're welcome to head

16

up there and have a look around. Or, if you prefer, I can show you.'

'I might have a look around by myself,' I said, taking the coffee from him. 'But I do have some questions for you.'

'Sure.' He smiled, and I realized it was a defence mechanism. A way to hide the pain. 'Whatever it takes.'

We moved through to the living room. At the back of the room, the Carvers' son Leigh was on all fours directing a plastic car under a telephone stand. He looked up as we entered, and when his father told him to say hello, he mumbled something and returned to the car.

I removed a pen and pad. 'So let's talk a little more about 3 April.'

'The day she went missing.'

'Right. Did you always drop her off at school?'

'Most mornings.'

'Some mornings you didn't?'

'Occasionally Caroline did. If my business has a contract further afield I like to go along to the site for the first couple of weeks. After that, I tend to leave it to the foreman to take care of, and do all the paperwork from home. That's when I took . . .' He paused. 'When I take Megan to school and drop Leigh off at nursery.'

'So you had a site visit on 3 April?'

'Yes.'

'Which is why Caroline dropped her off?

'Correct.'

'Did she pick Megan up as well?'

'No, that was me.'

'What happened?'

'I parked up outside,' he said. 'Same spot, every day. But Megan never came out. It was as simple as that. She went in, and never came out.'

I took down some notes. 'What was Megan studying?'

'The sciences – Physics, Chemistry, Biology.'

'Did you ever meet her teachers?'

'A couple of times.'

'What were they like?'

'They seemed nice. She was a good student.'

He gave me their names and I added them to my pad. Then I changed direction, trying to keep him from becoming too emotional. 'Did Megan have a part-time job anywhere?'

'She worked at a video store on alternate weekends.'

'Did she like it?'

'Yeah. It earned her some money.'

'Who else worked there?'

'Names? I don't know. You'd have to go and ask.'

'What about places she used to go?'

'You mean pubs and clubs?'

'I mean anything,' I said. 'Anywhere she liked to go.'

'You'd have to ask her friends about the places they used to go on a weekend. When they all got paid, they'd often go into the city. But I'm not sure where they used to go.'

'What about places you used to take her?'

'We often used to head up country – the Peak District, the Lake District, the Yorkshire Dales. Caroline and I love the open spaces there. London suffocates you after a while. We started taking Meg up north as soon as she was old enough to walk.'

'Do you think she could have gone to one of those places?'

He shrugged. 'I don't know whether she would have gone north when I don't know why she left in the first place.'

I'd asked them both about boyfriends the day before, but I wanted to ask them again individually. What you learned quickly in missing persons was that every marriage had secrets – and that one half of the couple always knew more than the other, especially when kids were involved. 'As far as you know, she didn't have a boyfriend?'

'As far as I know.'

'What's your gut feeling?'

'My gut feeling is it's a possibility she met someone.' He moved a little in his seat, coming to the edge of it. 'Do you think that's our best hope?'

'I think it's worth pursuing. Kids Megan's age tend to disappear for two reasons: either they're unhappy at home, or they've run away with someone – probably someone their parents don't approve of. It doesn't sound like she was unhappy at home, so that's why I'm asking about boyfriends.

We may find out Megan hasn't run off with someone.' I paused, looked at him. 'Or we may find out she has.'

'But if she'd run off with someone, wouldn't she have seen the press conferences we did? The Megan I know wouldn't have ignored them. She wouldn't have ignored the pain she was putting us through. She would have called us.'

I looked at him, then away – but he'd seen the answer, and it wasn't the one he wanted. It was the one where she didn't come home alive.

Megan's room was beautifully presented and had barely been touched since her disappearance. A big bay window looked out over Hampstead Heath, wardrobes either side of it. A three-tiered bookcase was on the right, full of science textbooks. Opposite the window, close to the door, was a small desk with a top-of-the-range MacBook sitting on it, still open. Photographs surrounded the laptop: Megan with her friends; Megan holding Leigh when he was a baby; Megan with her mum and dad. There was also a rocking chair in one corner of the room, soft toys looking out, and a poster of a square-jawed Hollywood heart-throb on the wall above that.

I booted up the MacBook and went through it. The desktop was virtually empty, everything tidied into folders. Homework assignments. Word documents. University prospectuses as PDF files. Clicking on Safari, I moved through her bookmarks, her history, her cookies and her download history – but, unless you counted a few illegal songs, nothing stood out. There was a link to her Facebook profile in the browser – the email and password automatically logged – but the only activity in the last seven months was the creation of a group dedicated to her memory. Judging by the comments, most people were assuming she wasn't coming home.

Both wardrobes were full of clothes and shoes, but the second one had a couple of plastic storage boxes stacked towards the back. I took them out and flipped the lid off the top one: it was full of pictures. The younger Megan got in the photographs, the less like her father she became. As a young girl, she was a little paler with strikingly white hair, and without any of the similarities that were so startling in more recent pictures. Later pictures were less worn by age, her parents older, her face starting to mirror some of the shape of her father's.

I opened up the next box.

A digital camera was inside. I took it out, switched it on and started cycling through the photographs. There were twenty-eight in all, mostly of Leigh. A couple near the end were of Megan and what must have been her friends, and in the final one she was standing outside what looked like the entrance to a block of flats. I used the zoom and moved in closer: the entrance doors had glass panels in them that reflected back the day's

21

light in two creamy blocks. A sliver of a brick wall on the right-hand side. Nothing else.

I returned to her MacBook and booted up iPhoto, hoping to find a bigger version – but none of the pictures on the camera were on the computer. She hadn't got around to downloading them. I checked the date on the camera: 6 March. Twenty-eight days before she disappeared. Zooming in again, I studied the photo a second time, but the reflection in the glass would have been the most useful identifier of where she was and it was full of light. Then, when I came back to her face, I noticed something.

Her smile.

It was a smile I hadn't seen in any of the other pictures of her. For the first time, she didn't look like a girl. She looked like a woman.

Because she's posing for someone she's attracted to.

'Find anything?'

I turned. Carver was standing in the doorway.

'I'm not sure,' I said, and held up the camera and the storage box. 'Can I take these?'

'Of course.' He came further in. 'I've been through those pictures hundreds of times. So have the police. Some days you feel like you've missed something. You think you've let something slip by. Then, when you go back, you only find what you found before. But maybe this whole thing needs a fresh pair of eyes.'

He moved further in and picked up an early photograph of Megan. I watched his eyes move across the picture, soaking up the memories. When he finally looked up, I could see he was trying to prevent his eyes filling with tears.

'Do you know where this is?' I asked him, handing him the camera.

He looked at the picture and studied it; shook his head.

'No.'

'You didn't take it?'

'No.'

'Any idea who might have?'

He shrugged. 'Maybe one of her friends.'

The phone started ringing downstairs. Carver apologized and disappeared. After he was gone, I went through the rest of the box. More photos, some letters, old jewellery.

Every trace of a life Megan had left behind.

It was almost lunch by the time I left. The sun had gone in, clouds scattered across the sky. In the distance I could see rain moving up from the heart of the city.

I opened my old BMW 3 Series, threw my pad on to the passenger seat and turned back to Carver, who had walked me out.

'I'd like to speak to your wife,' I said. *Alone.*

'Of course. It's just, I'm out on a site visit tomorrow . . .'

'That's fine. I'd like to keep things moving if possible, so if you can tell her that I'm going to call in, that would be great.'

'Sure. No problem.'

Afterwards, as I drove off, I watched him in the rear-view mirror disappearing back through the gates of his house. He looked like he'd had the wind knocked out of him. Give it a few weeks, and it might look like he'd had his heart ripped out too.

CHAPTER 3

There was a diner half a mile down the road from Megan's school. I sat at the window, ordered a bacon sandwich, then took out Megan's Book of Life. The previous night, when I'd glanced at it, it had been difficult to gain any kind of clarity. It was just sixty pages of random notes. The book was sectioned alphabetically, but none of her entries corresponded to the relevant letter. Where names should have been, there were phone numbers. Where phone numbers were supposed to be, there were names.

I flipped back to the start. On the first page she'd written her name and *Megan's Book of Life* in red ballpoint. *Contact Me!* had been scribbled underneath that, with two numbers alongside: one I recognized as her home phone number, the other her mobile. The police would have been through her phone records, and checked her last calls, incoming and outgoing. They would have been through her email too. I'd need to get hold of her phone records through my contacts, but the police had passed on login details for Megan's email to her parents, presumably at the Carvers' request.

They, in turn, had passed them on to me. If there was anything worth finding there, or anything crucial to the investigation, it was hard to believe the police would have been giving the login out, even to her parents, but – like her phone records – it was something else that needed to be ticked off the list.

Midway through the book, I spotted a name I recognized. *Kaitlin*. Carver had mentioned her over lunch the day before. She was the girl Megan was supposed to have met up with on the way to her Biology class. Except Megan never arrived. Kaitlin's name was in a big heart, as was a third – Lindsey Watson. I wrote down the names and phone numbers for both of them.

When I was done, a waitress with a face like the weather appeared at my table and threw my plate down in front of me without saying anything. Once she was gone, I took a bite of the sandwich and watched a news report playing out on a TV in the corner of the diner. A camera panned along the Thames. It looked like London City Airport.

'. . . taken to intensive care with hypothermia. Her condition was originally described as critical, but she has continued to improve, and hospital staff told Sky News they expected her to be released tomorrow. Police still haven't issued personal details for the woman, but sources have told us they believe her to be in the region of forty-five to fifty years of age. In other news, a farmer in . . .'

I finished my sandwich and moved through the book again, front to back. There were a lot of names. Maybe as many as thirty. Only six were male. I added the guys to the list, then paid the bill and headed for Megan's school.

Newcross Secondary School was a huge red-brick Victorian building midway between Tufnell Park and Holloway Road. I left the car out front, and headed for the entrance. Inside, the place was deserted. I passed a couple of classrooms and saw lessons had already started, kids looking on, half interested, inside. The main reception was at the far end of a long corridor that eventually opened up on to big windows with views of the school's football pitches. The interior decor had time-travelled in from 1974. A couple of thin sliding glass panels on a chunk of fake granite separated three secretaries from the outside world. They were all perched at teak desks on faded medical-green chairs.

I knocked on the glass. All three were fierce-looking women. Two of them paid me no attention whatsoever, the other glanced in my direction, eyed me, then decided I was at least worth getting up for. She slid the glass panel back, glancing at the pad in my hands. Her eyes – like Carver's the day before – drifted across my fingernails. What no one got to see were the other, even worse scars from the same case. It had been almost ten months and, although I'd made a full recovery, some days I could still feel the places I'd been beaten and tortured. My back. My hands. My feet. Perhaps a dull ache would always be there, like a residue, reminding me of how close I'd been to dying and how I was going to make sure it never happened again.

I got out a business card and placed it down on the counter in front of the woman. 'My name's David Raker. I'm doing some work for the parents of Megan Carver.'

The name instantly registered. Behind her, both women looked up.

'What do you mean, "work"?'

'I mean I'm trying to find out where she went.'

They all nodded in sync. I had their attention now.

'Is the headmaster around?'

'Did you make an appointment?'

I shook my head. 'No.'

She frowned, but being here because of Megan seemed to soften her. She ran a finger down a diary.

'Take a seat while I page him.'

I smiled my thanks and sat down in a cramped waiting area to the right of the reception. More medical-green chairs. Posters warning of the dangers of drugs. A vase of fake blue flowers. Some kids passed by, looked at me, then carried on. Everything smelt of furniture polish.

A telephone rang; a long, unbroken noise. One of the receptionists picked it up. The glass panel was now closed, but she was looking at me as she spoke. 'Okay,' she said a couple of times, and put the phone down. She leaned forward, and slid open the glass. 'He'll be five minutes.'

Fifteen minutes later, he finally arrived.

He walked straight up to the reception area, a hurried, flustered look on his face – like he'd run full pelt from wherever he'd come from – and followed his secretaries' eyes across the hall to where I was sitting. He came over. 'Steven Bothwick.'

I stood and shook his hand. 'David Raker.'

'Nice to meet you,' he said, using a finger to slide some hair away from his face. He was losing what he had left, and not doing a great job of disguising it.

'I'm here about Megan Carver,' I said.

'Yes,' he replied. 'A lovely girl.'

He directed me to a door further along the corridor with his name on it. His office was small, crammed with books and folders. A big window behind his desk looked out over the football pitches. Bothwick pulled a chair out from the wall and placed it down on the other side of his desk. 'Would you like something to drink?'

'No, I'm fine, thanks.'

He nodded, pushing some folders out of his immediate way and shuffling in under the desk. He was in his fifties and barely scraping five-eight, but had an intensity about him, a determination, his expression fixed and strong.

I reached into my pocket and got out another

business card. 'Just so you're clear, I'm not a police officer. I used to be a journalist.'

A frown worked its way across his face. 'A journalist?'

'*Used* to be. For two years, I've been tracing missing people. That's my job now. The Carvers came to me and asked me to look into Megan's disappearance for them.'

'Why?'

'Because the police investigation has hit a brick wall.'

He nodded. 'I feel so sorry for her family. Megan was a fantastic student with a bright future. When the police came here, I told them the same.' He took my card and looked at it. 'Yours is quite a big career change.'

'Not as big as you might think.' I watched him look at what was written on it – DAVID RAKER, MISSING PERSONS INVESTIGATOR – and across the desk at me.

He handed me back my card. 'So what can I help you with?'

'I've got a couple of questions.'

'Okay.'

I took out my pad and set it down on the desk.

'Her parents told me they dropped her off on the morning of 3 April, and she never came out again that afternoon. Do pupils have to sign in?'

'Well, we take a register first thing in the morning and again after lunch, yes. But only for those in years seven through to eleven.'

'That's eleven to sixteen years of age, right?'

30

'Right.'

'So Megan was too old?'

'Yes. Our A-level students are treated more like adults. We encourage them to turn up to class – but we won't come down on absences.'

'So say I missed a couple of days of school – would anyone notice? And who would it get reported to – you?'

'Yes. If a pupil was continually missing lessons, the teacher would inform me.'

'But a few absences here and there . . .?'

He shrugged. 'They may get reported, or they may not. It depends on the student. Some contribute so little to lessons that their presence may be felt less. I guess a teacher may not, in that instance, notice them as quickly. But Megan . . . I think we'd have seen straight away if she'd been missing a lot of school time.'

'She was a good student?'

'In the top three per cent here, yes.'

'And never got into any trouble?'

He shook his head. 'Absolutely not.'

'I understand she had Physics and then Biology for the last two periods of the day, and that she attended the Physics part of that?'

'Right.'

'Her teacher confirmed that?'

'Yes. And the fifteen other students who were in there with her.'

'How long's the walk between classrooms?'

'No walk at all. They're in the same block.

Chemistry's on the top floor, Physics on the second and Biology on the ground.'

'There's no CCTV in that part of the school, right?'

'Sadly not. We have cameras, but we can't afford to have them in every building – not on the budget we're handed.' He turned in his chair and pointed to a diagram on the wall. It was a plan of the school campus with tiny CCTV icons scattered across it. 'Those are the cameras we have. One at the entrance, one on the car park, one at reception, one outside the English and Maths block, and one trained on the playing fields.'

'Why only English and Maths?'

'It's the block furthest away from here.'

'Are there multiple entrances to the school?'

'Not really. Well, not *official* entrances, anyway. Some of the students live in the estates beyond the football pitches, so they climb over the fence and come across the fields. There's a rear car park behind the Sixth Form block as well, where some of the students in Years 11 and 12 park their cars, if they're lucky enough to have them. That's fenced off too, but only to about waist height.'

'So if she was going to leave the school grounds, and not be caught on CCTV, her best bet would have been jumping the fence at the back of the Sixth Form car park?'

'Correct. I think that's what the police concluded too.'

I reached down and got out Megan's Book of

Life. 'Would it be possible to speak to a couple of students?'

'Megan's friends?'

'Yes.' I looked down at the pad. 'Lindsey Watson and Kaitlin Devonish?'

He nodded, picked up the phone and punched in a four-digit number. On the other side of the door, I heard a phone ring in reception. 'Linda, I need Lindsey Watson and Kaitlin Devonish sent around as soon as possible, please.' He put the phone down. 'Anyone else?'

I looked down at the pad, turned it around and slid it across the desk to him. 'The six people at the bottom,' I said, pointing to the boys' names. 'Are any of them students here?'

He removed a pair of glasses from the top pocket of his jacket and popped them on, studying the names for a moment. 'Yes.'

'All of them?'

'I recognize all of them but one.'

'Who's the odd one out?'

'Anthony "A. J." Grant.'

'You don't recognize that name?'

'No,' he replied, taking off his glasses. He got up and went to a filing cabinet at the back of the room. It had three drawers, each filled with the same Manila folders, each folder tabbed. Presumably he liked doing things the old-fashioned way. He went to G, but didn't find anything.

'He's definitely not a student here.'

'Every student in the school is in there?'

'Every current student, yes.'

I brought the pad back across towards me and put a question mark next to A. J. Grant. 'The other names on here—' I pushed it back towards him '—are they all in the same year as Megan?'

'Yes.'

'Is it going to be possible to speak to them?'

'Certainly – but only Lindsey and Kaitlin today. Four of them are on a field trip to Normandy. The other . . . Well, the truth is, I don't know where Charles Bryant is. He missed a lot of school last year because his mother died. This week is the one-year anniversary of her passing, and he hasn't been in at all. I've tried calling his father, but have had no response. I even sent one of the teachers round to his house, but no one was home. I've no idea where he is, and to be honest, I think this week he's best left alone.'

'Would it be possible to get an address for him?'

'I can't give out addresses, I'm afraid.'

There was a knock at the door. Bothwick looked up.

'Come in.'

Two girls entered. They shuffled forward, their eyes flitting between the both of us. One was beautiful: petite with a dusting of make-up, slim and womanly. The other was plainer, bigger, dressed more conservatively, but smiling.

'Kaitlin, Lindsey, this is Mr Raker. He's looking into Megan's disappearance for her mum and dad.'

I stood. 'David.'

'Lindsey,' the bigger girl beamed.

The other girl hesitated.

'Kaitlin,' she said quietly. She had an accent.

I turned to Bothwick. 'Is it okay if I take them somewhere?'

He looked completely taken aback, as if I'd threatened to burn down the school. 'What do you mean?'

'I mean, is it okay if I take the girls for a coffee?'

'Why?'

'I'd just like to speak to them in private.'

He eyed me suspiciously. 'I'd prefer them to stay on school premises.'

'Fine. So is there somewhere we can go where we won't get interrupted?'

'You could go to the canteen.'

'There won't be any kids in there?'

'We've already had lunch.'

I looked at my watch. Two-thirty.

'Okay, we'll go there.'

CHAPTER 4

The canteen was long and narrow, the floor tiled in old hardwood, the ceilings high and sculptured in white plaster. Along one side were four huge windows. Light poured in, even as rain started spattering against the glass. Opposite was the kitchen, with big women in white uniforms cleaning out huge vats full of half-finished food.

On the walk over, Lindsey had done all the talking. The last time she'd seen Megan was before the Carvers went to Florida.

'She seemed fine,' she said, turning to her friend. 'Didn't she, Kay?'

Kaitlin glanced at me, then at her friend, and nodded.

'So how come you didn't see her between the time she got back and the time she disappeared?' I asked Lindsey.

'I was on a student exchange in Italy.'

'What about you, Kaitlin?'

Kaitlin glanced briefly at me. She looked nervous, like she might be in trouble. The police had probably been to her home, asking questions and trying

to work the angles. Sometimes that had the opposite effect. You ended up pushing harder because
you felt like they were closing up, but they were
only closing up because they felt like they weren't
helping. Maybe, in some way, Kaitlin felt responsible. If she'd met Megan outside the penultimate
class of the day, instead of by the lockers, she might
never have vanished. Instead she said goodbye to
her friend after lunch and never saw her again.

'Can you tell me what happened?' I asked her,
after we were all seated.

'I told the police.'

'I know you did. I know you helped them out a
lot. I'm just trying to see if there are any small
things that they might have missed. You're not in
trouble. I'm just here to help Megan's parents and
find out what happened to her.'

She nodded but still seemed nervous. Her hands
were flat to her legs, one of them rubbing the top
of her thigh gently.

'Where are you from, by the way?'

She looked at me, frowned. 'Tufnell Park.'

'No. I mean, originally.'

She was still frowning. 'South Africa.'

'I thought so. Nice part of the world. I used to
live in South Africa.'

For the first time something shifted in her
expression: the hardness, the stillness, replaced by
a slight softening of the muscles. 'What part?' she
asked.

'Johannesburg.'

She nodded, but her face hardly moved this time, as if she wasn't actually listening to me. I studied her for a moment, the look in her face, her hand moving against her leg, and for the first time wondered if it was shyness preventing her from opening up or something else.

'Kaitlin?'

She turned and faced me.

'Can you go over what happened?'

'I spent lunchtime with Meg,' she said quietly. 'Then, first period, I had History, and she had Physics. Between periods, we were meant to meet at the lockers in the Science block, but I waited there and she didn't turn up.'

'Why meet at the lockers?'

She frowned, looked at Lindsey. 'We always did that.'

'Before Biology?'

'Yes. Unless we had a free period together before. If we had a free period, Linds, Meg and me would probably go to the library or the Sixth Form block.'

'Did Megan seem all right that day?'

'Fine.'

'She didn't seem off colour or worried about anything?'

'No.'

'Just like her normal self?'

'Pretty much.'

I paused. 'Pretty much?'

Kaitlin shrugged. 'Like I told the police, she said

she'd had a headache for a couple of days. Nothing major. Just kind of a fuzzy head.'

I wrote that down, and then we started talking about Megan generally – what she was like, her personality, how she'd scored straight As in her GCSEs. Lindsey did all of the talking. It didn't amount to much. Most of it dovetailed with what the Carvers had already told me: serious about school, serious about making a career for herself, serious about not letting anything get in the way. Basically the most unlikely runaway you could get.

'Did Megan get on all right with the teachers here?'

'Who gets on with *teachers*?' Lindsey said.

'She wasn't close to one of them in particular?'

Lindsey frowned.

'I'm looking for reasons why she might have disappeared.'

Her mouth formed an O, as if she suddenly got the line of questioning, then she shook her head. 'I don't think so. In science, a lot of the teachers are women anyway.'

I nodded. 'Her dad said she used to work in a video store . . .'

'Yeah,' Lindsey replied. 'She did two weekends a month. But I think that place closed down about three months ago.'

'Okay. But did she ever meet anyone while she was there?'

'I don't think so.' She paused, looked at Kaitlin,

got no help and turned to me again. 'No one apart from Charlie – but she already knew him.'

'Who's Charlie?'

'Charlie Bryant.'

'*Charles* Bryant?'

Lindsey nodded again.

'The kid whose mum died?'

'Yeah.'

'Were the two of them friendly?'

'They went out for a while.'

'For how long?'

'I don't know . . . couple of months.'

'When was this?'

'After his mum died.'

'A year ago?'

'Yeah. He was hard work, though.' She paused, as if she might have just realized why. 'I mean, he'd just lost his mum. You can understand that.'

'Is that why they split up?'

'Megan said she felt sorry for him, but she didn't really fancy him. After a couple of months, she called it off.'

'How did he take it?'

'He was upset. He really, really liked her. But he seemed to be okay.'

'Was he still working in the video store when Megan disappeared?'

'I think so.'

'So they still spoke?'

'Yeah.'

'And got on pretty well?'

40

'Yeah, I'd say so . . .' Lindsey glanced at Kaitlin. 'Wouldn't you, Kay?'

Kaitlin looked at me and nodded. I underlined Charles Bryant's name. 'Does the name A. J. Grant mean anything to either of you?' The blank expressions told me everything I needed to know. I changed tack. 'Did you have any favourite pubs or clubs you used to go to?'

'Tiko's,' Lindsey said immediately.

'That's a club?'

'Yeah. In the West End.'

I made a note of it. 'Any others?'

They looked at each other. 'Not really,' Lindsey continued. 'I mean, we go to lots of places, but Tiko's is the place with the best music.'

I took out Megan's digital camera and scrolled through to the picture of her standing in front of the block of flats. 'Did either of you take this?'

They studied it, Lindsey holding the camera. 'Where is she?'

I shrugged. 'I don't know. You don't recognize it?'

'No,' Lindsey said, shaking her head.

'Kaitlin?'

'No,' she said.

I nodded, took the camera back and briefly glanced at Kaitlin. Her eyes had left mine, and she'd gone cold again. Shut down.

Something was definitely up.

Bothwick wasn't there when I got back. I glanced at the reception where one of the secretaries was taking a phone call, and then quickly moved inside his office, pushing the door shut behind me. I didn't have much time.

Two files were perched on the edge of the desk, where he'd left them. Kaitlin and Lindsey. I left Lindsey's where it was and picked up Kaitlin's. A school photograph of her, probably a couple of years younger. Below that, a list of the subjects she was taking and an attendance record. At a quick glance, it looked pretty good. No long absences, no comments in the spaces provided. On the next page was her home address in Tufnell Park, and on the final one her last school report. At the bottom: A for Drama.

So she definitely wasn't shy.

I snapped the file closed, placed it back on the desk and opened up the top drawer of the filing cabinet. The Bryant file was about eight in. Inside was a photo of him. He was a handsome kid; dark hair, bright eyes. Underneath was a top sheet with his address on. He lived with his father near Highgate Wood.

Then, outside, I could hear footsteps.

Bothwick.

I closed the file, dropped it back into the cabinet drawer and closed it as quietly as I could. A second later, he appeared in the doorway. 'Ah!' he said. 'Sorry about that.'

'No problem.'

'Did you get everything you needed?'

I smiled, briefly eyeing the files again to see they

were definitely where he'd left them. Then I shook his hand and told him I did.

Lindsey was right: the video store Megan used to work in was shut. Not just shut for the day. Shut for good. I drove past it and headed along Holloway Road to the Bryant home in Highgate, a three-storey townhouse with a double garage and a wrought-iron porch.

There wasn't a single light on anywhere inside.

I rang the doorbell and waited. Nothing. No movement. No sound from inside. As rain started to fall, spitting at first, then coming harder, I stepped down from the porch and wandered around to the side. A path led parallel to the property, behind a locked gate. I could see a sliver of garden but not much else. Walking back to the front door, I rang the doorbell again – but when no one answered for a second time, I headed back to the car in the rain.

CHAPTER 5

Three weeks after Christmas, a leaflet got posted through my door. It was advertising a support group for widows and widowers under forty-five. I wasn't a great believer in fate. In fact, I hardly believed in it at all. But I understood why people might when that leaflet landed on my doormat. At the time I was fresh off a case that had almost killed me, and I'd spent Christmas alone watching old home movies of Derryn. Physically and emotionally, I was low. So in the second week of January, I decided, on the spur of the moment, to go along, not expecting it to make much of a difference. Nine months later, it was still part of my weekly routine.

Most Tuesdays we met in a community college in Acton, in a room that smelt of stale coffee. But once a month, we all chipped in and went for a meal somewhere. If I hadn't already agreed to go, I might have cancelled it to concentrate on the Carver case, but it was too late to back out now. Instead, I headed from the Bryant house to my office in Ealing, picked up a change of clothes and some deodorant, and then drove to the restaurant. It was a Thai place in Kew, close to the river.

Something sizzled in the kitchen as I entered, the smell of coconut and soy sauce filling the air. There were fourteen of them sitting at a big table by one of the windows. The woman who ran the group was a short, dumpy 32-year-old called Jenny. Her husband had suffered a heart attack running for a train at King's Cross. She saw me, came over and pecked me on the cheek. I'd liked Jenny pretty much from the first time I'd talked to her. She was lively, quick-witted and fun, but she had an understanding of people; an ability to read and connect with them. We walked to the table together, and I apologized to everyone for being late, shaking hands and saying hellos to some of the regulars. There were two spaces left: one was in the middle next to an accountant called Roger, who, after a couple of glasses of red wine, always started talking about the brake horsepower of his Mazda RX-8; the other was right at the end, next to two faces I hadn't seen before.

'David, we've got a couple of new arrivals tonight,' Jenny said. She leaned in to me as we walked towards them. 'I was hoping you could keep them entertained for me.'

Jenny introduced them as Aron Crane and Jill White. They'd both lost their partners, and had got to know each other by sharing a morning coffee-shop routine. I wondered whether they'd since got together, but they sat apart from one

45

another at the table, and – as we got talking – reminisced about their partners in a way that made it obvious they weren't a couple.

We ordered, and spent the next half an hour drifting through polite conversation: the weather, the traffic, a local MP who had been caught with a rent boy and his trousers round his ankles in a toilet in Bayswater. Both of them seemed pleasant enough. She was closer to my age, maybe just the wrong side of forty, and had deep blue eyes – how you imagined the sea would look in places you couldn't afford to go – slight imperfections in her skin, like acne scars, and a small mark just above the bump of her chin. Both she was acutely aware of. When she talked, her hands automatically went to her face, the fingers of one hand resting against the curve of her jaw, the other tucking her blonde hair behind her ears. It was an appealing quality: a kind of underlying shyness.

He was in his mid-to-late thirties, dark brown hair, the same colour eyes and a slightly bent nose, as if it had once been broken and not reset properly. He was dressed conservatively – collared shirt, grey trousers, plain jacket – and if I'd had to take a guess, I would have said he was a City suit, burning in the fires of middle-management hell. He had a put-upon look, as if he could never quite get his head above water.

'So what is it you do, David?' he asked as the food arrived.

'I find missing people.'

'Like an investigator?'

'Yeah, a bit like one.' I smiled. 'Except I don't have a badge to flash and I don't get to kick down doors. Much.'

Aron laughed. Jill gave a thin smile, as if I'd just offended her. I tried to work out what I'd said. *Maybe the police comment.*

Aron looked at her, then back at me. 'Jill's husband used to be a policeman. He was . . .' He looked at her again and she nodded, giving him permission to tell the story. 'He died while on duty. Shot.' He paused. 'And she's still trying to find out who did it.'

'Oh, I'm really sorry,' I said.

She held up a hand. 'It's okay. It's been nearly a year – I really should be better at hiding my emotions.' She smiled for real this time.

The conversation moved back into more general subjects – films, sport, more on the weather – before it led to why we were all in London. Jill was in marketing, and had only recently moved to the city after her husband got a job with the Met; Aron confirmed what I'd suspected – that he was in finance – and worked for an investment bank in Canary Wharf. Eventually, things came full circle and returned to my work.

'So do you enjoy what you do?' Jill asked.

'Yeah, most of the time.' I held up my left hand and wiggled the fingers where the nails were damaged. 'Though not always. Sometimes it just hurts.'

'How did you do that?'

I paused, looking down at my fingers. 'Some people just prefer to remain hidden,' I said, trying to make light of it, trying to deflect any further questions.

It was just easier that way.

Outside, while a couple of them – including Aron – were sorting out the bill, I got talking to Jill on her own. The night was cold. Above us, the skies opened for a moment and the moon moved into view; then it was gone again behind banks of dark cloud.

'Thank you for keeping us company tonight, David,' she said. 'I realize it's probably not fun being lumbered with the new people.'

'It was good to meet you both.'

'I'm really glad Aron persuaded me to come along. I wasn't sure about it, I must admit. But I think this'll be good for me. As you know, we were fairly new to the city when Frank died; I mean, we have friends dotted all around the country, but not too many here in London. And I've basically spent the last year not going out.'

'Everyone here will understand that part.' I glanced inside at Aron and then back to Jill. 'So did you two just bump into each other?'

'Pretty much. Aron gets his morning coffee from the same place as me. I just said hello one day and then, after that, we gradually started chatting and, well . . . here we are.' She stopped. Studied me, as if turning something over in her head. 'Actually, we were thinking of going out for a drink Friday night. You're quite welcome to come.'

She looked at me, her eyes dancing in the light from the restaurant. I looked inside at Aron, laughing at something Jenny had said to him, then back to Jill.

'I don't want to step on any toes.'

Her eyes followed mine. '*Aron?*'

I nodded.

'Oh, no – we're just friends. I'm not ready for anything like that.' She glanced inside. 'Why don't I take your number? I can drop you a text, or give you a call, and if you decide you'd like to come along, then you can. But there's no pressure.'

I gave her my number. As she was putting it into her phone, she looked in at Aron again. Maybe she wasn't ready. Maybe he wasn't either. But they definitely felt something for one another, even if it was only a kinship. And I didn't want to get in the way, because I knew a little of how that felt; of finally finding a connection with someone in the shadows left behind.

CHAPTER 6

My parents had been gone for three years by the time Derryn died, and I'd been an only child. No brothers. No sisters. I'd relied mostly on friends at first, and – for a while – they would drop in on rotation. But then things gradually started to change. Before Derryn died, we'd all joke around, laugh at each other, get into beer-fuelled arguments about football and films. After I buried her, none of that seemed to matter any more.

Only one person ever understood that.

When I got home just after eleven, I looked across the fence into next door's front room and saw my neighbour Liz leaning over her laptop. Liz had been different from everyone else, despite the fact she'd never had any right to be. She'd moved in three weeks after Derryn died and didn't know me at all. But, as we started to talk, she became the person who would sit there and listen to me – night after night, week after week – working my way back through my marriage.

About three or four months in, I started to realize she felt something for me. She never said anything, or even really acted on it. But it was there. A sense that, when I was ready, she would be waiting. When I had needed it, she'd given me practical help too. She was a brilliant solicitor, running her own firm out of offices in the city. When my case before Christmas had gone bad, she'd sat with me in a police interview room as they tried to unravel what had happened and why. In the aftermath, I'd lied to the police and, deep down, I knew Liz could tell. But she never confronted me, and never mentioned it. She understood how the loss of my wife had changed the need for me to confide in someone, and seemed willing to ride it out.

As I stepped up on to the porch, my security light kicked in. Next door, she clocked the movement. Her eyes narrowed, and then I passed into the full glow of the light. She broke out into a smile and got to her feet, waving me towards her. I nodded, moved back down the drive, and up the path to her front porch. The door was already open, framing her as she stood in the kitchen searching in a cupboard.

'Hello, Mr Raker,' she said, looking up as she brought down a top-of-the-range grinder. On the counter was a bag of coffee beans, wrapped in silver foil.

'Elizabeth. How are you?'

She shook her head. She hated being called Elizabeth.

'I'm good. You?'

'Fine. You been in court today?'

'Tomorrow.'

'Oh – so are you sure you want me bothering you?'

'You're a nice distraction,' she said, and flashed me a smile.

The house was tidy and still had that 'just moved in' feel, even though she had lived there for nearly two years. The living room had a gorgeous open fireplace, finished in black marble with a stone surround. Logs were piled up in alcoves either side, and a small wooden angel, its wings spread, was standing where a fire should have been. The rest of the room was minimalist: two sofas, both black, a TV in the corner, a pot plant next to that. There was a Denon sound system beneath the front window. On the only shelf, high above the sofas, were four pictures, all of Liz and her daughter. She'd married young, had her daughter shortly after, and divorced soon after that. Despite Liz only being forty-three, her daughter Katie was already in her third year of university at Warwick.

I sat in the living room. She closed the top on the grinder and set it in motion, the noise like tractor wheels on stony ground, the smell of coffee filling the house. When she came through, she pulled the kitchen door most of the way shut and perched herself opposite me.

'So what have you been up to?'

'It was support group night.'

'Ah, right, of course. How was that?'

'Pretty good. I wasn't sat next to Roger this week.'

She smiled. 'He's the Mazda RX-8 guy, right?'

'Right.'

'Where did you eat?'

'Some Thai place in Kew.'

'Oh, I know where you mean. I took a client there once. He'd been charged with receiving stolen goods.' She paused, and broke out into another smile. 'Shifty so-and-so, he was. Luckily, what jail time I saved him was made up for by the big fat bill I posted through his letterbox at the end of the trial.'

'Are you expensive?'

'If only you knew *how* expensive.' She winked. 'You find yourself in possession of any dodgy DVD players, David, you know where to come.'

She smiled again, and we looked at each other, the noise of the coffee grinder filling the silence.

'So are you on a case at the moment?'

'You remember Megan Carver?'

She paused for a moment. She knew the name, but couldn't think where from. 'Wasn't she that girl who disappeared?'

'Right.'

'Wow. Big case.'

'Big enough. I'm trying to find her.'

'If she's even still alive.'

'Yeah, well, I think there's a distinct possibility she's not.'

She didn't pursue it any further, although as her eyes lingered on me I knew she wanted to. It was more than a natural curiosity. There were obvious parallels between our work – the damaged clients, the unravelling of lies and half-truths, the building of a case – but, deep down, I knew her reasons were much simpler than that: she wanted to feel we were moving somewhere.

'Oh, I almost forgot,' she said after a while, and disappeared down the hallway.

I looked up at one of the photos on the shelf again. In it, Liz had her arm around Katie's neck, and was dressed in a skirt and vest. She looked fantastic. Dark, playful eyes; long chocolate-coloured hair; slim, gentle curves. We'd never talked about the relationships she'd had since her daughter was born, but it seemed impossible that there wouldn't have been some. She was beautiful without ever suggesting she knew it, which only made her more attractive.

She returned a couple of minutes later. In her hands was an envelope. 'Here,' she said, and handed it to me.

'Are you charging for the coffee?'

'Ha ha – you're a funny man, Raker. No, one of my old clients just opened a new place. I don't know what it's like, but maybe you can treat a few of the guys at the group one week. Working in law, I have no real friends, so it makes more sense for you to have them.'

She was smiling.

I looked inside the envelope. There were eight vouchers with the name of a newly opened Italian restaurant in Acton at the top. Each one got you a free main course.

'Are you sure?' I asked.

'Yeah, absolutely.'

I glanced at her, then down at the vouchers again. *Don't think it through. Just do it.* I looked up. She was watching me again, that same look on her face.

'Are you free Friday?'

She paused. Didn't say anything. 'Don't feel like you need to ask me—'

'I'm asking you because I want to.'

She moved back to the sofa, brought her legs up under her so they were crossed, then broke out into another smile. 'Yes,' she said. 'I'm free.'

'Then it looks like we're eating Italian.'

CHAPTER 7

Megan's plastic storage box was still on the kitchen counter when I got in. I took it through to the living room and sat down at the table, spreading the contents out in front of me in three separate piles: jewellery, letters and photographs.

I went through the jewellery first. Some gold chains. A bracelet. A couple of rings. In the middle of them all was a necklace. It was unusual, almost out of place among her other things: a shard of dark glass, possibly obsidian, on a long black cord. I held it up in front of me and, as I watched it turn slowly in my hands, realized Megan's initials were inscribed on the back. I set the necklace down, away from the rest of the jewellery, and turned to the letters.

Handwritten letters were pretty rare now so I imagined the ones in the box would be at least a couple of years old. But I was out by another two. There were five, all unsent, all to her grandparents in Norfolk, the last written in the week after her thirteenth birthday.

Next, I headed to the spare room and fired up

the computer. Megan's camera used a standard Sony USB lead, the same as mine. I plugged it in and copied the pictures across to my desktop. Most of them mirrored the Megan in the photographs I already had of her, so I turned to the last one at the block of flats.

Everything was much clearer. Two metal doors, reinforced glass panels in them. Blobs of sunlight shining in the glass, with only the merest hint of anything else: maybe a tree reflected, and perhaps the edge of another building. There were sandy-yellow bricks behind Megan, on the right-hand side, and she was dressed in a dark pair of jeans, a black V-neck sweater, a thick bomber jacket and a red scarf.

And there was that smile.

I opened one of the other pictures of her with Leigh at the beach, and positioned them side by side. Different times. Different places. Different smiles. The smile on the beach was warm, but created. A smile for the camera, not for anyone beyond that. This one was different. There was nothing put-on about it. This smile carved across her face, filled up her eyes and brought colour to the surface of her cheeks. I needed to find out where she was in the picture.

But, more than that, I needed to find out who had taken it.

Using the password the police had given the Carvers, I accessed Megan's email. There were forty-two messages in her inbox, most of them automatically generated newsletters from companies she must have bought from or visited in the past. Three others caught my eye: two from Kaitlin, and one from Lindsey. All of them had been sent in the aftermath of Megan's disappearance, and – when I opened them up – they were all asking her to come home, or at least call her parents. The police had probably questioned the girls about the emails, and checked their accounts for replies.

Right at the bottom was a mail from a charity called the London Conservation Trust. It seemed slightly out of sync with the high-street stores, fast-food restaurants and cinema times that made up her other emails, so I clicked on it. It opened on to a bland-looking newsletter detailing the LCT's concern about urban development, and the impact it was having on wildlife in the city's parks. It thanked Megan for her donation of £10 and said the money would be put to use ensuring wildlife was protected in the face of the continued expansion of the city.

Suddenly, my phone started ringing.

'David Raker.'

'David, it's Spike.'

Spike was a Russian hacker living in a tiny flat in Camden Town, whom I'd known since my paper days. Back then, I'd used him a lot. He could get you an address, a phone number, a credit card statement, even bank account details – basically anything you wanted. The riskier the job, the more you had to pay him, but back then – when the story was all that mattered – he'd helped me break some big ones. I'd only ever met him once in the flesh: he was painfully thin and pale, as if he barely saw daylight. It was probably something to do with the fact that he was five years past the expiration of his student visa and never ventured outdoors.

I'd called him earlier in the evening, before I went out to the restaurant, and asked him to get me Megan's mobile phone records for the three months running up to her disappearance, and for the six months since.

'Spike – thanks for calling me back.'

'Hey, no problem – sorry it's so late.' I could hear him tapping something into a keyboard. 'So I got what you wanted here. There's a *lot* of calls.'

'How many?'

'Two hundred and seventy-four, plus four hundred and ninety-two texts.'

'That should be a fun evening in. Any after 3 April this year?'

'Uh . . .' He paused. 'No. None. How come?'

'That's what I'm trying to find out.' I logged out of Megan's email account, and moved to mine. 'Any chance you could email me that information? Can you turn it into a PDF or a JPEG or something?'

'Yeah. I'll PDF it. It'll be there in a couple of minutes.'

'Nice one, thanks.'

'You got my new drop-off details?'

Spike was a cash-only man, for obvious reasons. He had a locker in a sports centre close to his flat, and he gave his customers the access code, which he changed every day. The locker was his bank.

'I got it. I might need you for something in a bit, though.'

'Yeah, no problem. You know I'm not a nine-to-five man.'

I hung up. By the time I'd put in the username and password for my Yahoo account, the email and PDF were waiting there for me. I dragged off the PDF and opened it up. Thirty entries per page. Twenty-five and a half pages.

I went back through to the kitchen and turned on the coffee machine.

Two hours later, at almost two o'clock in the morning, I'd narrowed her list of calls down to eighteen different numbers. A couple I recognized off the bat: her home number; her mum's and dad's mobile phones; a few others from her Book of Life. The rest I'd never seen before.

I redialled Spike's number. 'I'm going to email you back a list of eighteen different phone numbers,' I said once he answered. 'Can you get me as many details for each one as you can lay your hands on?'

'Sure.'

'I need names and addresses for each. Anything else you come up with, you can chuck in there too as part of the fee.'

'This isn't gonna be a quick job.'

'That's fine. Just get what you can and give me a call back. I'll be out and about tomor—' I stopped, looked at my watch '—today, so just give me a shout on my mobile, okay?'

'You got it.'

I hung up, and looked back at Megan's face on the monitor. I'd never failed to find a missing person. I suppose, in some ways, I had a gift for it, some sort of magnetic pull that drew them to me, even if their bodies were the only thing left to find. I studied her face, her features, and hoped she would be luckier than that, just as I hoped all of them would be when I took on their cases. Because the worst moment of all was returning to the nest, sitting down opposite the people who had hired me, and having to tell them the child they'd brought into this world had just been pulled back out again.

CHAPTER 8

Tiko's – Megan, Kaitlin and Lindsey's favourite night out – was squeezed between a gay pub called Captain S and a tattoo parlour, just off Charing Cross Road. Beyond a door decorated in Aztec masks and dark wood, I was met by a bone-breaking R'n'B bassline and a thousand televisions blasting MTV into my eyes. There was one barman and a single customer. The customer had two beer bottles in front of him and both were already finished. It had just gone 11 a.m.

'Morning,' the barman said as I approached.

At the bar there was a sign saying they served breakfast.

'Morning. What's on the menu?'

'Anything you want.' He looked around him as he dried a glass. 'The chef ain't exactly rushed off his feet.'

'I'll have egg, bacon, some toast and a black coffee, then.'

'No problem,' he said. 'Take a seat.'

I slid in at the bar, about five stools away from the guy with the beer bottles. He looked up, his eyes red and mottled. I nodded. He nodded back. Then he dropped his head back down and stared into the empty bottles.

I took in the club. It was on two floors, with a winding staircase between them and a cramped balcony above the bar area and dancefloor. There were probably worse ways to spend a Saturday night, but I wasn't sure what they were.

A couple of minutes later, the barman re-appeared. The first thing he did was reach into one of the fridges and take out another bottle of beer. 'Food's ordered, coffee's on,' he said, flipping the cap off the beer and handing it to the other guy. 'You want anything else to drink while you're waiting?'

'Yeah, I'll have an orange juice.'

He nodded. I reached into my pocket and got out a photograph of Megan I'd taken from the box. One of her at home in her school uniform. The photo was probably a couple of years old, but she didn't look massively different from how she did in the most up-to-date pictures. Sometimes you had to work the percentages, though. The younger the victim, the more emotion you gener-ated, and the more help you were likely to get. I held up the photograph as the barman placed my juice down in front of me.

'I'm not only here for breakfast,' I said. 'I'm doing some work for the family of a girl who used to come in here a lot.' I placed the picture down and pushed it across to him. 'Do you recognize her?'

He glanced at the photo. 'Judging by that school uniform, looks like she shouldn't have been getting in at all.'

'I won't tell.'

He nodded, smiled a little. 'She doesn't seem familiar.'

'I imagine the police came in at one stage, about six months back.'

He raised an eyebrow. 'Police?'

'She used to come in with a couple of other girls her age.'

'Is she missing?'

'Her name's Megan Carver.'

His eyes widened for a moment. The name rang a bell. 'She was that girl on the news. The one that disappeared.'

'That's her.'

He looked at her picture again, as if trying to see something he hadn't managed to pick out the first time. Then he shook his head and pushed the photo back across the counter to me. 'I remember the news stories, but I was still sitting with my feet up on a beach in Thailand when she went missing. I've only been working here four months.'

I nodded, took the photo. 'I guess I'll just wait for my breakfast then.'

It arrived a couple of minutes later and was surprisingly good. The eggs were runny, the bacon was crunchy and both slices of toast were drenched in butter. When I was done, I pushed the plate back across the bar and set about finishing my coffee and juice. The barman was away cleaning tables on the other side of the room. Five stools down from me, my drinking partner had just finished his third beer.

I glanced at him. He was looking down into the empty bottles, one eye open, one eye closed. Stubble was scattered across his face. His hair looked like it had gone weeks without shampoo. But he was dressed in good clothes: Diesel trousers, a Ted Baker sweater, a Quiksilver bodywarmer and, sneaking out from under his sleeve, a Gucci watch. Basically the best-dressed drunk in London.

'Nice breakfast?' he asked without looking up.

'Pretty good, yeah.'

'You sound surprised,' he said, his voice quiet.

'I am.'

'You shouldn't be. It's a good breakfast in here.'

'I know,' I said. 'I just tasted it.'

I pulled a twenty out of my wallet.

'Your girl,' he said, turning on his seat, pushing the bottles away from him like he wanted to forget he'd spent his breakfast necking three beers. 'Megan. She sounded like a nice girl.'

Now he had my attention. 'You knew her?'

'No, I didn't know her.' He took one of the bottles and separated it out from the group. 'But I had the Old Bill in here asking me questions about her a couple of days after she went missing.'

I eyed him. He sat up straight, smiled and turned towards me. He could see I was trying to put it together in my head: the *drunk* owns this place?

65

'You're the manager?'

'The owner. I employ a manager.'

'What did the police ask you?'

'The same sort of questions you just asked. Did she come in here? Did I recognize her? Did she ever get into any trouble?' He paused, pulled the beer bottle back into the group, then looked up at me again. 'I didn't have any answers for them, just as I won't have any for you. She could have come in here for years, and she would have meant as much to me as someone who comes in here for the first time.' He shrugged, a little regret in his eyes. 'That's the nature of these places.'

'Did the police take anything away?'

'CCTV footage.'

'How much?'

'As much as we had.'

'Which was how much?'

'We keep a year's worth. That's what our legal people and security team advise us to do, in case anything kicks off in here and we have to go to court. We keep an additional year as well, but only one copy of that, and in a deposit box at a bank near St Paul's. Anything outside of those two years, we dispose of.'

'So the police took a year's worth of footage from you?'

'No. They took the six months up to, and including, the date of her disappearance, and the month after.'

'Did they find anything?'

'You'd have to ask them that,' he said. 'But as it's sitting in the drawer of my desk upstairs now, I guess not.'

He looked up at me then, and a smile spread across his face like glass cracking. I realized then that this was a man for whom drinking wasn't enjoyable, or an addiction, or just something to do. It was a way of finding an exit. For a brief moment, as we locked eyes across the bar, it was like seeing my reflection in a mirror.

'Are you okay?'

He nodded and looked away. 'Maybe I can help you.'

And when he looked back, his eyes were filling up. He got down off the stool and gestured for me to follow him up to the second floor.

His name was Paulo Janez, and his office overlooked a tiny London backstreet, full of townhouse doors and slivers of office space. On one wall was a huge black-and-white painting of Tony Montana. On the other were a series of photographs. Paulo was in most of them, as was someone I presumed was his dad. They looked the same: dark skin, black hair, brown eyes, immaculately dressed. He caught me looking at them.

'My father,' he said quietly, and sat at his desk. He opened one of the drawers and started going through them. I sat opposite and watched in silence. Eventually he brought out seven DVDs, bound together with two elastic bands. He closed the drawer and placed them on the desk in front of me.

'Be my guest,' he said, gesturing to them.

'That's the seven months the police took?'

'Correct.'

I got out a card and passed it across the desk to him. My guarantee I would return the DVDs. He took the card, studied it, then nodded that he understood.

'You married?' he asked.

'Not any more.'

'Divorced?'

I paused. Maybe he could sense something in me, like I could sense something in him. A connection between us. A sadness that bubbled below the surface of the skin.

'My wife died of cancer,' I said finally.

He nodded, seemed almost relieved, as if he'd started to doubt his initial feelings. 'My father passed away two months ago. The only person I ever really cared about.'

'I'm sorry.'

A sad smile wormed across his face, and then he was quiet for a moment. 'Take the DVDs and see if you can find anything. I hope you do – for that family's sake.'

CHAPTER 9

Just before 3 p.m., Caroline Carver buzzed open the front gates of her house and watched me pull into the gravel driveway. She smiled. But, as at the restaurant a couple of days before, it was only a smile in name. Before Megan vanished, I imagined she had turned a lot of heads, but as she led me into the house, gaunt and drained, I realized she was only a partial reflection of that woman now.

We moved through to the kitchen, where Leigh was sitting cross-legged on the floor, pushing cars across the lino.

'Would you like something to drink?' she asked.

'Just water would be great.'

She nodded but made no effort to say anything else, and as she filled a glass from the tap, I realized I was finding it difficult to get a handle on her. Normally I was pretty effective at reading people. I could see through to what made them tick. I wasn't sure whether it was a natural talent, or a skill cultivated through years of watching politicians lie through their teeth. But, either way, Caroline Carver was different. She wore herself the way you'd expect a grieving parent to: distant, fragile, the disappearance pulling at the seams. But sometimes I saw someone else. A woman of strength and steel who could bury her feelings as deep as they needed to go.

'How are things going?' she asked finally, as she led me into the living room. She touched Leigh's head on the way through and got no reaction in return.

I seated myself opposite her. 'At the moment I'm just following the same leads as the police. I need to make sure they haven't missed anything.'

I placed my pad down on the table between us and flipped it open. She looked down at it, back at me and nodded, seeing I was ready to start.

'Maybe you could tell me about those last few weeks.'

She paused, shrugged. 'I'm not sure there's a lot to tell. Jim was on a job up in Enfield, at a new contract there, so I took Meg into school for most of that last fortnight. Certainly the morning she disappeared.'

'She seemed all right to you that day?'

'Yes,' she said. 'Perfectly fine. She was always such a positive force. I'm not sure where she got it from, because both Jim and I can be a bit . . . well, temperamental, I suppose.' She smiled a little – a proper smile for the first time since I'd met her. Then it vanished again. 'That was why she was such a good student, I think. She just maintained an even keel the whole time. Never got over-excited or depressed. She was just an amazing girl.'

'What can you tell me about Charles Bryant?'

Caroline glanced at me. I wasn't sure whether she was telling me she never liked him, or was surprised I had brought him up in the first place.

'Megan dated him for a while.'

'Did you meet him?'

'Only once.'

'How long did they go out for?'

'Not long. Maybe two or three months.'

'What was he like?'

She shrugged. 'He seemed okay. It was a tough time for him.'

'Megan didn't love him?'

'Definitely not,' she said, shaking her head. 'I think that was the problem. She went out with him because she felt sorry for him. Felt sorry that he had lost his mother like that. And also because she was a good person. She looked at him and saw that he needed someone to help him through the grieving process.'

'How did he take the split?'

'What do you mean?'

I looked at her. She wasn't playing ball with me, even though she could see where I was trying to drive the conversation. Perhaps the idea of her daughter dating someone wasn't one she liked to think about, especially if it had somehow initiated her disappearance. 'I mean, I'm trying to work the angles here,' I said to her.

'He was upset.'

'Did he try to talk her round?'

'Not really. I think, in his heart of hearts, he knew the relationship wasn't built to last. He knew why Meg was around for him. He definitely had a thing for her, a very strong affection, but he seemed a level-headed boy. I think . . .' She paused, looked at me. 'I think if you're heading down that road with Charlie Bryant in mind . . . well, it's the wrong direction.'

'The police talked to him?'

'Yes. I think they had a similar theory to you.'

'Did she start seeing anyone else after that?'

A slight hesitation. 'No,' she said, but didn't look at me. 'Jim and I talked to her about it and suggested it might be better if she concentrated on her studies. She was three good grades away from getting a place at Cambridge. That was worth a little sacrifice.'

I nodded, but didn't write anything down.

Something was definitely up.

'What about the names Anthony Grant, or A. J. Grant – do they mean anything?'

She shook her head. 'No.'

I reached into my pocket and took out a printout of the photograph I'd found on Megan's camera. I'd blown it up on the computer.

'Do you recognize this photo?'

She took the printout. 'Yes. It's on her camera.'

'Right. Any idea where she is there?'

She brought the picture in closer to her. 'No. I

72

remember this is one of the photos we looked at right back at the start, because Jamie Hart asked us the same thing.'

'Did he find anything out?'

'No. The police went through all her photos, all her friends' photos, everything they could lay their hands on.' She paused, a flash of a tear in one of her eyes. 'But they got nowhere.'

'So they never found out who took this one?'

She glanced at the photo again, then back up. 'No. Why?'

'Don't you think her face looks different there?'

'Her face?'

I pointed to Megan. 'Her smile.'

'In what way?'

'I don't know. You know her best. But this smile, and the smile in some of the other photos . . . they seem different to me.'

'Different how?'

I shrugged. 'I'm not sure. Maybe it's nothing. I just think it would be helpful to find out who took this, that's all.'

Something passed across her face.

'Are you okay?' I asked.

She frowned at me. 'Of course. Why?'

Because something's up with you. 'You just seem a little . . . distracted, I guess.'

'I'm fine.'

I let it go. 'Just backtracking for a second, she definitely never made mention of being in any relationship *after* Charles Bryant?'

73

Another small hesitation.

'Caroline?'

'No.'

'She never made mention of one?'

Movement in her eyes. 'No, she definitely—'

'Caroline.'

She stopped. Looked at me.

'Do you want your daughter found?'

'Of *course*. What sort of question is that?'

I glanced at a photograph of Megan, in a frame on a small glass table at the end of one of the sofas. 'I'm just asking because I get the feeling I might be missing something here.'

'What do you mean?'

'I mean, I'm not sure you're being totally honest with me. I need you to tell me *everything*. Even if it's just a suspicion, a hunch.'

She paused, looked down at my pad, then dabbed a finger against her eye. If I was wrong, I'd have to apologize to her – but I had to be sure. I couldn't be working the case if one of the two people in the world who knew Megan the best wasn't prepared to give me everything she had.

Finally, after what seemed like minutes, Caroline looked up, sadness and disappointment in her eyes. She turned and faced the photograph of Megan I had been looking at a few moments before. Then, determination back in her voice, she said quietly, 'I think you should leave now.'

CHAPTER 10

By the time I got home it was almost dark. Autumn was moving in quickly now: once the sun faded from the sky, the night washed in and the temperature went with it. I put the football on in the living room, then turned the radio on in the kitchen. One of the things you dread the most when you've been left on your own is the silence.

After showering, I went through to the kitchen and started preparing some dinner, emptying a packet of stir-fry vegetables into a wok along with some sliced chicken. As I watched it brown, I kept coming back to Caroline Carver. I couldn't shake the feeling that she was holding something back. Even if I couldn't read her as clearly as I would have liked, I knew I wasn't mistaken. Something sat there between us, just as it had the first time we'd met at the restaurant. A secret. A half-truth. A lie. Something.

I was sitting down in front of the TV, twenty minutes into the match, when my phone started buzzing. I set the plate aside and hit Answer.

It was James Carver.

'Caroline told me about what you accused her of today,' he said, cutting to the chase. 'You think she would hold back something important? You *seriously* think she would do that? What planet are you on?'

'Hold on a min—'

'No, *you* hold on a minute.' He lowered his voice. He must have been in another room, trying to keep the conversation away from her. 'Don't *ever* accuse my wife of trying to get in the way of finding Meg.'

'I didn't accuse her of—'

'Don't tell me you didn't. I *know* you did. I'm paying you to be an investigator, not some amateur-hour psychologist.'

'Just let me explain.'

'You *really* believe Caroline doesn't want her found?'

'Of course not.'

'Then what the hell are you playing at?'

I paused, let him calm down for a moment. 'She seemed hesitant.'

'About what?'

'About everything.'

'Our daughter has been missing *six months*. You know what that's like? You know what that does to you? No, you don't. You've got no idea.'

I didn't reply. Let him feel like he'd had his victory.

'Are you going to apologize?'

'Listen, James . . . I don't know either of you

well, but I went with a gut reaction and if it turns out to be wrong, then I'll apologize.'

'You *insulted* her. Do you understand what I'm telling you?'

'It won't happen again.'

'No, it won't.' He cleared his throat. 'I think we should call it a day.'

'What are you talking about?'

'I want you off this. We entrusted you with the most precious thing in our life, gave you money, all you'd need to get the job done. But you've destroyed my confidence in you, David. And you've insulted my wife. I won't have that. I won't have you speak to her like that.'

'This is ridiculous.'

'Put Megan's things in an envelope and mail them to us. Whatever you have found out so far, please put it down on paper and include that too. The last thing Caroline needs now is to see you at the house again. I will pay you for the three days you have done, and an extra day as a goodwill gesture. Not that you deserve any goodwill from us.'

'Don't you think this is a little extreme?'

He hung up.

CHAPTER 11

At 2 a.m., something woke me. For a moment, the noise was distant and distorted, just a sound on the edge of my sleep. Then, when I opened my eyes, I saw my mobile was gently vibrating on the bedside cabinet. I reached over and scooped it up.

'Hello?'

'David?'

I rubbed an eye. 'Yes.'

'It's Jill.'

It took me a couple of seconds to realize it was Jill from the support group.

'I'm so sorry to call you like this.'

'Uh . . .' I looked at the clock again. *She really is calling me at two o'clock in the morning.* 'Uh, no problem.'

'I tried Aron, but he's not answering. I think he's away with work tonight. I tried a police friend of Frank's too, but he's not answering either. I didn't know who else to call. I guess I just thought, because of your job, you might know what to . . . to, uh . . .'

I sat up in bed, still feeling a little woozy. 'Are you okay?'

'I'm so sorry to wake you.'

'No, no – don't worry.'

'It's just . . . I don't know who else to . . .'

'Really,' I said, flicking on a bedside lamp, my brain working over the reasons she might be calling, 'don't worry. What's the matter?'

'I'm, uh . . .' She paused. The more awake I became, the more distressed she started to sound. 'There's, uh . . .'

'What?'

A pause. 'I think someone's watching my house.'

'What are you talking about?'

'There's someone across the street. He's just been sitting in his car all evening, looking across at my house. I don't know what to do.'

'Is he still there?'

'Yes.'

'Okay,' I said, and turned around in bed, flipping back the sheets. *She wants you to come over.* 'Uh, would you like me to come over?'

'Oh, *thank you.*'

Her voice wobbled. She was scared.

'Where do you live?' She gave me the address. 'Make sure all the doors and windows are locked. If you're unsure, at any time, call the police. I'll be there as fast as I can.'

The night was cool. On the drive over I had the heaters on full blast, rain spattering against the windscreen the whole way. Her road was narrow, cars parked on either side. She'd told me she had a black door, but in the darkness every door looked black. I found a space about halfway down the road, got out and saw I was about ten houses away. I scanned the street for any sign of someone watching her place, but it was difficult in the rain. Gutters were filling. Water pelted off glass and bodywork. Visibility was low.

There were no lights on in her house. I knocked twice, then turned and looked up and down the street again, this time from under the protection of her porch. Lots of cars. No sign of anyone sitting inside one.

The door opened.

Jill was dressed in tracksuit trousers and a big baggy fleece. Her eyes wandered past me, to a spot on my right. I turned and followed her gaze. There was no one there. When I looked back at her, I could see the confusion in her face.

'He's gone,' she said quietly.

I looked back out at the street again.

'Seems that way.'

'But he's been there all night.' She looked at me, then out into the street. 'He was sitting there in a red car. I think it was a Ford.'

I didn't say anything. She wasn't crazy, and I doubted she was seeing things. But being on your own changed things. Small things. Knowing someone else was in the house with you was a security blanket, even if – ultimately – you were just as vulnerable as ever. She looked at me and tears formed in the corners of her eyes.

'I wasted your time.'

'No,' I said. 'Not at all.'

'I must be going mad.'

'No,' I repeated, and touched a hand to the top of her arm. 'You aren't mad. He could have been watching another house. He could have been a cop. Or a government agent. Or maybe they think you're a terrorist.'

A smile. 'That makes me feel *much* better.'

She glanced at me, brought her hand up to her face, then looked down at herself. In her eyes, now the tension had passed, I could see what she was thinking: *Why the hell did I answer the door dressed like this?*

'Would you like to come in for some tea or a coffee or something?'

'Sure,' I said. 'Coffee would be great.'

Her house was small but modern; a show home ripped from the pages of a magazine. There were beautiful wooden floors running through to the living room, where a thick rug sat beneath a beech-and-glass table piled with glossy books. An original brick fireplace dominated one wall, a wood-burning stove perched in it. Opposite were two bookcases, filled with classics, either side of a black flatscreen TV. DVDs were piled up underneath, most of them foreign language. It didn't look like we'd be discussing the action scenes in *Predator* any time soon. She pointed to one of two cream leather sofas, and disappeared into the kitchen.

There were photographs of her husband on some of the bookcase shelves, and again on the mantelpiece above the fire. I walked over and picked one up. They were at a police get-together somewhere. She was in a flowery summer dress, her hair up. He had his arm around her, and was dressed in full uniform, two silver stars on his shoulder. I put the photograph back on the mantelpiece just as Jill brought two cups of coffee through, setting them down on the table. She perched herself on the other sofa.

'Your husband was an inspector,' I said.

'You know your police stripes.'

'Was he a detective?'

'Yes. He worked for Thames Valley before he moved to the Met. That's when we came up to London.'

'He was a cop the whole time you were married?'

'The whole time,' she said, pouring milk into her cup. After she was done, she lifted a necklace out from her top. There was a small silver angel dangling from the end, a long spear in one hand. 'This is St Michael.'

'The patron saint of policemen.'

'*Right*.' She smiled. 'I'm impressed.'

'I got to know the police pretty well as a journalist.'

'It was Frank's. I was going to bury him with it, but in the end preferred the idea of keeping it close to me. It seemed . . .' She slowly stirred her drink. 'It just seemed right.'

I nodded that I understood.

A thin smile worked its way across her face. 'Sometimes I still buy his favourite food when I go to the supermarket. I still leave the key in the wall out back, just in case he comes home. I guess . . . I guess I can't accept he's gone.'

'Do you mind if I ask what happened to him?'

She frowned. Looked at me for a moment. Then, as she blinked, her eyes filled up. She wiped them and sat back on the sofa, both hands wrapped around her coffee cup. 'They told me he was part of a task force looking into Russian organized crime. There was some link up with . . . is it SOCA?'

I nodded. The Serious Organized Crime Agency. In my previous life as a journalist, I'd had a couple of contacts inside the National Criminal Intelligence Service, which later became part of SOCA. At the time it came into being in 2006, the media labelled it 'the British FBI', but as few of its officers had the power to arrest, and most of their work was surveillance and co-ordination, they were closer to the MI5 model.

She shifted, sadness welling in her eyes. 'A couple of weeks after the funeral, one of his friends came here.'

'Off the record presumably?'

'Oh yes, definitely. I think he felt sorry for me. The way in which things had been . . . communicated. I mean, I tried to find out what happened to Frank in the weeks after his death, but the official version his bosses gave me, it just never . . .'

'Never felt right.'

'It just felt like there were gaps still to be filled.'

'How do you mean?'

She shrugged. 'They told me they were closing in on a big figure in one of the Russian gangs, and they'd been given a tip-off that he might be at a warehouse in Bow.'

'And was he?'

'I don't know.'

'They didn't tell you?'

She shook her head. 'No.'

'Because they wanted to contain the case?'

'Right. But I knew enough about police work to understand that. I didn't want to know the details of the investigation, I just wanted to know what had happened to Frank, and who killed him.' She took a few moments to find her feet again. 'All they told me was that he and another officer were shot in the chest.'

'By who – this Russian guy?'

'They said it happened fast.'

'So they didn't know?'

Her voice wavered. 'Officially, they said they didn't.'

'And unofficially?'

She paused for a moment. 'Frank's friend said the big figure they were after was a man called Akim Gobulev.'

Gobulev. 'The Ghost.'

She glanced at me. 'You've heard of him?'

'He's been on SOCA's most wanted list for the entire time it's been in existence.'

'Why do they call him "The Ghost"?'

'Because no one's even sure if he's alive.'

'Oh.'

'The NCIS used to joke that Gobulev was either buried somewhere, or had the power to turn invisible. They pinned stuff on him – trafficking, prostitution, drugs, money-laundering – but no one has seen him in years. The only evidence he even exists is an entry in a computer at Heathrow over a decade ago. He landed on a flight from Moscow – and then vanished into thin air.'

'Frank's friend said they were closing in on him.'

'Really?'

'That's what he said.'

'Gobulev was the guy at the warehouse?'

She picked up her cup of coffee again. 'No, I don't think so. He said he'd heard from some guys on the task force that this Gobulev man had had surgery.'

'What kind of surgery?'

'I'm not sure. But they'd found his surgeon.'

I sat forward in my seat. 'And that was who was in the warehouse?'

'Yes.'

'Gobulev's *surgeon* killed Frank?'

'Yes,' she said again. 'His friend said the task force didn't know much about the surgeon, but they went to that warehouse to get him – and then use him to get Gobulev.'

'What else did he say?'

'I think that's all he knew.'

'Did he know the surgeon's name?'

She shook her head. 'No.'

She quickly wiped a tear away with a finger; but then a second one followed, breaking free and running down her cheek.

'I'm really sorry, Jill,' I said gently.

Eventually she looked up, an apologetic expression on her face. She was conscious of embarrassing me, but couldn't do anything to stop herself crying. I watched her for a moment, studying her, turning things over in my head.

'Look, I'll tell you what: I'll make a few calls for you and see if I can find out anything more. I can't promise anything.'

'David, you don't have to—'

'It's fine. I have another case, and that one has to take precedence. But after I'm done with that, I'll ask around for you, okay?'

She nodded, choked up on tears.

'It might be . . . it might be painful, some of it.'

'I know,' she said gently. 'But it can't be any more painful than not knowing.'

I got back from Jill's at four o'clock. The rubbish bin I always kept at the front of the house had been tipped over, black bin liners spilling out across the pathway – and the sliding door at the front porch was open. I tried the front door.

It was still locked.

Backing out, I did a quick circuit of the house. Nothing was out of place. No sign of any disturbance. I often left the porch door open, without ever noticing; and, as I got back around to the front, a cat darted out from the shadows, across my lawn and out on to the street. It had some food in its mouth, removed from a hole in one of the spilt bin liners. I put the bags back inside the bin, and headed to bed.

CHAPTER 12

After staying out until 4 a.m. the previous night, I slept late. By the time I was showered and fed, it was almost midday. I headed into the office.

I didn't use it anywhere near as much as I once did. At the start, it had been a way to separate my home life from my work life. A way to legitimize my career. Now Derryn was gone, it was just an expensive inconvenience, and I was thirty days away from watching the lease lapse. Once that happened, I'd work out of the house permanently, and another little piece of my previous life would have washed away.

Swivelling in my chair, I looked up at the corkboard behind me. A wall full of the missing. Right at the top was Megan Carver. I stood and pulled the picture out, then sat down again and studied her. *What's going on, Megan? What's your mum hiding?* I turned gently in the chair, tracing the shape of her face; letting my mind turn over.

A couple of seconds later, my phone burst into life.

I looked at the display. NUMBER WITHHELD. Pulling it towards me, I switched to speaker phone.

'David Raker.'

No response.

'David Raker,' I said, louder.

No sound at all. No static, no background noise.

I sat forward in my seat. 'Hello?'

Just silence.

'*Hello?*'

'Mr Raker . . .' A soft voice. Female. 'It's Kaitlin.'

'Kaitlin?'

'You said to call you if I . . .'

I glanced at the photograph of Megan. *Things have changed*, I should have said. But then I remembered the way Kaitlin had been when I'd gone to the school, and realized a part of me wanted to find out what she had to say.

'I, uh . . . There's something . . .'

'It's okay, Kaitlin.'

'Something you should know.'

'Okay.'

'About Megan.' A pause. A long one. 'I'm just sick of having to lie.'

More silence. For a moment, all I could hear was the slight crackle of her breath against the mouthpiece.

Then, finally, she spoke.

The Carvers' gates were closed when I pulled up outside. I'd tried calling ahead, but no one had answered. I locked the BMW, stepped up to the intercom and pressed the buzzer. They had a small camera embedded in the number pad. I looked into it. It was moving from left to right, then – as it got to me – stopped. A crackle on the intercom.

'What do you want?'

James Carver.

'I need to speak to you.'

'We've got nothing more to say to one another.'

'You're going to want to hear this.'

The camera hummed. This time, in its centre, I could see the lens open up. He was zooming in on me. I stared straight into the eye of it.

Then the gates buzzed open.

Carver met me at the door, but didn't offer me anything to drink. Didn't even ask me in. The two of them stood in the doorway, arms crossed, defensive, waiting for whatever I had to say. Carver was in front of his wife, protecting her, as if he thought I might try to start something.

'I got a call this morning,' I said, keeping my eyes fixed on him. 'From Kaitlin – Megan's friend. Did the police ever tell you what she said in her statement?'

'What's this got to do with anything?'

'*Did* they?'

Anger flared in his eyes. 'She was the last person to see Megan.' He paused, a flutter of sadness in among the irritation. 'That's it.'

For the first time, I glanced at Caroline. Her eyes were fixed on mine, but there wasn't any of the animosity of her husband.

'That's not it,' I said, glimpsing a little fear in her now.

'What are you talking about?'

'Before Megan disappeared, she confided in Kaitlin.'

'About what?' Carver said.

'And I think she might have confided in your wife as well.'

Carver's mouth dropped a little, as if he couldn't believe I had the balls to come into his home and insult his wife again. Then, when Caroline didn't respond, didn't even attempt to register her disgust, he looked over his shoulder at her.

'Caroline?' he said. 'What's going on?'

She couldn't look at him.

'James,' I said, and waited for him to turn back to me. When he did, the anger had gone from his face. 'Megan was pregnant.'

SONA

S ona woke. Next to her, Mark was lying on his stomach, the sheet gathered at the small of his back, breathing so quietly she could barely hear him. On the floor, their clothes were scattered everywhere: a blouse, a skirt, a pair of jeans, a T-shirt, a jacket. Shoes at the door. Underwear still clinging to the ends of the duvet.

She sat up and caught sight of herself in the reflection of the mirror. Naked, and still a little conscious of it, even though they were nearly six months into their relationship. It was a feeling that was slowly starting to pass. Mark made her feel good about herself in a way few men had before. That didn't mean he complimented her a lot either, but she'd made allowances for that. He was incredibly shy, so different from the other men she'd known, and she liked that about him. She'd always had reactive men before. Men who told her she was beautiful and then ended up tearing her heart out. She found Mark's stillness – his sense of quiet – new, exciting and secure.

She headed to the bathroom and closed the door, looking at herself again in the mirror. In her twenties she'd done a little modelling and, as she'd passed into her thirties, she'd lost none of her looks. The blonde hair, blue eyes and high cheekbones could still turn heads, even if she saw changes elsewhere. Maybe a little more weight than she should have had. A few more lines at the corners of her eyes. Some of the definition around her stomach had gone. She'd be thirty-six in two days, and knew she had imperfections now. But she'd found a man who was able to look past all of it.

A man she was falling in love with.

They'd been driving for about twenty minutes when Mark told her she could remove the blindfold. Sona reached up and pulled the tie away. Her head throbbed slightly. She wasn't sure if it was the start of a headache, or the sudden switch from dark to light. Sun poured into the car as she looked around, and saw they were in a parking space on a narrow residential street. Identical terraced houses ran along either side of the road. Most hadn't been maintained with any sense of pride: paint blistered on windowsills, plants were dying in small concrete yards, broken gutters hung loose.

'It gets better,' Mark said, turning to her. 'Promise.'

'Where are we?'

'I used to come here sometimes.' He pointed a finger towards a small alleyway running between two houses further down. It was the only break in the buildings, on either side, for as far as they could see. 'To the woods down there.'

'Woods?'

Mark killed the engine.

'They used to make munitions in this area during the Second World War, at a factory further up the road. This whole place was once one of the centres of British industry. Now look at it . . .' He studied the houses opposite. When he turned back, he glanced at Sona and smiled. 'Oh shit, I've just turned into my dad.'

She laughed. He smiled, then reached down to the side of his seat. A second later, he brought out a single red rose. 'Happy birthday, Sona,' he said quietly.

She took the rose, a cream ribbon tied to the stem. Something moved across his face – as if he was on the verge of telling her something important.

He wants to tell me he loves me.

She waited for a moment, and when it didn't come, leaned into him and kissed him gently on the lips. 'Thank you, baby,' she said. When she drew away, she saw the same expression. 'Are you okay?'

He glanced towards the alleyway, then turned back to her.

'I just . . .' He paused. 'I'm just really . . .'

In love with you.

She smiled and squeezed his leg, kissing him on the cheek.

He nodded to the back seat. 'I hope you're hungry.'

She turned. She'd heard him sliding something into the back after he'd blindfolded her and guided her to the car. Now she could see it had been a hamper.

'Shall I take you to our picnic spot?' he asked.

'Yes,' she said, her voice trembling a little. 'I'd love that.'

Mark led her away from the car, carrying the picnic hamper. They turned into the alleyway and followed it until it opened up on to a concrete bed with a series of half-demolished brick walls across it. She realized then that it had once been a factory. To her left and right were more ruined walls, remnants of another age; some still just about standing, some nothing but piles of bricks and dust, grass and weeds crawling through the foundations. Rubbish was dumped everywhere: beer bottles, drinks cans, crisp packets, sweet wrappers, dustbin liners full of rotting food. The smell was awful.

'Don't worry,' he said. 'It really *does* get better.'

Ahead of them, carved like a mouth into a line of huge fir trees, was the entrance to the woods Mark had talked about. Everything was overgrown. As they moved past a warped, broken gate and along the path, trees leaned in over them, their foliage thick and dark. Grass was everywhere, sprouting up waist-high around the tree trunks, and breaking through the cracks in the gravel path. The further in they got, the less defined the trail became until, eventually, the gravel turned into hard mud.

'Everything's so thick,' she said.

'Yeah. Nothing ever seems to die here.'

Sona glanced right. Through a gap in the trees, she could make out huge letters on the side of another factory: MUNITIONS. There was row after row of smashed windows, jagged glass still in the frames, nothing inside but darkness.

'I always think they look a bit like eyes,' Mark said.

She nodded. 'What a creepy old building.'

He put his arm around her shoulder and brought her into him. 'Don't worry – I'll protect you from the scary factory.'

She laughed, and gave him a playful slap on the shoulder.

Crack.

A noise from behind them. She stopped. Mark walked on a couple of steps, his arm slipping away, then he paused and turned to look at her.

'What's the matter?'

She looked around her. Wind passed through the trees, whispering gently as the leaves fluttered against the branches.

'Sona?' he said, taking a step closer to her. 'Are you okay?'

She took his outstretched hand.

'Sona?'

Finally she looked at him. 'Yeah. I guess I'm fine.'

They carried on walking. The path was starting

to arc left, moving in a gentle curve. Before long, the hardened mud started to disappear beneath their feet, and in its place came more grass. But then Sona spotted a clearing about eighty feet in front of them. The canopy wasn't as thick, and sunlight was punching through the branches and leaves in hundreds of pollen-filled rectangles. It looked beautiful.

'Wow,' she said. 'Look at that.'

Mark smiled. 'That's our picnic spot.'

When they reached the clearing, he started to unpack the hamper, laying down a blanket on the knee-high grass, and removing packets of biscuits and cheese.

Sona looked around her. 'How do you know about this place?'

'I used to come here as a boy.'

'Are we far from home?'

Mark looked up. 'Not far.'

'It's so quiet—'

Crack.

The same noise again. Like fallen branches snapping and breaking underfoot. And now something else too. A sound behind it. *What is that?*

She stared across the clearing. Where the trees began again to her right, it was dark: hundreds of trunks gradually fading away into blackness; thick, tangled branches preventing sunlight getting through from above.

'Can you hear that?'

Mark continued unpacking. 'Hear what?'

She looked back at him. 'It's like a . . .'

He glanced at the spot she'd been studying, and back to her. 'Like a what?'

'Like a . . .' She looked worried now. 'A whimpering.'

She turned back to the woods, her eyes narrowing. Then something moved.

A skittle of darkness darting between tree trunks. She took another step forward, leaning slightly, trying to look beyond the initial row of trees. It moved again. Swapping between cover, one trunk to the next.

'There!' she said. 'Did you see that?'

Mark stood and fell in beside her.

'Something moved in there.'

He was turned to her now.

'Is it an animal?'

No response.

'Mark?' More silence. She turned to him. 'Mark?'

Something flashed in his eyes, the same expression she'd seen earlier. He wanted to tell her something important again. But it wasn't that he loved her, just – she suddenly realized – as it hadn't been earlier. It had never been a look of love.

It had been a look of regret.

'I'm sorry, Sona.'

'Sorry for wha—'

He grabbed her around the neck and yanked her into him. Locked his arm around her throat and clamped a hand over her mouth. As she tried to scream, he squeezed harder with his fingers so that no sound escaped. Then he pulled her down with him, her legs desperately kicking out as she hit the grass. She looked up, her eyes pleading, trying to find a trace of the man she'd known for almost six months. Instead, he released the arm from her throat and punched her in the side of the head.

She rolled over, dazed. On to her back.

When she opened her eyes, Mark was standing over her.

'I can't do this any more,' he said, looking away at something.

And then everything went black.

PART II

CHAPTER 13

It was late afternoon by the time I left the Carvers' house, the sky grey and streaked with black cloud. I opened the BMW and threw my notes on to the passenger seat. Then I slid in at the wheel and pulled the door shut. In the silence, I went over everything.

All the lies that had been told.

And all the lies that would still have to come.

Carver had led me into their house, pointing to one of the sofas. He glanced at Caroline, a look that told her everything. He was angry and embarrassed, and she was to blame.

'Would you like something to drink, David?' he asked quietly.

'Just some water will be fine, thanks.'

He nodded and disappeared into the kitchen. Caroline circled the sofas and then perched herself on one of the arms. I could see she was trying to work things through before her husband came back. What she knew. What she should have done. Why she didn't say anything. Eventually she looked at me, and I could see whatever fractious relationship

103

had begun to exist between us had just cracked a little more.

Carver came back in and handed me a big glass of water and then sat down next to his wife. There was a gap between them.

'Was Kaitlin sure?' he asked.

I sat down on the other sofa. 'Yes.'

'Why didn't she tell the police?'

I got out my notepad and pen and set them down on the table. On the top sheet were the words *Megan – pregnant*. I looked up at Carver. 'Kaitlin told me she was going to speak to the police . . . but then decided not to.'

'Why?'

'She was hesitant on the phone, so that's what I need to find out from her. I'll meet her and get the reasons why.'

'Who was the father?'

'Again, I don't know.' I paused, thought about it. 'Megan's friends never talked about any serious relationships. You haven't either. If she slept with someone, I think we can assume it was a guy no one had met.'

Carver flinched a little, as if the idea of his daughter sleeping with anyone was like a punch to the throat. Then, for the first time, he glanced at his wife.

'And you knew about this?'

'No,' she said.

'I need you to tell me the truth.'

'I *am* telling you the truth,' Caroline replied, desperation creeping into her voice. She looked at me, then shifted on the sofa, turning inwards to face her husband. 'She never told me she was pregnant. I *swear* to you.'

'But you knew anyway?'

'I could tell something was up. She was complaining of headaches, of feeling tired all the time. At first I just thought she'd been studying too hard. You know what Meg was like. But then, after she went missing, I was going through some of her things . . .' She paused. Looked at me again. 'I found some pregnancy tests hidden in one of her drawers.'

'Bloody hell, Car – and you didn't think to *tell* me?'

'I didn't know what to do.'

'Our daughter was *pregnant*.'

'I know.'

'You should have told the police.'

'I know!' she shouted.

'So why didn't you?'

'It was an unopened box,' she said. 'The cellophane wrapping was still on it. It didn't mean anything.'

'She was *seventeen*, Caroline.'

She didn't reply.

'Since when do seventeen-year-olds buy pregnancy kits just to be on the safe side? She was ten *years* away from starting a family. You should have told me. You should have told someone.' He glanced at me, then back to her. 'I defended you.'

'I know.'

He sat back on the sofa. Both of them fell silent.

I gave them a couple of seconds to cool off, thinking about what might have happened if Caroline had said something to the police.

'Okay,' I said eventually, sitting forward. 'We need to make sure of a couple of things now. Firstly, the police can't know about this. At least, they can't know about the fact that Caroline suspected something. If they think you were with-holding information, this whole thing goes down the toilet. I'll bring this information to them – but only when we're ready. I'll say I found it out for myself. That'll give us the time we need to try and dig a little deeper.'

Carver nodded. 'What else?'

'Kaitlin never told us anything. We need to protect her in the same way we're protecting you. We need to find out what's going on here, and why she remained silent. We can't do that if DCI Hart is parking himself on the case again.'

They both nodded this time. I looked between them.

'Lastly, I need to know that you have both told me absolutely everything you know about Megan. Every fact. Every detail. I'm not here to judge your daughter. I'm here to find her. I don't care what she's done, or who she's been out with, or mistakes she might have made. All I care about is finding her. So if there's anything else you think I need to know, I need you to tell me what it is now . . .'

Carver turned to his wife. She looked back, as

if she understood the gesture. When she shook her head, he faced me again.

'There's nothing else,' he said quietly. 'Please, David, find our daughter.'

CHAPTER 14

As I left the Carvers, I knew it was too late to call Kaitlin, especially at home. It was just after 5 p.m., which meant one or both of her parents would probably be around, and I didn't want to arouse any suspicion. But I definitely needed to speak to her; to find out more about what Megan had told her. And I needed to find out where Charlie Bryant fitted in as well.

Once I was back home, I showered, had some dinner and then took the pile of DVDs from Tiko's through to the living room. I dropped the first one into the disc tray. Seven months of footage. Two hundred and fourteen days. Nineteen hours a day. That meant there was over four thousand hours of video to get through. Even with a team of twenty, that would still mean two hundred hours each. It would have been quicker to put in a call to Kaitlin or Lindsey and ask them what nights they went, but – as that was out of the question until the morning – I decided first to concentrate on weekends, specifically Friday and Saturday nights; the nights Megan was most likely to be out.

I hit Play.

October's footage – six months prior to Megan's 3 April disappearance – stuttered into life. It was in colour and pretty decent quality, but it was also on a time lapse of three seconds, which gave everything an alien, staccato feel.

The footage began on a Wednesday, so I fast-forwarded to the Friday. As the club was open all day, there was a constant stream of people coming in and out. The younger crowd – late teens and early twenties – started arriving after eight. I got to closing time at 3 a.m. with no sign of Megan. An hour and a half later, I'd finished the weekends in October altogether and found nothing. No sign of Megan. No sign of her friends.

I thought for a moment about going back over the week days in October just in case I'd missed her. But then, on the second disc – November – Megan, Kaitlin and Lindsey arrived in Tiko's. It was 11 p.m. on the first Friday of the month.

They moved in a line through the crowds, Kaitlin leading. Men watched them, their eyes mostly fixed on Kaitlin, but a few watching Megan and Lindsey too. When they got to the bar, the girls waited. Talked to each other. In one frame Megan was leaning into Lindsey saying something; in the next Lindsey's head was back, laughing. The girls ordered drinks, then moved up the winding stair-case to the second floor.

The position of the camera wasn't great, but I could still see them, their heads visible in the crowds. Sweeping disco lights, choppy because of the time lapse, passed from side to side. People danced around them. The girls remained in the same position, next to a set of three sofas, all occupied. They returned to the bar three times to get more drinks. Then they moved back downstairs for good, to the dancefloor, and stayed there until they left at two o'clock.

I fast-forwarded it on twenty-four hours, but they didn't return on the Saturday. Then I remembered something James Carver had told me: *When they all got paid, they'd often go into the city.* Assuming they got paid at the end of the month, that probably meant the last few days of one, or the very beginning of the next.

I skipped on three weeks to the last weekend in November.

Nothing on the Friday, but on Saturday they returned to Tiko's. Eleven o'clock, just like before. They stuck pretty much to the same routine. In through the crowds. Up to the bar. Up to the second floor, in the same position next to the sofas. Five trips back to the bar, before ending up on the dancefloor permanently. The other discs – December, January, February and March – all followed exactly the same pattern.

The first day of footage on the sixth disc was Saturday 1 April. Forty-eight hours before Megan disappeared. The girls entered the club just before eleven, headed to the bar, and up the spiral staircase to the top floor. They talked for a while and then, as the clock in the corner of the screen hit midnight, Megan turned slightly to let someone through. Suddenly, a feeling of familiarity washed over me.

I paused the footage. Megan was facing the camera, flanked on either side by the others. I'd spotted something; something worth picking out. But I couldn't pull it out of the darkness. I moved closer to the screen and used the remote control to inch the footage on. In one frame, Lindsey leaned towards Megan. In the next, Kaitlin took a step away.

That was when I saw him.

I realized then that I'd glimpsed him earlier, on another disc, but not really registered him. He'd only been in view briefly, just as he was now. Hidden behind a tangle of bodies; perched on the edge of the sofa furthest from the girls. Dark hair. Black jacket. Black shirt. Jeans. Black shoes.

He was staring right at Megan.

He sat completely still even as one frame jumped to the next. It was like he was frozen in place. His head was angled slightly, his chin almost pressed against his throat, looking up from under his brow. He had pale skin but incredibly dark eyes. Through the scan lines of the footage, they were just holes in his head.

Then Lindsey moved again and he disappeared behind her.

I carried on watching, the footage jumping between frames. More people moved up the stairs.

At one point, a group of eight or nine men stood adjacent to Megan, Lindsey and Kaitlin. Twelve minutes later they finally moved again.

And the man was gone.

I fast-forwarded it, past the point the girls left the club at half-two to closing time at four o'clock. He didn't reappear. I rewound it to the beginning of the evening when they'd first come up the stairs to the second floor. He wasn't waiting for them then. It was like he'd ghosted in for those few short moments, shielded by the crowds – and then vanished again.

I dropped in March's DVD for a second time. Skipped forward to the evening of the first Friday in the month. An hour and a half passed. When the onscreen clock showed 00:37, a crowd spread out behind the three girls – and he emerged. I'd missed him the first time. But not now. For five and a half minutes, he sat there watching Megan through the crowds. Same as on the April DVD. Same clothes. Same expression. Dark eyes never leaving her.

Not once.

I went back over all the footage I'd already watched. Every month but the first one, October, he was there. Short periods of time. Never less than five minutes, never more than eight. It would have been incredibly easy to miss him – which is why I assumed he'd gone unnoticed by the police. They would have checked all four thousand hours; been through every single weekday; checked the footage all day, every day for six months, just to be sure. And apart from mornings, the whole time the place was jammed: so many people, so much going on. The man was only in shot for thirty-six minutes of the four thousand hours, with that fraction of time split up into even smaller chunks a month apart. I'd picked him up almost by accident. A fluke.

But he was there.

And he was watching Megan.

CHAPTER 15

Friday. After getting up at eight and making some coffee, I sat at the living-room windows, looking out at the garden, and studied the photograph of the man from Tiko's. I'd taken a picture of the TV screen, paused on the best view I could get of his face, and printed it out on the computer. Blown up big, the quality deteriorated.

But it was good enough.

He looked like he was in his thirties. Incredibly pale, jet-black hair combed into an old-fashioned side parting. A very angular face, all bone and sinew, his cheeks slightly hollow, his nose thin and straight. The ridge of his brow was prominent, raised, reducing his eyes to two tiny pinpricks of light. It gave him an odd, otherworldly feel: a man painted only in the darkest blacks and whitest whites. Physically, he didn't look much. Five-ten, maybe even less. No muscle, or at least no indication of any.

But something was off about him. Something ominous.

He looked at Megan the way a hunter looked at its prey. Deep concentration. Patience. His eyes constantly tracking her movements. His posture was slightly bent, as if he spent the whole time trying to make himself smaller, like a bear trap being primed. Because of that, he carried a kind of threat, a suggestion that his build and size wouldn't matter when it came to it. Because when it came to it, nothing would stop him.

He would get what he wanted.

I called Kaitlin and agreed to meet her during a free period she had at eleven o'clock. After that, I'd try and speak to DCI Jamie Hart. It was going to be a balancing act. I needed his help, because I needed to find out how far the case had progressed before it went cold, but I didn't want Hart getting too involved or interested in Megan's disappearance again. Perhaps I was doing the police a disservice. Perhaps they'd already pinpointed the man in Tiko's as someone to watch. But it was possible, and in fact more likely, that they'd totally missed him. And I didn't want them finding out about the man before I'd had a chance to try and find out who he was myself.

When I got to the school, I pulled in around the side in the Sixth Form car park, close to the fencing Megan must have scaled in order to avoid being picked up on CCTV. Kaitlin was waiting for me. Her bag was on top of a battered Ford Fiesta, a folder next to it, a set of textbooks next to that. I got out of the BMW. The morning was dry but heavy with the threat of rain. Dark clouds moved across the sky in thick coils. In the distance, beyond the rooftops of the houses surrounding the school, a mist hung, grey and oppressive like a blanket being pulled across the city.

I smiled at Kaitlin. 'Morning.'

She smiled back, but there was a slight hesitancy to her. Maybe she was expecting me to launch into a tirade about how she should have told the police what she knew.

I held up a hand. 'I don't care what you've done.'

She seemed to relax a little and then suggested we go to a coffee shop about half a mile from the school. It had two floors. The top one had big floor-to-ceiling windows and small circular tables lined up in front. I bought Kaitlin a latte, and then we took one of the tables, furthest away from everybody else. I got out my pen and pad, and turned to her. She was looking down at the people passing on the pavements.

'Are you okay?'

She glanced at me, a flicker of uncertainty in her eyes, as if I might be leading her into a trap. 'I'm fine,' she said eventually.

'So when did you first find out Megan was pregnant?'

'The week before she disappeared.'

'What happened?'

'I went round to her house, so we could work on a Biology assignment we'd been given. About an hour after I got there, she said she needed to puke.'

'Was that the first time she'd felt like that?'

'No. She said she'd been sick that morning, and

116

had been puking every day for a week. She said it was something she'd eaten.'

'But you didn't believe her.'

'No.'

'So she told you?'

'Eventually. She said she'd done a pregnancy test a week after the sickness and the headaches hadn't gone away.'

'Did you ask her who the father was?'

'Yes.'

'And what did she say?'

Kaitlin glanced at me. 'I guess this is where it gets confusing.'

'Okay.'

'This is the reason I lied.'

I nodded for her to continue.

'Megan was always very into, like, helping people. You know, charities, that kind of thing. She used to spend her summers helping out at a youth club down the road from her house. I think it was for people with, like, cerebral palsy or something.' She paused, glanced out of the window. 'Anyway, she said she'd met someone.'

'At the youth club?'

'Yeah.'

'Did she tell you his name?'

'No.'

'Why?'

She paused again, this time for longer. 'He was quite a few years older than her. Like, ten or fifteen or something. She thought he'd get into trouble.'

117

'With who?'

'Megan was seventeen. What do you think her parents would have said if they found out she was seeing some guy in his thirties?'

I leaned back in my seat. 'Did she tell you anything about him?'

'Just that she thought he was really sexy, and really clever, and that they were in love.' She shrugged. 'I'd never heard her talk about a guy like that. Megan was . . . well, she didn't meet very many men. When we used to go out, she was never interested in getting together with anyone.'

'Did she describe him at all? How he looked?'

'No.'

'Nothing?'

'No.'

I thought of the man in the club again. Had that been him? He wasn't attractive in any way, but he must have been at least fifteen years older than her. Even if the age vaguely matched, though, it didn't feel right. If she knew him, why would he be waiting there in the shadows? Why would he be there at all? I reached into my jacket pocket and got out the photograph. I pushed it across the table to Kaitlin.

'Do you recognize him?'

'Is that Tiko's?'

'Yes.'

I'd cropped it in, so the girls were out of shot, but her eyes still flicked to me, then back to the photograph, as she tried to put it together in her head.

'You recognize him?' I asked again.

'No.'

'You sure?'

'Positive.'

I took the photo back and folded it up.

'Did she tell you how many times they'd had sex?'

Kaitlin flushed a little.

'You don't have to be embarrassed.'

She shifted in her seat. 'Four times.'

'How far along was she?'

'In her pregnancy?'

'Yes.'

'Not far. I think about five or six weeks.'

'Did the guy she was sleeping with know she was pregnant?'

'Yes.'

'She told him?'

'Yes.'

I wrote that down. When I looked up again, she was staring at me, and for the first time I glimpsed the girl underneath.

'What's wrong?'

'I just wish I hadn't lied. Maybe if I hadn't lied, the police would have found her. Do you think she went off with the man she met? Do you think he . . .' She faded out.

'Listen to me, Kaitlin,' I said. 'If, for whatever reason, the police come calling, don't tell them about the pregnancy. I don't know if they'll be back or not. For all intents and purposes, the case

119

is dead. But they could get interested again if they find me snooping around, and the first thing we need to do here is protect you. So if they come calling, tell them about the youth club, and that you think she might have been seeing someone there, but leave it at that, okay?'

She nodded.

'Good. What was the name of the youth club?'

'Barton Hill.'

'It's close to Megan's house?'

'Yes.'

'Did you ever go?'

'No. She asked me along a couple of times, but . . . it's not really my thing.'

I drummed my fingers on the table, thinking. 'So did you decide not to tell the police about Megan being pregnant because – what? – she wanted to protect the identity of this guy?'

Kaitlin glanced at me. A movement in her eyes. 'No,' she said finally. Something else was at play.

'So why did you lie?'

'Because I . . .' She stopped. Glanced at me again. 'The day she disappeared, before the police came to talk to me . . . I got a phone call.'

'From who?'

Another pause. Longer this time. 'Charlie Bryant.'

This time it was my turn to pause. I studied her for a moment. 'Did he know about Megan's pregnancy?'

'Yes.'

'How?'

'She must have told him, or he must have found out somehow. He just called me and told me we couldn't tell the police anything.'

'Why?'

'Because we'd be in danger.'

'From who?'

'I don't know.'

'You didn't ask him?'

'He wouldn't tell me. He said it was best I didn't know.' She stopped. 'At first, I thought it was him getting all weird again.'

'What do you mean?'

'I mean, he was, like, in love with Megan. *Totally* in love with her. Sometimes he'd go over the top and creep us all out.'

'With the stuff he said to her?'

'Yeah, and the way he acted around her. He'd follow her around sometimes. Not like a stalker, but just . . . I don't know, just *following* her, you know? He'd do these drawings for her, paintings, write poems and shit like that. He was always telling her he'd be there for her. He could be a real weirdo sometimes.'

'So why did you believe him when he called you?'

She stopped, took a long drink of her coffee, then eyed me nervously. 'He just seemed different that day. Sounded different. He never really cared what the rest of us thought of him. Me and some of the others used to take the piss out of him all the time at school, but he was never bothered by

121

it. He just laughed it off. But that day . . . I don't
know. He sounded different. When he told me we'd
be in danger if we talked, I totally believed him.'
She took a deep breath. 'For the first time ever,
he seemed really scared.'

I was pulling the car out of the school gates when
my phone went. I picked it up off the passenger
seat and slotted it into the hands-free. It was
Spike. He had names and addresses for the eighteen
different numbers I'd sourced off Megan's mobile
phone. I told him to put them in an email. There was
an internet café about half a mile from Charlie
Bryant's house. I'd pick them up there.

I found a parking space off Holloway Road,
opposite a bank of new apartments, and headed
towards Highgate. The internet café – apparently
without any sense of irony – was called *Let's Get
Digital!*, but there was a PC right in the corner
where it would be hard for anyone to see the
screen. I logged into my Yahoo.

There was a PDF attached to Spike's message.
I opened it up.

Eighteen numbers, surnames with each, listed
alphabetically. It looked like a copy of a phone bill,
except this phone bill had names and addresses as
well as numbers. The information had probably been
ripped directly from phone company databases and
then pasted into the document. His ability to get
beyond firewalls wasn't the only reason Spike got
work. He had a certain attention to detail, such as

arranging names in alphabetical order, which made things even more appealing to his customers.

I went through the list.

There weren't many surprises. The mobile and work numbers for both James and Caroline Carver, which I already knew; a mobile and a landline for Kaitlin and the same for Lindsey; four other friends, all girls, whose names I recognized from Megan's Book of Life, each with a landline and a mobile. That left two. The first was a mobile phone number for Charlie Bryant. The second was a landline, outer London, no name attached to it, and no street address. Just a PO box number. Spike had written next to it: *Working on this – will get a street address and call you back.*

I got out my phone and dialled the number. It clicked and connected. After four rings, it clicked again and the echoey, distant sound of an answer machine kicked in. 'Please leave your message after the tone,' said a bored-sounding male voice. There wasn't much more I could do until Spike got me the street address.

But there was something I could do about Charlie Bryant. I knew where he lived – and now it was time to find out exactly how much he knew.

CHAPTER 16

It was two-thirty by the time I got to the Bryant house. I rang the doorbell, pressing my face against a glass panel in the door. Rain hammered against the hard plastic roof of the porch, a sound like nails being poured from a bucket. It would have been impossible to hear movement inside, even if there was anyone home. But there wasn't. The house was dark and silent, and had the cold, lifeless feel that came from being unoccupied. No light. No warmth. No sign of being lived in.

I looked along the house and back up the driveway. It was well protected from the road. Trees at the entrance and lining one side of the property, the neighbours a nice distance away over a mid-sized brick wall. It was unusual for a house in London to have so much space to itself. It made me wonder what Charlie Bryant's dad did for a living.

Finally, the rain started to fade a little, turning into drizzle.

And then I could smell something.

I stepped down off the porch and walked around

to the side gate. The smell started to get stronger. On the other side, I could see a series of bin liners, grass cuttings spilling out of the top. The grass had turned to mulch, sliding across the concrete and staining the brickwork on the house. Next to that were more bin liners, torn by animals, food scattered across the path. The gate was heavy oak, good quality, with a thick wooden bar across the middle. A big padlock was on the other side, visible through one of the slats.

I glanced both ways to make sure I wasn't being watched, then pulled myself up and over. I stood for a second, looking along the house, grass squelching beneath my feet.

The smell was stronger now.

There were two windows and a single door on this side of the house. The first window looked in at the kitchen. Semi dark. Wooden cupboards, metal finishes. A picture of Charlie Bryant's mum on top of the microwave in a green frame. Everything was clean. Nothing was out of place. The next window was for a toilet. Air freshener on the windowsill. Frosted glass made it difficult to see anything else. I moved to the door and, through a glass panel, saw it led into a pokey utility room. Washing machine. Tumble dryer. Fridge freezer. A wine rack full of wine bottles. Boots and shoes lined up next to a tray full of dog food. It was squirming with insects.

I moved quickly around to the back.

The garden was small and surrounded on all

sides by high wooden fences. Huge fir trees lined the back wall. It was very sheltered and very private. The back of the house had a big window and a set of patio doors. Cupping my hands against the glass of the doors, I could see into a long room that ran all the way to the front of the house. Leather sofas. Bookcases. Modern art on the walls. A TV surrounded by DVDs, with a games console slotted in underneath. As I stepped away from the glass, the patio door shifted slightly. It was open.

I reached for the handle and slid it across.

And the smell hit me.

It spilled out of the living room on to the patio, like a wave crashing. As it did, a feeling of dread began to slither through my chest. I put my hand to my mouth and stepped into the house. It was as quiet as a cemetery. Hardly any noise at all, except for the hum of the fridge in the kitchen.

'Mr Bryant?'

I waited, didn't expect an answer, and didn't get one.

'Charlie?'

No reply. No movement. No sound at all.

I headed for the stairs. The smell got stronger as I moved up. At the top I could hear a tap dripping. Nothing looked out of place in any of the rooms I could see into. Only the fourth door was closed. Bluebottles buzzed around the top of the frame, sluggish and dozy in the airless house. I pulled the sleeve down on my coat, over my fingers, and then wrapped my covered hand around the door handle.

Slowly, I opened it.

It was a small room. Maybe ten feet by ten feet. The curtains were partially drawn but – through the gap – I could see down to the side of the house. Inside it was warm, suffocating, and there were more flies at the glass and more insects crawling through the carpet. The family dog was in the corner of the room, a gaping wound in its side. In front, lying exactly parallel to one another, were Charlie Bryant and his father.

They were both dead.

His father was face down, arms tied behind his back with duct tape. Blood had spread out beneath him. Now it was dry and the carpet fibres were rigid. His skin had a green tinge to it, and there were maggots wriggling out from beneath his face.

Across from him was his son.

Charlie faced up to the ceiling, his chest awash in blood. Somehow, in death, he seemed younger than seventeen. I stepped further into the room. His legs were over to one side, bent in an A-shape. He'd been tied at the ankles as well. His mouth was slightly open, almost in a cry for help. And his eyes were the same.

Begging his killer to stop.

CHAPTER 17

I called the police and waited for them at the front. They arrived ten minutes later. Once the whole place was cordoned off, the scenes of crime officer asked me to retrace my footsteps in and out of the property. When a route was established, tents were erected at the side and the rear, and it became the route everybody used. No one deviated from the line. Despite the rain, they wanted to try to preserve as much evidence as they could.

After that, a uniform walked me out to the front of the house, where a second officer was standing with a clipboard, recording anyone entering and leaving. At the front gate, police tape flapped, twisting and whipping in the wind. 'Here,' one of them said and handed me an umbrella. I put it up. 'Someone will come for you in a bit.'

Fifty minutes later, two CID officers emerged from the side of the house. One was in his late thirties, dark hair, slim and lithe, dressed smartly in a black raincoat, black suit and salmon tie. The other was bigger, older and greyer, in his early fifties. He hadn't made such an effort: a dirty brown jacket, jeans, a thick red woollen top and a pair of white trainers. The younger one led the way towards me. He had the air of a man in charge.

'Mr Raker?'

I nodded. He was Scottish.

'I'm DCI Phillips,' he said, and pointed to his partner. 'This is DS Davidson. We need to have a chat. We can do it here, in the middle of this mayhem, or we can do it back at the station, where I can offer you a cup of coffee and something to eat.'

He spoke softly, in a controlled tone, and had his hands laced together at his front in an almost respectful gesture, the fingers of his right occasionally turning the wedding band on his left. But I could see it for what it was: an act. He was trying to tell me he was a reasonable man. Someone I could trust and confide in. But a different man existed beneath the surface.

'Mr Raker?' he repeated.

'Am I under arrest?'

Beside Phillips, Davidson snorted. I glanced at him. He wasn't as good at the drama as his partner. He stood slightly back, his stance more aggressive. Small, dark eyes. Arms folded. Head tilted, as if he was looking down his nose at me.

'Arrest?' said Phillips, and briefly turned to his partner. 'Why would we want to arrest you? You haven't done anything wrong, have you?'

When I didn't reply he seemed to realize his usual methods weren't going to work on me.

Maybe we were interested in the same things. Maybe we'd both read the same books. I'd spent years trying to understand people better; trying to find ways to see past the lies. The politicians, the celebrities, the headline-makers. He'd probably done the same. Trying to get inside the heads of the worst humanity could dredge up.

'Why don't you follow me?' he asked quietly, eyes lingering on me.

I was half tempted to say no and walk away, but refusing would make me look suspicious. I wasn't legally obliged to go, but I didn't need them digging around in my case and I definitely didn't need them thinking I had something to hide. They'd want to bag what I was wearing, so I told them I'd go with them once I got some spare clothes from the BMW.

After I was done, it was a quiet, fifteen-minute journey to the station. Davidson sat in the back with me while Phillips drove. Neither of them said anything. As we moved south through Camden, I began to put things together in my head. A plan. An approach. I imagined how they would come at me. I doubted they seriously thought I was the killer, but, at the moment, I was their only lead.

The station was an old 1970s building, with a horrible industrial look. Part factory, part prison block. Phillips pulled into a parking bay and killed the engine. Two spaces down I noticed a sign had been nailed to the wall: RESERVED FOR DCI HART. Jamie Hart. The lead on the Megan Carver case.

This isn't coincidence.

They would have discovered the link between Charlie and Megan months ago. The only question now was: How much did they know beyond that?

'Wait there a second,' Phillips said to Davidson as we were getting out. 'I left my phone in my car.' Davidson nodded and we both watched Phillips move across the car park to where a battered red Mondeo was parked. He flipped the locks, fiddled around in the glove compartment and then returned to us with his mobile phone. 'Okay,' he said. 'Let's go.'

The two of them led me inside to a small, cramped waiting area, with a raised front desk that looked down over everything. The custody sergeant – early sixties, with silver hair and half-moon glasses – was sitting there, filling in some paperwork. His eyes flicked up to watch as we approached.

'Aren't you dead yet?' Davidson said. It was the first time he'd spoken. He had a broad East End accent.

The sergeant smirked. 'You'll be dead before me, Eddie. I mean, just look at what you're wearing. No way the fashion police are going to take that lying down.'

Phillips burst out laughing.

'Who have we got here?' he asked, looking at me.

'He's just here for a chat,' Phillips replied.

The sergeant nodded, reached for a button under the desk and then went back to what he was doing. A codelocked door to our left buzzed, and we moved through into a thin corridor. On my right was a big, open-plan office, 'CID' printed on the door. Further down the corridor, in front of me, were four interview rooms. Phillips pointed towards Room 1.

As he opened the door, two strip lights flickered into life above us. The inside was stark. White walls, a dark blue carpet, no windows. A table, two chairs on one side, one on the other. Everything was bolted down, and there was a crash bar midway up the wall on all four sides of the room in case anything kicked off and one of the officers needed to raise the alarm. Next to the door was an intercom. Once the door had locked shut, that was how you got back out. Not exactly the cosy chat Phillips had promised.

'Do you want a drink?' he asked.

'Black coffee.'

He nodded, then disappeared.

Davidson watched me from the open doorway as I sat down. He didn't look like the type for polite conversation, so I drummed my fingers on the table as we waited in silence. It seemed to annoy him, which I liked. Phillips re-emerged after ten minutes with three cups of coffee and pushed the door closed. It was on a slow spring and took an age to click shut. Neither of them moved until it had. Once it locked, there was a gentle buzz, both of them sat down and we began.

CHAPTER 18

In the business, this was called a 'voluntary attendance'. I wasn't under arrest, so I didn't need a solicitor, and I could get up and leave whenever I wanted. But even here there were rules. Number one was covering your ass. The first thing Phillips did was pass a form across the table towards me that confirmed I was here voluntarily. I read it over and signed it. Davidson slouched in his chair, resting his coffee cup on his belly.

'Okay,' Phillips said, both hands flat to the table. 'Let's establish a few ground rules here, so there are no grey areas. You're not under arrest and we haven't charged you with anything. You're helping us with our enquiries. We have no legal responsibility to inform a lawyer you're here, but if you want a lawyer, you can make that call.'

They both looked at me. Phillips genuinely didn't seem to care whether I called anyone or not, as if it made no difference to the opinion he'd already formed of me. Davidson looked like he'd take it personally. If I called a lawyer, it would immediately cement his view that I was involved in something.

'Do you *want* to call a lawyer, Mr Raker?'

I shook my head. 'No. I'm good.'

'Great.' Phillips wrapped his hands around the coffee. Steam rose from the oily surface. 'Well, let's start at the beginning then. What were you doing at the house?'

'I'm on a case.'

Davidson snorted. 'Case?'

I looked at him and then back to Phillips. 'I work missing persons, including kids who have disappeared. Charlie Bryant was linked to the case I'm currently on.'

'Linked how?'

'He knew the girl I'm trying to find.'

Phillips nodded. He started turning his wedding band. A flash of that same steel in his eyes, as if he knew what was coming. 'Who are you trying to find?'

I paused, looked between them and then leaned forward. 'Megan Carver.'

Davidson snorted again. 'You gotta be fucking kidding me.' Next to him, Phillips didn't move. Davidson sat forward, placing his coffee cup down in front of him. 'Since when?'

'Since five days ago.'

'Why did they come to you?'

I shrugged. 'I guess her parents felt like the police investigation had hit a wall. You guys would probably know better than me if that's true.'

Davidson's eyes narrowed. 'What do you mean by that?'

'I mean, DCI Hart's in the next room,' I said, staring at him. 'Why don't you ask him?'

A short pause.

Then, Phillips again: 'You made any headway?'

'Some. Not much. Mostly I've been going back over ground Hart and his team were covering six months ago.'

'Like what?'

'Like everything. Family, friends, her school.'

'So you turned up at the Bryant house because . . .?'

'Because, as you know, Charlie Bryant used to go out with Megan.'

And because he knew she was pregnant.

Phillips was staring at me, his expression fixed, his body still. He didn't seem surprised by any of this. Next to him, his partner was twitchy and aggressive, his fingers tapping the plastic coffee cup, his body shifting in the chair.

'Things must have been getting a bit desperate,' Davidson said eventually. I glanced at him, frowning. 'I mean, you don't break into someone's house if a case hasn't already started going south.'

'You sound like you're speaking from experience.'

Davidson's skin started to redden. I could see a corner of Phillips's mouth turn up in a smile.

'Nothing was going south,' I said.

'So why did you break into their house?'

'There's no sign of a break-in anywhere in that house. You know the back door was unlocked. The only thing I did was scale the gate.'

'Trespass, you mean?'

'Which would you prefer? Me jump over that gate, or those two bodies lie in that house for another two weeks? Or a month? Or a year?'

'Still doesn't make it legal.'

'Yeah, you're right. Better that they stayed like that until the room filled with blowflies.' I picked up my coffee cup. 'Better that the police never get to find out why someone would want to murder a seventeen-year-old.'

Davidson's face reddened again.

'So why *would* someone want to murder a seventeen-year-old?' Phillips asked.

'I've no idea.'

He eyed me. 'Really?'

'Really. I told you: I've been on this case for less than a week.'

'You been sitting on your hands for a week, then?'

Davidson again. The colour had started to fade from his cheeks, but he still looked pissed off. I watched him. Eventually he sighed, as if my silence somehow confirmed what he'd said, and turned his attention back to the coffee cup resting on his belly.

'Charlie didn't seem a prime candidate for a murder victim,' Phillips said.

'I agree.'

'So why would someone do that to him?'

'I don't know.'

'And his father.'

I shrugged. *I don't know.*

136

'Do you think this is related to Megan Carver?'

It was obvious he'd already decided the answer for himself, and I realized that a red flag had just gone up again on the Carver investigation. I could have lied to them both from the start and pretended I hadn't been led to the Bryant house through Megan's disappearance, but none of us would have believed it. What was definitely obvious was that they'd be pulling Jamie Hart into a meeting room as soon as I left the building.

'I don't know if it's related to Megan,' I said eventually.

Davidson snorted again. 'Of course you don't.'

'Shall I make something up?'

'All right,' Phillips said softly, and placed a hand on his partner's arm. 'DS Davidson, why don't you take five minutes?'

Davidson's eyes lingered on me before getting up and leaving the room. Phillips waited for the door to click shut, then turned back to me.

'You were a journalist, is that right?'

I stared at him. *So that was why you took so long to get the coffees.* He'd spent some time going through my history. After my last case, I'd had to sit in a police station giving interviews for two days. Everything I'd told them over those forty-eight hours would be logged in their database for him to find. He'd know about me, about my background, about my cases.

'Why the career change?'

I shrugged. 'Why not?'

'You didn't enjoy journalism?'

'I enjoyed it up until my wife got cancer.'

'Is she still around?'

I shook my head.

'I'm sorry to hear that,' he said gently. He waited for a moment, once again laying both hands flat to the table. 'You know the Carver disappearance is an ongoing investigation, right? Her parents told you that, I expect.'

'I'm not sure it makes much difference to them.'

'Oh?'

'Megan hasn't been found. That's all they care about.'

He didn't reply.

'Look, I don't know what game you're playing here – but it's not me against you. It's not me against *anyone*. I'm trying to find Megan Carver, just like DCI Hart was trying to find her.'

'But you can see how your presence complicates things?'

'How does it complicate things? Hart stopped calling the Carvers when the case hit a wall. You should be talking to him, not me.'

He rubbed a couple of fingers against his forehead, as if he were trying to reason with a child. 'Truth is, David, you've – whether unwittingly or not – stepped into a situation here – and I need you to step back out again.'

'What are you talking about?'

'I need you to drop the Carver case.'

'Why would I do that?'

He sighed. 'I'm asking you as a favour.'

'A *favour*?' I sat back in my seat and studied him. His eyes were dark, focused, looking right at me. 'Have you got a lead?'

'I can't talk to you about that.'

'I'm not dropping the case as a favour to someone I met for the first time an hour ago. Has anyone here even *talked* to the Carvers in the past two months?'

'Of course we have.'

'I don't mean calling to tell them there's nothing new to report. You might want to go around to their house some time and see what sort of state they're in. They spent four months waiting for Hart to bring their daughter home, and another two months waiting for the phone to ring. If you have a lead, then you need to act on it.'

'Are you telling us how to do our job?'

'No, I'm telling you you're messing with people's emotions here. You need to give them something to hang on to. The reason they came to me is because they need to see the case moving forward. They need to believe they're getting closer to finding their daughter, even if they're not. You need to share whatever you have with them.'

He smiled. 'It's not that simple.'

'Nothing's simple,' I said. 'What's the lead?'

'It's an ongoing investigation.'

'Maybe I can help.'

'I don't think so.'

'How do you know?'

'Because I know,' he said, his voice simmering for the first time. 'I'm going to level with you here, David. I need you to step back from the case. The only reason I can give you is that, by you sticking your nose in here, you're jeopardizing a parallel investigation.'

'You've got another case linked to Megan's disappearance?'

He leaned forward. 'I can see your mind ticking over there, David. But whatever you *think* is going on here, it isn't.'

'You've got another disappearance?'

'No.'

'Then what?' He didn't reply, and this time I sighed myself. 'You might want to take a refresher course where negotiation is concerned, DCI Phillips. We've all got to make a living.'

'This is going to turn out bad for you, David.'

'Is that a threat?'

'No,' Phillips said, giving me his best innocent look. 'We're not in the business of threats here. We're the police. We *respond* to threats. But I'm telling you now: if you get in the way, we won't hesitate to push you aside.'

'Thanks for the heads-up.'

He got to his feet. 'I'm going to make this easy for you, okay? Charles Bryant and his father are part of a murder investigation now. You can throw the dog in there too, for all I care. The one thing I want to make absolutely crystal clear for you is this: you don't even *think* about looking into the

140

Bryant murder, and you don't come near us on anything to do with the Carver disappearance if it overlaps with lines of enquiry we're following with Bryant. Understood?'

I didn't move. Just stared back at him.

'Your *case* . . .' He shook his head. 'We worked all the angles you're working. We worked them better, with more manpower and more experience. We found nothing. But that doesn't mean the case is finished. It just means we're coming at it from another angle. And, like I said, if you get in the way . . .'

I smiled at him. 'So you *do* have another lead?'

He shrugged. 'You mull it over. I can't tell you anything else, but I can assure you that this DIY detective shite *is* going to come back and bite you on the arse.'

His eyes lingered on me as I tried to figure out exactly what it was he was hiding. Then he turned and left the room.

CHAPTER 19

I'd been waiting about five minutes when the door opened again. It wasn't Phillips or Davidson this time, but another man. He was in his mid forties, at least six-two, broad – but thirty pounds overweight with messy red hair and blotchy skin. He looked like he hadn't slept in months. Once he might have been a good-looking guy, but something had rubbed away at him so only the shadows of that man remained.

In one of his hands, he was cradling a mug of coffee. In the pocket of his jacket, a small spiral notepad poked out with a pen wedged in the top. He held the door in place, about two inches shy of the frame, and placed the pad on the floor in the gap to keep it open. Then he left it there and came over and sat down opposite me.

'Mr Raker?'

I nodded.

'My name's Colm Healy.'

He was southern Irish. He sipped on the coffee and flicked a look back towards the door. The pad was still there, holding it open. I studied him. *He doesn't want to use the intercom to buzz back out.*

Which means he's either lazy – or he's not supposed to be here. He turned back to me. 'How you doing?'

'I'm sitting in a police station.' I said. 'What could be better?'

He smiled. 'They been treating you nicely?'

'Five-star service.'

'Good.' He looked again at the door. 'I'm not going to take up much of your time here. I just need to ask you a few questions.'

'Your pals just asked me a few questions.'

'I know,' he said. 'Luckily for you, I've got some more.'

'Why?'

'Why what?'

'Why are you here?'

'Like I said, I've got a few quest—'

'I know what you said.'

He paused, a serious expression settling across his face. Then a smile cracked; he wasn't amused, he was just trying to tell me he was a reasonable guy. 'Are you playing hardball, Mr Raker? Is that it?'

'Where's Phillips?'

'Never mind about Phillips.'

'You two don't get on?'

He pushed his coffee aside and reached into his back pocket. Took out his warrant card and laid it down in front of me. Next to a picture of a younger version of him it said DETECTIVE SERGEANT COLM HEALY.

'I worked on the Megan Carver case,' he said, and glanced towards the door again. 'So I'd like

143

you to answer a few questions for me. That way we can stop messing around and get on with the business of finding her.' He smiled his best shit-eating grin. 'Is that okay with you?'

'I've already told Phillips everything I know.'

He sighed. 'I'm going to level with you, Mr Raker. Me and Phillips . . .' He leaned forward, his voice dropping to a whisper. 'We don't get on. If I have to spend more than a couple of minutes in his company, I want to put my fist through a bloody wall. He rubs me up the wrong way. He rubs a lot of people up the wrong way here. The guy's got a rod up his arse.'

'At least we agree on something.'

'Do you think Megan Carver is still alive?'

I looked at him. There had been a tremor of desperation in his voice. I leaned in even closer to him and this time I could smell the aftershave on the collar of his shirt and the coffee on his breath.

'Mr Raker?'

'I don't know.'

His eyes narrowed. 'You don't know – or you won't tell?'

'I don't know.'

He glanced towards the door again. 'We might be able to help each other here.'

'How?'

'You scratch my balls, I scratch yours.'

I smiled. I didn't particularly want any man scratching my balls, but I was intrigued by what his play might be. Five minutes after Phillips warns me off my case, another cop turns up and tells me he can help me if we meet halfway.

'So . . . you want to dance?' he asked.

I didn't reply.

Healy's eyes narrowed again, like he'd second-guessed me. 'That's disappointing.' He stood. 'I could have helped you.'

'I don't even know you.'

'You don't need to,' he said. 'We don't have to move in together. You tell me what you know, I tell you what I know. After that, we go our separate ways.'

'Why?'

'I already told you why.'

'No, you didn't. You told me you worked the Carver case, but we both know that's not true.' I nodded towards the pad wedging open the door. 'We both know you're not supposed to be here.'

We looked at each other; a face-off. After a while, he shrugged again, and made a move for the door. *Give him something. See what his angle is.*

'Wait a sec.'

He turned back to me. I reached into my jacket pocket and removed the folded-up printout of the man from Tiko's. I placed it down on the table, turning it so Healy could see. 'You want to help me?'

He stepped back in towards the table. Nodded.

'Tell me who this is.'

He picked up the photograph, his eyes moving from left to right, taking in as much of the face, and the scene around it, as possible. There wasn't

145

a lot else to see but the features of the man. I'd cropped it in as close to his head as I could get. Kaitlin had recognized the surroundings as Tiko's. Healy wouldn't.

'What's this?' he said.

'You didn't come across him during the Carver investigation?'

His eyes flicked to me. Frowned. 'Now why would I have done that?'

A weird answer. I leaned back in my seat.

'I don't know,' I said. '*Why* would you?'

'Do you know who he is?'

'No. Do you?'

He didn't answer.

'*Do* you?'

He placed the picture back down on the desk. 'You want my advice, David?' he said, ignoring my question and calling me by my first name now.

'Not really.'

'Well, I'm gonna give it to you.' He picked up his coffee cup for the final time, and nodded at the picture. 'You want to spend less time with your nose in the history books, and more time trying to find out where the hell Megan Carver is.'

'What are you talking about?'

'This prick,' he said, pressing a finger to the face of the man in the photo. 'How's *he* going to help you?'

'What do you mean?'

He looked at me, like he couldn't decide if I was

joking or not. 'What do you think I mean? Your guy in the picture there – how's he going to help find Megan when he's been buried in the fucking ground for a hundred years?'

CHAPTER 20

I stared at Healy across the interview room. 'What are you talking about?'

He glanced at the door, then back to the photo on the desk in front of me. 'You ever heard of Milton Sykes?'

I frowned. 'The serial killer?'

'Right. Old school. Kidnapped and killed thirteen women just over a hundred years ago and buried them so well no one's ever been able to find them. Sat there happily admitting he'd taken them, but wouldn't tell the police where he put the bodies. Probably thought he was Jack the Ripper – all smoke and mirrors and mystery – but all he really was, was a fucking arsehole.'

I glanced at the photo. 'So?'

'So if someone's given that to you, they're taking the piss.'

'It's not Milton Sykes.'

'It looks exactly like him.'

'It's not Sykes.'

'It's *Sykes*. Open your eyes.'

I shook my head. Short of screaming in his face,

he was unlikely to understand how certain I was. 'I'm telling you now, this isn't Milton Sykes.'

'Face it. You've been taken for a ride.'

'This is a still from CCTV footage taken six months ago.'

He took a step back towards me, the smell of aftershave and coffee coming with him again. His eyes flicked across the photograph, as if satisfying himself he was right. Then he shrugged. 'Look, believe whatever you want to believe. I don't care whether it is or it isn't. It doesn't help me either way.'

'So what helps you?'

'What?'

'You're not interested in Megan. So what *are* you interested in?'

He was at the door now, fingers wrapped around it. He opened it a fraction and looked out through the gap. When he saw no one was coming, he turned back to me. Glanced at the photograph. Picked up his pad. Didn't say anything.

'Come on, Healy.'

Two uniformed officers had stopped outside the door, chatting.

'Why are you standing here now?' I asked.

He looked out into the corridor again, nodding at the officers. They nodded back, before saying goodbye to one another and disappearing from view.

'I have my reasons,' he said.

And then he was gone.

*   *   *

They made me wait outside the CID office when we were done. Through the door I could see Phillips and Davidson at the back of the room, close to a wall full of photographs, chatting to someone. I recognized his picture from the papers: DCI Jamie Hart.

He was thin, gaunt, with closely cropped blond hair, and wore the tired, put-upon look of a man who spent most of his life inside the walls of the station. His eyes, though, were different: fast, bright, lively, darting to meet mine every few seconds as Phillips, perched on the edge of his desk, spoke to him.

As I waited for them, I took in the walls of the office: the photographs, most too small to make out; a map of the city, littered with tacks and scrawled all over in marker pen; pieces of note-paper pinned adjacent to that; and – off to the side – a thin, vertical series of stickies with numbers on each: 2119, 8110, 44, 127, 410, 3111, 34. Something next to that also caught my attention: a blown-up black-and-white photocopy of Megan. It was the same picture I'd found of her on her digital camera, standing outside the block of flats. *What have they got on her?*

I glanced at Phillips and Hart, then removed my mobile phone. The best bit about voluntary attendance was that you didn't have to sign over your personal effects. I raised the phone in front of me so it looked like I was texting, then quickly went to the camera option, zoomed in and took the best shot of the wall that I could manage. It was blurry and half lit – but it would have to do.

Seconds later, Phillips led Hart out towards me.

'David,' he said, as he came through. 'This is DCI Hart.'

We shook hands. I made a show of pausing briefly, as if to send a message, and took in Hart properly. Then something else registered with me: Hart and Phillips were both DCIs. They worked out of the same station. They even worked out of the same office. Usually there was one ranking officer and a series of sergeants and constables. Here, the balance was off. Ten officers maximum, two of whom were DCIs. It was top heavy in a way I'd never seen before.

'I understand you're working my case,' Hart said, disrupting my train of thought. There was a smile on his face. I didn't know him well enough to tell whether it was genuine or not – but somehow I doubted it.

'Yeah, looks that way.'

'You think this Bryant kid was murdered because he knew Megan?' he asked, launching straight in.

'I doubt it,' I lied.

'So what's your take?'

'Charlie Bryant had a disrupted last year or so. From what I can tell, he wasn't spending a lot of time at school, so he had to be spending his time somewhere.'

'And?'

'And maybe he got in with the wrong crowd.'

151

'His father too?'

I smiled at Hart. He was trying to corner me. I didn't want to lead myself anywhere I didn't have to go, so I just shrugged and said nothing.

'Petty stealing,' Phillips said, picking things up, 'a little vandalism, underage drinking – that's the wrong crowd where Charlie Bryant comes from. Having an eight-inch blade put through your chest? Not so much.'

I shrugged again for effect, but Phillips was right. Charlie Bryant wasn't from the bad part of town. He wasn't even from the okay part. His corner of north London was affluent and safe. Crime in his road was swearing at old women. Despite that, I stuck to the argument: 'It's been a while since we were teenagers, DCI Phillips. It's not the good old days any more. You leave your back door open now, you come home to no house.'

Phillips studied me, eyes fixed, brain ticking over. He didn't look convinced, and I made a mental note to watch him. He was switched on and bright. That made him dangerous.

'So,' I said, 'if we're done, I'll be off.'

'Fair enough,' he replied, and held out his hand. I shook it. 'Remember, the Bryant murders are a police matter now, David. That means the police are dealing with it, and we don't need anyone getting in the way. And we absolutely, one hundred per cent, will *not* be sharing any information until we're ready to do so.'

I nodded. 'Sounds like a plan.'

'It does, doesn't it?' he replied, then jabbed a thumb over his shoulder to the office. Davidson was sitting at a desk, watching us, an expression like a pitbull. 'You have a think about what we discussed. We're all after the same thing here. We all want to know why Charles Bryant was killed like that – *and* we all want to find Megan.'

Inside the office, I suddenly saw Healy appear, a fresh mug of coffee in his hands. He glanced towards us, momentarily stopped, then moved away and out of view.

Yeah, we all want to find her, I thought. *Just some of us more than others.*

CHAPTER 21

Phillips had someone drop me back at my car, which I'd left outside the Bryant house. A uniformed officer was still positioned outside the front gates, another one further up the drive, and lights were on in the living room. Crime-scene tape shone in the street light.

On the drive back home, I placed my phone in the hands-free and made a couple of calls. The first one was to Liz. It was Friday night, and we were supposed to be going to the new Italian restaurant her client owned in Acton. I told her we were still on, but I'd got caught up at work and would have to re-book the table for eight-thirty. She said that was fine. As I killed the call and thought about what lay ahead, something bloomed in my stomach. Excitement. Or doubt. Or both.

As the traffic ground to a halt, I reached inside my jacket and took out the photograph of the man from Tiko's, studying the features of his face: the lines, the shape, the prominent brow sitting like a shelf of flesh above a pair of oil-black eyes. It wasn't Sykes. Milton Sykes was long dead. But there must have been enough of a similarity for

Healy to believe it was him. Once I was home I'd find out more about Sykes – his victims, his crimes, his history – but, in the meantime, I could start filling in the gaps. I reached across to the phone and scrolled through to T.

Terry Dooley.

Dooley was an old contact I'd used during my paper days. His career was twenty-four hours away from being flushed down the toilet after I'd found out him and three of his detectives had spent a couple of hours at an illegal brothel in south London. I stepped in and offered to save his career and his family life all at the same time in exchange for information when I needed it. He reluctantly agreed, realizing the trade-off was better for him. Dooley was all bluster and front, but basically repentant. The one thing he cared about more than his job was his kids, and the idea of seeing them once a week after his wife had dragged him to the divorce courts was more terrifying than any crime scene.

'What a great end to the day,' he said when I told him who it was.

'How you doing, Dools?'

'Yeah, fantastic now I've heard from you, Davey. What do you need this time? Your car cleaned?'

The last time I'd called him, I'd got him to sort out a problem I'd had with a stolen hire car. Dooley's days of dealing with petty crime were about fifteen years behind him. He'd been working murders ever since.

'Nothing like that, Dools – although my kitchen needs painting.'

He blew air down the line. 'Funny.'

'This won't take long.' I glanced at the photograph of the man from the club. 'You familiar with anyone from the Megan Carver team?'

'The Carver team?' He paused. 'Not really. They mostly worked out of the stations in and around north London.'

'How come?'

'The chief super wanted things to look like they were focused locally so her family and the public would think we were on the frontline, asking all the right people all the right questions. Made it look better in the papers if the teams stayed local.'

'It was all bullshit?'

He snorted. 'What do you think? I know a few of the faces up there, but not well. I've seen Hart around. He used to work Clubs and Vice with one of the boys on my team. They called him "Skel" – as in "Skeleton". You seen him?'

'Yeah. He's thin.'

'*Thin?*' Dooley laughed. 'I don't trust anyone who looks like they just crawled out the fucking ground.'

'Anyone else?'

'I know Eddie Davidson. We came through the ranks together, but I haven't seen the Burger King for a few years. The others . . . only what I've heard. There's some Jock going off like a rocket up there.'

156

'Phillips?'

'Yeah, that's him.'

'Any idea why him and Hart are working out of the same office?'

'What do you mean?'

'I mean, he's a DCI and so is Hart. There's two of them leading a tiny team of about eight detectives. I've never come across a set-up like that before – have you?'

'Can't say I have.'

'So what's your take?'

'My take? Sounds like a one-way ticket to a great big shitheap of politics and personality clashes. I mean, who's the SIO? Who sets out the Policy Log?'

The senior investigating officer ran the case and was also responsible for determining the parameters of the Policy Log, a set of rules unique to every case, which set out how the investigating team dealt with things like roles, responsibilities, HOLMES searches and the media. Dooley had a point: who made those choices when there were two officers of equal rank working in such close proximity? Something was definitely out of kilter. I just had to find out what.

'Can I go now?' Dooley asked.

'What about a guy called Healy?'

'*Colm* Healy?'

'Yeah – you know him?'

'Yeah, everyone knows Colm. He was a good copper back in the day. Worked murders with me for a while. Nose like a bloodhound.'

'He's not good any more?'

'He's had . . .' He stopped. 'He's had a few personal problems.'

'Like what?'

'His wife left him, his kids hated his guts. He had this unsolved which pretty much broke him for a year. He had to take a month off on stress leave, and when he came back he was about half the cop and twice the man. He looked like the Goodyear blimp last time I saw him.'

'Why'd his wife leave?'

'Cos he spent most of his life chained to a desk working murders. She ended up banging some other guy, and when Colm found out he flipped.'

'And did what?'

'Punched her lights out and put her into a neck brace for eight weeks. She lost the hearing in one of her ears for a while. The kids had already turned on him, so he didn't do himself any favours there. I think he had three – two boys, one girl. Girl ends up having a massive barney with him; tells him she can't even stand to be in the same room as him any more. Just ups and leaves a couple of days later.'

'Moves out?'

'Disappears.'

'As in, vanishes?'

'Into thin air.'

'Really?'

'Yeah, really.'

I stopped for a moment. Healy's daughter was gone, just like Megan. *So that's why he was so interested*. Maybe he thought there might be a connection between them. Or maybe he'd already found one.

'Was she ever registered as a missing person?'

'Why, you hoping to make some money?' Dooley laughed at his joke. 'Yeah, Healy and his missus got back together for one last gig and tried to find her. Healy drafted in a couple of guys from the Met to help him out for a few weeks, but the whole thing hit the skids. When nothing turned up, the hired help drifted away and the bosses put them back on other investigations.'

'Can you email me the missing-persons file?'

'Yeah, if I wanna get sacked.'

Bluster and front. This was how Dooley played things, just so he felt like he still had some control. 'Send it to my Yahoo.'

I got silence as a reply this time.

In front, brakes lights winked in the night, then disappeared, and I inched the car forward a few more feet.

'So is that it?' Dooley asked.

'One more thing.'

'It's Friday night.'

'You won't be late for the disco, Dools, I promise.'

He sighed, his breath crackling down the line.

'What can you tell me about Milton Sykes?'

'*Sykes?*'

'Yeah.'

'I didn't realize you were digging up cold cases

159

now, Davey. Things must be slow. Who wants to know about him?'

'I'm just interested.'

'Ever heard of the internet?'

'Yeah, I remember someone talking about it once.'

'Stick his name into Google. You'll get about a trillion hits.'

'Anything that didn't get released to the public?'

'I know I might look it,' Dooley said, 'but I ain't *that* old. How the fuck should I know? They were communicating with smoke signals when Sykes was running around.'

'Come on, Dools. I know how it works. Knowledge passed down through generations of police officers, like the family secret. You old-timers love to talk about what you would have done differently.'

He paused, then blew more air down the line. 'What do you wanna know?'

'You ever had any copycats?'

He paused. 'You got someone running around pretending to be Sykes?'

'No. I'm just asking.'

'No.'

'No copycats?'

'No. He's old school now. Most people under forty probably wouldn't even be able to tell you who he was. Sykes is the grandparents' story. Once that generation dies out, no one will even know what he did.'

'So tell me about him.'

'What do you want to know?'

'Everything.'

The line drifted a little. It sounded like he was moving. When he started talking again, it was virtually a whisper: 'Okay, you want my theory?'

'That's why I phoned.'

Another pause. 'He buried them in the woods.'

I heard the line drift again. He was moving to a place where absolutely no one would hear him talking. I reached across to the hands-free and turned the volume all the way up. 'Just give me the condensed version,' I said.

'The condensed version's the same as the long version: he was screwed from day one. His father pisses off the moment he zips himself up, and his mother pops her clogs from tuberculosis two months after young Milton is born. Sykes goes to live with his psychopathic aunty and uncle down the road; she's the bitch from hell, and he's a violent pisshead. Cue sixteen years of being beaten shitless and locked in the dark. School was a total write-off as you might have expected, although he got an A for killing animals and being a weird loner no one liked or spoke to.'

'What happened after he left home?'

'He landed a job at a dyeworks near East India Docks. Then women started disappearing. You think *we're* bad at our jobs; police back then didn't even notice for six years.'

'How come?'

'All the women were Indian immigrants working in the textiles factories. Their families reported them missing, but their English was bad or non-existent. Police excused themselves after Sykes was arrested by pretending they couldn't understand what they were being told – but, truth was, they probably didn't give much of a shit.'

'So how'd he get caught?'

'He stopped taking Indian girls.'

'And took a white one instead.'

'Right. Girl called Jenny Truman. Nineteen. Blonde-haired, blue-eyed. Goes to work at one of the factories in the morning and never comes home again.'

'Why change?'

'He was clever. He knew the police wouldn't go hard at the Indian disappearances, so he played things safe. But after a while he couldn't help himself and went after Truman. That was when the police finally decided to get serious. Eventually a couple of witnesses told them they'd seen her leaving with someone matching Sykes's description. So they head down to Sykes's place at Forham Avenue. You know where that is?'

'No.'

'That's because they've knocked it down now and built an industrial estate where the road used to be. It was right on the edge of Hark's Hill Woods, this big, overgrown area full of old factories in east London. When the police turned up at Sykes's house, he excused himself and headed to

162

a toilet at the bottom of his garden – and then made a break for it. Vanished into the woods.'

'Did they find him?'

'No. They lost him. But they searched his house and found a dress belonging to Jenny Truman with blood all over it, and a shovel – all hidden in a wall cavity in his kitchen. Three days later, he hands himself in to a police station in Camberwell.'

'Why?'

'Said he was tired of running.'

'So they never found the bodies?'

'Nah,' Dooley said. 'After he got the rope in 1906, they did another search of the woods and came up empty-handed like before. But he *must* have buried them in there.'

'Why d'you say that?'

'He knew those woods like I know the way to the bar. He used to escape there as a kid to get away from his nutjob family. There was this place he talked about in his interviews with police. Locals used to call it the Hanging Tree; this weird, T-shaped oak, all gnarly and messed up, that looked like a giant set of gallows. There are photos of it online. Most people were completely freaked out by it, but not young Milton. He loved it so much he built a tree house in it. You ever been there?'

'Hark's Hill? No.'

'It's a strange place. Got this . . .' Dooley paused, then dropped his voice even further. 'Got this kind of . . . atmosphere.'

I smiled. 'You a psychic now?'

'Laugh it up. You don't believe me, ask the teams they sent down there in the 1920s to try and put a train track through there.'

'What do you mean?'

'Back in 1921, the local authority decided they wanted some track running from the factories up on Hark's Hill to the mainline on the other side of the woods. They sent teams in there to clear a path and start laying the foundations for the train tracks, only . . .' He paused again. 'Only, they got spooked.'

'Spooked?'

'They kept seeing things and hearing things.'

'What sort of things?'

'No one was ever sure, but enough to put the shits up them. That little project lasted four weeks before the entire workforce decided enough was enough.'

'They walked?'

'Like I said, that place . . .' Dooley sucked in his breath. 'First time someone told me that story I laughed my arse off. But you want to try going down there some time.'

'Are you serious?'

'Go down there,' he said, no hint of humour in his voice. 'You know me: the only thing I believe in is a beer on a Friday night. But you go to enough crime scenes, you start to get a real sense of life and death. And sometimes . . .'

'What?'

'I've worked murders for fifteen years, and some of the places you end up . . . I don't know, you're standing over bodies in these holes, and you can just *feel* a place is bad. That's the only way I can describe it. You get a sense for places; kind of attuned to things. That's why I'm telling you he buried those women in the woods. Because I went down there, and that place . . . something's seriously wrong with it.'

CHAPTER 22

When I got back to the house, I checked for answer phone messages and then switched on the TV. A reporter was standing near the Royal Docks, the Thames framed behind her. At the bottom of the screen, a ticker tape was running right to left: MET POLICE: WOMAN FOUND IN THAMES RETURNED TO FAMILY. FAMILY HAVE REQUESTED NO NAMES/DETAILS BE RELEASED TO PUBLIC. I remembered the same reporter covering the same story a couple of days before while I was in the café close to Newcross Secondary. I didn't know much about it, but I did know that, if it had any legs, it wouldn't have been tucked away right at the end of the hourly bulletin.

After showering, I went through my wardrobe. Laid a shirt out. Trousers. A pair of shoes I hadn't worn since the funeral. Then I sat on the edge of the bed and looked at my reflection in the mirror. That same flicker ignited in my stomach, and I felt all the doubt and the guilt and the fear move through my chest.

It's too soon, I thought.

And then I realized, until I did it, it would always be too soon.

Ten minutes later, Liz answered her door. She looked beautiful. She was wearing a black halterneck dress that followed the shape of her body all the way down to the middle of her calves. Her hair was curled at the ends, falling against her shoulders in ringlets. She had a little make-up on, but not much, and her eyes were dark and playful, looking me up and down.

'Wow,' I said.

'Thank you.' She fluttered her eyelids jokingly and reached for a long black coat laid over the back of one of the sofas. 'You look very dashing too.'

I looked down at myself. I had a black buttonup shirt on, a smart pair of denims and a long, black, *very* expensive Armani jacket I'd bought at a shiny supermall in Dubai when I'd had to spend a week out there with the paper. It had looked great on the hanger, even better on, but decidedly less good coming out of my bank account. Since then, I'd worn it three times, terrified I'd irreparably damage it by subjecting it to fresh air.

'I feel underdressed,' I said, looking at her.

'Oh, rubbish,' she replied, slipping on her coat. 'You look great.'

I handed her a brown paper bag.

She took it and looked inside. Her face widened in delight. 'Kona coffee?' she asked. 'Now it's my turn to say "wow".'

'It's just coffee.'

'It's *Kona* coffee, David.'

'Now you'll be forced to think of me as you drink it.'

She smiled. 'That won't be a hardship.'

The restaurant was three miles away, right on the edge of Gunnersbury Park. On the way over, we talked about our days. When it was my turn, I left out the bit about ending up at a crime scene and spending three hours at a police station. Liz looked at me a couple of times, as if she knew I'd not told her everything, but she didn't probe.

At the restaurant, the owner – her client – gave her a kiss and a hug, then found us a table near the back, with views out across the park. On the walls there were black-and-white pictures of old Italy: cobbled streets; shuttered windows looking out over small town squares; stony-faced men and women outside cafés, their skin etched with age, their colour darkened by the Mediterranean sun. I ordered a bottle of white wine and some water, and then – once the waiter had gone – I turned to find her looking at me.

'You okay?'

'I'm fine,' she said. 'Are *you* okay?'

'Yeah, I'm good.'

There was a slight hesitation between us. This was a very different road from the ones we'd walked before. She could see the apprehension in me, and I could see it reflected. It was nearly two years since Derryn had died, and in that time it had been a meal, or a coffee, or some company at the end of a hard day. Now it was the beginning of something more.

I eased us back into conversation by asking about her daughter.

Liz had met her ex-husband straight out of university, and been married at twenty-two. A year later, Katie was born. She'd told me a bit about her background before. Her husband had battled her for custody of their daughter, but came out second best. 'He could be a little . . .' She looked up at me. *Violent.* I nodded that I understood. 'Never seriously. And he never, *ever* touched Katie – but any future I had seen for us rapidly went down the toilet when he started on the booze.'

'When did you decide to get out?'

'When Katie was two. I packed her off to my parents for the weekend, and sat him down and told him I was leaving. He took it badly, as you might expect. I think any man, even a drunk, feels wounded when you tell him he's not providing for his family.'

'Does she still see him?'

'He moved up north. She hasn't seen him for eight years.'

Our meals arrived a few minutes later. 'So what about you?' she asked, as we started eating.

'What do you want to know?'

'Did you ever think about starting a family?'

'We talked about it a lot, especially when we hit our thirties. I always imagined my work would put me off wanting to have kids – all the tragedy and the heartbreak I got to see – but it never did. We definitely always wanted them. In the end, though, Derryn found out she had cancer and . . . well, it became less important.' I smiled at her, letting her know everything was fine. She seemed to understand the gesture, but I could tell the conversation had led somewhere neither of us wanted it to go. I made an attempt to redirect it: 'My mum used to tell me she loved me more than anything in the world – but that I'd put her off having another baby for the rest of her life.'

Liz smiled. 'Really? So you've *always* been naughty then?'

'Apparently they could never find my heartbeat when she was pregnant.'

'So, what – you're a vampire?'

I laughed. 'Not a vampire. But definitely a pain in the arse.'

'When did your folks pass on?'

'Mum was just over five years ago. When I was young, my dad used to take me out shooting in the woods close to our farm. Dad had this whole thing about me being a marksman in the army. When I became a journalist and crushed his dream, I agreed to go shooting with him on Sunday mornings as often as I could get down to see them. One morning we got back to the house and mum was lying on the bench outside the house. She'd had a stroke. Dad died a couple of months later.'

'I'm sorry.'

I shrugged. 'It's weird. The only time it ever

really registered with me that my parents were getting old was when they talked about their age. I never really noticed otherwise.'

'You must miss them.'

'Yeah, I do.'

'Do you ever get over that feeling?'

'You want the honest answer?'

She nodded.

'When you love someone, I'm not sure you do.'

I left Liz chatting to the owner while I walked to get the car. The rain had eased off, but there was still a chill in the air. The BMW was parked close to a cemetery and in view of the motorway, cars flashing past beneath a permanent orange glow.

'David.'

I turned around, my key in the door. On the other side of the road, just coming out of a pub, were Jill and Aron. They crossed the road towards me.

'Wow,' Jill said, smiling as they approached. 'Talk about coincidence!'

I shook hands with Aron. 'How are you guys?'

'We're good,' Aron replied.

Jill held up her mobile. 'I tried calling you earlier, but you weren't picking up. I figured you were busy with work.'

I fished in my pocket for my phone. It wasn't there. Then I remembered I'd left it on the bed at home.

'That's because, brilliantly, I've forgotten to bring it with me.'

Aron smiled. 'Forty – it happens to us all.'

Jill laughed. 'Oh well, never mind. I was just calling to see if you wanted to come out for a drink. Remember I mentioned it?'

'Oh, of course.'

I did remember. I hadn't purposefully forgotten, but I was glad to have gone out to dinner with Liz instead. Even from the limited conversations I'd had with them both, it was obvious their friendship was developing in a way both of them were enjoying. I didn't want to get between that.

'I'm really sorry,' I said, lying. 'That would have been great.'

'Next time maybe,' Jill said.

I glanced at Aron. He was smiling, and looked as if he wasn't worried whether I said yes or no. If it was for show, or to avoid making me uncomfortable, he was doing a good job.

'Next time,' I said.

'I wanted to thank you, actually, David,' Aron said.

'Really?'

'For going round to see Jill the other night.' He looked at her. She smiled at him. 'I was up in Manchester at a work function, and had my phone off all night.'

'It doesn't matter,' she said.

'It does matter,' he replied softly. He turned back to me. 'Anyway, I wanted to thank you for stepping in and helping out.'

I held up a hand. 'Really. It was nothing.'

'Well, it was very good of you.'

I nodded at him. 'Can I give you guys a lift somewhere?'

'Oh, no, don't worry,' Jill said.

'It's only about a quarter of a mile to my place,' Aron added, nodding across the cemetery to where a bank of newly built homes had gone up on the other side. 'You should come over one day. We can celebrate the onset of old age together.'

I smiled. 'I like to live in denial.'

'Then we can live in denial together.'

I shook his hand, but Jill seemed hesitant as I turned to her. I'd promised her I'd make a few calls, though had also said it would be after I cleared the Carver case. It had only been a day since I'd offered. But I could understand her impatience. She wanted to know what happened to Frank, and she didn't want to have to wait now she'd found someone willing to help. I'd left a message with an old contact of mine, who used to work in the National Criminal Intelligence Service before they became part of SOCA. But I hadn't chased it up.

'I haven't forgotten about Frank,' I said.

'Oh, thank you so much.'

I nodded to them both, said goodbye again and got into the BMW. As I headed back to the restaurant to pick up Liz, I looked in the rear-view mirror and saw them side by side, laughing at something, fading into the night.

Liz offered to make me a cup of Kona coffee from the packet I'd bought her so, after parking the car,

I wandered around to hers. One of the sofas had folders and loose legal papers scattered across it. I sat down on the second one and could see books with names like *The Dictionary of Law* and *Solicitor Advocate* stacked up by the fireplace. She came back in, armed with two coffees, sat down next to me and glanced at the books.

'Fascinating, huh?'

I took one of the mugs. 'I think I'm too terrified to find out.'

'Fortunately I've got a photographic memory.' She winked. 'Actually, that's not true. But I do seem to be good at remembering lots and lots of really boring, really technical things.'

'So if I'm a vampire, does that make you . . . a robot?'

She laughed – and then a momentary silence settled between us. 'Thanks for the meal tonight,' she said.

'Thank your friend.'

'No, I mean . . .' She paused, took a sip from her mug. 'I mean, thanks for asking me out. I know you didn't have to.'

'I didn't have to – but I wanted to.'

She nodded. 'I know how hard this must be.'

I looked at her. Her eyes were dark. She moved a hand to her face and tucked some hair behind one of her ears, and I felt a sudden, unexpected pull towards her.

'Are you okay?' she asked.

I put down my coffee. Liz followed my hand,

then looked back up at me. I placed my fingers on hers and eased her mug from her grasp, putting it down next to mine.

Then, slowly, I leaned in and kissed her.

At first she backed away a little, her mouth still on mine, as if she didn't want me to feel like I had to. Then, as I moved a hand to the back of her head and pressed her in harder against me, she responded. We dropped back on to the sofa, me on top of her, feeling her contours and her shape beneath me. I breathed in her scent as we kissed, one of her legs moving between mine. She moaned a little, and a feeling raced through me, like every nerve ending in my body was firing up. When I looked at her, she was staring up at me, her eyes sparking.

And that was when I broke off.

Slowly, the look dissolved in her face.

'I'm so sorry, Liz.'

She reached for one of my arms and squeezed it. 'You don't have to be sorry,' she said gently, but I could see the disappointment in her eyes. Derryn flashed in my head, a series of images that were there and then gone again: the night I first met her, the day we married, the two of us on a beach in Florida, and then at the end of her life – wrapped in sweat-stained sheets – as she lay dying in our bed. I shifted closer to Liz and apologized again, but I'd razed the moment, and what remained between us was exactly what had always been there.

My doubts. My fears. My guilt.

CHAPTER 23

When I woke at nine the next morning, the house was cold. I started the fire in the living room and put on some coffee. While I was waiting for it to brew, I padded back through to the bedroom to find my phone. It said I'd missed two calls. The first had been from Jill, as expected, at eight the previous evening. I'd also got a text from her: *Hi David. We're meeting in the Lamb in Acton, at 8.30. See you there? Jill.* The second missed call was from Ewan Tasker at 7.55 a.m.

Tasker was the contact I'd mentioned in passing to Jill. He was working for the Metropolitan Police now, in an advisory role, but previous to that he'd been part of the National Criminal Intelligence Service, before it was assimilated into SOCA. Like the other sources from my paper days, our relationship was built on being mutually beneficial, but over ten years we'd gradually become good friends. The last time I saw him was at his sixtieth birthday almost a year previously. He'd held it in a golf club in Surrey. We sat by the windows, looking out at the course, both of us nursing whiskies. He was mourning the onset of his sixties. I was mourning the death of my wife.

I tried returning the call, but no one answered, and I allowed my thoughts to quickly turn back to Megan, the man in the nightclub – and Milton Sykes.

In the spare bedroom I booted up the computer, logged on to the internet and printed out everything I could find on Sykes. I wanted as much information as I could get on his life, his upbringing, his crimes and his arrest. I wasn't sure how it fitted into what I had, but the obvious physical similarities between Sykes and the man in Tiko's couldn't be ignored – and neither could the idea of a copycat. I noted down the most important information and moved carefully through the rest, making sure nothing was missed. When I was done on the first read-through, I flipped back to the start and reread it. Then a third time. Two hours later, I had sixteen pages of notes.

I turned back to the computer and logged into my Yahoo. There was an email waiting. It was sent from Terry Dooley's home address: no subject line, no message, but a PDF attachment. I dragged it to the desktop and opened it up. It was the missing-person's file Colm Healy had set up for his daughter, and a few miscellaneous pages tagged on to the end covering the subsequent search for her.

I started going through it.

Leanne Healy disappeared three months before

Megan, on 3 January. She was older, at twenty, and not nearly as capable at school. She'd left at sixteen with middling results, and gone to college to study Beauty and Holistic Therapies, before dropping out after six months. From there she got a job in a local supermarket, which she stuck for another year and a half, then went back to college, this time to do a National Diploma in Business. She completed the course two years later with decent, if unspectacular, grades, and had spent the time between the end of her course and the date she disappeared struggling to find work. On 2 January she'd finally got something: as a full-time office junior at a recruitment agency. Twenty-four hours later, she was gone.

Physically she wasn't too dissimilar to Megan. Neither of them were overweight, but they definitely weren't skinny girls. They had a nice shape to them, but their height – five-five to five-six – would have prevented them from turning heads in the way they might have done at a few inches taller. Megan was definitely the better-looking of the two. She had a natural warmth, obvious in her pictures, which added to her attractiveness. Leanne looked harder work, and less inclined to make the effort, which came across in the only photograph in the file; she was standing outside a house, straggly blonde hair covering part of her face. In the light, and because of the fuzzy quality of the picture, her smile looked more like a scowl.

Surprisingly, Healy's version of the events leading

up to Leanne's disappearance didn't differ all that much from his wife Gemma's. Neither account mentioned him hitting her, although Gemma said he'd become 'angry and aggressive' when he found out she'd been having an affair. Healy himself tried to claim the moral high ground early on in his own statement, talking about the sanctity of marriage, before admitting he 'may have scared' his wife when she told him the truth about her affair. He described 'getting a little closer to her' than he should have done, and 'swearing at her'. At one point, midway through the transcript, Gemma told her interviewer, 'If Colm dedicated as much time to his family as his work, Leanne probably wouldn't have left that night.'

The last person to see Leanne alive was one of her brothers. They'd been home together on the afternoon of Sunday 3 January, watching a DVD. In the middle of it, Leanne told him she needed to pop out. She left at three-thirty, and never came home again. At eight, her brother called Gemma, who was at a friend's house having dinner, and told her what had happened. Gemma phoned Healy, who was at work. Seven hours later, Healy called in her disappearance, and she was registered as a missing person.

Right at the back of the file was a black-and-white MISSING poster, the same photo of Leanne in the corner. *Leanne Healy. Age at disappearance: 20. Leanne has been missing from St Albans, Hertfordshire, since 3 January. Her whereabouts remain unknown.*

There is growing concern for her welfare. Leanne is 5ft 6in tall, has shoulder-length blonde hair, blue eyes and is of medium build. After that it listed a confidential helpline number and, right at the bottom of the page, a list of places she most often went before her disappearance.

The list of places were mostly pubs and clubs, as well as the address of the college she'd gone to, and the name of a coffee shop just around the corner from her parents' house, where she'd spent most Saturday mornings studying in the run-up to her exams. But then, in among them, I spotted a name and address I recognized: *Barton Hill Youth Project, 42 Chestnut Road, Islington, London.*

The same youth club Megan had gone to.

And the place she'd met the man who'd got her pregnant.

THE HOLE

Sona woke. The first thing she could see was a line of light above her, about an inch wide and maybe six feet in length. As her eyes adjusted to the darkness, she realized she was lying on a mattress in some kind of hole. It had a dirt floor and brick walls, water trails running down them. Above her, out of reach, was a trapdoor. The thin line of light was where it didn't fit properly against the mouth of the hole.

The hole must have been eight feet deep. It was cut out of the floor, and through the sliver of light above she could see snatches of a steel cabinet, a sink and a clear bottle of something sitting on a counter.

It looked like some kind of utility room.

'Help me!'

No sound came back. No response. No movement. She got to her feet, using the wall for support, and then stopped for a moment: her head still throbbed, and she could feel bruising around her jaw. She closed her eyes, trying to compose herself, then started circling the hole, angling her head in order to get a better look at what was beyond

181

the trapdoor. All she could see were parts of the same unit: more of the steel sink, more of the same cabinet. Nothing else. No shadows shifting. No sign of life.

'Mark!'

Silence.

'Mark, *please*!'

More silence.

This time she screamed until her voice gave way, until her heart was racing in her chest – beating a rhythm against her ribcage – and tears were blurring her vision. After she wiped them away, she closed her eyes and saw him there in the darkness: lying next to her in her bed and then leading her into the woods.

Bzzzzzz.

Her eyes snapped open.

A noise from above. She reached up, her fingers clawing at the walls, nails dragging through the water trails. 'Help me! I've been kidnapped! Help me!'

Then everything – her voice, the water against her fingers, the gentle buzz from somewhere up above – was drowned out by the sound of feedback. It burst from the walls of the room above the hole, turned up so loud it was distorting whatever speaker it was being piped from. She covered her ears. Even eight feet under the ground, it was like having her face glued to an amp the size of a house.

Then, as suddenly as it had begun, it stopped.

And the trapdoor shifted away from the hole.

Her heart shifted, the noise still ringing in her

ears, and a flutter of fear took flight through her chest. When she swallowed it felt like shards of glass were passing into her stomach.

'Hello?'

The trapdoor came away completely and the room appeared. She could see the rest of the steel cabinet extending across the length of an entire wall. A bare wall next to that, a huge crack running down it. Another sink. A glass-fronted bathroom cabinet, full of pill bottles. A red door, the paint blistered, with a glass panel in it. It was open, but there was only blackness beyond. From the top of the trapdoor cover, a rope snaked off, into the dark of the doorway.

'Hello?' Sona said again.

Out of the darkness of the door came a small, transparent plastic tube. It hit the floor of the room above her, rolled across it and tumbled into the hole. She caught it. The tube was about six inches long and packed with cotton wool. She looked up.

'Mark?'

Something else emerged from the black of the doorway. It rolled across the floor, over the lip of the hole and fell towards her. It made a dull *whup* sound as it landed.

A plastic bottle.

She picked it up. Inside was a pale blue liquid, the consistency of water. There were no other labels on the bottle, just a handwritten message: *Apply* ALL *of it to your face, then throw it back up.*

'Mark,' she said, looking up again. 'Mark, this

is ridiculous, baby. Why are you doing this?' She wiped one of her eyes. 'Why are you doing this?'

Silence.

'Mark, tell me what you want.' She paused. 'This isn't you, baby.' Her voice was starting to break up. '*Mark.*' She waited for any sign of movement in the darkness. 'Mark,' she said, tears running down her face now. 'Mark, you bastard! Why are you doing this to me? Why are you doing thi—'

'Put it on your face.'

She stopped, heart lurching. A whimper passed her lips. Fear moved down her back like a finger tracing the ridge of her spine. She swallowed again.

'Mark?'

Something shifted in the blackness of the doorway. She could see a small patch of white now, about the size of a coin.

A face.

Then he stepped out of the darkness.

He moved slowly, looking down at her, his feet stopping right on the lip of the hole. It wasn't Mark. It was another man: black hair in a side parting, pale skin, pinprick black eyes. In his left hand he held something big.

'Where's Mark?'

'Put it on your face.'

She took another step back and bumped against one of the walls.

'Mark!'

'Put it on your face.'

'Mark!'

'*Put in on your fucking face.*'

Another surge of fear exploded beneath her ribs, and she shrank into the corner of the hole. *His voice. What's wrong with his voice?* It was tinny and robotic, and there was a constant wall of static behind it. The confusion pushed her over the edge: tears started running down her cheeks, over her lips, tracing the angle of her neck.

Mark, she went to say again – but this time she stopped herself.

Because, above her, the man raised what was in his hand – and dropped it into the hole. It came at her fast, landing hard on the ground about three inches to her right. She shuffled away from it, trying to figure out what it was.

And then she could see.

The torso from a mannequin.

Cream and rigid. Punctured and broken. The middle of the chest had a hole in it, gauze spilling out from the hollow inside.

'You see that?' he said from the top of the hole, fingers twitching, a smile like a lesion worming its way across his face. 'Do you see that dummy?'

He paused. The word *dummy* glitched a little, and then there was a fuzzy noise, like interference. Sona whimpered, sinking all the way down into the corner of the hole.

'I'm going to sew your fucking head to it.'

CHAPTER 24

I got the number for the youth club, but, after the tenth unanswered ring, killed the call. I then dialled the Carvers' number and asked if I could stop by. James told me they'd be in until midday, but Saturday afternoons were when they took his mother out for a drive. She spent the rest of her week in a nursing home in Brent Cross.

The journey over took forty minutes. I went via Barton Hill, to get a sense of where it was. It was closed. A brass sign on the front said it was open Monday to Friday, 9 a.m. to 9 p.m. The building was about a quarter of a mile from the Carvers' place – close to King's Cross station, in a thin triangle of land between two main roads – and had all the aesthetic beauty of a shipping container: no windows; corrugated steel panels to about the eight-foot mark, where uniform red brickwork took over; and a big rusting door with an oversized padlock. Maybe all the money had been spent on the inside.

I got back on to Pentonville Road and headed for the Carvers'. At the house the gate was already open. I walked up the drive and saw James Carver standing in the entrance, filling it with his huge frame, his eyes watching the skies as dark clouds finally began to rupture and rain started to fall. We shook hands and moved inside.

Caroline was in the kitchen. She looked up and said hello to me. Immediately I could feel an atmosphere between the two of them. Carver obviously still felt betrayed by her. I imagined, in a strange way, he also felt like he didn't know his daughter as well as his wife had; a feeling magnified further now she'd disappeared.

We sat in the living room while Caroline put some coffee on. Behind us, in the corner of the room, Leigh was playing with a wooden train set.

'How are things going?' Carver asked.

'They're progressing. I've got a couple of good leads. One is the reason I'm here today.'

He held up his hands. 'Whatever it takes.'

Caroline came through with a tray of coffees and some biscuits. She laid them down on the glass table between us. I thanked her, and took one of the mugs.

'Is one of the leads Charlie Bryant?' Carver asked.

Their eyes were both fixed on me now, waiting for the answer. On the drive over, I'd decided I wasn't going to bring up the events of the previous day – even though they'd probably read about it in the morning papers. But now they were looking at me and asking me what they *really* wanted to know: Is Megan dead as well?

'At the moment there's nothing to connect this to Megan, other than the fact that she knew him.'

Deep down, in their darkest moments, they'd

probably glimpsed a similar end for their daughter. Her in a field, or in a backstreet. Them standing in the subdued light of a morgue while Megan's body, naked and broken, lay rigid in front of them.

'Does the name Barton Hill mean anything to you?'

Carver frowned. Caroline started nodding.

'Yes,' she said. 'Megan used to go there until she disappeared. It's a youth club, some kind of community project. They help teenagers with cerebral palsy.'

'Ah, the youth club,' Carver said, trying a little too hard. I'd been right: he definitely felt like he was standing on the wrong side of the glass now; staring in at a daughter, and her mother next to her, wondering what else lay buried at their feet.

'So can you tell me anything else about it?'

Caroline shrugged. She was still prickly. Carver flicked a look at her. She picked up on it and turned back to me. 'Only what Megan told me. They laid on activities for kids with cerebral palsy, gave them a chance to do something normal, while giving their parents a break.'

'So what made her decide to start going?'

'There was a work placement scheme going on at her school,' Caroline said, glancing at her husband. He looked like he didn't know any of this either. 'She really wanted to do something with disadvantaged kids, and kids with disabilities. So she spoke to her teachers and they came back with a list of places where she could go and get some experience for a fortnight. Barton Hill was where she ended up.'

'And she kept going after the work placement ended?'

Caroline nodded. 'She liked it.'

'Did you ever meet the people who ran it?'

'Only in passing. Jim usually did his weekly accounts on a Wednesday night, so I ended up being the one that ferried her back and forth. I met a few of the people there, just from taking her and picking her up again.'

'Anyone you remember?'

She paused, thought about it. 'The guy who ran it was called Neil Fletcher. There were two or three others, but I never really talked to them much.'

'Did Megan ever talk about meeting anyone there?'

They both looked at me, eyes brightening, brains ticking over. Suddenly, James Carver was right back in a conversation he'd been slowly drifting out of.

'Do you think she went off with someone she met there?' he said.

'No, I don't think so,' I lied.

I could have told them the truth: that I had a reason to believe she did. That the youth club, and someone who worked there, may have been linked to her pregnancy and her disappearance. But there were things I needed to find out first. There were questions that needed to be answered. And there was a man, somewhere, who knew the truth about where Megan was – and whether we'd ever find her alive.

CHAPTER 25

An hour later, I was opening the door to the office and my phone was going. I looked at the display. It was Spike.

'David. Sorry it's taken me a while.'

'No worries. What have you got for me?'

I heard him tapping. 'Okay, the PO box number you asked me to look at . . .' He paused. More tapping. 'It's for a charity called . . . uh, the London Conservation Trust.'

Megan had had an email from them. I sat down at my desk and booted up the computer. I'd called them when Spike had first got Megan's telephone records over to me, and all I'd got in return was a short answerphone message. No mention of the charity. No thank you for calling. Just a bored-sounding man in an empty room.

'Anything else?'

'The street address is 150 Piccadilly.'

'One-fifty?'

'Yeah. The building's called Minotaur House.'

I pulled a pad across the desk and started to write down the address. Then stopped. *150 Piccadilly.*

'That's the Ritz,' I said quietly.

'Huh?'

'150 Piccadilly. That's the address for the Ritz.'

'The hotel?'

'Yeah, the hotel.'

The computer pinged as the desktop appeared. I fired up the internet browser and entered the URL for the Ritz. At the bottom was their street address: 150 Piccadilly. I went to Google and searched for Minotaur House, got nothing, then headed to the Charity Commission website. No mention of the London Conservation Trust there either.

The address was false.

And the charity didn't exist.

I thanked Spike, hung up and went to Megan's Hotmail. The email from the London Conservation Trust was right at the bottom. It had been sent on 27 March. Seven days before Megan disappeared. The design of the newsletter was plain and uninspiring: a green banner across the top with a clean but basic logo, all in a pale green. The 'T' of the Trust was a tree. Beneath the logo was a short message, thanking her for her donation of £10 and telling her the money would be put to protecting parkland. There was no street address or phone number. No links or attachments.

I read the message.

Dear Megan,

Thank you for your donation of £10. We want to protect the city's parkland and make a genuine difference – and that means we don't just want to imagine a world where animals are running free in their natural habitat, we want to see it in action!

At the time of writing, we are engaged in ten different campaigns, and every pound you send to us helps maintain parks and parklands in our capital, and in turn brings flora, animals and people together.

If you want to be on the frontline, join our march to Parliament next Monday where we will be trying to persuade government ministers to make the protection of local wildlife more of a priority in the coming year. See the website for more details or enter your email to sign up to our weekly newsletter and get the most up-to-date info delivered straight to your inbox!

Yours sincerely,

G. A. James

I put the London Conservation Trust, LCT and the name G. A. James into Google. The LCT got no hits, and the name got nothing in relation to the charity. The incongruous nature of the email had stopped me briefly the first time I'd read it earlier in the week, but only because it was totally out of sync with every other message in Megan's inbox. In truth, it sounded enough like a charity newsletter to pass under most people's radar; a little too jokey and vague, but nothing that would immediately stand out. I scanned it again, reading it over for a second time. *See the website for more details.*

Except there was no website.

Or was there?

The email address the message had been sent from was info@lct.co.uk. I put www.lct.co.uk into another tab on the browser and hit Return. Within seconds, a website was loading. It was a plain site. No real design. No flair. It mirrored the newsletter in its pale green colouring, but the banner at the top, which was presumably where the logo was supposed to be, had corrupted and failed to load. Down the left was a menu with five options: HOME, ABOUT US, OUR PROJECTS, CONTACT, DONATE. The rest of the page had nothing on it except UNDER CONSTRUCTION! in big black letters and some random letters and numbers right at the bottom. When I tried the options on the left, they all took me through to 404 Error pages, except for the last one: DONATE. Clicking on that brought up a secure login box, asking for a username and password. *What charity asked you to enter a username and password before donating? And where was the option to sign up to the newsletter?* I doubted there was one. Everything about the site was off – but it must have been created for a reason, to serve some purpose.

As an experiment, I put in Megan's email address as a username and the password for her Hotmail account below that. The box juddered, flashed up *Incorrect username and password*, and closed. I clicked on DONATE again. This time, I tried Megan's email prefix, 'megancarver17', for the username and the same Hotmail password.

Wrong again.

Think.

The police would have worked Megan's phone records in the same way I had. They would have seen that the street address for the PO box was phoney and the building name false. They would have been led to the email, then to the website. Their technicians would have eventually bypassed the security on the website and found what was beyond. But they still hadn't found Megan. Maybe it meant there was nothing beyond the security box – or at least nothing that led to Megan's whereabouts. So why would someone go to the trouble of creating the website and the email if there was nothing worth finding?

Think.

I looked at the random numbers at the bottom of the webpage: 21112303666859910012512612 71321331341421441480320 6. It wasn't an error message – or, at least if it was, it was unlike any error message I'd ever seen. Grabbing a pen, I rewrote all fifty numbers on to my pad, and then circled an area in the middle that immediately stood out: 125126127 and 132133134. One hundred and twenty-five through to one hundred and twenty-seven, and one hundred and thirty-two through to one hundred and thirty-four.

They were both sequential.

I went back to the start and worked through from the beginning, applying the same logic throughout. If I assumed the list was one long, gradually increasing series of numbers, fifty suddenly became eighteen: 2 11 12 30 36 66 85 99 100 125 126 127 132 133 134 142 144 148. Except I'd cheated, because right at the end was 03206, and I didn't know how they fitted in so had left them out. Even taking each number on its own, or every two, there was no obvious pattern.

Tabbing back to Megan's inbox, I read over the newsletter again.

There were no numbers in the message. Nothing to tie the sequence to the site. Not one scrap of evidence to suggest the numbers even meant anything. *So why are they there?* I looked around the office, trying to pull inspiration out from somewhere. My eyes passed pictures on the walls, photographs, the front pages I'd written and the stories I'd broken. *What aren't you seeing?* Without a username or password, I'd have to enlist the help of Spike to get past the security for me. And that meant time. It meant hours sitting on my hands. It meant wasted days.

I looked down at the numbers written on the pad again, then back to the email in Megan's inbox, then back to the numbers. *What the hell aren't you . . .*

Then I saw it.

Copying and pasting the contents of the email into a Word document, I started going through the message again. The first number in the sequence was two. I capitalized and emboldened the second word in the email. The second number was eleven. I capitalized and emboldened the eleventh word. Then I did the same with the twelfth, thirtieth, thirty-sixth, sixty-sixth and the rest.

Two minutes later, everything had changed.

CHAPTER 26

I leaned in towards the monitor and took in each line of the email, every bold word suddenly coming alive. Three minutes before it had just been a charity newsletter.

Now it was the reason Megan had disappeared.

Dear **MEGAN**,

Thank you for your donation of £10. We **WANT TO** protect the city's parkland and make a genuine difference – and that means we don't just want to **IMAGINE** a world where animals are **RUNNING** free in their natural habitat, we want to see it in action!

At the time of writing, we are engaged in ten different campaigns, and every pound you send **OFF** to us helps maintain parks and parklands in our capital, and in turn brings flora, animals and people **TOGETHER**.

If you want to be on the frontline, join our march to Parliament **NEXT MONDAY**

where we will be trying to persuade government ministers to make the protection of
local wildlife more of a priority in the coming
year. **SEE THE WEBSITE** for more details
or **ENTER YOUR EMAIL** to sign up to
our weekly newsletter **AND** get **THE** most
up-to-**DATE** info delivered straight to your
inbox!

Yours sincerely,

G. A. James

A feeling of dread flared in my chest. *Megan,
want to imagine running off together next Monday?
See the website. Enter your email and the date.*

I tabbed back to the LCT website, clicked on
DONATE, and put Megan's full email address in as
the username. *Enter your email and the date.* What
date? Today's date? The date the email was sent?
The date she disappeared? I tried them all and
every time the pop-up box juddered and closed.
None of them was right.

You're stumbling around in the dark here.

The date. The date. The *date*. I let my mind work
back over the last week, trying to recall anything
I'd found that might give me a clue as to what
that meant: Megan, her parents, her school, her
friends, the youth club, Charlie Bryant, the man
at Tiko's, his similarity to Sykes . . . and then I
stopped.

Sykes.

The last five digits of the numbered sequence. 03206. I hadn't been able to see where they fitted in before. But now I did.

03 2 06. 3 February 1906.

I flipped back a couple of pages on my pad, to where I'd made the notes about Sykes. 03 02 06. 3 February 1906.

The day he was hanged.

I entered Megan's email as the username, and 03206 as the password. And I hit Return. The security box disappeared and the website began to load a new page. It took a couple of seconds. When it was done, a small map appeared in the centre, about five square inches in size. It had been drawn by hand with black marker pen and scanned, and looked like an approximation of a car park, vehicles – as if viewed from above – on one side, a long thin line opposite them. On the other side of the line was an *X* and a typewritten message: *Meet here at 2.30 p.m. for a romantic woodland picnic!*

It was the Sixth Form car park at Newcross Secondary.

He knew what he was doing. He knew there was no CCTV coverage in that part of the school and he knew what time her lesson finished. He picked her up and he took her away, and no one even noticed.

The ultimate disappearing act.

Except he'd left a trail. Because while the woodland he described could have been anywhere as far as the police were concerned, I'd spotted him in Tiko's, I'd found out who he looked like, and I knew the significance of the website password.

I knew his next move that day.

He'd taken her to Hark's Hill Woods.

CHAPTER 27

There was a coffee shop that doubled up as a deli a couple of doors along from the office. I headed downstairs and ordered a steak sandwich. While I was waiting, my phone started buzzing. It was Ewan Tasker calling about Jill's husband. I was tempted not to answer, not because I didn't want to speak to him, but because I didn't want another case to add to my workload minutes after a major break in the Carver one. But if I didn't answer, Tasker would just assume I wasn't around – and then keep on calling.

I hit Accept. 'Help the Aged.'

A laugh crackled down the line. 'Raker.'

'How you doing, Task?'

'Good. How are you?'

'Can't complain. I tried you earlier this morning, but I imagine you were winding your way towards the nineteenth hole. You're not hammered already, are you?'

He laughed again. 'Not yet.'

Rain pounded against the window of the coffee shop, making a noise like an army marching. I bent slightly and covered my other ear.

'So what have you got for me, old man?'

'You didn't hear any of this from me.'

'Goes without saying.'

The sound of paper being shuffled around.

'Okay. Frank Robert White. Forty-one years of age. Married to Jill, no kids. Detective inspector for three years before he got popped, nineteen months of which he spent at the Met. On the evening of 25 October of last year, he was shot once in the chest, high up near the left shoulder, and once in the head, just above the bridge of the nose. He was part of a task force investigating Akim Gobulev. You've heard of him, right?'

'Yeah. The Ghost.'

'Right. Gobulev runs Russian organized crime in London, except no one's seen him since he landed at Heathrow ten years back.' More paper being flicked through. 'You know what his first name means back in Mother Russia?'

'No.'

' "God Will Judge". Fucking right about that. He was a pain in my balls at NCIS, but it looks like SOCA managed to get close to him through an informant.'

'So SOCA were working with White's Met team?'

'Right. White was SCD.'

The Specialist Crime Directorate. They were a Metropolitan Police department working across the city on serious and high-profile cases. Homicides, gangs, child abuse, e-crime, money-laundering – it all came under the SCD umbrella. It was split into eight Operational Command Units, and SCD7, which covered organized crime, would have been where Frank White was based.

'White had put a task force together to support SOCA and work alongside them, and they were about to put the cuffs on Gobulev's . . . What the hell have I written here?'

'Plastic surgeon?'

'Yeah, surgeon.' He sounded surprised. 'You already know all this?'

'Not much, but some.' I kept it at that. I didn't want an overview from Task; I wanted everything he had. 'What do we know about this surgeon?'

'Intelligence suggests he's kind of like a gun for hire – except he comes armed with a scalpel and a syringe full of Botox.'

'So he isn't Russian?'

'No. Informants put him as English. He did the works on God Will Judge's face – as in, completely changed the way he looked – which is probably why we never found the arsehole in ten years at NCIS.'

'And presumably why Gobulev took a shine to the surgeon.'

'Yeah. He uses his medical expertise on a free-lance basis – nose job here, brow lift there – but mostly he's just sewing up knife wounds and scooping out bullets for low-level shitheads. It's a way for the Russians to keep their employees out of A&E. Once you hit the hospitals, people start asking questions.'

'So what happened the night Frank died?'

'SOCA got a tip-off that the surgeon would be at that warehouse down in Bow, helping Gobulev take delivery of some guns.'

'But Gobulev wasn't there.'

Tasker snorted. 'Gobulev doesn't go to his own birthday party.'

'So why send the surgeon?'

'No one was really sure. But the Russian informant reckons there was something else with the guns as part of the delivery.'

'What?'

'Currently unclear. White's team screwed up and got spotted early doors and then it turned into the OK Corral. White and the other officer who died got separated from the rest of the task force, and the next time anyone saw them they were bleeding out on the floor of the warehouse and the surgeon was haring away from the scene of the crime in a stolen car.'

'What about the rest of Gobulev's men?'

'Three dead at the scene. One was DOA; one decided not to speak in the interview, or during his subsequent trial.'

'At all?'

'Not about his involvement in anything, no. The Ghost's a scary man. Maybe Mr Dumb thought a life in clink was preferable to whatever Gobulev would do to him if he talked.'

'What about forensics?'

'Not much. The warehouse wasn't exactly a

sterile environment. They recovered a ton of fibres, a shitload of hairs, some trace stuff. No matches.'

'Fingerprints?'

'Lots of prints, but mostly from the people working in the warehouse, or Gobulev's men. Nothing for the surgeon. Looks like the murder team were pretty exhaustive too. Every print the SOCO came back with, they put through IDENT1.'

The scene of crime officer was the conductor. He documented everything that happened on site, from the moment the first officer arrived to the moment the lights were turned out. At the end, he handed in his report, including fingerprints lifts. After that, all the prints were put through the national automated fingerprint system – which meant the surgeon's prints failed to match up with any of the six million already logged.

'So he hasn't got any priors,' I said.

'No. Although that's working on the assumption he even left his prints at the scene in the first place. They had some prints they couldn't attribute to anyone – but that doesn't necessarily mean they were his.'

'Everyone leaves prints.'

'Not if you're wearing surgical gloves. Forensics found traces of cornflour at the scene. Looks like it's the same story with ballistics as well. White was shot with a hollow point 9mm, and the markings on the shell . . .' Tasker paused. I could hear him looking through his notes. 'The markings put the weapon as a GSh-18. Also Russian. Imported illegally, so pretty much impossible to trace.'

'Okay. So, physical description of the surgeon?'

'Medium height, medium build.'

'Anything else?'

'No. He's a mystery man.'

'Anyone see his face?'

'You're gonna like this. The informant said the surgeon used to turn up to meetings wearing a white plastic mask. No markings on it. Just holes at the eyes, nose and mouth.'

'Are you serious?'

'The man without a face.'

I paused and looked around me. Rain continued hammering against the window. Across the road, people ran past, caught in the storm, their coats pulled up over their heads.

'What did Gobulev's people call him?'

'Dr Glass.'

'Anyone know if that was his real name?'

'Doubtful given that he turned up to meets in a mask.'

'You put the alias through HOLMES or PNC?'

The Home Office Large Major Enquiry System was a database used by UK police forces to cross-check major crimes. The Police National Computer held details on every vehicle registered in the UK, stolen goods, and anyone reported missing or with a criminal record.

'Nothing,' Tasker said.

'Nothing flagged up?'

'Nothing for that alias.'

I thought of Jill. I knew the alias of the man who'd

206

killed Frank now, but that wasn't much more than she had already.

'Sorry, Raker – I know it's a whole lot of nothing.'

'No, Task, that's great. I appreciate your help.'

'You need anything else?'

'Any chance you could send me a copy of the file? I made a promise to someone that I'd look into this and I just want to make sure I've ticked all the boxes.'

'I've got a golf competition in Surrey tomorrow morning. We tee off at 6 a.m. I'll put the printouts through your letterbox on the way through.'

'All right, old man. I appreciate it.'

I killed the call and pocketed the phone. I felt sorry for Jill, but the dead end suited me fine. Right now, Megan was my priority.

CHAPTER 28

Back at the office, I slid in at my desk, started on my steak sandwich and went to Google Maps. Within seconds, I had a top-down satellite view of Hark's Hill Woods. It was a weird slab of land. A square mile of overgrown woodland right in the middle of an incredibly dense swathe of city. North of the woods was a road that looked new, leading to some kind of industrial estate on the north-western corner. A quarter of a mile south was tightly packed housing, unfurling across London all the way down to the curve of the Thames. And immediately surrounding the woods, in the spaces around its edges, were the skeletons of old factories – dyeworks, foundries, munitions plants – some standing but damaged, most collapsed or in a serious state of disrepair. It was obvious that the whole area, save for the redevelopment to the north and the homes to the south, had been completely forgotten about since the end of the Second World War; and the only constant was that the woods had grown bigger and the factories had crumbled further.

After finishing the sandwich, I began filling in

some of the background on the area. Putting Hark's Hill Woods into Google got me 98,400 hits, most detailing the Milton Sykes case. I moved through the results. On the third page, a hit halfway down caught my eye. An encyclopedia of serial killers.

I clicked on it.

Heading to S, and then down to Sykes, I found a photograph of him, slightly blurred, and a badly spelt description of what I'd already found: his upbringing, his victims and his connection to the woods. Right at the bottom was what had caught my attention in the two-line description on Google: *Sykes was reported to have sometimes used the alias Grant A. James.* Grant A. James. The letter sent to Megan from the London Conservation Trust had been from G. A. James. And then I remembered the name in her Book of Life too. The name no one had been able to shed any light on: A. J. Grant.

I leaned back in my chair.

Staring out at me from the computer monitor was a blurry photograph of Milton Sykes and, sitting in the space in between, a succession of unanswered questions. I drummed my fingers on the desk, trying to fit all the pieces together. The man at Tiko's. The Grant alias. The email.

The map.

That's why I'm telling you he buried those women in the woods. Because I went down there, and that place . . . something's seriously wrong with it. Dooley's words came back to me as I tabbed back to the satellite photograph of Hark's Hill Woods. From the air it didn't look like much: just a square mile of land built on rumour and folklore. But it had affected people, scared them, and then drawn them into its heart.

And, six months before, one of them had been Megan Carver.

CHAPTER 29

It was three by the time I found Derry Street – the nearest road to Hark's Hill Woods on its southern side – and it was a truly miserable network of terraced houses. Everything had a derelict, run-down feel to it, compounded by the fact that there was absolutely no one around. No kids playing. No people talking on doorsteps. Just a grey autumn still.

As the road began to rise, beyond the rooftops of the houses to my left, I could see the empty factories I'd spotted in the satellite photos. They too were deserted, but in a more obvious way: decaying brickwork, hollowed-out windows, some entrances boarded up, some lying open in an invitation to drug addicts, the homeless and teenagers on a dare. When the road dropped off again, the factories disappeared, but – a quarter of a mile on – I spotted a small alleyway where the terraced housing broke for the first time. A tattered sign pointed along it. It was illegible, blistered by the sun and worn by rain. A kid, about fifteen, was sitting on the steps of his house watching me. I parked up, got out of the

211

BMW and set the alarm. The kid continued to watch.

I looked at him. 'Afternoon.'

He didn't say anything. His eyes flicked from me to the alleyway, as if I was about to do something stupid. I moved level with the entrance. It was paved until about halfway along, then became a gravel path. Beyond that was a bed of concrete, the half-demolished walls of an old factory still standing in places, almost defiantly. Even from where I was, I could see the place was a mess. Rubbish strewn everywhere, pushed into the corners where the walls still stood, or just left on the ground in the open spaces between them. The smell of bottles, wrappers, cans and bin bags came in on the wind.

'You're not going down there, are you?' the boy said.

I looked at him. 'Yeah. Looks nice.'

For the first time he smiled. 'It ain't nice.'

'Oh, I don't know.' I breathed in. 'It's mountain fresh up here. Not many places can give you that delicate aroma of rubbish dump *and* public toilet.'

He smiled again. I nodded a goodbye to him, and started along the alleyway. As I passed, he watched me, the smile gradually fading from his face. 'The Dead Tracks.'

I stopped. 'Sorry?'

'That's what they call it.' He looked from me, along the alleyway. 'The woods over the back. That's what they call that place: the Dead Tracks.'

★   ★   ★

212

On the other side of the factory bed, the entrance to the woods loomed ahead of me. It was completely overgrown. Nature had claimed back what was once its own, covering everything, eating away at its surroundings like a virus. Either side of the path, trees leaned in, forming a canopy. Further along, daylight stabbed through whatever spaces it could find, hitting the floor in squares of watery yellow light.

I started along the path.

The grass became more aggressive as the path started turning to mud, carving through the earth, breaking the surface like hundreds of fingers. The deeper I got, the less light there was. I looked at my watch. Three-thirty. In an hour and a half, the day would start to fade. By six, it would be pitch black under the trees.

Ahead of me, rain dripped from the leaves of a huge sycamore, hitting the mud like a distant drumbeat. Then a little way down I spotted something on the path: a train track, rusted by age, weeds crawling through its slats. It broke through the grass on my left, fed across the path and then disappeared between the trunks of two giant oak trees on the opposite side. It was part of the railway Dooley had talked of; laid but never completed. I carried on, the canopy breaking briefly above me.

Crack.

I stopped.

What the hell was that?

Suddenly, wind clawed its way out from the trees

to my left, whipping across the path – and the temperature seemed to drop right off. Goosebumps scattered up my arms, down the centre of my back, and I felt a shiver pass through me like a wave. But then, as quickly as it had arrived, the wind disappeared again.

Swivelling, I looked back down the path.

'Hello?'

The route I'd followed had started to darken, as if lights had blacked out behind me, one after the other. But nothing moved, and no sound came back, and after a while I felt ridiculous. *You're standing in the middle of the woods talking to the bloody trees. Get a grip on yourself.*

I turned and carried on. After a couple of minutes, the foliage started thinning – and then a clearing appeared on my left. It was about thirty feet long, running in a semicircle adjacent to the path. There were no trees, but it was awash in knee-high grass. It looked momentarily beautiful compared to the approach, and seemed like the first, and most obvious, place for the picnic that Megan had been promised on the website.

Then, through the corner of my eye, movement.

A blur, where the trail continued on past the clearing. I stepped back on to the path, and looked deeper into the woods. Everything was dark: the path itself, the trees lining it.

A branch broke behind me.

I turned and looked back along the way I'd come. In the woods to the side of the path, about thirty feet down, something shifted in the trees. The wind came again, cutting across the clearing in an icy blast. The whole time, my eyes never left the spot between the trees. But there was no other movement. No sound. Just the *drip, drip, drip* of rain. And then, when that stopped briefly, a pregnant hush, as if something was sitting behind the silence, waiting to scream.

I watched for a few moments more, then stepped further into the clearing and began looking around. I wasn't sure what I expected to find, but even when people vanished, they didn't *vanish*. And yet, ten minutes later, I'd found nothing, the light had faded a little more, and now I could hear thunder in the distance and see steel-grey clouds moving across the sky above me.

Crack.

I span on my heel. Exactly the same noise as before. And now something else too, just behind it. *Is that whimpering?* Ahead, in the direction I'd come, trees moved. Leaves snapped and turned. Rain hit the path.

Then I sensed something behind me.

A shape darted into the clearing, about twenty feet from where I was standing. The grass moved. Left to right, then back. Whoever it was, was crouched. The shape moved another couple of feet and then stopped again.

The grass in the clearing settled.

Silence.

'I can see you,' I said.

I couldn't, but I took a step forward. My heart moved in my chest, as if it was readjusting; readying itself for a surprise. Another step. A patch of the clearing, about six feet in front of me, moved. Grass rustled. Shifted left and right again.

'I can see you.'

Silence.

Then: a scratching noise. I took a step closer, glancing down the path. Around me, the woods suddenly seemed bigger and darker, as if awoken by the imminence of night. More scratching. Definitely whimpering.

Then a dog emerged.

It hobbled a little, pushing between two clumps of waist-high grass either side. It was just a silhouette against the pale green of the clearing. As the first hint of dusk had started to settle, the brightness of the grass was the only thing pushing against it.

The dog moved gingerly towards me.

Even as a silhouette, I could see it was shaped like a greyhound: small, narrow head; a belly that curved up towards its hind legs; no body fat at all. It stopped about six feet from me, its face obscured by the developing shadows. I dropped to my haunches in front of it and held out a hand.

'Hey boy,' I said gently. 'Is it you who's been running around?'

Thunder rumbled again. I glanced up through the gaps in the canopy. In the distance, the clouds seemed to close up, obscuring the sky.

The dog licked my hand.

I looked down at it.

'Fucking hell.'

I jumped to my feet and stumbled back, my eyes fixed on the greyhound. It took another couple of steps towards me, its right hind leg dragging in the mud.

And then it was no longer a silhouette.

One side of its face had no fur on it at all. Flesh glistened in whatever light was left in the woods, a sliver of teeth showing through even though its mouth was closed. As it took another step to me, I could see there was something else in the flesh on the side of its face: a square of pink, at odds with the red of the sinew. It took me a couple of seconds to work out what it was.

Skin.

The dog hobbled forward some more.

'Who did this to you?'

It moaned a little. But now I realized there were other noises as well: wind passing through the trees, falling rain, grass whispering as it moved. I looked along the path, into the advancing darkness. *Dooley might be right about this place.*

The dog made a soft whimpering sound.

I turned back to it, dropped to my haunches again and slowly made a movement towards it, so it knew I offered no threat. But it hardly flinched. It seemed lethargic and distant, and just looked from my hand to my face; a slow, delayed action.

'Who did this to you?' I said again.

It turned its head slightly, grey fur matted with

water. Then I saw its eyes fix on something, over my shoulder, back the way I'd come. I turned. Trees moved, rain spotting against the canopy. Soft sounds played in the background.

'What can you see?'

Standing up, I had a view of about thirty feet in either direction. Thunder stomped across the sky. Five seconds later, lightning flashed, freeze-framing the clouds. The dog whimpered and moved towards me, brushed against my leg. I touched its head and felt my fingers run across the dried flesh of its face. Its nose arched upwards, into the cup of my hand.

'Come with me,' I said to it quietly.

It hesitated at first and then – when I beckoned it – it followed me, its leg stiff and dragging in the grass of the path. I moved back the way I'd come. Around me, all I could hear now was a constant patter as rain started to hit leaves, like hundreds of footsteps coming from every direction. A little further on, I could see the gate again. I picked up the pace, but – as I did – I felt the dog hesitate. I looked back. It was standing still and had turned to face back along the path into the woods.

'What's the matter?'

It didn't move. I stepped towards it.

'What can you see?' I asked.

It sniffed the air, as if it had picked up a scent. I dropped down and placed a hand gently on its back. It didn't move. Rain hit my hand and ran off on to its coat.

'What can you see?' I said again.

It whimpered once more, for longer this time. And then it started moving off, back along the trail, its leg dragging behind it. I whistled gently for it to return to me, but it either ignored me or couldn't hear me.

Thirty seconds later, it was gone.

I paused for a moment. Tried to see into the darkness to where the dog had gone. I hadn't really thought what I would do with it once we got back to the car, but it needed to be looked at. It needed to see a vet. I whistled louder this time, but the rain and the wind and the noise of the woods took the sound off into the night. For a moment, I thought about going back for it – but then a strange feeling passed over me.

Like someone was watching.

I gazed along the track. Eyes moving from one side of the woods to the other. There was no movement and no sound. But the feeling of being watched didn't disappear. It buzzed just beneath the surface of my skin even as the sounds seemed to wash out of the trees and the dying embers of the day gave way to evening.

And then, finally, the Dead Tracks settled.

CHAPTER 30

The quickest route home would have been through the centre of the city, but instead I headed in an arc, up through Whitechapel, Shoreditch and Finsbury, rain popping against the windscreen like shotgun spray. By seven o'clock, I was parked outside the youth club. It was Saturday, so I knew it would still be closed, but it was another thirty-six hours until someone opened the doors, and I couldn't wait that long. It felt like I had some momentum now – but, more than that, I wanted to look around without someone standing over my shoulder.

To the side of the building was a thin alleyway. I made my way along it, all the way through to a car park at the back. The entrance to it was from a road running parallel to the one I'd parked on. Everything was badly lit: a nearby street light was flickering on and off and there was a square of light from the kitchen of the restaurant next door.

The rear doors of the youth club were set back in an alcove. I took out my phone, flipped it open and used the light to examine the entrance. Double doors. A cylinder lock. No handle on the outside.

I backed up and examined the building. There had been no alarm on the front and there didn't look like there was one on the back either. But everywhere had an alarm these days. If there was no box, it probably meant the alarm was wired up to an old-fashioned open-circuit system; an alarm built with magnets that reacted to the doors opening, but turned off again when they closed and the circuit realigned.

I looked both ways, back across the car park, then took out a couple of straightened hairpins that I kept in the car. Picking locks was an art. You had to get the pins in exactly the right place, and apply the right amount of tension. You had to know the sounds and be able to feel the slightest of movements travelling back from the pins to your hand. I avoided picking locks if I could. Not because it was illegal, but because it was hard. As if to prove the point, it took me twenty frustrating minutes before I heard the pins finally falling into place.

I pressed the door shut for a moment while I readied myself – and then, as fast as I could, yanked it towards me, stepped inside and pulled it shut again. There was a brief noise: a high-pitched squeal lasting a second. I gripped the handle and waited. Placed an ear to the door. The alarm hadn't lasted long, but it might have been long enough to get someone's attention. I gave it five minutes to be certain, and then flipped open my phone and directed its light into the darkness of the building.

Immediately inside, on the left, was a kitchen and a serving hatch. Opposite, in a small ante-room, were some wheelchairs. I moved along the corridor and into the main hall. A stage to my left, a set of double doors to my right and the main entrance in front of me. Next to the entrance, nailed to the wall, was a planner. As I got closer, I could make out the names and photos of everyone who attended the youth club; above that, dressed in identikit green polo shirts, were the people who ran it.

I illuminated the pictures with my phone light. Neil Fletcher was at the top: the man in charge. Caroline had mentioned his name earlier. He was in his forties, black and grey hair, bright eyes, beard, trim. He wasn't the man in Tiko's – but neither was anyone else on the board. There was a woman below him, then two other men: Connor Pointon and Eric Castle. Both looked the same, without obviously being related. Mid twenties, square jaws, same hair, generically good-looking. Neither fitted the age group of the man Megan had been seeing. But I made a mental note to double-check both.

Swinging the light round, I walked across the hall to the doors at the far end, my footsteps echoing, the door squeaking on its hinges as I pulled one of them open. On the other side were toilets and an office. The office was sparsely decorated and cold. There was a desk up against one wall, a seat pushed in under it. A computer on the desk that looked at least five years old. Behind the desk, right in the far corner, was a filing cabinet.

I opened it up. Inside were files on every kid who had ever attended the youth club, set out by surname. I went through them, just in case, but nothing stuck out. In the next drawer down were the files on anyone who had ever worked there. Each had undergone an extensive Criminal Records Bureau check, which meant – if the man Megan had met *had* actually worked at the club – he wouldn't have had a record.

I pulled the files, set them down at the desk and turned the lights on. It was a windowless office, so no one would see me from the outside.

In all, there were seventeen files. I went through those on the three men who worked at the youth club first. The more I read about Fletcher, the less like a potential suspect he seemed. Forty-eight, married with two kids – one almost seventeen herself. Of the other two, Pointon was married, with a young daughter; and Castle was Australian, here on an ancestral visa, and wasn't even in the country when Megan first went missing.

I looked through the rest of the files.

The next eleven were female volunteers. Two I recognized immediately: Megan Carver and Leanne Healy. Megan was working part-time in the evenings at the club when she disappeared. Leanne had left two months before she vanished to concentrate on getting a full-time job, though a couple of entries on some kind of attendance form suggested she'd returned several times to help out. There was nothing else to add to what I already knew.

That left the nine other women. If I was assuming whoever had taken Megan had also taken Leanne, then I had to assume any female that had ever passed through the doors of the club was a potential victim. I wrote down the names of the women, and made a note to cross-check them with disappearances.

The last three files all featured men.

I laid them out in front of me. One was in his early fifties. I immediately dropped that on to the pile with the women. According to Kaitlin, the man I was looking for was in his thirties or – at a stretch – early forties. The two remaining were good fits. Both thirty-five. Neither was married. Both had clean bills of health from the CRB, and both had worked at the youth club in the period when Megan and Leanne went missing. I looked at their names. Daniel Markham. Adrian Carlisle. According to their files, Carlisle had left the youth club three months ago. Markham, though, still worked on a Monday afternoon. His CV listed his full-time job as 'consultant', whatever that meant.

There were phone numbers and addresses for both. I put them into my phone, and ripped out the pictures of the men attached to the files. From the surrounds of a five-centimetre-high photo, Carlisle looked like the kind of guy who'd perfected the art of smiling without meaning it, but was the better-looking of the two: slick, tanned, nice hair, expensive teeth. Markham seemed friendlier. He was also good-looking but in a studious kind of way, with sensible hair and horn-rimmed glasses. I went through both files again and tried to see if there was any mention of where Carlisle went after he left the club. Spike would probably be able to find out for me if I fed him the details when I got home. I collected all the files together and put them back into the cabinet.

Then I heard something.

Two short beeps. Then silence.

Was that the alarm?

Quietly, I pushed the filing cabinet closed and killed the lights. Stepped back from the door and let my eyes adjust to the darkness. After a couple of seconds, I moved into the corridor and up to the doors into the hall, sliding down the wall until my backside touched the floor. I opened the doors about half an inch. Stopped. Listened again. Pulling one of the doors all the way back, I slipped through the gap and into the hall. Paused. Let it fall back gently into place behind me. Without the light from my phone, the room seemed huge and endlessly black. I waited, crouched down, one knee against the floor. I tried to force myself to see things: shapes, doorways, any sign of movement.

But nothing stood out.

Slowly, I moved across the hall. I studied the

anteroom with the wheelchairs in it. Then the door into the kitchen. Then the serving hatch.

Now I could see something.

I moved closer. Got out my phone again.

Shone the light towards it.

At first I wasn't sure what I was looking at. It was pink and misshapen, its front turned away from me. Then, as I took another step closer, I realized what it was.

A plastic doll.

Another step, and suddenly it was looking up at me with glazed blue eyes. Its mouth, turned up in a permanent smile, had been smeared with lipstick. One of its legs had been cut off, leaving a dark hole. Its body was facing the other way to its head, away from me.

I shone the phone back into the hall, and then along the corridor to the back doors. Nothing was out of place. The rear doors were still closed.

It was like no one had ever been inside.

Outside the youth club it was cold. In my pockets were the photographs. In my hand was the doll. When I looked down at it, its glassy blue eyes stood out against the night, briefly glinting, and then rolled back under the eyelids.

The car park entrance opened on to a thin sliver of backstreet. I veered left, towards the road I'd parked on, keeping to the shadows cast by the buildings. Somewhere behind me a horn blared. A couple of seconds later another car joined in, this time louder and longer. I glanced back over my shoulder, an automatic reaction – and, in the darkness, something moved.

I stopped. Turned.

In the shadows of an overhanging building, I could make out a shape within the darkness. The toe of a shoe. Part of a leg. Above that, the curve of an elbow. I started to move back towards the alley, slowly at first, and then faster as I tried to close the space between us. But the silhouette just remained there – unmoving, turned in my direction – until I was about twenty feet away.

Then it broke into a run.

A figure appeared from the shadows like it was torn from the night. Ten feet further on, as I broke into a full sprint, it passed beneath a street light and I could see it was a man, about six foot, dressed in a long dark coat, dark trousers, black boots and a dark beanie. He kept his back to me the whole time, angling his head away, so that even as he turned a corner, running at full pelt, I couldn't see his face.

He disappeared from view as the street we were on narrowed and darkened, before suddenly veering right. And by the time I hit the traffic, noise and crowds on Euston Road, he was gone.

CHAPTER 31

Sunday morning, seven-forty. Waiting for me on the floor below the letterbox was the police file Ewan Tasker had promised he'd drop by: everything the Met had on the night Frank White died. It would have to wait for now.

I put some coffee on. Next door, Liz was leaving her house, heading for her car. Friday night came back to me: pulling away from her and then watching her hope go out like a light. For the second it took to make that decision, everything had felt right. It was too soon, too immense, the guilt too much of a weight to bear. But now all that remained was regret. It fizzed in my belly, a dull ache that I couldn't suppress.

I watched her go and then carried the coffee through to the living room, set it down and spread out the photos I'd taken from the youth club on the table. I brought Adrian Carlisle and Daniel Markham to the front. Using the notes I'd logged on my phone the previous night I scribbled down the addresses and numbers for them both. Carlisle lived up near the reservoirs in Seven Sisters.

Markham was in Mile End, close to the tube station. There was a landline and a mobile for Carlisle, but only a mobile for Markham.

On the other side of the table, the doll lay on its side. One of its eyes had dropped closed. The lipstick had smeared a little more. I brought it towards me and turned it, studying the hole that had once been its right leg. Then I noticed something inside the body cavity. I grabbed a pair of scissors, made the hole bigger and pulled it out.

My heart sank.

It was a photograph, folded to quarter size: a top-down shot of the shoulders and neck of a female. It had been taken in subdued light. Not darkness exactly, but not far from it. No part of the head or face was visible. No hair creeping into shot. Nothing above the neck. The skin was blotchy, like whoever was being photographed had just stepped out of a shower. A bruise, starting to yellow, was on the edge of the shot, close to the hardness of the shoulder blade. Shadows cut in from the sides, moving in towards the neck and around the indent at the bottom of the throat. And right in the top corner, someone had carved something into the glossy finish with either a compass point or the tip of a knife blade. It was the number two.

I flipped the picture over. It had no identifying marks on the back. None of the reference numbers or dates that shop-developed pictures were sometimes tagged with. Which meant it had been printed out on a colour photo printer – or developed at home.

But whose home?

Whoever it was had followed me to the youth club and left the doll there. The doll itself had to hold some significance, otherwise why use it? But for the time being, I was more concerned about the fact that someone was tracking my movements, watching from the darkness without me being able to see back in. Because if someone knew I was at the youth club, and this was some kind of message, it meant there was a hole in the case. And if there was a hole in the case, it would only get bigger until I closed it up.

I leaned in closer to the picture, studying the areas surrounding her body, and the background. It looked like she was sitting up. Behind her, despite the lack of light, the room seemed to extend out. It was granite grey close to her body, but – further back – descended into a wall of complete darkness. Maybe the girl in the photograph wasn't even Megan. Or maybe it was. Both possibilities made my blood run cold.

Then I paused.

Brought it in even closer to me.

Right at the edge of the photograph, just above her right shoulder, there was a shape in the dark. I used a finger to trace it.

Cardboard boxes.

They faded off dramatically, but there was a definite L-shape. I could see a thin line, where the horizontal and vertical axes met on the highest box. There was something else too: a small, pale label stuck to its side, half in the shot, half out. The writing on it was obscured by the darkness of the picture. But I could make out a two-line header in thick black letters. Part of it looked like a pi symbol; the rest was Cyrillic.

I grabbed my phone and dialled the number for Spike.

'We must stop meeting like this,' he said, using Caller ID.

'I need your help. Again.'

'Just name the server.'

'It's not computer work.'

'Oh.'

'I've got something here which I need translating. I don't feel comfortable taking it to a high-street service, so I was hoping you might have a look at it for me.'

'What is it?'

'Definitely Cyrillic. I think part of it might be a number.'

'Yeah, okay. Send it over.'

'Thanks, Spike.'

I killed the call and then used my cameraphone to take shots of the photograph, trying to leave out as much of the woman as possible. The fewer questions I got about who she was and what she was doing, the better. Once I had a couple of clear pictures, I messaged them over to Spike. He called me back inside three minutes. When I picked up, the background music he'd previously been playing had been turned off. No sound of tapping keyboards now. No jokes. This was Spike in full-on concentration mode.

He launched straight in: 'You were right. That symbol, the one that looks a bit like pi, it's the number 80. As for the rest . . .' He paused. 'You got a pen?'

'Yeah, shoot.'

'The lighting's terrible, but from what I can make out . . .' He paused for a second time. I could hear movement and then a couple of clicks of a mouse. 'Okay. There's the main header and then another line underneath. The one underneath . . . Man, I'm not even sure how to pronounce this.' More mouse clicks. 'C-A-R-C-I-N-O—'

'Carcinogen?'

'Yeah. Could be. What does that mean?'

'It means it'll give you cancer.'

'Shit,' Spike said quietly.

I looked down at the photograph. Spike had translated the easiest, cleanest part. But the header on the top line would be harder to make out.

'Any idea what the other bit says?'

'Difficult to tell. Maybe the name of a company. Looks like an F, maybe an O. An R, an M. Not sure about the fifth or sixth letters. The seventh is definitely an I.'

I wrote that down. *F-O-R-M-?-?-I.*

'Okay, that's great, Spike. I really appreciate—'

I stopped. Looked at the letters I'd just written

down. Scribbled out both the question marks and replaced them with an A and an L. *F-O-R-M-A-L-I.*

'David?'

I dropped the pen down next to the pad and leaned back in my chair.

'David?'

'It's not the name of a company,' I said.

'No?'

'It's the name of a chemical compound.'

'Form . . .?'

'Formalin.'

'What's that?'

'Liquid formaldehyde.'

Spike paused. 'That's what they use in embalming, right?'

'Right.' I circled the word a couple of times. 'And preserving remains.'

CHAPTER 32

By half-ten, I was moving along Whitechapel Road, into Mile End, and I had the heaters on full blast. I'd already been to Adrian Carlisle's house in Seven Sisters. He wasn't home. I tried his landline and mobile and no one answered. I waited outside his place – a three-storey mid-terrace in which he occupied the top floor – for an hour. But there was no sign of him. Now, as I passed into Mile End, I could make out the sandy brick and gunmetal roof of the building Daniel Markham lived in.

It was the first of six identical five-storey apartment complexes. Each one stood parallel to the next, all facing west so that anyone with a home on the east of the building spent their life without sun. In what must have surely been an ironic touch, they were all named after different types of roses. Markham lived in Alba on the ground floor. At the entrance, the glass doors had steamed up and two women were standing talking, coats and scarves tightly bound around them. I parked up and headed towards them.

Then, ten feet short of the doors, a flash of recollection hit me.

The entrance.

It was the block of flats in Megan's photo. She'd been standing where the women were now, looking into the camera of the man she'd been with, that smile etched on her face. *Markham*. Was he the one she'd been seeing? The man who'd got her pregnant? The man who'd taken her? I quickly headed inside, through the doors to the ground floor and along a small, grey corridor, to flat number eight.

I knocked twice. Elsewhere in the corridor there was the muffled sound of television. Laughter. A baby crying. But no answer from Markham's flat.

'Daniel?'

No response.

'Daniel, my name's David Raker.'

Nothing.

I stepped forward. There was no spyhole in the door. I put an ear to it and listened. After a couple of seconds, I could hear a noise.

'Daniel, I need to speak to you.'

Again, with my ear pressed to the door, I could hear a noise. The same one: a creak, or maybe a click. When it came again, it sounded more like a click.

'Daniel?'

I leaned in again and tried to separate out the sounds. There was a constant buzz; possibly a fridge. Some peripheral noise from outside the flat. Behind that, whatever was making the clicking sound. Except this time it was preceded by a gentle whirr.

'Daniel?'

Click.

Distantly, there were police sirens. I stepped away from the door and waited until they got closer, until the noise started to cover some of the other sounds inside the building. Then I took another step back – and launched a foot at the door.

It cracked and swung open, hitting an adjacent wall and bouncing back towards me. I stopped it with a hand. Paused. Looked along the corridor.

Then I stepped into the flat and closed the door.

Immediately to my left was a bathroom. Next to that was the bedroom door. In front of me was a short hallway, feeding into a living room and open-plan kitchen. It looked like someone had half moved out and never returned. Dust clung to walls. Windows had been whitewashed, but not very well. Through one, I could see out to the path leading up to the flats, and the entrance itself. It was a good position for Markham: he'd be able to see if anyone approached the building.

'Daniel?'

Silence. There was a two-seater sofa in the living room. A lamp next to that. A half-filled bookshelf. Otherwise, the flat was empty. No TV. No music centre. No games consoles, satellite decoders or DVD players. Nothing a single man should have owned.

The kitchen had been mostly cleared out as well. Only a few things remained. A kettle. A couple of plates stacked in a drying rack. A fruit bowl. A refrigerator in the corner, humming. It was on, but it had been defrosted. The doors were open to both the fridge and the freezer. There was no food in either. Same story in the bedroom: a bed base, a mattress, no sheets, no duvet. Built-in cupboards, all open. There were some clothes inside, but not many. A couple of shirts. Some trousers.

Click.

That noise again. I moved out into the hallway. Looked around. There was very little sound now: no noise from the flat, no noise from outside. Heading into the bathroom, I turned on the light. Toilet. Bath. Basin. Bathroom cabinet with a small mirror on the front. Above me, the extractor fan kicked into life. I opened up the cabinet and looked around inside. A can of deodorant, a razor, some shaving cream. Nothing else. I pushed the cabinet shut – except now it wouldn't close. When I tried again, it just slowly crept back open. I leaned in and looked at the catch. It was broken. The moment I'd pulled the cabinet open, the catch had come loose.

As if it had been set up to break.

And someone was trying to draw attention to it.

I stepped in closer to the cabinet and looked inside. In the corners, it had been attached to the wall with four screws. I placed a hand on either side of the cabinet and levered it away. It stuck for a moment, the screws clinging to the holes that housed them. But when I applied more pressure they began to come out as it shifted off the wall.

It had been deliberately left loose.

Dust spilled out from around the screw heads, landing inside the cabinet. Plaster made a scraping sound behind it. And then, a couple of seconds later, the cabinet came away.

In the space behind it was a patch of cream paint – the original colour of the bathroom – and the holes that had once housed the screws.

In the centre was a message, written directly on to the wall.

It said: *Help me*.

CHAPTER 33

Back at the car, rain continued falling. I started up the engine and left the heaters running. In the pop-out drinks holder was a takeaway coffee. Steam rose from a hole in the lid.

I grabbed my phone. On it was a picture of the message I'd found on the wall. I'd placed the cabinet back as best I could and wedged the front door of the flat shut with a folded piece of card. If someone returned to it, it would only take a second for them to realize there had been a break-in. But that was *if* they returned. It felt like a place that had gone a long time without being lived in.

As I exited the photo again, the phone started buzzing in my hand. The number was withheld.

'David Raker.'

'David, my name's Corine. I'm a friend of Spike's.'

'Corine – thanks for calling me.'

After he'd translated the writing in the photograph for me, Spike had offered to put me in contact with a friend of his who had some sort of science degree. He was deliberately vague. He didn't involve the people he liked in his work.

'Spike said you had some questions.'

She sounded English; softly spoken with a slight northern twang. I wondered how she'd come to meet an illegal immigrant who never went outside.

'Yeah. I was hoping you could tell me about formalin.'

'Formalin?' She paused. 'What do you want to know?'

'It's what they use in embalming, right?'

'Not so much any more. Formaldehyde's kind of frowned upon these days. In fact, some European countries have banned it altogether.'

'Because it's carcinogenic?'

'Right. Formalin's only thirty-seven per cent formaldehyde. The rest is methanol and water. But it's still ridiculously good at what it does. Drop an animal into a vat of it and you've got an instant tissue preserver. Just ask Damien Hirst.'

'How's it work?'

'Basically, the formaldehyde hardens you up. It eats away at the cell tissue, drying out the protoplasm and replacing the fluid with this firm kind of gel-like compound. So it not only solidifies the cells and maintains the shape of the skin, but disinfects the tissue at the same time. And even better than that – it's incredibly resistant to bacteria.'

'Where would I get some?'

'Formalin?'

'I'm talking theoretically – and on the quiet.'

'Well, because it's carcinogenic, it's heavily policed, so your best bet would be to import it from outside Europe – or from somewhere *inside* Europe that isn't properly regulated. You're taking a chance whichever route you decide. And you'd obviously need someone who'd be willing to bring it in for you, with all the associated risks. I don't know where you'd find those kind of people.'

An hour later, I pulled into Kensal Green Cemetery: seventy-two acres of gravestones, mausoleums and parkland, rolling across the city like a blanket. Nosing the car around to a long colonnade, I bumped the BMW up on to the grass beside the pillars and killed the engine. A face looked out briefly, and then disappeared again. I got out and headed across. Beneath the colonnade it smelled old and musty. About twenty feet to my right, a skinny black guy wearing a yellow beanie and a shiny green bomber jacket was moving towards me.

His name was Ray Smith.

Smith was a small-time crook the police had got their hooks into after a botched bank job in Mayfair five years ago. He'd been the getaway driver, but hadn't got away fast enough. Smith actually wasn't a bad guy – he'd just got in with the wrong people. In exchange for a new life as a paid informant, he got to roam the streets a free man. That was when I got my hooks into him and told the paper to double whatever the Met paid him. He was small-time, but he had a good pair of ears. Which was how he got his name. Ray wasn't short for Raymond. It was short for Radar, as in, he always knew what was going on.

I looked him up and down.

He was a ten-stone bundle of energy, powered by a mixture of adrenalin and paranoia, and known for his appalling fashion sense. His bomber jacket was a nuclear explosion, and on the middle finger of his right hand was a huge, diamond-encrusted ring.

'You travelling incognito, Ray?'

He rolled his eyes and looked around him. 'Fuck you. I shouldn't even be here talkin' to you, man. You're a bad luck charm.'

'How do you figure that?'

'You remember the last time I helped you out?'

'Sure. Must have been about two years back.'

'Correct. And you know what happened the next day? I get my face kicked in. And then my fuckin' dog dies. You got the Medusa touch.' He was looking to the side, but his eyes flicked back to me. 'Listen,' he said. A pause. 'I, y'know . . . heard about your girl.'

I nodded. He turned and looked along the colonnade behind him, turning his back to me. I let him have a moment. That second of eye contact was Ray trying to tell me he was sorry about Derryn. It was about as poignant as our relationship had ever got.

I changed the subject. 'So you still bleeding taxpayers dry?'

He turned back to face me. 'Yeah, still doin' it.

242

And the only reason I'm still standin' here breathin' is 'cause my boy keeps me outta the limelight.'

About fifteen years ago, the police started asking detectives to register their confidential informants, which as most of them would tell you was one of the worst ideas in the history of law enforcement. As soon as CIs thought details of their snitching was available somewhere to find or pass on, the intel dried up. What most detectives did instead was log two or three CIs they knew they'd never use, and keep their best ones off the books. Radar was one of the best ones.

'You do much for them?'

'Yeah, a fair bit,' he replied, shrugging. 'Gotta be done. It's either that or the boys in blue turn up at my front door and slap the chains on me. And I don't much fancy a bumming in Pentonville.'

'Really?'

He frowned. 'You sayin' I'm bent?'

I laughed, but tried not to make too much of it. Ray had never killed anyone in his life, but he still maintained a strict code of conduct as if he was the world's most dangerous hitman. And like most criminals, it was a code all twisted up. No women. No children. Anything to do with drugs was fair game, as long as the product didn't end up in the hands of kids under sixteen. Guns were out, but knives were in. And no jokes about him deliberately dropping the soap in the showers as homosexuality was against God.

'So, I need your help.'

He nodded. Stepped closer to me.

'I'm an importer looking to bring some chemicals into the country on the quiet. Nothing that's going to flatten a city, but bad enough that they'd be too difficult to get hold of in the UK.'

'What kind of chemicals we talkin'?'

'Formaldehyde.'

'What the hell's that?'

'It's what they'll coat you in when you die.'

'Like dead people and shit?'

'Right.'

'Not ringing any bells.'

'It probably came in as a liquid. Would have been called formalin.'

Ray stopped jigging about momentarily, his eyes fixing on mine. Then he started up again, but didn't make a move to say anything.

'What is it, Ray?'

Another dramatic pause. 'There's this guy. Got a building over in Beckton, near the airport. He's from up north. Manchester. Somewhere round there.'

'And he does what?'

'Imports shit – but ninety-nine per cent of it's legit. He runs a clean company outta his place. I think he's, like, a supplier for restaurants. Some of the stuff is actual food, but most of it's plates and engraved bowls and all that kinda shit.'

'So what's the other one per cent?'

'The way I hear it, he's got some serious connections. He's like a fixer. You go to him with what

244

you want and he gets it; brings it in with the bowls and the china plates.'

'I'm still waiting for the bonus ball.'

He rolled his eyes. 'You hearin' anythin' I'm sayin' here? He ain't handin' me a fuckin' inventory every week. The guy ain't a personal friend of mine. But if there's chemicals comin' into the city, you can bet your arse they're comin' through him.'

I didn't reply. His eyes flicked to me. His face seemed straight: no movement, no obvious sign that he was hiding anything.

'Okay,' I said. 'What's the name of the business?'

'Drayton Imports.'

'That's the guy's name as well?'

'Yeah, Derrick Drayton.'

I took a pen out of my pocket and wrote the names on the back of my hand. 'So, who's been using him?'

'I don't know.'

I sighed and looked up at him. 'Stop feeding me bullshit, Ray.'

'I ain't.'

'I don't believe you.'

'I ain't holdin' back!'

'I don't believe you,' I said again.

This time there was a brief hesitation and then that movement in his face I'd been waiting for. He knew something.

'Ray?'

Another pause. 'Okay. I shouldn't be tellin' you this.'

'Telling me what?'

'The police came askin' about all this shit a few months—'

'Wait a sec, wait a sec. The police?'

'Yeah.'

'What were they asking about?'

'If I'd heard anythin' about this Drayton guy.'

'They tell you why they were asking?'

'No.'

'What did they say?'

'Nothin'. Just asked me if I'd heard anythin' about this guy, Drayton, who ran it. When I told 'em what I knew, they said I needed to keep my trap shut if anyone asked.'

I paused. Let my mind return to the photograph and the formalin in the background. 'Did the police ever ask you if you'd heard anything about a missing girl?'

Radar frowned. 'No.'

'They just asked about Drayton?'

'Yeah.'

I paused. 'So if they know he's on the take, why haven't they closed him down?'

'He disappeared. Most people think he bought a one-way ticket out of the country when he could smell pork on the wind. And the business is squeaky clean. So his family run the place over in Beckton in his absence. You'd have to dial 999 to find out what the police have got planned for him if he ever returns. Especially after the . . .' He trailed off.

'The what?'

'Doesn't matter.'

'The *what*?' He didn't respond. 'Speak up, Radar.'

He sighed; slid a couple of fingers beneath his beanie and tried to rub his frown away. Eventually he took the hat off altogether and dragged a whole hand across his head, his shaved hair bristling beneath his palm. Another sigh, this time louder.

'Especially the what, Ray?'

'This Drayton guy, he's got a series of properties all over that part of the city. Not just the place at Beckton. And in one of them . . . somethin' got fucked up.'

'What are you talking about?'

'It's why the police were interested. Way I hear it is that Drayton sourced some guns for some OC outfit and allowed 'em to use one of his buildings as a pick-up point for the weapons.'

'Organized crime?'

'Yeah. Russians. The police got wind of it and sent in the cavalry. Only it went wrong.' He paused. Looked at me. 'And a couple of coppers got a bullet in the face.'

I looked at him, struck into silence.

Bloody hell.

He's talking about the night Frank White died.

CHAPTER 34

The Frank White file was sitting inside the boot of the BMW, still in the envelope Tasker had mailed it in. I'd brought it with me in case I found the time to skim-read it while chasing leads back to Megan. But now, somehow, Frank White had moved in from the periphery – and he'd tethered himself to her disappearance.

I slid in at the wheel, closed the door and tried to clear my head. The cemetery was quiet. I put the wipers on intermittent, listening to them sweep across the glass. For the moment, there wasn't a direct connection that I could see. There was a line running from Frank's death, to the Russians, to Drayton Imports, to the formalin, and on to the girl in the photograph. But the circle wasn't complete. It felt like *something* was at work – like on some level the two of them were bound to one another – but even if Megan *was* the girl in the picture, which wasn't even certain, the only thing that connected her to Frank White was the fact that the formalin in the background of the shot had probably been imported by Drayton – the man who owned the warehouse Frank was shot in.

And yet I didn't like the convenience of it all; the coincidence. Because I didn't believe in coincidences. I believed in structure and meaning. I believed in connections.

People connected. Events connected.

Everything tied up.

I started going through the file. It echoed exactly what Tasker had already told me over the phone. The task force was spotted early on by Russian lookouts, and the operation descended into a shoot-out. Three specialist firearms officers had accompanied White's SCD7 team to the scene, and one of them had managed to hit the surgeon's getaway vehicle, a stolen black Lexus. But he still got away. At 11.17 p.m., Frank White was declared dead. Another detective, Kline, was already gone. Two of Akim Gobulev's men made it through the firefight. One died in the ambulance on the way to the hospital; the other refused to talk. There were five separate attempts by detectives to interview him, and the five transcripts included in the file weren't more than a page long.

So all they had was the surgeon.

And they didn't even have him.

Pathology, fingerprint lifts and ballistics confirmed what Tasker had already told me, but the evidence inventory was one of the longest I'd ever seen. The lack of a smoking gun – and the fact that two police officers were lying dead on the floor of the warehouse – had galvanized the forensic teams. It looked like every fibre in the building had been processed.

For the people working there, it had become personal the moment White and Kline stopped breathing.

I leafed through the list. Everything bagged at the scene had been catalogued, and it all quickly became a blur: numbers, names and descriptions rolling down one page and on to the next. Hairs. Mud. Dust. Powder. Skin. The eleventh and twelfth pages listed evidence recovered from Gobulev's men – dead and alive – at the scene. More fibres. Fingerprints. Illegal firearms, the serial numbers removed. Below that, there were two entries for the two 9mm bullets that had killed Frank White. Both were hollow point, which meant they'd expanded in his chest and head as soon as they'd made contact. He would have died quickly.

I moved on through the rest of the file – interviews, photographs of the scene, what they knew about the surgeon – and when I got to the end dropped it on to my lap and looked out at the cemetery again. It was still quiet. No people. No cars. Only the gentle wheeze of the wipers.

Picking up my phone, I dialled the Carvers. James answered, but Caroline was there as well. I asked him to put me on speakerphone, so I could talk to them both.

'Very quick question,' I said. 'Do either of you recognize the name Frank White – maybe someone Megan knew, or perhaps the police mentioned the name in passing?'

'Doesn't ring a bell for me,' Carver replied.

I could feel the tension travel down the line. He was answering for himself, not the two of them now.

'Same here,' Caroline said quietly.

People connected. Events connected. Nothing is co-incidence. I said goodbye, then dialled Jill's mobile. She was out somewhere. In the background I could hear people talking.

'I'm not disturbing you, am I?'

'No, not at all,' she said. 'I'm doing some shopping.'

'Can I ask you a couple of questions?'

'Of course.'

'Do you ever remember Frank mentioning the name Megan Carver?'

A pause. 'Wasn't she that girl who went missing?'

'Right.'

'I don't think so.'

'He never mentioned being involved in the search for her?'

'No. Why do you ask?'

I paused. *You have to ask her – and there's no easy way to phrase it.* 'Mind if I ask why you decided to come to the support group this week?'

'What do you mean?'

I mean I'm already working the Megan Carver case, and then you turn up and I end up looking into your husband's death as well. And now I find out there might be some kind of connection. 'I just wondered about the timing, that was all.'

She hesitated. I rode out the silence. There didn't seem to be a lot of mystery to Jill. The grief she

251

felt for her husband seemed real; the shyness seemed genuine. I couldn't see anything behind her reasons for coming to the group other than to get over the death of someone she'd loved. But, even so, the timing was too perfect. She'd all but asked me to look into Frank's death forty-eight hours after the Carvers had first brought me Megan. London was a city of seven million people, and yet somehow I'd ended up with both cases within two days of each other.

'David, I don't know . . .' She paused. 'I don't know what you're asking me.'

'Frank's name came up in relation to Megan, and I'm trying to work out why. Because Megan is the case I'm working at the moment. The one I told you about. I'm not accusing you of anything, I'm just trying to find the connection.'

'I swear to you, I didn't know they were connected.'

All I had to go on was her voice. The tiny movements in it; the rise and fall of the words. She was either telling the truth or she was a flawless liar.

'I was struggling to cope,' she said. 'That's why I came to the support group. It's been nearly a year, and it's just not getting any easier. I thought the group might help.'

'Did you know I attended the group?'

'No.'

'Had you heard of me before?'

'Absolutely not.'

I paused for a moment. 'Okay.'

'That's the truth, I swear.'

'I believe you,' I said, but wasn't sure if I was committed to what I was saying. Even if she was telling the truth, something was out of kilter somewhere. 'I just needed to be sure.'

'I understand.'

Now she sounded like she was lying. I'd offended her by suggesting she'd arrived at the group with an ulterior motive. Some hidden agenda.

We said goodbye, her voice quiet and distant, and then I turned to the file again, flipping back to the start. I worked it hard: every line, every entry, every detail. But, after twelve pages, the second read-through was the same as the first. No connections. Not to people, not to events and, most importantly, not to the girl I was trying to find.

Then, on page thirteen, I found something.

Midway down, one of the techs had recovered a series of grey hairs. DNA tests revealed that they didn't belong to anyone present at the scene – because they weren't even human. They were from a dog.

A greyhound.

No one recalled seeing a dog at the scene, and the warehouse was kept locked up so wouldn't have been home to any strays – which meant someone brought the hairs with them. Police would have assumed they'd come from a living room somewhere, or a kitchen. But I knew instantly they didn't come from a house.

They came from the Dead Tracks.

CHAPTER 35

As I moved into my road, I could immediately tell something was up. People were standing at the top of the street in the pouring rain looking down towards my house. Blue light painted the buildings and flashed in the windows. Crime-scene tape fluttered in the breeze. An officer was stationed just behind the tape. He watched me approach, eyes narrowed, trying to get a fix on who I was, and what I might want. As I continued my approach in the car, he looked like he was about to tell me to turn around. Then he got a glimpse of my face and recognition sparked in his eyes. He looked behind him. There was a crime-scene van and three cars parked outside. Two were marked. One, a Volvo, wasn't, but had a lightbar flaring on the front dash. As I stopped the car short of the tape, the officer shouted something and two men emerged from my driveway.

Phillips and Davidson.

I got out of the car. 'What the hell is this?'

Neither of them said anything. Phillips led the way, a long black coat trailing behind him like a cape. Davidson followed, a cup of takeaway coffee in his hands, the merest hint of a smile on his face.

'David,' Phillips said.

We were either side of the crime-scene tape. Phillips looked back at the house. A crime-scene tech was coming down the driveway now, carrying a shoebox. It was one of the ones I'd had stacked in the spare-room wardrobes; full of stuff belonging to Derryn that I hadn't yet sorted through. It was inside an evidence bag.

'Where's she going with that?'

Phillips didn't reply. Davidson shrugged.

I glared at Phillips. 'Everything in there belongs to my *wife*.'

'Calm down, David,' he replied.

'Calm down?'

'Calm down.'

'I want that box back *now*.'

'*Listen* to me,' Phillips said, and his eyes flicked to the crowd at the end of the road. Automatically, I turned and looked towards Liz's house. It was dark. No one home. I didn't want her to see this. 'Just calm down,' he said again, 'before you make this worse.'

'What are you doing in my house?' I said, ignoring him. 'Have you even got a warrant?'

Phillips felt around in the pocket of his coat and brought out a piece of paper, sealed inside a water-proof sleeve. He held it up.

'Did you lie on oath to get this?'

He didn't reply, just handed it to me.

I looked at it. In the lack of light it was difficult to see the specifics, but I spotted my name at the top and a signature at the bottom.

'Who the fuck signed off on that?'

'I need you to come with me,' Phillips replied.

'Why would I do that?' There was definitely a smile on Davidson's face now. I looked at him. 'You got something to say to me, fat man?'

He shrugged, still smiling.

Phillips audibly sighed. 'Okay, David, we're going to have to make this official.'

Davidson now had a pad in his hands and – despite the rain – was busy writing down what I'd just said. Even as the rage boiled in me, I knew I had to cool off to avoid saying something I'd regret. But when I looked again at the tech loading the shoebox into the back of the van, anger fired in me for a second time. I ducked under the tape. The uniformed officer made a move towards me. Phillips noticed and held up a hand.

'David,' he said.

'You better have a damn good reason for being here.'

Phillips nodded. 'David Raker, I'm arresting you on suspicion of the abduction of Megan Carver. You do not have to say anything—'

'*What?*'

'—but it may harm your defence if you do not mention, when questioned, anything which you later rely on in court. Anything you do say may be used in evidence. Do you understand what I've just said to you?'

'You've got to be kidding me.'

'Do you understand, David?'

I glanced at the two of them. Davidson was still writing. Phillips looked between me and the PC standing to my side.

'David?'

I stared at him.

'David, do you understand – yes or no?'

Behind him, Davidson continued writing.

'Yes or no?'

I looked at him. 'Yes.'

He nodded at the PC again. I heard the metallic rasp of a pair of handcuffs and then felt the officer come up behind me. He guided my arms around to my back and sat them at the base of my spine. Cold, wet metal fed around my wrists and locked into place. In front of me, Davidson made a point of forcibly adding a full stop on to the end of whatever he was writing.

'This is crazy,' I said.

Phillips placed a hand on my arm. 'Time to go.'

THIS IS THE BEGINNING

She had a mattress and two blankets for when she slept. An hour after his second visit of the day, when he would throw down the liquid for her face and the cotton wool to apply it with, the lights would go out, plunging the room into total darkness. The lights would come on again the next day, for the first visit, when he came with her food. With the lights out, all she had was silence.

Some nights, early on, she would yell at the top of her voice, trying to get someone to hear her. When a week passed, she started trying to reason with him when he came in. At ten days, she told him the mattress was uncomfortable. Finally, at two weeks, she changed tactics when he came in with her food.

'I'm going to kill you, you bastard!'

She only tried once.

After she screamed at him, he paused. Straightened. Looked down at her. A smile broke out on his face; a thin line, like a slash from a knife. As it formed, his mouth peeling open, she realized it wasn't a smile at all. It was a warning. He was telling her that, even if she never slept again, she wouldn't see

258

him approach. He'd do what he wanted to her, come for her when he needed her.

And all she would see was a flicker in the darkness.

Sona woke. It was pitch black; the middle of the night. She rolled over on the mattress, springs popping beneath her, and pulled the blanket up to her neck. As she did, she heard something beyond the silence for the first time since she'd been taken: the gentle patter of rain. It was coming down somewhere distantly, softly, consistently. When she shut her eyes and tried to concentrate on the noise, it sounded like it was hitting a metal grate.

pffffffff

Her eyes snapped open.

The hole was bricked in dark colours all the way up, so there was no definition to her surroundings. No chinks of light. She couldn't even see her own hand in front of her face. Everything vanished in the darkness, and all that remained was sound: a very gentle rumble now, reverberating through the floor of the room above and down the walls of the hole; and the rhythmic beat of the rain.

She lay there with her eyes open. As she counted the time in her head – thirty seconds, a minute, two minutes, five minutes – the rain started to get harder. At ten minutes, she could feel herself getting tired again. Her eyes drifted closer together. She opened them and stared into the darkness for another sixty seconds. Then she closed them, too tired now to fight the onset of sleep.

pffffffff

She moved quickly, sitting up on the mattress. *What was that?* The sound had been closer this time. She expected to be able to see something, maybe just the smallest mark against the darkness. But there was nothing. No light. No shapes. Everything was black. She reached out in front of her, to where the sound had come from. Leaned a little way forward. Pressed her other hand against the floor for support.

And then it came to her.

She realized what the sound had been.

Static.

Torchlight erupted from the corner of the hole, blinding her briefly. She brought a hand to her eyes, automatically reacting, but a leg kicked her supporting arm out from under her and she fell forward, hitting her face against the floor. It dazed her for a moment, white dots flashing in front of her. When she rolled on to her back, he was standing above her, a foot either side of her body, a smile cutting across his face.

Behind him, propped against the wall, was a ladder.

He'd come down, into the hole, and she hadn't even heard him.

She tried to wriggle away from him, getting as far as she could, but he placed a boot on her throat and pinned her to the floor. Static from the speakers in the room above.

'This is the beginning,' he said.

Even up close, it was hard to make out his features clearly. He'd turned the torch away from himself, shining it to the left. Shadows cut across him, little pieces of the night clinging to every fold and crease in his face.

'This is where you give me my life back.'

In the blink of an eye, the man took his foot off her throat and lifted her up off the floor of the hole. She went to fight him, went to kick or punch or bite, but he was too quick. He punched her in the side of the head – a fast, efficient jab, right at the corner of the eye – almost hissing at her as he moved.

And then she toppled sideways on to the mattress and blacked out.

PART III

CHAPTER 36

They took me to the same station as before, but this time I wasn't going to be walked straight into an interview room. The same custody sergeant that had greeted my arrival the first time was perched at the front desk, looking down through his half-moon glasses. He glanced at me, then at Phillips and Davidson, and buzzed them in. The three of them led me in the opposite direction to the interview rooms, through two sets of doors, into the custody suite. Behind me, Phillips pushed a metal gate shut until it locked. Davidson moved off to my left. The sergeant slid in behind a desk, introducing himself as Fryer, and asked Phillips to undo my cuffs. Up front, he told me my rights. Every couple of sentences, he paused to ask if I was clear. They hated the Police and Criminal Evidence Act more than any of the men and women they arrested. Anything missed, any mistakes, and a solicitor would dismantle the case.

Fryer produced a camera from under the counter. Police liked to get the pictures out the way in case, for any reason, injuries were sustained inside the station later on. He took three photographs. Once he was done, he invited me across to a table where the fingerprint kit sat. The whole time, Davidson watched. I glared at him, but he just stared at me blankly.

Next, Fryer asked Phillips to go over his account of the arrest. It was the reason Davidson had been taking notes. Except Phillips didn't need them. He'd committed pretty much everything to memory. When he was done, Fryer turned to me and asked if I had anything to add; in effect, he was asking me if I wanted to dispute Phillips's account. I shook my head.

The rest of the booking in took twenty minutes. I emptied out my pockets and everything was logged, gave them my belt and shoelaces, then Fryer reminded me of my rights again, and asked me if I wanted to call anyone or inform a solicitor. This time I said I wanted to make a call, and Phillips directed me to a room behind the booking-in area. It was small with reinforced glass panels, one table and one chair – both bolted down – and a telephone on the wall. They left me there. I watched them go, and then dialled Liz's mobile. After three rings, she picked up.

'Hello?'

'Liz, it's David.'

'David,' she said, and sounded pleased to hear my voice. 'How are you? I popped over yesterday, but you must have been out.'

'Liz . . .'

266

She immediately sensed something was up. 'Are you okay?'

'I'm under arrest.'

'*What?*'

'The police turned up at my house earlier . . .' I paused. 'They've made a mistake. They've somehow tied me to the disappearance of Megan Carver. I don't know how, but . . . Look, I don't want to talk about it too much over the phone. I just need your help. Can you get here?'

'Yes, yes, of course,' she said. 'The only thing is, I'm not in London.'

My heart sank.

'Where are you?'

'I'm up in Warwick seeing Katie.'

I remembered her walking down the drive to her car before eight that morning. Warwick was eighty miles away. An hour and a half on a clear run. Except Sunday night on the motorways into London wouldn't be a clear run. Even if she left now, it would probably take her a couple of hours. If I was unlucky, even more.

'David,' she said, and her voice was suddenly quiet and controlled. 'What is it they think you've done?'

'Abducted Megan.'

She paused. '*Did* you abduct her?'

'No. Absolutely not.'

I heard her exhale softly. 'Okay. Listen. I'm going to ask you a couple of questions. Don't leave anything out.' She stopped. Let that last sentence settle. She was reminding me of the times she'd helped me out before when both of us had known I'd left some of the truth buried. 'So, first: do you think Megan's dead?'

'She's been gone six months.'

'Is that a yes?'

'Statistically, there's a good chance, just because of the time she's been missing. I've got no evidence to support that. And neither have they. But the case is still active.'

'So if the case is still active, they're working from the assumption that she could just as easily be alive?'

'Right.'

'Because here's the thing. You are entitled to free legal advice. They'd have told you that already. The police *have* to provide that as part of PACE. You can go that route and, because it's a Sunday evening and a solicitor won't magically appear at the station in five minutes flat, that will delay any interview taking place for a while. And it will give me some time to get back.'

'But?'

'*But*,' she said, and paused. She blew out some air, and it crackled down the line between us. 'If they think that there's a real and immediate danger to the life of someone connected to this case – i.e. the girl they're accusing you of taking – they can start the interview without having to wait for a solicitor. If they think Megan's alive – if the evidence they have points to that – and they think any delay will adversely affect them *finding* her alive, then they can start the interview once you get off the phone to me.'

I looked out through the glass to where Phillips, Davidson and Fryer had booked me in. They'd been joined by Hart now – and someone else I didn't recognize. He was wearing uniform. Early fifties but lean. On the shoulder of his shirt was his rank insignia. A crown, with red trim. Beneath that, a four-pointed star. As I studied him, he seemed to sense it and returned the look.

'David?'

I watched him for a moment more. 'So who makes that call?'

'What call?'

'To bypass the solicitor.'

'It has to be superintendent rank or above.'

Standing between Fryer and Hart, a printout of my custody report in his hands, the station's chief superintendent was still looking at me.

CHAPTER 37

Twenty minutes later I was inside Interview Room 4 and the tape was rolling. There were three cups of machine coffee between us. None of them had been touched. The room was smaller than the one I'd been in before. It was all part of the play. Smaller room. Less space to breathe in. Psychologically, they were trying to secure any kind of advantage they could.

After pushing Play, Phillips introduced himself and Davidson for the benefit of the tape, and then asked me to confirm my name and address. On the desk in front of him was a thin brown Manila folder. From inside, I could see the corners of photographs poking out. His hand was flat on top, as if he were scared it might suddenly disappear. Next to him, Davidson had resumed the casual stance of the first interview: leaning back in the chair, jacket off, too-tight T-shirt, arms crossed and resting on his belly.

'Okay, David,' Phillips said, 'let's get started. I'm going to ask you a few basic questions first, all right? So . . . can you confirm your occupation for us?'

Davidson smirked. I looked at him. 'Something funny?'

'David?'

I turned back to Phillips, but didn't answer.

'David?'

'I'm a missing persons investigator.'

Davidson nodded. Mock sincerity. He leaned forward in his chair and dragged one of the coffee cups towards him; just to be seen to be doing something.

'So, why missing persons?' Phillips asked.

'About four months after I left the paper, one of my wife's friends asked me to look into the disappearance of her daughter.' I paused. Both of them looked at me. Phillips made no movement. Davidson shifted again. 'So I did. After that, a couple came to see me. Then another one. Then another. Somewhere after that, it became a job.'

'Are you registered?'

'With who? The ABI? No, I'm not registered. I haven't signed up for my free newsletter and quarterly copy of *Investigators Journal*.'

'How do people hear about you then?'

'Yellow Pages, the internet, word of mouth.'

'Did the Carvers hear about you through word of mouth?'

'You'd have to ask them.'

'They didn't tell you?'

'Normally it's not that important to me.'

'What do you mean?'

'I mean, the people who come to me have usually

had their hearts ripped out because their kids haven't come home for a month. I'm not conducting market research. I'm trying to find the most important person in their lives.'

'And do you?'

'Do I what?'

'Find them?'

I nodded. 'Always.'

'So you're good at your job?' Phillips asked.

I glanced at Davidson, but spoke to Phillips. 'I think you and I probably have different definitions of whether a person's good at his job or not.'

Davidson sat forward in his seat. Laid both hands on the table, like he was trying to hold himself back. If the tape hadn't been running, he might have said something.

'What have you found out about Megan Carver's disappearance?' Phillips asked, staring at the file, still closed, in front of him.

'Not much.'

'Care to elaborate?'

I didn't respond immediately, and when he looked up, he could see my face: *Not really*. 'She disappeared from her school on 3 April this year,' I said, before he could say anything that would get committed to tape and make me look unhelpful. 'I've interviewed her friends and family. I've been through her email and her phone. As of yet, I haven't found anything.'

Phillips's eyes narrowed. 'Really?'

'Really.'

'Nothing at all?'

'Nothing substantial.'

There were three things I had that the police didn't. One was Megan's link to the Dead Tracks. When they'd got into her email, and been beyond the security on the LCT's site, they would have found the map of the school car park and the message (*Meet here at 2.30 p.m. for a romantic woodland picnic!*), but with no idea which woodland it referred to, it wouldn't have led anywhere. Because they didn't have the guy in Tiko's. If they'd picked out the man in the footage at any point during the six months since Megan vanished, then seen the message on the map, eventually they would have put it together. But without him, what they had was worthless.

The second thing was the youth club. They had that too – they just hadn't gone deep enough. They'd almost certainly interviewed Daniel Markham, but because Kaitlin never mentioned Megan's pregnancy to them, he'd probably managed to slip through the net. And if he'd talked himself out of trouble once, it was a fair bet he'd do it again. What the police had was an obvious connection between Megan and Leanne: two missing girls, both part-time workers at the same place. But if Healy was sniffing around, working his daughter's case off the books, it meant he was desperate for a lead; and that, in turn, meant police were still trying to find out who had taken Megan and Leanne. Markham was key, and – for the

273

moment – only I knew about his relationship with Megan.

And then there was Frank White, out there in the margins of the case. They'd found dog hairs in the warehouse the night he was shot. Hairs I was willing to bet matched up with the dog I'd come across in the woods. Beyond that, though, I was still looking for what tied him directly to Megan. Perhaps I could use Healy. He wanted answers about Leanne, and I wanted to know where Frank White fitted in.

'What about Charlie Bryant?' Phillips asked, disrupting my train of thought.

'He's connected to her disappearance somehow, but I haven't figured out how or why. I'd suggest, though, that whoever killed him probably took Megan.'

'Why kill him?'

'Like I say, I haven't figured that out yet.'

'You must have a hunch.'

'Maybe he witnessed something he shouldn't have.'

'Like what?'

I frowned. 'You want me to list a few fantasy theories? Or do you just want to stick to the facts? No witnesses. No CCTV. No accounts that Megan was particularly unhappy or depressed. No sign her grades were dropping at school. As I'm sure your colleague DCI Hart has already told you, this is a complex case.' I paused. *Hart.* He was supposed to be the lead on the Carver investigation. So where was he? I looked at Phillips. 'Shouldn't Hart be taking this interview? He was heading up the Carver disappearance, wasn't he?'

Phillips nodded. 'Chief Inspector Hart is busy elsewhere.'

'I saw him earlier.'

'He was checking in.'

Now it was my turn to look suspicious. 'The biggest unsolved of the last twelve months and he doesn't want a piece of it?'

Phillips sighed. 'If you must know, David, DCI Hart is currently taking a long, hard look around your house.'

I frowned. 'Why?'

Phillips ignored me and spun the folder around, so it was facing me. He slowly opened it up. Inside were five photographs, face down, one on top of the other.

'Why do you think?' he asked.

He flipped the top picture over. Crime-scene photography. It was a picture of the doll I'd found at the youth club, sitting on my living-room table, just as I'd left it. He turned the next one over. The photograph I'd discovered inside it – the woman's shoulders and neck – in a transparent evidence sleeve.

'Those were left for me.'

'Where?'

'In my front garden,' I lied.

'By whom?'

I looked at him. 'I don't know.'

'When?'

'I don't know.'

'Do you know where the doll came from?'

'No.'

'Do you know who the female in the picture is?'

'No.'

He leaned back in his seat. 'There's a lot you don't know.'

'Would you rather I made up an answer?'

Phillips shook his head. 'No. No, I don't want that, David. But let me remind you: you're in trouble here.'

'Because some nut left a doll on my lawn?'

He studied me for a moment, then looked down at the rest of the photographs. A couple of fingers tapped the table. He started playing with his wedding band. Turning it. Turning it. 'Do you know what the number two signifies on that photograph?' Phillips asked, placing a fingertip on the scrawled two in the corner of the picture of the woman.

'No.'

'I think you do.'

He slid a finger under the third photograph and turned it over. It was another picture of a photograph, this one bagged as evidence, sitting on the kitchen counter in my house. It had been taken in the same location as the previous picture of the woman's neck. Same subdued light. Taken either seconds before, or seconds after. In the corner was the number one, written in exactly the same way.

And looking out was a woman I didn't recognize. Not Megan, but not dissimilar to her. Blonde hair, tied up behind her head. Blue eyes open, but slightly glazed. She wasn't dead, but it looked like she might be drugged. She was pretty, but her skin was grimy and it looked like there might be a faded bruise to the side of her right eye.

'Who's that?' I asked.

'You don't know?'

'No.'

'You didn't take this?'

'No.'

Phillips flipped over the fourth photograph. It was a picture of Derryn's shoebox – the one I'd seen a crime-scene tech leaving with – taken from above, bathed in the white of a flashlight. It was full of her stuff: photographs of us, photographs of her, some jewellery, a notebook. On top, right in the centre of the box, was the photo of the woman Phillips had just shown me; in situ. Dirty, drugged face. Blonde hair. Bruise.

They'd found it in the shoebox.

'That's not where it was,' I said.

'That's where we found it.'

'I've never even seen that—'

'We found that photograph *in* the shoebox *in* your cupboard *at* your home,' Phillips said. 'This woman . . .' He looked from me to Davidson. 'We believe you abducted and tortured her.'

'You've got to be kidding me.'

'No, David,' he said. 'I'm deadly serious.'

'I don't even *know* her. I've never seen this woman in my fucking life. I don't know who she is, or how her picture got into that shoebox, but it's nothing—'

A blink of a memory formed in my head. The night I got back from Jill's at four o'clock in the morning. I'd forgotten all about it, but now it was coming back to me. The rubbish bin at the front of the house had been tipped over, and the bin liners had spilt across the pathway. And the porch had been left slightly open.

'Somebody broke into my house,' I said quietly, almost to myself.

'David—'

'Somebody broke into my house.'

'Who?'

'I don't know. I was at a friend's. When I got back it was the early hours of the morning and there were bin liners all across the path, and the door to my porch had been left open. I didn't leave it open that night.'

'Did you report it?'

'No.'

'Why not?'

'I didn't think about it.'

'Or you just lied to us again,' Davidson offered.

'Why would I lie?'

'I don't know,' he replied. 'Why *would* you?'

'I'm not lying.'

'You're lying,' Phillips said.

I stopped. Looked at him. It was more definitive

coming from Phillips, more of a statement than if it had come from Davidson. Phillips had played everything out on an even keel. No posturing. No promises. No showboating. Now he was accusing me of lying in a police interview.

'I'm not lying,' I repeated.

Phillips watched me for a moment, and something flickered in his eyes; maybe a little disappointment, as if he'd expected more from me.

Then he flipped the final photograph over.

It was a picture taken in my kitchen. An evidence marker had been placed on the floor at the base of some varnished wooden panels that ran for about six feet under one of the counters. The very top one had come away on the right side. I'd noticed it a couple of nights before while making myself dinner and had vowed to reattach it, but then forgotten. In the space behind the panel there was a nail in the cavity wall.

And something was hanging from it.

I pulled the photograph towards me. It was a piece of white clothing, the cotton speckled with blood.

'What's that?'

'That,' Phillips said, thumping a finger against the picture, 'is what Megan was wearing the day she disappeared.'

CHAPTER 38

The first thing I thought about was how far away Liz would be now. There were no clocks inside the interview room, and though Phillips wore a watch, it was hidden beneath his shirt cuffs. It was maybe an hour since I'd called her. That would put her somewhere north of Oxford if she'd left the moment I put the phone down. I looked between Phillips and Davidson and considered asking for the free legal advice I was entitled to. It wouldn't stop the interview altogether if they thought Megan was alive somewhere and in immediate danger, but it would break the two of them up and complicate the interrogation. By the time they were back on track, Liz would be that bit closer.

'You going to deny you put it there?' Phillips asked.

I nodded. 'Yes.'

'You suggesting someone's setting you up?'

I nodded again. 'Yes.'

Davidson shook his head. 'This is bollocks. You know where Megan Carver is. You've got her clothes in the walls of your fucking *house*. Where is she?'

I looked at him. 'Think about it. Why would I take on her case if I'd abducted her? Why would I risk the exposure? Someone's trying to put this on me. Whoever it is broke into my house and planted all this shit for you to find.'

'You're just digging yourself in deeper here, David,' Phillips said.

'I'm not digging myself in anywhere. Someone thinks I've got too close to the truth, and now they're trying to screw me to the wall.'

'Got too close?' he replied. 'But earlier on you said you hadn't found anything more than we did. Are you saying that's not the case?'

He tilted his head a little, like I'd just slipped up.

'No,' I said, and began to weave another lie: 'I'm saying I may have inadvertently hit on something I haven't managed to figure out yet – or drifted too close to him somehow.'

'Him? Who are we talking about here?'

I sighed. 'Everyone in this room knows it's a man.'

'Yeah,' Davidson said. 'You.'

'No,' I said. 'Not me. But every stat on the planet will tell you this is a man. It's not a leap of faith.'

Davidson shook his head again.

'How did you even know to look in my house in the first place?' I asked him. 'How did you know this stuff was there? Six months along the line, you suddenly decide I look good for this? No way would a judge sign off on that.'

'Maybe it's the fact that the first time we met

281

you you're stumbling out of a house that ain't yours with two dead bodies inside,' Davidson said, leaning in to me. 'And to up the ante, one of them's just a kid and, four inches from his body, we find a piece of plastic – which turns out to be from *that*.' He punched a finger at the photograph of the doll. 'Oh, and you know who that doll belongs to, David?'

I didn't – but his question had just told me.

'Megan,' Phillips said.

It was Megan's doll. *Shit*. I was struggling to keep my head above water.

'The police investigation is over,' I said, trying to maintain the control in my voice. 'You know it, I know it. If you had anything on Megan's where-abouts, any leads, I wouldn't have been hired by the Carvers. Whoever it is that's doing this knows you aren't a threat to him any more.'

'And what?' Davidson smirked. 'You are?'

'Why else would he leave this stuff in my house? He's setting me up. I've hit on something some-where, and he's trying to protect himself.'

'So what have you hit on?' Phillips asked.

'I *told* you. I don't know.'

'You don't know because you won't tell us?' he fired back. 'Or you don't know because you've just made up a load of shite and are hoping we'll buy it?'

'You want alibis?'

'Sure, why not?' he said, his voice simmering. 'Give us your alibi for the day Megan disappeared. And why not deliver a few witnesses too while you're at it? One for when the doll *magically* turns up on your lawn. And another who can back up your story of someone breaking into your house, taking out a board in the kitchen, hammering a nail into the wall and placing an item of Megan's clothes on there.' He shook his head. 'You better start dancing with us, David.'

I realized then that I'd have to give them something. Something to get them thinking.

'The youth club.'

Phillips had been looking away, at the photos. He turned back to face me, as if sensing the conversation was about to shift. Davidson's eyes narrowed again, his default expression. If I wasn't on the defensive, he immediately got suspicious. He leaned forward a little, waiting to see what I had.

'You went to the youth club, right?'

Phillips nodded.

'Whoever abducted Megan met her through there.'

Neither of them spoke. Phillips glanced at the photos, at his partner and then back to me. 'What makes you say that?'

'Something one of her friends said. Kaitlin Devonish. She told me Megan used to really like this guy who went there. That they may have even dated.'

Phillips studied me. 'She never mentioned that to us.'

'Maybe you never asked her.'

He pursed his lips. He looked like he was trying

to figure out where I was going with this. Whatever conclusion he came to, it had temporarily altered the dynamic. For a moment, both of them had lost forward motion. Now they were on the back foot.

'Who was the guy?' Davidson asked.

'Kaitlin didn't know. Maybe that's why she didn't mention it. I mean, why would she report as suspicious someone who made Megan happy?'

'Because we asked her if Megan was dating.'

'They may not have even dated officially.'

Silence now. Phillips began turning his wedding band again, and Davidson was watching me like I was a waxwork in his least favourite part of the museum.

'Megan's parents didn't know about it,' I continued, 'and they knew about the other guys she'd dated. If she went out with this guy, it was on the quiet. Even Megan's friends might not have known. I think Kaitlin was speculating that they dated, rather than knowing for sure.'

'And Kaitlin will back this up?' Phillips asked.

I nodded. 'One hundred per cent.'

Listen to me, Kaitlin, I'd said to her when she'd first mentioned the youth club, and the guy who'd got Megan pregnant. *If, for whatever reason, the police come calling, don't tell them about the pregnancy . . . The first thing we need to do is protect you . . . Tell them about the youth club, and that you think she might have been seeing someone there, but leave it at that, okay?*

Eventually I'd expected the police to take an interest in what I was doing. Maybe not this way, but when you worked the periphery of an unsolved, you stepped on toes and you pissed people off. I didn't want to involve Kaitlin. She was just a kid, and a scared one at that, but I had to rely on her not telling them about the pregnancy and being convincing enough to steer the course of the interview, and the evidence, away from me.

There was an added problem too: the youth club. They'd see it had been broken into over the weekend. And although I'd been careful not to leave prints, and the pictures I took from the club were next to the spare wheel in the back of the BMW, not lying around at home, it would open up another line of enquiry, adjacent to the Carver disappearance – and the seams would come apart a little more. The only thing I could do was continue pushing back at them. Because I wasn't about to go down for this. Not now. Not ever.

I turned to Phillips. 'Did you get an anonymous tip-off?'

'When?'

'Today. Is that the reason you were at my house?'

The two of them looked at each other. Phillips turned back to me. 'I'm not at liberty to discuss that.'

I nodded at the photographs. 'Put the photo of that woman's face through your labs and see if you can find any of my prints on it.'

'Maybe we put the photos through forensics,' Phillips said, voice taut, eyes fixed on me. 'Maybe we find your prints, maybe we don't. But you're mixed up in this somehow, we both know that. And when I find out how, I will bring you down.'

I didn't reply. He was as angry as I'd seen him, colour prickling in his skin. The lead I'd given them for the youth club hadn't been enough. It had stalled the interview, but it hadn't stopped it. They'd filed it away as an interesting line of enquiry, but it hadn't changed anything. I was in this up to my neck.

Then I thought of something.

Something Phillips had said in the first interview. *The only reason I can give you is that, by you sticking your nose in here, you're jeopardizing a parallel investigation.* 'Have you officially tied Leanne Healy's disappearance to Megan's?' I asked.

There was a long pause. 'Leanne Healy?'

'Colm Healy's daughter.'

'I know who she is.'

'She worked at the youth club. The same one as Megan. Even if you didn't know about the man Megan might have met there, you would have seen that the youth club connected Megan and Leanne.' Another pause. Davidson turned away from me. A flicker of something. Next to him, Phillips didn't move. 'So is her disappearance being tied to Megan's?'

Nothing from either of them.

Then Phillips: 'David, you don't know what you're talking—'

'They're both blonde. They both look vaguely similar. They both worked part-time at the same place. They both disappeared and never came home.'

286

Davidson glanced at Phillips. Phillips looked back. 'No,' he said. 'We're not tying the two together.'

'Really?'

'Really.'

'You must know something about Leanne then.'

'Why would you say that?'

'Because you'd link them otherwise.'

'Would we?'

'You know you would. You'd have two girls. And then you'd have a pattern.' I looked between them. I was building the theory as I went, adding together everything I'd learned as I tried to push back at them. 'And, eventually, you'd have more.'

'More what?'

'More women. If there's a pattern, there's a man responsible. And if he's magicked two of them into thin air, you can bet he'll do it again and again until he's stopped.'

Phillips shook his head and started turning his wedding band. 'This isn't *CSI*, David. You don't get a Hollywood ending.'

A parallel investigation.

I looked between them again. I'd given them the youth club. I'd told them I knew about Leanne. Now it was time to make a leap of faith.

'So where does Frank White fit in?'

Davidson's eyes flicked to me and then away. A moment of surprise, followed by a ripple of alarm. Phillips stopped turning his wedding band momentarily. 'I don't know what you're talking about,' he said evenly.

'You remember him though, right?'

Phillips nodded. 'Of course I remember him.'

'They're linked.'

'Who are linked?'

'Frank White and Megan.'

'Everyone's linked according to you.'

'Something happened at that warehouse the night he was murdered. You dig far enough in, and you'll find a connection to Megan.'

They both looked at me. I couldn't decide if it was disbelief or panic in their faces. I decided it was panic. I was on to something.

'His death is connected to Megan, isn't it?'

Phillips started collecting up the photographs, feeding them back into the Manila folder. He looked at me. 'We ask the questions around here, David.'

'Is it something to do with the surgeon?'

A brief pause. Then Phillips leaned over, spoke into the recorder to confirm the time and the fact that he was taking a break – and they both got up and left.

CHAPTER 39

As they were walking out, I requested a toilet break. Phillips asked Davidson to show me where it was, and disappeared through a security door that connected the interview rooms to the main office. Davidson didn't say anything, just led me past the other doors into an L-shape kink in the corridor. There were two further doors around the corner: one for men, one for women. 'I'll wait here,' he said.

Inside, it was cold and sterile. Old metal-framed windows, with iron mesh over the glass. China basins screwed to the floor. No soap. No hot water. Grey-green cubicles minus the toilet seats. Basically nothing you could rip off and use as a weapon. There was the overpowering stench of urinal cake and, as I moved into one of the cubicles, I realized I could see my breath in front of my face. It couldn't have been more than five degrees.

After about half a minute, I heard Davidson start talking to someone. Above the traffic noise from outside, and the constant gurgle from the cistern, I could only make out a few words, but it sounded like Davidson was asking a uniform to stand guard.

I flushed and walked across to the basins. As I was washing my hands, I heard another voice. Male. Low. Almost a whisper.

He was sending the PC off on an errand.

A couple of seconds later, I watched the door open in the mirror above the basin. It squeaked on its hinges. A foot appeared. Then a face.

Colm Healy.

He looked at me, our eyes meeting in the reflection. Then he glanced over his shoulder, out into the corridor again. Ran a hand through his red hair and rubbed one of his eyes. He had the chewed nails of a man who sat up all night unable to sleep – and the yellowing fingertips of a smoker.

I swivelled to face him, flicking my hands dry.

'We've got ten minutes tops, so I'll spare you the small talk,' he said. 'I don't believe you did it. I've read your file. I've heard about you. No record. No blips on the radar. Two years back, your wife dies. And now I'm supposed to believe you're on some kind of . . . of what? *Revenge* mission? No. You're not this guy. So you're going to tell me what I want to know, and then I'll help you out in return. Okay?'

'You said all you needed to say last time.'

'Yeah, well . . .' He faded off. Stood there with his hand on the door. 'That guy you had in that photo you showed me. Milton Sykes. Who is he really?'

I shrugged. 'I don't know.'

'Why's he look like Sykes?'

290

I shrugged again. 'I don't know.'

'Well, let me give you a head start,' he said. 'I'm gonna give you enough credit to assume you've read up about Sykes.'

I nodded, trying to figure out where he was headed.

'So you remember how the police pinned the murder of Jenny Truman on him, right?'

I went to nod again. Then stopped. He was talking about her dress. I'd overlooked the connection, forgotten it in the blur of the last couple of hours.

'They found her dress behind a board in his kitchen,' I said.

'Bingo. And now they've found Megan's blouse behind a board in *your* kitchen. I think we can safely assume whoever's pinned this on you has a hard-on for Sykes. He looks like him, and now he wants to *be* like him.'

'Maybe the guy wants to be like Sykes. Maybe he's somehow involved in Megan going missing. But I don't think he's the man who took her.'

'Why?'

'Because the man who took her worked at the youth club.'

He stopped. Studied me. Looked outside into the corridor then pushed the door shut as far as it would go without fully closing it. 'Is that the lead you gave Phillips and Davidson?' He could see the answer in my face: *yes*. He rolled his eyes. 'Why?'

'Because I was screwed.'

He shifted on the spot. Looked out through the door again, then back to me. 'How do you know this Sykes guy didn't work at the youth club?'

'Because if he did, why isn't he on their records? For a place like that, you have to pass CRB checks. And if he did that, his picture and his details would be on file at the youth club. But he isn't anywhere near the place.'

'So if it's not him, who is it?'

I didn't answer. Eyed him. 'Why should I even trust you?'

'Because I'm your only friend inside this house. And you're gonna need a friend. Even if you get bail tonight, the evidence won't go away.'

'Forensics won't find anything.'

'You sure?'

'My prints aren't on the photos.'

'Maybe they're not,' Healy said, glancing out to the corridor again. 'Or maybe they are. Maybe the blood in that blouse is yours. Maybe whoever's setting you up has been hunting around in your soap and put one of your cock hairs inside the doll. Who the fuck knows? If he's good enough to set you up, he's good enough to finish the job. You wanna wait around to find out – or do you want to try and finish this before you get flushed for something you didn't do?'

'Finish it?'

He looked at me, but didn't say anything.

'What are we finishing, Healy?'

His eyes drifted outside to the corridor again. He was nervous. On edge. It looked like he was about to say something, but then he just cleared his throat.

'Why aren't they linking Leanne to Megan?'

He frowned. 'What do you mean?'

'We both know you're still working her case on the quiet. You're still trying to find out what happened to her. Why aren't they tying Leanne to Megan?'

A lingering look at me. But no response.

'She worked at the same place as Megan. She even *looked* a bit like Megan. You know all this already. You know the youth club is what ties them together. Everyone here knows that. So why is Phillips telling me they're not linked?'

Silence. I studied him, and realized his nervousness wasn't borne out of being caught; it was out of being caught before he'd had the chance to find out where his daughter had gone. He was fuelled by anger, sadness and revenge. Later on down the line that could become dangerous. But at the moment it was helping him focus. No mistakes. No errors. No slip-ups.

'Look, I'm neck-deep in shit,' I said to him. 'We can both see that. So I have an agenda just like you. You want to find your girl; I don't want to go down for what they're trying to pin on me. I need to be ready for what mud they sling in my direction next. I need to be armed. You understand that, don't you?'

After a couple of seconds he nodded.

'Good.' I paused, studied him. It was going to be hard to get beneath his skin. He wasn't used to giving things up or sharing information. He looked at me and away again. He was telling me I would have to go first. And I knew, at the moment, with the situation I was in, I didn't have much of a choice. 'Daniel Markham.'

He flicked a look at me. 'What about him?'

'I think that's the guy who took Megan.'

'But we interviewed him.'

'Obviously not well enough.'

'Why him?'

'Because Megan was sleeping with him.'

A pause. '*What?*'

'And she was pregnant.'

'*What?*' He hardly moved. Just stared at me. Then, finally, he rubbed a hand across his forehead and turned away. 'By Markham?'

'That's the assumption.'

Something flashed in his eyes. There and then gone. A moment's thought that it was Leanne and not Megan who had been pregnant. A young girl, scared and alone with a man she thought she'd known – but hadn't really known at all.

'Who told you this?'

'One of Megan's friends.'

'And she didn't think to tell the police?'

'She was warned off.'

'By who?'

'Charlie Bryant.'

'The dead kid?'

I nodded. Healy knew the case intimately: all the files, all the names, every word of every interview. He didn't need me to explain who they were or how they fitted in.

'How much of this do Phillips and Davidson know?' he asked.

'Just that Megan might have been seeing someone at the youth club. They don't know about the pregnancy.'

'Why would he warn her off telling the police?'

'I don't know yet.'

He looked at his watch. 'What have you found out about Markham?'

I thought of the flat. The emptiness of it. The message behind the bathroom cabinet. 'He's definitely involved.'

'Meaning?'

'His flat. He's not living there any more, but something's up. I can show you when I get out of here, but I need you to get what you can on him in the meantime. His CRB check came up clean, so there's nothing on record. But there must be something.'

Healy nodded. His mind was turning things over. Outside in the corridor, a noise. A door opening and shutting. Healy looked out. 'Where's PC Harrison?' said a voice.

It was Davidson.

'He's gone to look for you.'

'What are you doing here?'

'Keeping an eye on your suspect.'

A short silence. I could sense the suspicion passing along the corridor. 'What the hell's taking so long?' Davidson asked.

'He's having a shit,' Healy replied.

'Tell him he's got one minute.'

'You've got one minute,' Healy shouted, looking off to his left, where the stalls ran in a line. Outside in the corridor the same sound: a door opening and then closing.

'I gotta go,' Healy said.

'What do you know about Frank White?'

A tiny movement in his face.

'Healy?'

'He was one of the coppers killed in that shoot-out down in Bow.'

'I know Phillips is working another case parallel to this one. I know because he told me. I know Frank White and Megan are connected somehow. Something happened that night at the warehouse.' Healy didn't say anything. 'Am I right?'

Again he didn't reply, just pulled the door back and peered out into the corridor. When he saw no one was there, he pushed it closed again and looked at his watch.

'Do you want to find your daughter or not?' I asked him.

'What kind of a fucking question is that?' He shifted on the spot and looked out through the door again, then back to me. 'I'll call you. We'll meet somewhere safer.'

'This is bullshit, Healy. We had an agreement.'

He opened the door and paused.

And then he left.

About fifty minutes later, I was waiting on the front steps of the police station for a taxi. Kaitlin had come through for me. She'd told them that there was a guy at the youth club Megan had become friendly with – but that was as much as she knew. I'd been released on bail, without charge. Technically, I was out 'before charge', which meant that once forensics had finished their analysis and the police had chased down the lead at the youth club, they'd be back for me. Healy was right: I had a couple of days to try and find out the truth, or they'd be pulling my life apart and coming at me even harder.

I called Liz. She was stuck on the motorway, about ten miles out of London. When she answered, she sounded surprised and confused.

'I've been released,' I said.

She paused. 'How come?'

'On bail.'

'Yeah, but how come?'

'When you get back, when I've sorted out a few things, I'll take you for a drink,' I said to her. She didn't reply. 'And I won't leave anything out.'

Again she didn't reply, but I could sense a change, even along the phone line. She could hear my last words for what they were. A confession. I'd lied before; told her things that weren't true and hidden things that were. And all the time she'd sat at my side and defended me in front of the law, knowing there were parts of my life, decisions I'd made, that might never break the surface.

But now I was signalling a change.

I was telling her things would be different; and in a strange way, perhaps admitting that next time we were together I wouldn't pull away from her. I wouldn't have doubts. I'd take her hand, and I'd step off the cliff.

And I wouldn't look back.

CHAPTER 40

An hour after they'd come for me at the house, a separate team had been through my office. As I opened up and walked inside, I could see mud on the carpet and damp footprints where detectives had stood at filing cabinets and been through the drawers of my desk. My computer had been left on, the screensaver – a blue cube – bouncing back and forth across the monitor. I walked around, trying to figure out if they'd taken anything, but nothing had been removed.

I filled the percolator and then dropped into the chair at my desk. As coffee started to soak through the filter, I let my mind turn over, back to everything they'd found at the house; to the interview; to Healy hanging me out to dry.

I'd given him Markham. He'd given me nothing.

That wasn't how it worked.

As soon as I left the station, I'd called Spike and asked him to track down Healy's home address and mobile number. I didn't mind how it played out: with Healy, or without him, it didn't bother me. But I was going to get what I was owed.

299

Pulling my keyboard towards me, I brought up Google. Megan had disappeared on 3 April. I put the date into the search engine and punched Return. Over 115 million hits. Encyclopaedias, blogs, newsletters, press releases, Facebook posts, Flickr albums. I moved through the first few pages, trying to spot anything remotely connected to the case. But apart from news stories posted in the aftermath of her disappearance, there was nothing. Flipping back to the first page, I went to a site that listed every major historical event – births, deaths and everything in between – that had taken place on 3 April. I was hoping something would leap out from somewhere, a spark. But instead I got more of the same: nothing.

My eyes drifted from the monitor to some paper-work on my desk. Hard copies of the pages from the London Conservation Trust site. I'd printed them out for reference. Alongside that was the email the LCT had sent Megan six days before she disappeared. It was dated 27-03-11. I traced a finger along the numbers and, as I did, a feeling stirred in me, as if I'd drifted close to something. A recollection. A memory. I stopped, brought the paper closer to me. Studied the numbers.

Was there something in the date?

I let the feeling go for a moment and did a search for the date Leanne had gone missing: 3 January 2011. It took about thirty seconds to realize it wouldn't lead anywhere. It was exactly the same story as the Google search for Megan – except there was no major press this time. Megan had ticked all the right boxes: white, wealthy, bright, beautiful. Leanne was different. Physically not quite as attractive, educationally middling, working-class background and – unlike the Carvers – with parents who didn't have a picture-postcard marriage. Leanne was mentioned once in the *Evening Standard* and once in the *Metro*. I clicked on both stories, one after the other. Both were two paragraphs long, and both had the same quote from Healy asking Leanne to come home. At the end it listed the number for a missing persons helpline.

What am I overlooking here?

For a second time, I stared at the printouts on my desk. The date. The way it was written: 27-03-11. That same feeling blossomed. Maybe it was something I'd seen, or heard, and not fully taken in at the time. Or maybe it wasn't even the date.

Maybe it was the format.

Ripping a piece of paper from my notepad, I wrote down the dates the girls had gone missing – 3 April 2011 and 3 January 2011 – then, underneath that, the numerical equivalent: 03 04 11; 03 01 11. I leaned back in my chair, rolled my pen back and forth across the desk. Listened to the clock on the far wall ticking over. The whole time I didn't take my eyes off the numbers. There was something in the date.

Something I'd missed.

I leaned forward, pressing a finger against the date

of Megan's disappearance: 03 04 11. Grabbing the pen, I scribbled out the zeros and the year: 3 4.

Three and four.

Or thirty-four.

Then it hit me. I pulled my phone across the desk and went to the photos. There, right at the top, was the last one I'd taken: the wall in the police station, the first time I'd been in. Slightly blurred, Megan's picture looked out at me, pinned to a board in the CID office. Next to that was the map and more photographs. And then seven stickies, running in a vertical line, a separate number on each. I could only make out three of them, the first, sixth and seventh: 2119, 3111 – and 34.

They hadn't been numbers.

They'd been dates.

The first one – 2119 – was four digits. They'd included the year after it, so they'd know all the others followed in sequence, through 2010 and into 2011. I turned back to the computer and this time typed '2 November 2009 missing' into Google and hit Return.

Four links down I found what I was looking for.

It was a missing persons site, profiles of men, women and kids decorating the front page. Picture after picture. Face after face. So many missing people, all of them lost somewhere – or worse than lost. The Google search had taken me straight to the page corresponding to the people who'd vanished on 2 November 2009. I was thirty-two pages and almost three hundred profile pictures in. And bang in the centre was the woman I was looking for.

In her photograph, she was smiling at the camera, her blonde hair cascading down her face in long, thin strands. She was pretty. Slim but not skinny.

And she looked like Megan and Leanne.

I clicked on her profile.

Missing | Case Ref: 09-004447891
Isabelle Connors
Age at disappearance: 28
Isabelle has been missing from Finchley, north London, since 2 November 2009. She was last seen in Lemon Street in Islington getting into her car after a work function. She later spoke to a friend on the phone to confirm she had got home. It is believed she disappeared that evening or the next morning as she failed to turn up to work, where she was employed as a graphic designer.

There is great concern for Isabelle as her disappearance is out of character. She is 5ft 8in tall, of slim-to-medium build with blue eyes and blonde hair. When last seen she was wearing a pair of blue jeans, black heels, a white vest and a long black coat.

Another missing woman. And she was the same as Megan and Leanne. Same hair. Same eyes.

303

Same shape. The only difference was their age. I looked away and tried to picture the list of numbers on the wall of the office. Tried to recall the second, third, fourth or fifth stickies. I'd taken the dates in, but not realized their importance. They were just a random list of numbers then. A blur among the maps and the photographs and the paperwork.

I slowly started tabbing back through the pages, closely examining every female picture. Six pages later, I found her. Blonde. Blue eyes. She'd disappeared on 8 January 2010. I looked at the picture on my phone: although it was blurred, I could instantly make out what looked like 8110. The second number on the wall.

> Missing | Case Ref: 09-004447958
> April Brunel
> Age at disappearance: 45
> April has been missing from Hackney, east London, since 8 January 2010. Her whereabouts remain unknown. She called friends on the evening of 7 January to say she couldn't join them for a drink as she was feeling unwell. There is growing concern for April as her disappearance is out of character. She is 5ft 6in tall, of slim build with blue eyes and blonde hair. She was last seen at work that day, where she was employed as an accountant.

In the pit of my stomach, there was a growing sense of unease. Four missing women now, and it was obvious there were three more to come. It took me ten minutes to find them, and another five to scan their profiles. Jayne Rickards, thirty-three; 4 April 2010. She had been number 44. Kate Norton, twenty-nine; 12 July 2010. She had been number 127. Erica Muller, twenty-three; 4 October 2010. She had been 410. All slim-to-medium, with blonde hair and blue eyes. All gone.

And all connected.

CHAPTER 41

The pub was small, with low lighting and ambient music. A series of booths, decked out in black leather and walnut, ran along one side, next to windows that looked out over Camden High Street. I found a seat right at the back with virtually no lighting and only a partial view in and out. The barman said, as it was so quiet, he'd come to my table. I ordered two beers and waited.

Ten minutes later, Healy arrived.

He squinted and scanned the room. Then his eyes fell on me. He cast a glance around him – making certain there were no faces he recognized – and made his way across. He slid in at the booth without saying a word.

I pushed one of the beers towards him. He scooped it up and emptied it in about half a minute. When he was done, he swivelled in his seat, trying to catch the barman's eye. 'Just do me a favour,' he said when he'd finally put his order in for a second. 'Keep your eyes on the door. Because if anyone even vaguely familiar comes in, we're both in the shite.'

'I don't think anyone you know will be coming in here.'

He studied me, a frown forming on his face. Then he looked back over his shoulder and took in the room for a second time. Four men at the bar. Two in the booth a couple down from us. Two more beyond that, hands touching on the table. He turned back to me. 'Is this a gay bar?'

'Looks like it.'

'Then you're probably right.'

A silence settled between us.

He got out his phone, placed it on the table and watched the barman bring over his drink. He scooped it up immediately. By the time he was finished, it was half empty. He pushed it aside and leaned forward. 'So, what did you call me for?'

'I think you know.'

He eyed me. 'Look, I couldn't say anything to you earlier. It was too risky. If they found out I was telling you about . . .' He stopped.

'Telling me about what?'

He didn't reply.

'The five other women?'

A flitter of surprise on his face. 'I don't know what—'

'Save the circus act, Healy.' I reached into my jacket pocket and placed a folded piece of paper down on the table between us. He picked it up and unfolded it. In front of him were photographs of the five missing women I'd discovered on the site, as well as Megan and Leanne. 'I've found them. I know they exist. I've seen them on the wall of the incident room, so I know they're linked. Question is, why doesn't the public know about them?'

His eyes flicked to me but he didn't say anything. I leaned forward, pushing my beer aside. 'Do their families even know they've been linked? Do their families know *anything*?' I paused and waited for him to answer. He didn't. 'You want to know what I *really* don't understand? Why you're happy to play along with this bullshit cover story when your daughter's one of them.'

He looked up at me, his fingers resting on the beer bottle now.

'Healy?'

'You don't understand,' he replied quietly.

'*What* don't I understand?'

'What it's like.'

This time I didn't respond. His eyes drifted outside, and for a moment it was like looking right into his head: the anger, the sadness, the need to hit out, bubbling away below the surface.

'You think I don't care about my daughter?' he said finally, still studying the people passing on the street. 'You think I don't care about finding her? I care. I care so much it's like I'm being eaten up from the inside.' He looked at me, fire in his eyes now. 'I needed to find out what you had on Megan Carver, because I've hit a dead end. I don't know where to go next with Leanne. So that's why I needed you. But what I *don't* need, what I won't put up with, is you getting in the way. Because I'm going to find the person who took her – and I'm going to fucking kill him. And you aren't going to stop me, and neither are those other pricks.'

He meant Phillips and Hart. He meant Davidson. He meant everyone.

'So are you working her disappearance by yourself?' I asked.

'Yeah.'

'Why?'

'Because no one else cares about her.'

He turned in the booth, back towards the door, as if he didn't trust me to look out for him. Then he faced me again, his eyes focused beneath the ridge of his brow.

'The police don't give a shit.'

'About Leanne?'

'About any of them.'

'Why?'

He went to speak and then hesitated. I'd seen it in him earlier. No mistakes. No errors. No slip-ups. He'd worked his daughter's disappearance for so long, off the books and without the knowledge of his bosses, that he'd completely insulated himself. Everything he knew, anything he'd managed to find out about her, no one else got to hear about. He finished his beer and gestured for the barman to bring him another.

'Okay, here's how *I* see it,' I said, trying to jump-start the conversation. 'You've got seven women. They all look the same. They've been registered as missing persons, but they've not been linked – at least publicly. Thirty thousand people go missing in London alone each year, so I understand how they've managed to stay off the radar. But what I don't understand is why the police haven't gone public.'

The barman brought Healy's third beer. After he had gone, Healy looked up at me and a look of disgust moved across his face. 'They're just one part of the jigsaw.'

'And what's the other part?'

He turned his beer bottle around, that same look on his face. No mistakes. No errors. No slip-ups. But then he glanced at me again, and I could see what he was thinking: it was different now. The stakes were as high for both of us. He was illegally pursuing a case under the noses of his bosses. I was out on bail for the abduction and probable murder of a teenager.

'The other part is Frank White,' he said.

I looked at him. 'So I was right?'

'Yeah. You were right.'

'How are Megan and Frank connected?'

'Your number-one fan DS Davidson works for Jamie Hart, not Phillips. Hart's in charge of a murder investigation team looking into the disappearances of the women.'

'So it's definitely a murder investigation?'

'We're assuming they're all dead.'

He stopped. Realized what he'd said. He'd just committed his daughter to the ground alongside the others. A flicker of emotion in his face, and then it was gone again.

'Where does Phillips fit in?'

'Phillips works in the same office as Hart, but not on the same investigation. He's SDC7 – just like White was. He's heading up a task force trying to put the cuffs on Akim Gobulev.'

I frowned. 'Wait a second, Phillips works organized crime?'

'Yeah.'

'So why's he coming after me?'

Healy glanced over his shoulder again, checking the door. And as he did, everything suddenly shifted into focus. The link between Megan and Frank White.

'The surgeon,' I said quietly.

He looked back at me as the connections started to snap together in my head. The links between events – and everything in between.

'They think the surgeon's involved in the women's disappearances?'

'They don't think he's involved,' Healy said. 'They think he's the one taking them.'

CHAPTER 42

I stared at him, waiting for him to tell me it was a joke. But then I saw the anger in his face – and suddenly felt some of my own, burning in the middle of my chest. I'd been trying to peel away the layers of Megan's disappearance for six days and the whole time the police were sitting on the answers. They'd lied to me. They'd lied to the Carvers.

They'd lied to everyone.

'Why keep them secret?' I said, and – in that moment – I heard the timbre of my voice and saw Healy attach to it. For a second he thought he'd glimpsed a kindred spirit; someone with the same anger and sense of injustice. I realized then that I'd have to reel myself back in again. One of us had to remain in control.

'Phillips has people on the inside and they're all coming back with the same intel. The guy's a freak. Wears a mask to meets. Surgical gloves. Bandages around his arms, so he doesn't drop fibres or flakes of skin. And he doesn't even get paid in cash any more. Instead it's medical supplies and hospital equipment. Scalpels, forceps, hooks, retractors, mallets, beds, gurneys. Rumour has it, the Russians even agreed to bring in an ECG for him. He changes their faces and he sews up their wounds, but only so it pays for what he's *really* into.'

'The women.'

'Right. He's a killer. And now he's got two task forces on his tail. Phillips wants him for his connections to the Russians. And Hart wants him because they think he's got seven dead bodies stored somewhere.'

Even in the noise of the bar, the word *dead* seemed to hang in the air.

'So that's the reason there's two DCIs in that place?'

He nodded.

'Why hasn't any of this been made public?'

'He put a bullet in White's face, so that immediately promotes him to the top of the shitlist in every department at the Met. It's personal. But that's not what it's really about. What it's *really* about is Phillips getting the surgeon, squeezing him for everything he's got, and then shutting down the Russians in London.' He looked up. Turned his beer bottle. 'But go public with this prick's sideline in women, and the surgeon goes underground . . . and his little black book gets flushed down the U-bend.'

It took me a second to realize what he'd just said. 'Wait a minute, wait a minute. Do you even know what you just told me?' When he didn't react, I leaned in to him. 'You're saying closing down the Russians is – what? – the bigger win?'

'You know what I said.'

x

313

'Yeah, you're saying it's more important that the police get their nails into organized crime than find seven missing women – one of whom is your own *daughter.*'

I waited. Nothing from him again.

'That's it?'

'What do you want me to say?'

'This is a conspiracy of silence. The police are sitting on their hands while those women lie dead somewhere.'

'They can close down the Russians.'

'Them is you, Healy. *You're* the police.'

'I'm not the same as them.'

'But you think what they're doing is all right?'

'I don't think it's *all right,*' he spat, fingers squeezing the beer bottle. 'Why the fuck would I be talking to you if I thought it was all right? They're burying my girl in a fucking filing cabinet. So let me make it clear for you: when I find her, I'm going to kill the piece of shit that took her, and I'm going to rip out his heart and stick it down his fucking throat. Is that clear enough for you?' He eyed me. 'You can come with me, or you can back down. But if you come with me, be prepared for it to get bad.'

I wasn't sure if he was talking about finding Leanne or going up against the police. 'Do you know why the surgeon was there that night?'

'At the warehouse?'

'Yeah.'

'Something came in with the guns. Whatever it was, he made off with it.'

Everything's connected.

'It was the formalin.'

'The what?'

'Liquid formaldehyde.'

He paused. 'Like the tissue preserver?'

'Yeah,' I said. 'Like the tissue preserver.'

He pressed a hand to his forehead and started massaging it. If the surgeon had already taken seven women, Healy didn't need me to tell him why he wanted the chemicals.

'The police can't keep this quiet,' I said.

'Can't they?'

'No.'

'They've done a pretty good job up until now.'

'But the surgeon won't come up for air again until he's absolutely sure it's safe. He's not going to risk a repeat of what happened that night in the warehouse.'

Healy shrugged. 'They're not going to put the women out into the public domain. Because if the surgeon thinks they're about to collar him, they've lost him, and they've lost the names and numbers of every Russian arsehole in the city.'

I leaned back in the booth. He met my eyes.

'We can help each other,' he said. 'You want to find the Carver girl so you can give her parents the answers we couldn't get them, right?' His eyes narrowed. 'Right?'

I nodded.

'And I want to find him so I can . . .'

He trailed off. For a second, I could see some

of my own reflection. A man torn apart by loss. He'd never laid his daughter to rest. He didn't even know where she was and what had happened to her. His last memory of the two of them together was a screaming match. The blurred line between what the law told him he should do, and what he was going to do, was indistinguishable. Maybe there wasn't even a line now.

'How are they pinning the women on this guy?'

He looked as if he'd expected me to ask. 'Their necklaces.'

I remembered the shoebox containing Megan's belongings. I'd taken it from her wardrobe. Inside had been photographs, letters and jewellery – and a shard of smoothed obsidian on the end of a chain. *Glass.* 'You mean the glass necklace?'

'Yeah. Because he's wrapped up like the Mummy the whole time, no one knows what he looks like, or what he's called. So the Russians nicknamed him Dr Glass because of a chain he wears around his neck. It's a smoothed piece of obsidian with the inscription *PC* in the back. It's basically the only thing they know about him.'

Megan's had *MC* carved into it.

'Are they his initials?'

Healy shrugged. 'Who knows? But all the women had one in their possessions, with their initials inscribed in the back, so it's a fair assumption.' He stopped. A flicker of sadness passed across his eyes. 'All the women . . . except for Leanne.'

'She didn't have one?'

He looked down at the table. 'Phillips lied to you about a lot of stuff today. But he didn't lie about Leanne. They can't one hundred per cent link her to Megan, or to any of the others.'

'Because she didn't have a necklace?'

'Right.' He stared at me. 'There were a lot of problems at home too. We used to fight a lot. On paper . . . Leanne was a good candidate for a runaway.' A pause. More sadness – and then steel. 'But I know he took my girl. I *know* it.'

I nodded, let him have a moment. 'Is that it?'

'What do you mean?'

'That's how they're pinning seven women on this guy?'

I looked at him. He didn't reply.

'It's a link, but it's tenuous. What happens if they're on sale in Asda? Suddenly, him and fifty thousand other people have got one.'

A moment of silence settled between us.

'What else aren't you telling me, Healy?'

He glanced over his shoulder to the door. Looked like he was about to say something, then stopped. When he turned back, he held up a finger. 'There's more,' he whispered. 'But . . .' He paused again, checked his surroundings a second time. 'I'll tell you. But not here.'

'You've told me everything else.'

'I need to show you,' he said.

I let my mind tick over for a moment, trying to figure out what he meant. 'Have any of the other missing women got connections to the youth club?'

317

'No. Just Leanne and the Carver girl.'

'Which means you need to get some background on Daniel Markham,' I said. 'Because, at the moment, he's the best hope we've got of finding out what happened to them.'

CHAPTER 43

Healy picked up me at seven o'clock the next morning. It was still dark. He had a Vauxhall estate with straw all over the back seats and muddy paw prints on the inside of the doors. The car stank of wet dog. It looked like he was dressed in the same clothes as the night before, apart from the tie. He had the seat all the way back, but his belly still almost touched the wheel, and his legs were arched under it. He wasn't exactly fat, but he was a big man, and thirty pounds of extra weight added a lot of bulk.

The drive over to Mile End was about fourteen miles. Neither of us said much for the first half-hour. It was slow going, and I got the sense that, like me, Healy was mulling things over: everything we'd discussed the night before, and everything that awaited us. At one point he started fiddling around in the side pocket of the door, and after a couple of seconds brought out a file. He handed it to me.

'You want a coffee?'

I looked at him. 'You a coffee fan?'

We were moving east through Paddington, and there was a Starbucks ahead. He bumped up on to

319

the pavement outside and switched on his hazards. 'I need it to function in the morning,' he said, and pointed towards the file. 'And you'll need some to get through that.'

I looked at the folder and flipped it open. Inside were missing persons files for all seven women.

'How do you take it?' he asked.

'Black.'

He got out and headed into the shop.

I opened up the folder and pulled out the files. Megan's was on top. I read through it. The investigation added up to very little. They'd identified the email from the London Conservation Trust as a potential line of enquiry, and made mention of the map on the website, but both leads had hit dead ends. As I'd suspected, without pinpointing the guy in Tiko's, they didn't have Sykes, and they didn't have the connection to the woods. Attached were interviews with everyone who had ever worked at the youth club. I searched for Daniel Markham's and read over it. It was bland enough not to raise any alarms, and the answers he gave were solid and believable. Like the file at the youth club, it listed him as single – but this time it said he was divorced from his wife Susan.

There wasn't much space in the car, but I attempted to lay the seven different files out on the dashboard, next to one another. Then I discovered there weren't seven.

There were eight.

The eighth file was thin and different from the

others. Inside was a single sheet of A4, all the pertinent details blacked out. No name. No address. No personal information, other than the place of birth and family status. Mother dead. Father still alive. One sister. The only other thing that faced out at me was a photograph. Female. Blonde hair. Blue eyes.

I set the file aside and started to move through the others one by one. Photos of the women looked out at me. None of them had a record, so the pictures were all personal, taken by friends and family members. Megan, at seventeen, was the youngest by a clear three years. The rest fluctuated between twenty and forty-five.

It was unusual for serial crime to cover such a wide age range, but he was picking victims based on appearance, not age. What criteria did blonde, blue-eyed, medium-build women fill for him? And what else tied them together? I read on a little further and discovered that all the women were single or not dating seriously, and most were pursuing careers rather than jobs that just paid the mortgage. They were intelligent, attractive and well educated. Even Megan, still at school, could be put into that bracket. The only one who looked out of sync was Leanne: average at school, plainer than the others.

So where did Daniel Markham fit in? Megan – and presumably Leanne – he'd got to know through the youth club, but the others had no connection to Barton Hill, and judging by the files, no connection to each other. But they weren't random victims. This was an utterly methodical man. One who plotted, planned and scoped out. He was organized and sociable, he was intelligent and he didn't look out of place. Maybe that was Markham. Maybe that was Glass. Maybe it was both of them, and they were working together – or maybe they were one and the same.

For a second, I thought of the families, most of whom were still praying for sightings or – in their darkest hour – perhaps even hoping a body would be found so they could at least get some closure. But the police knew things ran deeper. Phillips, Hart, Davidson, they all knew. Anger worked its way up from my stomach.

Seconds later, Healy emerged from Starbucks, two giant coffee cups in a cardboard tray. I took the files down from the dashboard, collected them together and took the cup he handed me.

'Right,' he said, bouncing the car off the pavement. 'Time to go.'

We moved past Hyde Park to the south, and Regent's Park to the north. But then, two minutes further along Euston Road, we hit traffic. Healy braked gently, leaned over and turned up the heaters. It was cold. Mist had started crawling in across the windscreen, and rain had begun dotting the glass. With his foot on the brake, he peeled the lid off his coffee and looked down at it.

'You find out anything more about Markham?' I asked.

'Maybe. He's not on the National Computer,

but – like you said – if he cleared a CRB check, he won't have any kind of record anyway. His home address is listed as the one we already know about at Mile End.'

'No other addresses?'

'No. The guy's Mr Average. You read his interview, right?'

'Yeah, it listed him as a consultant.'

'Over at St John's.'

'The hospital?'

'It's about a mile from his flat.' Healy paused, looked at me. 'I called them to ask about him. He's a psychiatrist.'

'That's not much like a plastic surgeon.'

Healy nodded. 'I don't think he's Glass.'

'I was thinking the same.'

'So where does he fit in?'

'Were any of the women patients of his?'

'No.'

I drummed my fingers on the dash. 'He was divorced.'

'Yeah.'

'Did anyone try to find his ex-wife?'

'She wasn't too hard to find.'

'How come?'

'She got placed in a psych facility up in Hertfordshire a couple of years back. Markham tried treating her himself, but couldn't work his magic. When he got given the all-clear after the first round of interviews, it was decided she was a line of enquiry not worth pursuing.'

'So have you looked since?'

'I pulled her records after you made bail yesterday. She had some sort of Grade A nervous breakdown after the divorce. Ended up getting fired from her job, got sick, then spent a year trying to kill herself. Markham had to have her committed.'

'Is she still at the hospital?'

'No.'

'Where is she?'

'Looks like she was released in May last year.'

'She might be worth talking to.'

'If you can find her. I called the hospital yesterday to try and get a last known address but she never turned up to any of the post-release support groups, and they never saw her again.'

'At all?'

He shook his head. 'At all.'

We both looked at each other, and I could see we were thinking the same thing: it wasn't coincidence that another woman connected with Markham had disappeared into thin air. 'Did he have an alibi for the day Megan disappeared?'

'He was working.'

'Did you ask the hospital if he was working today?'

'Yeah. They told me that he'd been off ill for two days.'

'Really?'

'Really. Some sort of flu virus.'

'There wasn't much Lemsip at his flat yesterday. In fact, there wasn't much of anything. The place looked like it had been cleared out.'

'Maybe that's why he's been off work.'

Except his flat didn't have the look of somewhere completely abandoned. Items remained in place. Furniture. The heating was still firing up. The lights still worked.

Finally, the traffic started to move. I looked at Healy.

'There's an eighth file,' I said.

He brought the cup up to his lips and swallowed some coffee. When he put it down again, his fingers twitched, just as they had the day before. He'd definitely been a smoker once, but not any more. He didn't carry the smell and neither did the car. There were no cigarette packets inside, and – in over an hour of being on the road – he hadn't expressed the need to smoke once. But it still ate away at him, and his fingers still reacted to having nothing to hold.

'Healy?'

The files were stacked on my lap, the photograph of the woman in the eighth facing out at me. Healy looked at me, then down at her photo.

'Later,' he said quietly.

STATIC

When Sona opened her eyes, everything was filled by light. She immediately closed them again, rolled over and crawled across the floor to the wall of the hole. Except the wall wasn't there. And she wasn't in the hole.

She gradually opened her eyes for a second time and, around her, shapes started to form. The four white walls of the room she was in. Two thin strip lights above her, buzzing constantly. A glass panel built into one of the walls, running halfway down from the ceiling. When she looked more closely, she saw it was a one-way mirror: everything in the room was reflected back at her; nothing visible on the other side.

She sat up. There was a door in the wall, adjacent to the mirror, and – next to that – a table with a glass of water. Next to the glass was a small piece of card folded in half: an arrow pointed to the water, and the message *Drink this* had been written underneath. Along from that, hung across the table, was a medical gown. A second card sat on top of it: *Put this on*, it read. For a second, she thought of her mother reading *Alice in Wonderland* to her when she was a child. Then a creeping sense of dread washed away the memory.

Standing, Sona examined herself in the glass. She wasn't sure how long she'd been kept in the hole. She'd started to lose count after a week. But she could see a change in herself. She had a bruise on her face where he'd come for her last time. One of her eyes looked a little puffy too; the kind of look insomniacs wore. She'd slept most nights, but never well. Part of her was always switched on so she'd hear him approach.

But it wasn't the bruise, or her eyes, that was changing.

It was her skin.

She stepped up closer to the mirror and touched a finger to the glass. On the hardness of her cheekbones, on the bump of her chin, at the tip of her nose, little blobs of light formed, dull and matte. Her skin was waxy. When she touched it, it left a trace of itself on her fingers.

Then something moved.

She stepped back and gazed at the window. A flicker behind the glass. Or had she imagined it? Fear blossomed in her chest, prickling, moving through her blood and her muscles and her bones. 'Hello?' she said quietly.

Nothing.

Drink this. Put this on.

She pulled the medical gown off the table. It was thin cotton, and there were ties at the neck and midway down the back. Then she picked up the water and drank some. Gown in hand, she moved to the far corner of the room. Turned, so her back was opposite the glass. Then started undressing. She'd been in the same clothes for however long she'd been kept in the hole. But although she could smell sweat on herself, some of her other scents remained. Perfume. Moisturizer. She could even smell a little of the shampoo she'd used on her hair the day Mark took her to the woods.

When she was naked except for her underwear, she glanced back at the window. Another brief movement. A tiny blur, like the outline of a shadow. She studied it for a while longer, her own thoughts (*he's watching me*) sending a shiver down her spine, then slid her arms into the gown and began to tie it at the neck and back. When she was finished, she faced the door.

Something had changed.

She looked around the room, spinning on her heel. Walls. Window. Table. Water. Her clothes on the floor. In the mirrors, the only thing she could see was the room and herself.

Then she realized: it wasn't something she could see.

It was something she could hear.

She looked up. The strip lights above her had stopped buzzing.

Suddenly, the first one blinked, like a flash of lightning, then cut out altogether. The walls lost their brightness. The floor lost its shine. She backed up a couple of steps, her eyes fixed on the only remaining working light, fear squeezing at her throat. There was a pregnant pause. A long, terrible moment where she silently begged it to stay on. Then it blinked once, mirroring the first strip light – and went out.

Dark.

She moved in the vague direction she remembered the door being, and when she couldn't find it, she started to panic. Breath shortened. Heart pumped harder.

'Please,' she said, tears forming in her eyes.

Crank.

A noise from her left. Then a line of light opened up in the darkness. The door. A shape filled the gap. Behind its shoulders was a white corridor, lit by a dull bulb.

'Please don't hurt me.'

A tremor passed through her voice as she backed away from the door. The shape, still in the corridor, stepped into the room. And then it pushed the door shut.

'Please,' she said again.

No response. No sound of movement.

Nothing until, about five seconds later, a crackling sound started to emerge from somewhere.

Static.

To her side: movement.

'Mark?'

'You won't feel a thing,' a voice said from somewhere inside the room.

And then a hand slipped around her face, clamping on her mouth, a tissue pressed against her nose and lips. And within a couple of seconds, she'd blacked out.

CHAPTER 44

Healy and I walked up the path towards Alba, the block of flats in Mile End Daniel Markham had once occupied. The doors were open. Just inside, in the foyer, a woman was mopping floors, big puddles of water scattered around her. She didn't even look up as we moved behind her and into the ground-floor flats.

It was eight-thirty. Commuting hour. A couple of people left their apartments, dressed for work. At Markham's door we waited, listening to the sounds of the building. Televisions. A conversation next door. But no one about to exit their flat. I pushed at the door to number eight and it swung gently away from its frame. The piece of card I'd used to wedge it shut dropped to the floor. Healy stepped back and let me take in the flat – any changes, any suggestion Markham had been back. But it looked exactly the same.

Healy headed to the living room. I went back to the bathroom and flicked on the light. The bathroom cabinet remained open, the clasp still broken. Nothing else had been moved. I placed my hands either side of it and lifted the cabinet off the wall. The message emerged. *Help me.*

'Healy.'

He appeared a couple of seconds later, looking at me, then at the message on the wall. 'You think Markham wrote that?'

'You don't?'

He studied the wall, shrugged. 'Why's he asking for help? And why bother hiding it where no one's going to find it?'

'I found it.'

'By accident.'

'But I found it.'

'So what's your point?'

'Maybe he wants to be stopped,' I said, looking at the message again. 'Or maybe he's caught up in something, he's scared, and he wants someone *else* to be stopped.'

'Who, Glass?'

'That's what we've got to find out.'

Click.

A noise from behind me. From outside the bathroom.

As I moved to the door, a memory formed: standing outside the flat the first time I'd been around, my ear pressed against the door, listening to something click inside.

I walked out into the hallway and looked around. It was narrow and empty. One painting on the wall of a sunset, but nothing else. Healy passed me and went to the kitchen. I headed into the bedroom.

Bed base, no mattress. Empty bedside cabinets. No lampshade. In the living room, Healy was opening and closing cupboards. I walked through and looked around. Exactly the same as everywhere else. Nothing had been moved. Nothing had changed inside the flat since I'd last been in. Healy closed a cupboard, noticed me and looked up.

'You all right?'

'Did you hear something?'

He stood up. 'Like what?'

There was no sound in the flat now. The only noise was from outside: cars passing on the street below; people next door; distant sirens. I scanned the room.

'Like what?' Healy asked again.

'Like some sort of click.'

'A *click?*'

Then I saw it above the doorway.

It was sitting on a small black shelf, obscured by shadows, a wire snaking out of it and up through a tiny hole drilled in the ceiling.

It was a video camera.

'Someone's watching us,' I said.

Before Healy had a chance to fall in alongside me, I redirected him back towards the living room and out of sight of the camera. I hadn't spotted it the first time I'd been in, but I saw it now. Small and compact, black, sitting on an equally black shelf in the darkest part of the room. It was easy to miss. If it hadn't been for the click of the zoom, I might never have thought to look up there.

Through the corner of my eye, I followed the wire out of the back of the unit and into the ceiling.

It leads to the flat upstairs.

Healy disrupted my train of thought. He was moving across the living room to a stool in the corner of the room.

'What are you doing?'

He stopped and looked back at me like I'd asked the dumbest question he'd heard all day. 'What do you think I'm doing? I'm going to get that camera.'

'That's a bad idea.'

He let out a snort and rocked back on his heels, as if I'd just surprised him with my stupidity a second time. 'Yeah? And what's a good idea? Standing around here with our dicks in our hands?'

'We need to leave it where it is for the time being.'

'And why would we do that?'

'Because it feeds into the flat upstairs.'

His eyes drifted to the ceiling and then back to me, as if he thought I might be trying to trick him. 'Then what are we waiting for?'

'We need to play this right.'

'*Right?*' He shook his head. 'Who the fuck do you think you're talking to? In case you hadn't noticed, I'm not your apprentice.'

'Healy,' I said gently, 'cool down.'

Fire flared in his eyes, and for a moment I wondered whether enlisting his help had been the right thing to do. He'd brought me details of the case I might have spent weeks trying to find. But he also brought a lack of control, and a need for vengeance. I'd sensed it in him the first time we'd met, and I saw it again. For a second, I caught a glimpse of the two of us hours and days from where we were now. And all I could see was me trying desperately to rein him in – and, eventually, not even able to do that.

'Look,' I said, keeping my voice down, 'if you go off like a rocket, you're going to mess this up for the both of us. I know how you feel, remember that. I know what it's like to lose. But you need to look calm for the camera. You need to turn around and start scouring the flat like you were before, understand? It has to look like we either can't see what's there – or we don't know what to make of it.'

'And what are you going to do?'

'I'm going to head upstairs.'

'You're going to go looking for him?'

'Yes.'

'I'm coming with you.'

I shook my head. 'One of us needs to stay.'

'Then you stay.'

'*No*,' I said, my voice raised for the first time. 'You've lost focus. You need to stay here and calm down.' I stopped. 'We need to make it look like we're staying put.'

His eyes lingered on me. I wondered whether he had come to the conclusion I was right, or was formulating some sort of alternative plan that didn't involve me. I didn't know him well enough to choose between the two. And now I was starting to realize I *definitely* shouldn't have enlisted his help. Once the anger died down, Healy became a stone wall. No expression. No obvious clue to how he felt. I was good at reading people, but I couldn't read him. And if I couldn't read him, I couldn't trust him.

'Fine,' he said, his voice even. 'Do what you have to do.'

He turned away from me. I waited a moment, wondering if I'd handled it the right way. Then I started walking back towards the camera, keeping my eyes off the lens, trying to make it look as if I was heading back to the bedroom.

But then it all went wrong.

CHAPTER 45

As I got level with the bedroom, Healy appeared behind me and pushed me inside. For a second I was completely off guard: I stumbled into the bedroom, only just staying on my feet, and crashed into the nearest wardrobe. The door shut behind me. Beyond it, I could hear him heading out of the flat. Hard, fast steps. The front door crashing against the wall as he yanked it open. Footsteps in the corridor outside, fading quickly away.

Healy, you stupid bastard.

And then more movement, this time from upstairs.

I sprinted out of the flat and into the corridor. He was disappearing up the stairs, heading for the second floor, the noise of him echoing through the building. I took the steps two at a time, getting to the second-floor landing just as the door to the flat burst open and a figure emerged from inside, heading off in the opposite direction. It was a man. The same one I'd seen in the alleyway outside the youth club. Long dark coat, dark trousers, black boots, dark beanie. Healy was almost within touching distance; I was about ten feet back and closing.

At the end of the corridor were two doors, left and right. Both opened on to an external stairwell: the left one headed down; the right headed up. The man got to the end and tried the left one. It juddered in its frame, sticking and then coming out – but not far enough. He couldn't get through it. Switching to the right-hand one, he pulled at it hard – it didn't move an inch, his hand slipping from the handle.

He was cornered.

A second later, Healy was on him.

He grabbed the man by the arm, trying to pull him into his body. Face contorted. Coloured. Fierce, violent anger rupturing like a fault line. But the man moved fast. Jabbed twice. Once to the chest. Once to the throat. Healy stumbled back, his hand at his windpipe – but swiped a leg in an arc. It caught the man in the knee, knocking him sideways, back against the left-hand door. It slammed shut.

This time Healy came at him harder, hands out, teeth clenched. For a second, the size of him was immense. Not fat, not overweight, just *powerful*. Driven on by all the injustice and the heartbreak and the revenge; everything he'd felt in the past ten months, channelled. A second after that, he was at the man's throat, pushing him back towards the ground, fingers white. Squeezing. Pulling. But then everything slowed down. I was only feet away when something glinted in the sleeve of the man's coat. A syringe. He jabbed it once, up into the nearest piece of Healy he could find. In the split second it took Healy to react, the man had pushed him aside and was on his feet. He glanced back at me.

It was the man from Tiko's.

The man who looked like Milton Sykes.

He dropped the syringe into a coat pocket and reached into the opposite pocket for something else. A blade emerged. It was a hunting knife: about eight inches long with a rubberized handle and a guthook built into the end of the stainless-steel blade. He swivelled it inside his palm, so the right angle of the guthook was facing out in front of him, then swiped it across the air in front of me. I stepped back. My heels hit the door to someone's flat. But I didn't take my eyes off him. In the periphery of my vision, I could see Healy off to the side of me. He was slumped against a wall, his hand clutching an area above his heart where the needle had gone in. A speck of blood was soaking through his shirt. He looked like he was on the edges of consciousness, his eyes drifting in and out like a television reception.

The man started to edge around me, back towards the only way out, the knife up in front of him. As he glanced between the two of us, I noticed something weird: his eyes were moving fast, but the rest of his face was still. Completely still. Almost paralysed. It was a weird, detached kind of look. When I stepped towards him, he jabbed the blade forward again. A warning. He did it again as he passed beyond me. He'd come all the way around. Now all he had to do was turn and run.

I inched towards him.

'I wouldn't do that,' he said.

His eyes flicked to Healy, then back to me. His speech was quiet, but sharp and clipped, as if he was trying to disguise his voice.

'Where are you going to run?' I said, taking another step. He jabbed the knife at me a third time, his forefinger stretched along the edge of the handle and on to the metal of the blade. He was holding it like a scalpel. Like a surgeon. 'You can't get away.'

Something glinted in his eyes. 'You and me,' he said, glancing at Healy, but using the knife to indicate he was talking to me. 'We have something in common.'

'Put down the knife.'

'We have a connection.' A smile. Small and tight. 'Did you hear me?'

I studied him. 'Come on, put the knife down.'

'Did you *hear* me?'

'Put the knife down.'

He jabbed it towards me again. Another small smile.

'You can't outrun me,' I told him.

'I know.' He glanced between Healy and me. Healy was almost unconscious now. 'That's why you're going to stay here.'

'That's not going to happen.'

'Oh, it is.'

'No, it's not.'

He swished the blade, left to right. *Whoosh.* 'Yes, it is. You're going to stay where you are . . .' He stopped, looked down at Healy. 'Or his daughter gets her throat cut, ear to ear.'

Healy's eyes fluttered. Fixed on the man. 'Where is she?' he croaked, holding his chest. The man glanced at him and smiled again.

'You've got to get to her first,' I said.

'Wrong,' he replied, and jabbed the knife towards me. 'You don't control anything here, *David*. *I'm* in control. I always have been. If I don't make it back, I've made sure things are set into motion and his daughter . . .' He made a cutting gesture across his throat. 'She bleeds out like a stuck pig.'

Healy groaned from the floor.

The man didn't look at him this time, just stared at me. Then he seemed to hesitate for a moment, his eyes flicking back to the flat he'd come out of.

'It doesn't have to be like this,' I said.

He was still staring at the open door.

'Just give me the knife—'

'Shut the fuck up!' he screamed.

Suddenly he was on edge, angry about something. His eyes pinged from me, to the flat, and back again. Another step. More hesitation.

And then I realized what was wrong.

He'd forgotten something.

A trace of emotion passed across his eyes and, as he got level with the flat, he took another last, lingering look inside. Edged closer to the door, as if wondering whether he could take the risk. Then he turned back to me and realized he couldn't.

And he ran.

CHAPTER 46

Five minutes later, Healy was starting to come around, but his speech was slurred and one side of him – his foot, his leg, his arm, his fingers – lifeless and unresponsive. I propped him up against the wall and then looked into his eyes.

'How are you feeling?'

He glanced at me. 'Okay.'

'Good. And one other thing: don't *ever* stab me in the fucking back again like that, understood?' He nodded and massaged an area in the middle of his chest where the needle had gone in. 'I'm going to have a look around the flat.'

I didn't wait for the reply.

The flat was an exact replica of Markham's but completely empty. Naked walls, naked floorboards, no curtains, no furniture. A flat that had never been moved into. From the ceiling a white cord hung down, but there was no bulb attached; the windows in the living room were the only light. Right in the middle of the room was a wooden crate and a dustbin, turned upside down.

On top was a laptop.

A power lead snaked off to a plug, and another

moved off across the floor of the flat to a tiny hole in the corner. It must have fed downstairs to the camera. I walked over to the computer. The desktop was plain, and there were two folders on the right-hand side under the hard-drive icon: one labelled 'Feed Stills', the other 'Pics'. In the centre of the screen, obscuring most of the rest of the desktop, was a loading bar, gradually filling up. It had just hit the ninety-two per cent mark. I stepped in closer.

Then I realized it wasn't loading.

It was deleting.

He was erasing everything on the laptop.

I clicked Cancel, but nothing happened. Went to Force Quit and hammered the Return key. Nothing. It was a waste of time; the deletion had been locked, and the more time I spent trying to figure out how to stop it, the more data disappeared. I clicked on the desktop, and double-clicked on the first folder. 'Feed Stills' opened up. Inside were forty-two photographs. I opened the first one. Healy and me in the flat fifteen minutes before. I closed it. Opened the next one. Exactly the same, except this time I was looking up at the camera. Inside the folder, the stills started to delete from the bottom up, but all of them had been modified within the hour, which meant they were all freeze-frames of Healy and me, taken with the video camera.

Ninety-four per cent.

I opened up the 'Pics' folder. Inside were ten

photographs. I grouped them all, then double-clicked. Slowed down by the deleting process, they opened one by one.

Ninety-six per cent.

The first was a shot from the window of Healy and me approaching Alba. I tabbed to the next. Healy picking me up outside my house that morning.

Ninety-seven per cent.

The third was a photograph taken from the end of my street the night Phillips and Davidson had arrested me. Rain was falling. I was standing beside my car, behind the police tape, a finger pointing in Phillips's face. To the left of the shot were some people I recognized from the top of my road. He'd been among them the whole time.

Broken into my house. Set me up.

Watched it all unfold.

The next was me outside the youth club the night I'd got inside. Half obscured by shadows, hairpins in the lock.

Ninety-eight per cent.

Two photos disappeared from the folder and the desktop simultaneously. I moved more quickly through the remaining pictures. Pictures five and six were of me on the path in the Dead Tracks. I recognized the area. Just past the second length of railway track, close to the clearing. The picture was taken from behind one of the trees, about fifteen feet back from the path. In picture five, I was staring vaguely in the direction of the camera. As if I'd seen him.

Ninety-nine per cent.

Another photo disappeared. One left.

A man with his back to the camera, and a woman facing him. They were talking to one another in front of an entrance to some sort of office building. People were filing out around them. Everything was slightly off, slightly blurred. It had been taken on maximum zoom, and the camera had moved just as the shot had been taken.

I leaned in closer.

Looked at the man and the woman for a second time.

Her face wasn't defined properly. Her outline was smudged. The blur of the picture had turned her eyes into dark blobs. But I still recognized her.

She was the woman in Healy's eighth file.

Next to her, back turned, the man seemed immediately familiar. Then I saw the edge of his glasses, the waves of his dark hair, the choice of clothes, the studiousness – and I realized who I was looking at.

Daniel Markham.

I got out my phone, flipped it open and selected the Camera option. I wanted a picture of the two of them to show Healy. But as a pixellated version of the laptop appeared on the phone's screen, the deleting process hit one hundred per cent.

And the photograph disappeared for good.

I double-clicked on the hard-drive icon, trying to find any trace of the file. But all the information was gone. The laptop had reverted back to its factory settings. There were ways to extract the information if I wanted, ways to retrieve the pictures. Files were never fully deleted from a computer, only the entries for the files; the data itself remained. But the only person who could do that for me, quickly and on the quiet, was Spike.

I closed the laptop. And then, on the kitchen counter, I spotted something.

When I'd first swept the flat I thought it had been some kind of kitchen utensil – but the flat was empty. There *were* no utensils. I got up and moved across to it. It was a metal container, about twelve inches long, and had a removable screw-top lid at one end. As I started fiddling with it, a memory surfaced: the man's hesitation as we'd faced each other out in the corridor, his eyes flicking to the open door.

As if he'd forgotten something.

This was what he'd forgotten.

Healy was still in the same place I'd left him. He had a couple of fingers pressed against his chest. He turned and looked up, wincing at the movement. In one hand I had the laptop. In the other I was carrying the metal container.

'How you feeling?'

'I'll survive,' he said, and got to his feet gingerly. His eyes drifted to my hands, and then back up to me. 'So was that the guy from the nightclub?'

'That was him.' I held up the laptop. 'He left this. He'd set it to delete anything remotely incriminating, and most of it was gone by the time I got up there.'

Healy nodded. 'What's that?'

He was looking at the metal container. I crouched down, placed the laptop on the floor and the container next to it. Healy dropped to his haunches beside me, wheezing a little. I reached inside and pulled out a tube from inside the container.

It was a cylindrical glass cask, about ten inches long and six inches high, full of clear liquid. Both ends were plugged with airtight seals.

'Fuck me,' Healy said quietly.

Inside the cask were two human hearts.

One adult. One child.

CHAPTER 47

By twelve, Healy and I were parked in a street in Beckton opposite a row of seven identical warehouses. On one of them, a big red sign was pinned to the front: DRAYTON IMPORTS. It belonged to Derrick Drayton, the man who owned the warehouse in Bow that Frank White had died in. And the man who had brought in the crate of guns for the Russians – and, I was guessing, the formalin for the surgeon along with it.

'If you're hoping Drayton is going to drop out of the sky, you're gonna be waiting a long time,' Healy said, both of us with our eyes fixed on the warehouse. A lorry was parked up, its cab facing out. Inside the warehouse, men were removing boxes from the back and filing off out of sight.

'Drayton's gone. I know that.'

'His family don't know anything.'

I looked at him. 'You seriously believe that?'

'The task force spent three days down here interviewing the entire tribe,' Healy replied. 'Wife, mum, dad, brother, sister. They looked terrified.'

'Doesn't mean they don't know something.'

Healy had spent the journey over massaging the

spot on his chest where the syringe had gone in. Although he claimed to be feeling fine by the time we left Markham's flat, I wasn't about to take any chances – so I offered to drive. The laptop was on the back seat. The cylindrical cask was at his feet, back in its original container. So far, neither of us had made mention of the contents.

Healy studied me, then turned back to the warehouse.

'What?' I said.

'You think it's her?' He was still looking at the warehouse, at the men removing boxes from the back of the lorry. When I didn't reply, he turned to face me again. 'Do you think it's Megan?'

I glanced down at the metal container. 'It could be, yeah.'

'So the other one . . .'

'Would be her baby.'

He'd probably seen worse. The darkness in men; the moments in life when murderers and rapists and abusers reached into the earth and pulled a little piece of hell out with their hands. I'd been there too. Walked through blood. Stepped over bodies. Flashes of time when, for a second, you realized humanity had vanished, and no rules remained. We'd both known worse than a heart cut from what housed it. But things changed when a child was involved. And, in this case, maybe not even a child: an unborn baby. Healy carried on massaging his chest.

'Are they preserved in that stuff?'

I looked at him. 'Formalin? I'd imagine so. I'm guessing Drayton sourced all those weapons for the Russians, and the chemicals came in with the guns. That was the currency the Russians paid Glass with: the formalin.'

When I looked at Healy again, his mouth had flattened and his eyes seemed to project his thoughts: Leanne and the formalin, and whether he could bear to imagine the rest.

In the warehouse, someone started closing the rear doors of the lorry. The noise carried across the street towards us; a huge metal clang. We both turned and watched as the driver came around the front and disappeared inside the office door. Two minutes later, he re-emerged, got into the cab of his lorry and pulled out. The lorry was gone within thirty seconds.

Inside we could see people milling around. There was a wall of misty-coloured windows at the back of the warehouse. What little light the day could muster shone through them, turning everyone inside into silhouettes. I counted five people. Possibly six. The interior was hard to make out other than that, but it looked cavernous and empty.

'I hope you know what you're doing here,' Healy said, pressing his fingers against his chest again. 'You're out on bail, remember.'

In the rear-view mirror, a blue Nissan appeared at the top of the street, heading down towards us. 'I know,' I said, watching the car. It slowed up as it got to the warehouse, and bumped up on to the pavement outside. Healy heard the noise and turned to look.

'That's him,' he said.

'Drayton's son?'

'Yeah.'

'What do you know about him?'

Healy shrugged. 'Only what I've heard. I remember Phillips saying he thought the kid might be hiding something. But you know what Phillips is like.'

Drayton's son got out of the car. A couple of the people inside the warehouse waved to him, and then he disappeared through the office door.

'You ready?' I asked.

Healy looked at me. 'Let's do it.'

CHAPTER 48

The office was small and plain. There was a counter running most of the length of the room to our left, and a window behind it, looking out on to the warehouse. The place was a mess: invoices and paper pinned to the walls, a Page Three calendar, receipts, even photographs of the family. There were three worn seats, none matching, and a circular table in the waiting area. Everything smelt of food. Drayton's son was standing behind the counter, leaning on it as he wrote something down. He looked up as Healy approached. I could see his brain ticking over, trying to decide if he recognized him. I stood at the door the whole time.

'Luke Drayton?'

He studied Healy, then glanced at me. 'Do I know you?'

Healy fiddled around in the pocket of his jacket and got out his warrant card. When he laid it on the counter, he kept a couple of fingers pressed against the wallet. I could see what he was doing: the tips of both fingers were covering his name.

'We're with the Metropolitan Police.'

Drayton looked between us. '*Again?*'

'We've got some more questions.'

'About what?'

'About your father.'

Drayton rolled his eyes. 'We told you everything we knew the first time you came. And the second. And the third. Do you want me to make something up – is that it?'

Healy took a step towards Drayton. Leaned on the counter.

Didn't say anything.

'Dad screwed us,' Drayton continued. 'He destroyed the reputation of this business. Everything I told you the other times you people came to see me, it still stands. I hope he rots in hell. I hope he never finds peace, wherever he is.'

Healy nodded. 'Sounds like you miss him.'

Drayton frowned, and shook his head.

I left them at it, let the door close behind me, then made my way around the side of the warehouse. At the back was a concrete yard surrounded by a five-foot wall topped with barbed wire. I peered over: a small forklift truck; two cars and a van; a few unmarked barrels; and a massive pile of cardboard boxes, covered with a rainsheet. Two men were milling around the boxes. One was holding a clipboard, marking something off. A second was adding more boxes to the pile from a stack inside – presumably part of the delivery earlier.

I followed the path around the property and at the end was a stream, probably feeding in from the Royal Albert Dock. It ran the length of all seven warehouses and disappeared into a knot of trees at the end. I could see that the back wall of the yard was topped by three lines of barbed wire instead of one. No entrance. No way over unless you wanted to tear your skin to shreds.

Heading back up the path to my original position, I looked over the wall again. The only person left in the yard now was the guy with the clipboard. He was standing to the right of the pile of boxes, running a finger down a printed list. The boxes were all different heights and sizes, and stacked in a series of towers.

From inside the warehouse, the man who'd been carrying the boxes appeared again. He held a huge cube-shaped cardboard box in front of him, his arms barely stretching halfway along each side. He wobbled as he walked, slowly edging around the pile, careful not to knock anything. About three-quarters of the way along, side-on to where I was looking in, he reached down and placed the box in a space on the pile. The movement brought his weight forward, and the toe of his boot knocked against the bottom of one of the boxes underneath. It shifted. Turned slightly. Beneath the box, a line appeared, carved into the concrete floor.

The man crouched, placed a hand on either side of the box and then manoeuvred it back into position, over the line. Within a couple of seconds, it was in its original position and there was nothing visible on the concrete floor except tyre marks and dust.

We got back into the car. Healy kept his eyes on the warehouse.

'He knows something,' he said.

'What did he say?'

'Nothing.'

'So what makes you suspicious?'

'I'm not sure,' he said, and looked at me. 'Maybe you've just got me paranoid. But if he *is* weaving a story, he's a bloody good liar.'

The windows of the car creaked in the wind.

'Anything around the back?' he asked.

I nodded. 'We need to come here again when it's dark.'

'Why?'

I could see through to the rear doors at the back of the warehouse, and the yard beyond. 'Because there's a trapdoor hidden out the back.'

CHAPTER 49

There was a coffee shop just off the East India Dock Road. Healy found a space a couple of streets away, the Dome – framed by grey skies and drizzle – across the water from us. We were about to go inside when, a little way up the road, I saw someone I recognized: Aron Crane. There was no Jill with him this time, and he was dressed in a suit.

I told Healy I'd see him inside. Aron looked deep in thought, his eyes fixed further out to where the skyscrapers of Canary Wharf needled the low-hanging cloud. Twenty feet short of the coffee shop, he spotted me.

He broke out into a smile, stopping. 'David.'

'How you doing, Aron?'

'I'm good.' We shook hands. 'What are you doing in this part of the world?'

'Just having coffee with a friend.' I nodded inside. Healy was leaning against the counter looking out, his eyes flicking between us. 'Well, more of an acquaintance, to be honest.'

Aron glanced at Healy. 'He looks angry.'

'He's smiling on the inside,' I said. Aron laughed. 'So, do you work close by?'

'Yeah. Well, kind of. For the next fortnight, anyway. I'm doing some consultation work for Citigroup and HSBC. It's probably why I've got this thousand-yard stare.'

'I remember you saying you worked in banking.'

'Don't hold it against me.'

I smiled. In the brief silence that followed, we both realized what was sitting between us. 'How's Jill?' I asked finally.

'She's good.' A pause. 'She said you called yesterday.'

There didn't seem to be any animosity in what he said, but as he looked at me, I could see what he was telling me: *You upset her.* 'I didn't mean to offend her.'

He nodded. 'I know.'

'It's just . . .' I stopped myself. It was a natural guard against giving out anything more than I had to on a case that was still active. *But she would have already told him everything. They're close. He knows what I said to her.* 'There were just some unexpected links between what happened to Frank and what I'm looking into at the moment. It seemed too convenient. I needed to ask Jill what she knew, if anything.'

He nodded again and ran a hand through his hair, as if he wasn't sure what to do with himself. 'You don't have to explain.'

'Are you seeing her tonight?'

'No.' He looked at his watch. 'I'm heading over to Canary Wharf to pick up my stuff and flying out to Paris at four for a meeting. It's a pain, and I feel really bad about it. It's obviously the support group tomorrow night, and I promised Jill I'd go, but I'm not going to be back until Wednesday.'

I'd forgotten all about it.

'Are you going?'

'I'd like to,' I said. *I'd like a chance to talk to Jill, look her in the eyes and find out what she knows.* 'But I think I might have to see how things pan out. I was going to ask you to apologize again for me if you were going.'

'I'm not, but I'll phone her later and tell her.'

I nodded my thanks.

'Okay, well, I better be going,' he said.

We shook hands again, and as he headed off down the street, I got the feeling that he was trying his best to remain neutral but finding it hard. I regretted offending Jill, but I didn't regret asking her the question.

Because something, somewhere, wasn't right.

CHAPTER 50

The coffee shop was small. Stools at the windows looked out at a row of two-storey terraced houses and a brand-new glass and chrome apartment block. I ordered a black coffee and a cheese and pastrami sandwich, Healy a bigger coffee and a beef and mustard roll, and we sat at the window looking out. It was nearly two and had started raining. We had at least three hours before it started to get dark. A lot of time to kill doing nothing.

'This must be home away from home for you,' he said.

I took a bite of the sandwich. 'I was a bit further down the road in Wapping.'

'Reckon you'd have given up journalism if your wife—' he stopped, glanced at me '—if it hadn't have happened?'

'Probably not.' I brought my coffee towards me. Outside, rain began spitting at the glass, and a little of the light fizzled out of the day. I nodded to the water running down the window. 'One reason I might have stuck it out on the paper was being able to get away from shitty weather like this on a regular basis.'

'Did you spend much time abroad?'

I took another bite of my sandwich. It tasted good. 'Yeah, quite a bit. Most of the time I took Derryn with me. She was a qualified nurse, but worked short-term contracts, so she'd come and stay with me, as long as I wasn't in the middle of a war zone. We spent a year and a half in the States, a year in South Africa, but most of the time it was a month here, a month there. She'd just fly out and join me and keep me sane.'

Both of us fell quiet. Within a couple of minutes, the drizzle had eased off again, leaving a fine mist in its place.

'What about you?'

'What about me?'

I looked at him. He was picking the sliced gherkins out of his roll. After a few seconds, he turned to me and shrugged. 'You already know about me.'

'Do I?'

He smiled. 'I'll give you the benefit of the doubt. You knew about Leanne, so I'm going to take a wild guess and say you know about my recent history.'

I didn't say anything.

He smiled again. 'I'll take that as a yes.'

'Take it however you want,' I replied, and drained some of my coffee. 'You tell me or you don't. It's up to you.'

Silence again.

I ate through my sandwich. Healy continued picking at his food and staring at his drink.

'I had this case,' he said eventually. He picked the

last of the gherkins out of the roll and placed the bread back on top of the beef. 'Two girls killed down in New Cross. Twins. Eight-year-olds. Neighbour called the police after not hearing anything next door for a week. They'd been raped and strangled. Mother's cold in the next room. Stabbed in the chest. Father . . . fuck knows where he is. The girls had never met him. He'd never had any part in their lives. Even the mother didn't know his surname. He contributed one thing and one thing only to their lives – and that was nine months before they were born.'

He paused, emptied a packet of sugar into his coffee and started stirring it. 'So, obvious first suspect: the mother's dealer. Girls come home from school, find their mum and the dealer in the flat. Argument kicks off between the two adults. Dealer goes mental, stabs the mum, turns on the girls. *Or*, beats the shit out of the mum and forces her to watch him with the girls while she bleeds out, until she pays what she owes. Post-mortem put her death before the two girls.' He stopped, shrugged. 'Whether it's one or the other, they both made me feel fucking sick.'

He took a bite of his roll, wiped his mouth and shrugged again. 'We bring in the dealer, this weaselly piece of shit. He's probably responsible for half the misery in New Cross, but he's not the killer. So it's back to square one again. Forensics – nothing. They come back with fibres and prints, but there are zero matches. We ask around and no one's seen anything or knows anything. A week turns into two. Two into three. Three weeks into a murder investigation, and you start to get a bit twitchy. The doubts start creeping in. You think, "Have I missed something? What have I missed? What aren't I seeing?" And after that, you start going round and round in circles. Back to the scene. Back to the computer. Back to the forensics. Back to the statements. Suddenly, a month in, literally *all* you can think about is the fact that someone out there has walked away a free man after putting two innocent girls in the ground.'

Healy paused again. 'No one understands the debt you have to the people you stand over in these places. And when they're *eight years old* . . . Eight years old, and you can't find a trace of the arsehole who did these things to them anywhere in this worthless fucking city. No one understands what that feels like. Even some of the people I've worked with in the police. And if they don't get it, how the fuck are your family supposed to get it?'

I nodded but didn't say anything.

'It was about a month in when I found out she was seeing someone else,' he said, talking about his wife now. 'If I'd found out any other time, I would have been angry. I would have thrown some furniture around. Put my foot through a door. I know I've got a temper. It's who I am. I'm forty-six. I'm too old to change. But it wasn't just any time. I found out she was screwing around when I was up to my neck in photographs of two eight-year-old girls with injuries to every hole in their bodies. I had the media baying for blood, the chief super crawling up my arse . . .' He faded out, glanced at me. 'And worst of all, I had zero fucking suspects. No one. The debt I felt for those girls, I'd never had it as bad as that. So when Gemma told me, I just totally lost it.'

'We've all done things we regret.'

A smile without humour. 'You don't seem the wife-beating type.'

'We've all done things we regret,' I said again.

He turned to me. 'So what have you done?'

I looked at him. *I've killed people. People who deserved it. People who would have taken my life if I hadn't taken theirs. But I've still killed. I'll still be judged the same as them.* When I didn't respond, he stared out of the window. In front of him, his food was virtually untouched and his coffee had lost its warmth.

'You never really know anyone,' he said finally, 'even the ones you love. She thought she knew me, and I thought I knew her. But we didn't know each other at all.'

A couple of minutes passed. I watched the thumb and forefinger of his right hand rub together; he would have taken a cigarette now. After a while, he returned to the counter and ordered a fresh cup of coffee, then disappeared to the toilet. A few minutes later he came back, added some sugar to his coffee and took a long drink from it. I could see his mind turning over, and I wondered what he was thinking about. His wife. The night she told him about the other man. The moment he hit her. The twins. Leanne.

'When do you accept someone is finally gone?' he said quietly.

I turned and studied him. The question surprised me, but I tried not to show it. I hadn't expected it from him. I hadn't expected emotion like that to exist so close to the surface.

'It's different for everyone. But there's no shame in hanging on. There's no shame in believing they might walk through the door at any moment.'

Healy didn't respond.

I let him have a moment of silence and then pushed on. 'So, you going to tell me then?'

He looked at me. 'Tell you what?'

'About the woman in the eighth file.'

He faced out at the street. Movement and light played in his eyes, the world beyond the window reflected. 'Sona,' he said.

'That's her name?'

He nodded. It was an unusual name. I liked it, but I'd never heard it before. Healy started fiddling in his pocket for something. 'I think her mother was born abroad somewhere,' he said. 'Eastern Europe.' He brought out a piece of folded paper and handed it to me. It was the same page I'd seen earlier inside the file – except this time there was nothing blacked out. All the information was there.

'So where does she fit in?'

He looked at me. 'She's the one that got away.'

THE ONE THAT GOT AWAY

Sona woke with a start, so hard and so fast she felt something rip. Two strips of tape hung down from her eyelids where they'd been placed over her eyes. She looked around. She was on a hospital bed. On one side: a metal table full of surgical instruments and an ECG machine. On the other: a yellow defibrillator, two metal paddles coiled around a peg at its side. The room had five doors: one left, one right, three in front of her.

She sat up and something pulled at her chest. Wires snaked out from under her gown, feeding off towards the ECG, and she could feel two electrodes stuck to the spaces above both breasts. In the top of her right hand was a catheter that led to a bag of IV fluid hanging from a metal stand. For a second she felt woozy, as if she'd been torn too suddenly from unconsciousness. But then reality hit. Fear fluttered in her chest, a chill fingered up her spine. This wasn't how he worked. He would know when she was supposed to be awake down to the minute. He watched. He listened.

So why hadn't he come for her yet?

Because I'm not supposed to be awake.

She'd been anaesthetized. He'd left her there because he thought she'd been given enough to knock her out.

But he hadn't. She was awake.

And now I need to get out of here.

She removed the tape from her eyelids, disconnected the catheter and pulled both electrodes off her chest. Instantly, the ECG flatlined, its steady *beep beep beep* replaced by one long noise. She stood in the centre of the room and looked between doors. He *had* to arrive through one of them now. He *had* to come for her. But a minute later she was still waiting.

She glanced at the trolley again. There was a pair of scissors about six inches in length, the ends pointing out at a forty-five-degree angle. Surgeon's scissors. Next to that was a series of scalpels; a mix of different lengths and weights, of different blades and designs. More instruments: something that looked like a hammer; a syringe; and a drill. And finally, a bottle of clear blue liquid.

The same stuff he'd made her apply to her face.

She touched her cheek. She could feel the waxy sheen of her skin against the tips of her fingers – but she felt nothing in her face. Not a single thing. Everything was dead: no nerve endings firing up, no sensation of movement when she opened and closed her jaw. Nothing. It was completely numb. She reached to the other side, to see if it was the same, felt nothing and brought her fingers

366

back – and then a ripple of horror escaped through her chest. Her fingers were covered in blood.

Suddenly a horrible realization moved like an oil slick inside her: *He was using the liquid to prepare my skin for surgery. And he's cutting into my face right now.*

Sona grabbed one of the scalpels. *Come on then, you bastard.* She tried to force adrenalin through her body, tried to kick-start some sort of response, but she was halfway across the room when she heard movement.

Fast footsteps echoing in a corridor beyond the nearest door.

Then static.

She stopped, frozen to the spot. No footsteps any more. Just static. She transferred the scalpel from one hand to the other and held it up in front of her, in the vague direction of the door. Waited. Waited. Then she realized the static was coming from inside the room. She glanced to her left, high up into the corner. Hidden in the darkness was a speaker, built into the wall, painted the same uniform white to disguise it.

'*Sssssssssona.*'

A voice from the speaker.

And then in front of her the door handle began to turn.

Heart shifting in her chest, she stepped sideways and forward, so she was behind the door as it opened towards her. Swallowed once. Twice. The third time she almost coughed. She was so frightened now her throat felt like his fingers were already closing around it. She clamped a hand to her mouth, trying to stop any sound, any whimper, any breath that might force its way up and form a noise. Next to her, the door continued opening. *Don't make a sound.* It inched towards her. *Don't make a –*

It stopped.

She looked down. The edge of a black shoe was in view. Nothing else.

The ECG screamed. The static bristled. But all she could hear was her heart in her ears, thumping against her ribs, the noise so fierce it swamped everything else. From somewhere she summoned enough strength to raise the scalpel up, her fingers drained of colour, and hold it out in front of her, ready to use. She waited for him to come into the room.

Waited.

Still he didn't move. Then, from the speaker in the corner of the room, the static got louder for a second. Crackling. Reverberating. Changing pitch and tone.

'Where are you hiding, Sona?'

His voice, coming from the speakers above her, and next to her on the other side of the door. A wave passed through her legs, the fear temporarily paralysing her muscles. She stepped further back, towards the wall, to prevent herself from falling completely. The movement made the smallest of noises; a squeak as the ball of her bare foot slid across the polished floor.

It was enough.

The door swung towards her so fast she barely even had time to register it. Within a second, it smashed into her face, the hard wood of the door pounding against her cheekbone. She stumbled back, trying to keep the scalpel up in front of her, desperate not to let her guard down. For a brief second, her brain told her she should be feeling pain in her face now – but instead she felt nothing.

He came around the door at her.

He was in pale blue medical scrubs, a cap and a face mask. She could see his eyes, flashing bright blue inside, and a wire, coming out from under the mask, down under the scrubs. In the split second it took her eyes to flick from the wires back to him, he clamped a hand on her throat and squeezed.

Static.

He forced her down towards the ground. She looked up at him. At his eyes. They were narrowed, focused on hurting her. He pushed her down to the floor, her legs giving way beneath her. He was showing her he was in charge. Forcing her to make short, sharp choking noises as her lungs tried to push air up through her throat. His thumb pressed against her windpipe harder. She was bordering on the edges of a blackout.

Survival instinct kicked in.

Nerves fired. Muscles tightened.

She gripped the scalpel as tightly as she could and jabbed it into the back of his right hand. He yelled out, his cry initially dulled by the mask, but drowned out a second later as it screamed from the speakers in a distorted, broken copy of his reaction. Both hands released her. The sound died down. A wail of agony replaced by feedback and static.

Sona scrambled to her feet, headed around him and out of the door. A long grey corridor. Concrete walls. Strip lights all the way down. She looked both ways. The corridor turned at a right-angle to her left. All she could see around the corner was darkness. To her right was a heavy iron door, huge rivets tracing its circumference.

She headed left.

'You fucking *bitch*!'

She could hear him but not see him as she ran, his voice coming through a speaker in front of her, high up on the wall. But then: footsteps.

She glanced over her shoulder. He emerged from the doorway, his eyes immediately fixed on her. Blood ran from his hand down the front of his medical scrubs and on to his trousers. But he didn't care now. Above her, static hissed out of the speaker, and then, whispering, his voice travelled down to her: 'There's nowhere to run.'

She turned and broke into a sprint again. As the corridor kinked left, it opened out into another, shorter one. A couple of crates leaned against one wall. No lights above her. There were three glass panels on her left and more concrete walling on the right. At the end was a door, about forty feet away, connecting the corridor she was in with a better-lit room beyond.

'Where you going, Sona?'

She passed under another speaker.

'You've got nowhere to run!'

She heard his footsteps behind her, but this time didn't look back. Just kept her eyes on the door at the end of the corridor. Never letting up. Never dropping the pace. Ignoring the pain that was starting to emerge in her cheeks and across her forehead. Ignoring the screaming voice inside her that said she was never going to get away from him.

Then, as she passed them, she realized the glass panels were windows.

The first window belonged to a room she recognized. White walls. White ceiling. She could see the table, and the cards perched on top, pointing to the water and the place where the medical gown had been. In the corner of the room were her clothes. Left there in a pile. Everything but her underwear.

She pounded on.

The next room was exactly the same, except empty.

Then she got to the third room.

A woman was sitting on the floor in the opposite corner, legs up to her chest, face buried in her knees. Her hair covered her shoulders and arms, disguising some of the bruises on her skin – but not all of them. Sona slowed a little: an automatic reaction.

There's more like me.

A noise from behind her. She looked back.

He'd closed on her.

In front of her, she could suddenly see a brightly lit room beyond an open iron door. The room was about thirty feet square, with a thick fire door on the far side. 'Help me!' she screamed as she ran into the room. 'Somebody help me!' Through two thin glass panels on the fire door, she could see steel cabinets and the outline of the hole he'd kept her in.

She ran back, grabbed the heavy iron door and started pushing it closed. It cranked and juddered as it swung inwards. He was getting closer. Twenty feet, maybe less. She pushed harder, pain suddenly flaring in her face. In her nose. Her lips. Her cheeks. Then the door stuck.

He was ten feet away.

Shut.

Eight feet.

Shut.

Six feet.

'Shut!' she screamed.

The door shifted and swung shut against the iron frame. She glanced around the room for something to jam against it. It looked like a submarine door – huge, bulky and intricate – but there was no revolving lock mechanism, which meant all he had to do to open it again was push from the other side. Halfway across the room was a metal pipe – like a piece of scaffolding – propped against the wall. She went to grab it.

Then the door started squealing.

He was pushing from the other side.

She grabbed the length of pipe, placed one end against a kink in the floor and then forced the other end into a space about halfway up the door. It would hold for a while. But not long.

'Sona?'

She froze to the spot. Turned slowly. There was no one else in the room. But on the far wall, above the fire door, she could make out another speaker. She frowned. Took a step towards it.

'Sona?' the voice said again.

She stepped closer to the speaker. Watched it for a moment. Through the glass panels in the door she could see more of the hole she'd been kept in. Plastic containers were piled up in the corner of the room, and a ladder was against the far wall, out of sight. That was how he'd got down into the hole in the first place.

'You need to stop running.'

She looked up at the speaker again. His voice sounded soft now, almost caring. Tears filled her eyes. 'Let me go,' she said quietly. 'Just . . . let me go.'

'I will,' came the reply.

'I mean it!'

'So do I.'

She glanced back at the door, then at the speaker. 'I don't believe you.'

No reply this time.

'I don't believe you!' she screamed, and tears started rolling down her face. She was scared, desperate. She wiped the tears away, trying to compose herself.

A scratching sound.

Crank.

She turned to face the door. He was still pushing at it. It shifted a little, the length of pipe bending against the floor. Then, from somewhere above her, she could hear rain.

She looked up.

Six feet above, a circular hole had been cut out of the ceiling. A manhole. Fixed to one side of the hole was a drop-down ladder. She looked around her. On a wall next to the glass-panelled door were three switches. Two were for lights, presumably the room she was in, and the room with the hole. The other was set apart on its own.

Sona moved to it. Flicked the switch.

With a clunk, the ladder started dropping down, whirring metallically. When one part of it had extended its full length, the second part continued downwards. It stopped in front of her, two feet off the floor of the room.

'Step on that ladder and I will kill you.'

She glanced at the speaker.

'I will hunt you down and I will cut you into pieces. I mean it. I will carve you open if you put one *foot* on that ladder.'

She put her foot on the ladder.

'You stupid bitch!' A crank. The pipe at the door wheezed as he pushed, bending some more. He smashed his fists against the other side, hammering at it like a drum. 'You are dead! You are fucking *dead*!'

Halfway up the ladder, she paused briefly and looked down into the room. Above, the rain continued to fall. Below, the door edged inwards even more, and she glimpsed the pale blue of his medical scrubs.

'You will remember me,' he said from below her.

She pushed at the manhole cover above her. It moved away from the hole. Rain fell out of the sky and down past her, to the room below. She placed a foot on the next step. Then the next. Lifted her head up above the lip of the manhole.

'Every day, when you look in the mirror, you will remember me.'

And then she hauled herself out – and she ran.

PART IV

CHAPTER 51

By six o'clock it was getting dark and we were sitting in the shadows of an alley opposite the warehouse. In the office, framed in the glass panel of the door, we could see Luke Drayton still behind the counter, writing something. The warehouse itself was closed up now, the huge delivery doors pulled shut and padlocked.

'How big was the trapdoor?' Healy asked.

I shrugged, keeping my eyes on Drayton. 'Difficult to tell. Most of it was covered by boxes. It looked like a circular manhole cover. No bigger than two and a half feet across.'

We fell into silence again. Ten minutes passed. Twenty. Thirty. At six-forty, Drayton was still at the counter, writing. He had a calculator on one side of him now.

'Maybe he lives down the hole,' Healy said.

I smiled. Occasionally I'd look at Healy and see a brief glimpse of the man he once was. A different person, not built on revenge and regret, but on better qualities; on compassion and humour. I liked that Healy, and I wondered how long it would take him to reclaim that side of himself – and if he ever would.

A couple of minutes later, Healy's phone started ringing, buzzing across the dashboard towards him. He picked it up and looked at the display.

'Bollocks.'

'What?'

He didn't answer and flipped it open. 'Healy.'

Even with the rain, I could immediately hear the voice on the other end. 'Healy, it's Phillips. Where are you?'

'I've got the day off.'

'It's not marked on the board.'

'I told Moira.'

'It's not marked on the board,' Phillips said again.

'So I'll mark it up tomorrow.'

A pause. Healy glanced at me.

'You got any idea where David Raker is?' Phillips asked.

'Who?'

'David Raker.'

Healy paused again, looked out through the windscreen to where Drayton was still in the same position at the counter.

'Raker?' he said. 'He's the guy you brought in, right?'

'Right.'

'Why would I know where he is?'

'Davidson says he found you and Raker alone yesterday.'

'So?'

'So why were you alone with him?'

'Because Davidson had left him, and I didn't think it would look good if one of our best leads in the Carver case wandered out of the station, never to be seen again.'

'You don't have any cases of your own?' Phillips asked.

'Listen—'

'No, *you* listen,' Phillips fired back. 'I don't know what the hell you think you're doing, but whatever it is it's against the law, understand?'

Healy didn't respond.

'You know, there's a reason you're not part of this task force, or any other task force for that matter. And it's because you can't be trusted. You're a liar, Healy.'

'What did you say?'

'You heard what I said. We tried getting hold of Raker and his mobile's off. Been off all day. We went round to his house, and it looks like a mauso-leum. So we go round to your place because, you know, it's supposed to be your *day off* – and guess what?'

'I'm out with my wife.'

'Bullshit, Healy. I know you're with Raker.'

'I'm out with my wife.'

'Raker's playing you. He's playing everyone. He sent us on a wild goose chase down to that youth club today, and guess what we found?'

Healy didn't reply.

'Fuck all. Nothing. Just like the last time.'

Healy glanced at me again and slowly shook his head. *We're in trouble.* His eyes moved to Drayton for a second time.

'I don't know where Raker is,' he said finally.

Phillips blew air down the phone, the line distorting. 'You just finished your career – you *do* understand that, right?'

Healy didn't reply.

'*Right?*' Phillips said a second time. He got no response. 'You trust Raker above the people in this station? Above the people you've closed cases with, who stood by you and worked for free, when Leanne went missing?'

I watched him wince at the mention of his daughter's name. His cheeks started to flush, filling up like blood soaking through cotton.

'You didn't do anything for me. She's not even on your radar.'

'We tried to help you find—'

'Don't tell me you tried to help me find her!' Healy erupted, eyes burning now. 'The people who helped me, most of them weren't yours. You and Hart – you didn't give a shit about her. You didn't give me anyone. *No one.*'

'Leanne can't officially be linked—'

'Don't tell me that she can't be linked to this, you fucking prick!' he screamed down the line. 'That piece of shit Glass took my daughter. And you know what I'm going to do now? I'm going to find him – and I'm going to kill him.'

'Healy,' Phillips said slowly. 'You will go to jail.'

'I don't give a shit.'

Healy glanced at me. Then his eyes moved across the road to Drayton again, and he nodded to the office door. *We're going in now.*

I placed a hand on the door, opened it.

'You're in deep shit, Healy,' Phillips said. '*Deep* shit. And so is your partner-in-crime there next to you, wherever the hell it is you're hiding. But let me tell you this now, so we're all crystal clear: we're on to you. You get me? We've picked up your trail.' Phillips paused. 'And when we get to you, you're both going down.'

CHAPTER 52

We marched across the road towards the office, Healy in front. His face was flushed and burning with anger, his fists opening and closing, ready to push aside, pull apart and tear into pieces. 'Healy,' I said to him, trying to keep my voice level, trying to clear the fog that was forming inside his head. 'Wait a second.'

But he didn't. He stepped up to the office door and shoved it open. It swung back so hard it hit the adjacent wall, the pane of glass clattering inside its panel. From the counter, Drayton looked up, eyes widening. He backed away from the desk.

'What are you doing—'

Healy grabbed the back of Drayton's head and yanked him forward, smashing him down on to the counter. The side of his face made a slapping sound as his cheek hit the vinyl. He cried out in pain. Healy leaned into his ear. 'What's under the trapdoor?'

'What?' Drayton said, his words muffled by Healy's hand.

'You better tell me what's in there.'

Drayton's eyes darted between us.

'Healy,' I said again.

He glanced at me. '*What?*'

'Calm down.'

'Shut the fuck up,' he spat, and pulled Drayton towards him, dragging his small frame up and over the counter. Drayton hit the floor face-first, crying out, and then rolled up into a heap on the carpet as if expecting punches to rain down on him. When they didn't, he looked up at us, blood running down one of his cheeks.

Healy reached down, yanked him to his feet and pulled him in so they were nose to nose. 'Open the trapdoor.'

'What are you talk—'

'Open the trapdoor *now*.'

Drayton glanced between us. I backed up towards the office door and looked out. The road was dark and quiet; only the sound of rain on the metal roof. When I turned back, Healy had swivelled Drayton around and had a hand locked in place at the back of his neck. He guided him out of the office and along the front of the warehouse to the delivery doors. They were padlocked.

'Unlock them.'

'There's nothing—'

Healy pushed forward and Drayton's face hit the metal door. The noise passed across the building like a ripple.

'I'm telling you,' Drayton said, his voice wavering. 'Please. I'm telling you – there's nothing in there.'

'Open it, and we'll see.'

Drayton fumbled in his pockets and brought out a ring of keys. He selected a brass one with a red mark on the side and slid it into the padlock. It clicked. Healy reached around him, pulled the padlock out from the metal plate and tossed it into the street. Then he yanked open one of the doors and pushed Drayton inside. The warehouse was completely dark except for one faint rectangle of orange street light filtering in from a window above us.

'Where are the lights?'

'There,' Drayton nodded.

He was looking at a panel of white switches to my left. I flicked them all on. Strip lights buzzed in the darkness, then stark white light fed along the ceiling.

The rear door was the same size as the delivery entrance at the front. Drayton unlocked the padlock with a second brass key, also marked red. Then Healy used him as a battering ram, forcing him forward into the door until it opened enough to let them through. Out in the yard, four security lights flicked on simultaneously, shining down from poles built into the fencing. In their glow, rain sheeted past us.

Healy glanced at me and jabbed his head towards the pile. 'Show him.'

I looked between him and Drayton, then walked around to the spot I'd glimpsed earlier and pushed aside a couple of the bigger containers. Beneath one, the edge of the trapdoor emerged.

'What's that?' Healy said to Drayton, pushing at his neck.

'It's for storage.'

'No shit.'

I moved some of the other boxes. A minute later, I'd cleared a space. A circle, cut into the floor and about two feet across, was freeze-framed in the security lights. It looked like a manhole cover. There was a handle cut into it and a lock attached. I dropped down, slid my fingers in and pulled. It didn't budge.

I glanced up at Drayton. 'Which key unlocks it?'

No reply.

Healy forced Drayton forward, so he was almost standing over the manhole. 'Which key is it?' he said through gritted teeth.

Drayton threw the key ring over. It landed in a puddle on the floor next to me. 'It's the small silver one, marked with a blue dot.'

I selected the key and slid it into the lock on the manhole cover. It clicked. Sliding my fingers around the handle again, I pulled it out from its surrounds.

The space dropped down less than a foot.

And the only thing inside was a piece of A4 paper, folded in half.

The rain started getting heavier, hitting the corrugated iron of the warehouse. I took out the piece of paper, slid it inside my jacket and nodded to Healy that we should go back inside. He pushed Drayton ahead of him, and we re-entered the building.

I opened up the piece of paper.

'What is it?' Healy asked.

It looked like a map of a street. We both recognized the style immediately: black marker pen; just lines. No street names. No places. No identifying marks. It was the same style as the map of the school I'd found on the LCT website. This one was a single straight road, with houses – drawn as identically sized squares – either side. Halfway down, one of the houses was coloured in red. A line came out of it to a number twenty-nine. Apart from that, there was nothing else on it.

I glanced at Drayton. 'Who gave you this?'

He just stared at me.

'Who gave you the map?' Healy said.

Again, Drayton didn't reply. Healy squeezed his fingers tighter around Drayton's neck. 'You tell us who gave you this map, and you tell us what it's of, or I swear to you the next time you wake up it'll be with your balls in your mouth.'

Drayton's eyes fixed on me. For a moment it looked like he was going to say something. Then he stopped, glanced as best he could at Healy and shrugged.

Healy smashed a fist into the side of his head. The impact sounded dull, like a wet flannel hitting a wall. Drayton didn't make much noise; just collapsed on to all fours, and then rolled on to his back. He looked up at Healy, blood leaking from his nose.

'Healy.'

He turned to me. '*What?*'

388

I stepped forward, closer to him. *Calm down.* He saw my expression, and then glanced at my feet, as if I'd just stepped into his personal space. He took off his jacket and threw it on top of the nearest box. 'Who gave you the map?'

No reply.

'*Who gave you the fucking map?*'

Drayton glanced between us, but remained quiet.

Healy blew out some air. 'You're one stupid piece of shit, you know that?'

'Drayton,' I said, trying to rein Healy in. 'This is easy. Tell us who gave you the map, and then we walk out of here and you never see us again.'

He looked at me from the floor; a look that said he couldn't tell us, and that I was the only one who could intervene. Then he turned back to Healy, blood filling the gaps between his teeth, and looked him in the eyes.

Silence.

'I think we need to clean out your ears,' Healy said. Across from us, a set of metal stairs wound up to a viewing platform, where a desk and chair sat looking down across the warehouse. Healy's eyes locked on the chair, and then on a roll of duct tape on a box near to us.

He reached down, pulled Drayton up and dragged him across the warehouse, scooping up the duct tape on the way. When they got to the stairs leading to the platform, Healy shoved him up them. Drayton looked back at me, the same message in his face: *Stop this.*

389

'Healy—'

He flashed a look at me. 'If you don't like it, go and sit in the car.'

When they got to the top, they marched across the platform and Healy pushed Drayton into the chair. I followed.

'You wanna play games?' Healy said, unravelling the tape.

He used one of his hands to secure Drayton's wrist to the arm of the chair and started circling with the duct tape. Once that was done, he did the same to the other wrist. Then both legs. Drayton looked at me, then back to Healy, who was taking a handkerchief from his jacket and screwing it into a ball. He shoved it into Drayton's mouth, ripped off another strip of duct tape and secured the gag in place.

'You don't have kids,' Healy said, leaning in to Drayton, nose to nose. 'I mean, look at you: you're just a kid yourself. You've got no idea what you feel for something you created. The bond you have. What lengths you'll be prepared to go to, to protect them. What you'll do to avenge them.' He straightened, rolling his shirt sleeves up even further. 'But you're about to find out.'

He shifted forward quickly, arcing a fist up into Drayton's stomach. Drayton doubled over, the wind bursting out of him, arms locking into place on the chair.

This was starting to get out of control. I stepped forward. 'Drayton – stop screwing around. Just tell us who gave you the map and all this ends.'

He was leaning over, saliva and blood leaking from his lips.

'*Drayton*,' I said again.

Nothing.

Healy smiled at Drayton. 'You're a fucking idiot, you know that?'

Not even movement now. Just silence and blood and saliva and the sounds of shallow breathing.

Healy turned around and started going through one of the drawers of the desk. In the third one down, he found something. A letter opener. Long and thin. Double edged. He removed it and then lifted Drayton up by his hair so they were facing one another.

'You remember what I told you?' Healy asked him.

Drayton said nothing.

'That you'll wake up with your balls in your mouth?'

A flash of fear in Drayton's face now. Air jetted out of his nostrils. He tried to shift in the chair, looking between the letter opener and Healy.

'Well, now you get to find out I wasn't joking.'

CHAPTER 53

'Healy,' I said, but he ignored me, reaching to the belt on Drayton's trousers and loosening it. '*Healy.*'

This time he stopped, studying me. 'You think he's going to tell us anything if we ask him nicely? Does it *look* like that to you?'

'He's a fucking kid.'

'So what?'

'So, take a look at yourself.'

He paused, glanced down at the sweat coming through his shirt, and Drayton's blood dotted across the cotton. Then he studied me, his face blank. For a second, it felt like the fuse had gone out. Then he turned back to Drayton. 'I don't care if he's a kid,' he said quietly, and I realized the only way this was going to end was if I stopped it.

Drayton squirmed in his seat as Healy started fiddling with the belt again. Fear clouded his eyes. His breath came in short bursts through his nose. After a few seconds, Healy had undone the trousers and pulled them along Drayton's thighs, and the kid had started screaming. One long, terrible noise that was worse through the gag, like an animal in distress. Healy glanced at me, tugged at Drayton's boxer shorts and reached under his shirt, grabbing the penis. Drayton screamed even longer and harder this time, eyes like saucers: wide and terrified, and glistening with tears. When he saw he'd got the reaction he wanted, Healy let go, ripped the gag away and leaned in again.

'Talk,' he said.

'Okay, okay,' Drayton said, short of breath. 'Okay.'

'*Talk*,' Healy repeated.

'A man,' Drayton said, looking between us.

'What man?'

'He didn't tell me his name.'

'So what did he tell you?'

Drayton glanced to his left, a minor movement. Healy didn't seem to notice. He was boiling over. Fuelled by adrenalin. But I spotted it the first time, and then again a couple of seconds later: a swivel of the eyes, over his shoulder to the warehouse below.

'What did he tell you?'

'He just told me to keep the map safe, not to show anybody, never try to replicate it, photocopy it or write it down. Basically, just keep it under lock and key.'

'Why?'

Drayton hesitated.

'*Why?*'

'He's . . .'

Drayton's eyes drifted again. A split-second movement.

'He's what?' Healy said.

'He's a regular customer.'

'A regular whose name you don't know?' Healy snorted. He leaned in, placing a hand on either arm of the chair. 'You got two seconds, or I really *will* cut your balls off.'

Drayton sniffed. Moved his head from side to side gently, like he was trying to decide the best course of action. Then, quietly, he said, 'I don't know his name.'

Healy shook his head again. 'Wrong answer.'

'Wait a second,' Drayton said. 'Wait a sec—'

Grabbing the handkerchief off the floor, Healy shoved it back into Drayton's mouth and secured it in place again with the duct tape. Drayton started shouting through the gag. I stepped towards Healy, crossing the line into his personal space. He looked at me and then rocked back. 'You gonna try and stop me?'

I looked past him, out through the rear doors of the warehouse. It was hammering down outside, rain lashing in across the yard. The wind had picked up too, whipping in over the fences and lifting the plastic sheeting away from the boxes.

'Stay here,' I said. 'And don't do anything.'

'Where are you going?'

'Just stay here.'

I headed down the stairs and outside, pulling the hood up on my jacket. The boxes I'd already moved were stained darker with rain. I took out my pocket knife and stabbed the blade down

394

through the top of the nearest box, edging it around in an L-shape and peeling it away. Inside were woks, each separated by a layer of foam. I pushed the box aside and went for the next one. Porcelain dishes. The next one along: frying pans. I stepped back and looked further into the pile, under the plastic sheeting. A wind carved in from behind me and lifted the tarpaulin away. Right in the middle, surrounded on all sides, was a tall, thin box, with a small black symbol in the corner.

Shoving boxes aside, I moved further into the centre of the pile, trying to create a space where I could drag the box back out with me. When I got to it, I tried to move it. It was heavy. At least forty or fifty pounds. I dug the knife blade into each side and cut out a couple of finger holes, then tightened my grip again and pulled the box out. As it moved, even as the rain pelted down and the wind howled, I could hear something moving around inside. Liquid sloshing.

Back inside the warehouse, Healy looked down, a frown on his face. I could see Drayton trying to turn.

'What's that?'

I pulled the box to the bottom of the steps, so they could both see. Then I set it straight. Drayton stared at it, something in him receding, as if a great secret had just been blown away in the wind. There had only been a small movement in his eyes before. But it was enough for me to realize he was hiding something. Eyes weren't just the doorway to the soul. They were the ultimate polygraph test.

'What's that?' Healy said again.

I jabbed my knife down through the top of the box and cut out a hole. 'Formalin,' I said, prodding a finger against the symbol on the outside. 'This is the number eighty in Cyrillic.' *Just like the pi symbol.* I'd seen it before on the cardboard boxes in the background of the photo I'd found in the doll. The photograph that had been used to help frame me. 'There are about eighty canisters of the stuff in here. And I'm willing to bet that whoever drew that map for Drayton was hoping to take delivery of them.'

Drayton made no noise.

I made my way back up the steps.

'So,' I said, and picked up the map off the desk. 'Where's this?'

He looked at me and I could see he was just as involved in all this as his father; as good a liar as his father too. The problem was, he wasn't as organized and he wasn't as good at covering his tracks. He'd got sloppy, keeping the goods he'd imported on his premises rather than shipping them off to another storage unit. He'd thought hiding them among the imported kitchenware would be enough. And maybe it would have been if I'd never spoken to Spike and found out what the symbol in the photograph meant.

Healy reached over and tore off the gag.

'He said he had information on the business,'

Drayton said. 'He said he would send evidence of deliveries, of goods we'd imported, to the police. He said he would finish us.'

'Who was he?'

'I don't *know*,' Drayton replied, his voice tearful. 'I can't run this business like my dad. I can't do it. I *hate* it. But I promised him I could meet his expectations. I promised him I would look after the family. I promised him I would never let him down. But I can't even do that one thing for him.'

I pointed at the map. 'Where's this?'

'Walthamstow. Pine Terrace. Number 29.'

'You were supposed to drop the formalin off there?'

Drayton nodded.

'When?'

'Tomorrow.'

'What were your instructions?'

Drayton glanced down. 'Leave the box on the front steps of the house.'

'That's it?'

'That's it,' he said. 'The same instructions every time. I've been importing things for him for months now. When he comes here, he tells me the same thing. Memorize the road name. Don't write it down. Don't photocopy it. Keep the map secure. Tell anyone anything and he buries the business.'

'Is he home when you drop off the package?'

Drayton shook his head. 'The house is vacant. They had a fire there. Half of it's boarded up, but you can see in through one of the broken windows.

The living room has been burned to shit. No carpet. No furniture. The back garden's like a jungle, and out front it's just a dumping ground. Cans and wrappers and dog shit all over the place.'

'You ever stick around after the drop-off?'

'No. He tells us to deliver the package and leave immediately.'

I reached into the inside pocket of my jacket and took out a picture I'd torn from one of the youth club personnel files. I held it up for him.

'Is this the man who comes to see you?'

Drayton studied the picture. 'Yeah, that's him.'

It was Daniel Markham.

CHAPTER 54

Pine Terrace was a narrow, forgotten row of houses that looked like its best days weren't just behind it, but had never arrived in the first place. Each home had the same uniform white-bricked garden wall, but the actual houses were painted a mish-mash of clashing colours, like a work of modern art gone wrong: reds, creams, peaches, greens, all visible even under subdued street light and lashing rain. Halfway down, stained with soot and ash, was number twenty-nine. Drayton had been right about its appearance: its concrete path had turned to rubble; its door was blistered and warped; glass was scattered across what lawn there was left; and someone had spray-painted the walls. Council notices warning against entering, once stuck to the front door, had peeled away over time.

Healy pulled up a little way down the street. I got out, turning the collar up on my jacket, and studied the road. If Markham was asking Drayton to drop the box off on the front steps, then he was confident enough about getting to the package before any passers-by took an interest. That meant that when Drayton – or the people who worked for him – turned up at the house, Markham had to be watching. I looked across the street to the houses opposite. They were buildings without life. The whole road had a depressed air about it, a lack of internal light. It was obvious why Markham had chosen this street.

'What a shitheap,' Healy said as he passed me, studying the dark front window of the house. In his hands was a torch he'd got from the back of the car. He made his way up the driveway, the concrete beneath his feet crumbling, and looked in through a hole in the glass. A few seconds later, he flicked the torch on and directed it inside. In the cone of light, I could see blackened walls, a fireplace and – at the back – patio doors.

'You know how long this has been unoccupied?' He shone the torch at the council notice on the front door, then directed the light back into the living room. 'Three years. No wonder it smells like someone shat themselves to death in there. Half the tramps in London have probably used it as a bed and breakfast.'

I followed Healy, checking the houses opposite. The windows across the street would be the obvious place to watch the delivery being made: high position, clear view, good cover. If he used either of the places that flanked number twenty-nine, he'd have to be more careful, but he'd have an even better view of the drop-off. Neither seemed likely, though: in the one to the right, through a pair of net curtains, I could see an old couple sitting in front of their TV; in the house on the left, children's toys were on the windowsill and behind the closed curtains a light was on.

Healy looked at me. 'Better hold your breath.'

Along the edge of the door frame the council had once run luminous yellow tape in an attempt to keep people out. He tore some of it away, stepped back from the door and kicked it open. It juddered and shifted, then swung back into the darkness.

The hallway was small and narrow, and as black as the outside of the house. As we stood and looked in, rain swept in from behind us. It ran down the blistered, seared walls and formed puddles in the glass that lay, sparkling in the torchlight, at the entrance.

The smell hit us about three feet inside. The thick stench of fire. The stink of urine, sweat, alcohol and vomit. Healy shone a torch into the living room. Two men were lying on the floor under blankets, one facing us, one facing away. They were both drunk. He whistled at them. The one facing us opened his eyes; the other didn't even move. He looked vaguely in our direction, unable to focus, then his pupils rolled back in his head. A second later, he was still again.

There were patches of carpet on the floor beneath them, but mostly it was exposed floorboards and – in some places – black holes where the fire had eaten its way through. Beyond the men, tucked away on the other side of the room, was the stair-case. The steps were destroyed, and more council tape had been placed across the entrance to them. Close to the staircase was a fireplace, and beyond that was the kitchen.

Both men on the floor stirred, one mumbling, one making a sound like he was suffering his last, dying breath. Between them were a succession of empty cans and bottles. One of them had wet himself.

'Bloody hell,' Healy said quietly. 'It's like St Patrick's Day in here.'

We moved back across the living room. Healy headed straight for exit, but I stopped to look up the stairs. I could see some of the landing: walls were burned through and full of cracks, and holes came right the way through the ceiling into the living room.

The torch swung back in my direction. 'You coming or what?'

I ignored Healy and moved towards the fireplace.

'Give me the light,' I said.

He held out the torch. I glanced at him, not moving, waiting for him to bring it to me. Finally, he shook his head and moved across the glass shards and broken wood, to the fireplace. He slapped it into my hand.

'You after a new fire?'

I ignored him for a second time and used the torch to light it up. It was a standard gas fire: fake lumps of coal sitting in a tray, inside a once-smart silver surround. It wasn't plumb to the wall. A half-inch gap ran all the way around, and when I directed the light in behind, it looked like it was just an empty space. No fire interior. No wall cavity. No insulation. Just space.

'Give me a hand,' I said, and Healy went to the other side of the fire. We both fed our fingers into the gap and pulled the silver surround away from the wall. It stuck at first, making a dull scratching noise as we dragged it. Then it popped free, the coal tray coming with it.

I picked up the torch again.

There was a hole in the wall about three feet high and four feet long. I shone the light into it. Through the hole, the bricks, insulation and wall cavity had all been knocked through.

On the other side was the house next door.

CHAPTER 55

I got down on to my hands and knees and crawled through the space, through plaster and dust, glass and chunks of brick. Healy followed.

On the other side, the layout was exactly the same as number twenty-nine. It was sparsely furnished: a tall lamp across from us, currently on and plugged into a timer; a worn sofa; a brand-new TV in the corner on a cabinet, with a DVD player and a very old VCR; VHS tapes underneath that. The kitchen had cutlery on the worktops and food packets half open. The stairs were uncarpeted.

By the front windows were two mannequins. Both were naked, though an arm was missing from one – and something was hanging off its face. It looked like a sheet of thin plastic, part of it glued to the side of the mannequin's head.

I stepped closer and touched a finger to the plastic.

But it wasn't plastic.

It was latex.

One side of it was smooth and creamy, almost polished. The other side had more colour and

texture. I pulled it across the face of the mannequin and Healy came around behind me, looking
over my shoulder.

'What the hell is that?'

I smoothed it down, over the ridges of the
mannequin's head. 'It's a face.'

We stepped back, children's toys scattered along
the windowsill behind us, teddy bears and plastic
animals poking out between the curtains. Everything
was here to create silhouettes. To make people
outside think normality existed on the inside.

But it didn't.

In front of us the mannequin looked back, its
dead gaze peering through the eyeholes in the thin
latex mask. Small, pursed lips were visible through
the mouth slit. The mask started to slip away again,
the glue not strong enough to hold it any more.
But not before both of us had realized who was
looking back.

Milton Sykes.

I ripped the mask away from the curved plastic
dome of the dummy's head. Healy stood beside me,
both of us looking down at the latex approximation
of Sykes.

It was a skilled piece of work. Not perfect by any
means – some of the colouring had run and there
was glue and globules of varnish on parts of
the skin – but it was good enough to convince. The
mask ran from the top of the forehead to either ear
and down to just below the chin. Whoever made
it had ensured that the forehead was thicker than

the rest of the mask to match up with Sykes's most prominent feature. The depth of the latex at the forehead was almost four times as thick as it was on the rest of the face. If anyone had managed to get close enough they might have been able to tell that something was off. But through the glitchy, staccato black-and-white of the CCTV camera in Tiko's, it had looked perfectly lifelike.

I remembered the man at Markham's flat. The weirdness of his face: how his mouth and eyes had moved, but the rest of him had remained perfectly still.

Now I could see why.

We searched the living room. No clay. No sculpting tools. No liquid latex. No paints. No reference materials or pictures of Sykes. There was nothing to suggest the mask had been created inside the house. With something as complex and time-consuming as moulding and styling a latex mask, there would be evidence. Instead, the house was half empty. *So it must have been brought here.*

Healy walked across the room and looked up into the darkness of the staircase. He flicked on the torch, waving it up and down the steps to check they weren't in the same state of disrepair as the ones next door. Then he tried the light switches next to him on the wall. None of them did anything. He glanced at me and nodded that he was going to have a look around upstairs. I nodded back. As he disappeared into the shadows, just a cone of light as his guide, I headed to the rear of the house.

Clackclackclack.

Something moved in the darkness of the kitchen. Left to right. I side-stepped and leaned left, trying to get a better view around the counter. But there was nothing now. No movement. No sound other than Healy moving around upstairs, the floorboards creaking under his weight.

I took a step forward.

Clackclackclack.

Then there was a faint squeak, like a rusty hinge moving.

I took out my phone, flipped it open and directed the light from the display into the space on the other side of the worktop. A rat scurried away, its claws making a *clackclackclack* noise on the linoleum. It headed through a hole between one of the cupboards and the cooker.

As I went around the worktop I saw a second rat, its fat pink tail visible, the rest of its body hidden by one of the units. It wasn't squeaking and it definitely wasn't moving, but there was still a noise. A different one: moist, wet, like it was chewing on something. To my left I spotted Healy coming down the stairs, the torch in front of him. He looked at me and shook his head. Nothing upstairs. Then a fly buzzed past my face. As I went to swat it away I felt another, dozy and unresponsive. A second later, I could hear more.

They were everywhere.

And then my senses opened up: animals, blood – and decay.

I flipped open my phone again, swinging the blue light around to the space behind the counter. The rat moved this time, following the path of the other one.

Clackclackclack.

Except this one left a trail: a series of tiny red marks.

Footprints.

Lying on the floor, half slumped against the kitchen units, was the body of a man. His arms were at his sides, palms up, fingers curled into claws. His eyes stared off into the night, wide and pale, and his clothes, and the lino around him, were covered in blood. His T-shirt had been torn open about halfway down, and on the skin of his chest I could see a series of knife wounds, probably made with a serrated blade: long and thin, thrust in so deep and pulled out so quickly that flesh, muscle and fat had come with it. His trousers were riding up either leg, and one sock was on the other side of the kitchen, among blood spatters that looked like arterial spray.

'So what the fuck are we supposed to do now?' Healy said from behind me, shining the torch into the face of the man on the floor.

We'd found Daniel Markham.

CHAPTER 56

Healy traced Markham's dead body with the torch, careful not to disturb the crime scene. Eventually we'd have to call it in, but first we had to clear our heads. Press Reset. Our best lead was lying in a pool of his own blood on the floor of a derelict house.

'Difficult to tell how long,' Healy said, 'unless you want to shove a thermometer up his arse and take his temperature.'

He moved the torch beam down Markham's arm, blue veins prominent below the skin. The blood that hadn't left his body through his chest had pooled in his legs, his feet and the small of his back. Healy used the torch to signal one of his calves. The area directly in contact with the lino hadn't filled with blood. The area just above it had.

'That's hypostasis,' he said.

Once gravity kicks in, your red blood cells head south and settle; but the skin that's in direct contact with a surface won't fill up because the capillaries are compressed.

He swung the torch around the kitchen.

'The body hasn't been moved,' he continued. 'Once the red blood cells drop, they stay dropped. If he'd been turned over from his front, the blood would be in his shins, knees, top of his thighs and the front of his chest – not where it is now.'

'Looks like he's got rigor mortis too,' I said.

Healy stopped, turned to me, eyes narrowing. 'So what else am I telling you that you already know?' He was angry that we'd hit another dead end, and he needed someone to offload on. 'You going to tell me how it is you're a part-time pathologist as well as a part-time policeman?'

I let the insult slide.

'*Huh?*'

'What are we arguing about, Healy?'

'I just like to know who I'm dealing with.'

I rubbed my fingers across my forehead. I'd only known him for a short space of time, but Healy was nothing if not predictable.

'I wanna know who I've got along for the ride,' he said. 'I don't want surprises. I don't want a knife in my back.'

I stared at him. 'What's that supposed to mean?'

'You know what it means.'

'I don't even know what you're getting your knickers in a twist about. So I know what rigor mortis looks like. So what?'

'*So*, I don't trust you.'

'You don't have to trust me. You just have to work with me. When this is all over, I'm sure there'll be plenty of time for us to find a cosy corner somewhere and discuss what we do and do not know about the human body after it dies.'

His eyes narrowed again. 'What the fuck do *you* know about death?'

He realized what he'd said within about a second of it coming out of his mouth, but Healy wasn't the type to apologize. The best he could do was a vague flattening of his mouth. It was a typical Healy moment; a pointless argument borne out of him realizing he wasn't in complete control.

He fixed the torchlight on Markham's face.

'Yeah, he's stiffened up,' he said quietly.

Rigor always starts in the facial muscles, before crawling its way through the jaw and the throat and then out into the rest of the body. It can give you an approximate time of death, but even a pathologist would have struggled to pinpoint it exactly based on the kind of conditions we were dealing with. The fact that rigor mortis had set in certainly put him at under thirty-six hours, and the hypostasis in the lower parts of his body was a dark purple. I'd shadowed the Forensic Science Laboratory in Pretoria for two months as part of a feature I was writing about post-apartheid South Africa in the late nineties, and had been to a few crime scenes. Maximum lividity occurred about six to twelve hours after hypostasis set in. Which meant Markham was alive when he woke up this morning.

'If we call this in, it's over,' Healy said, the torch back on Markham's body, running the length of one of the knife wounds. 'This whole thing goes down the toilet.'

I nodded. He was right. At the moment, we were ahead of the curve and the police were playing catch-up.

I started pulling the room apart, pushing furniture aside, dragging the sofa out from the wall, trying to zero in on anything that would give us a lead. Healy started as well, stepping around Markham in the kitchen, and opening and shutting drawers.

Moving to the TV cabinet and the stack of videotapes, I knelt down and started pulling them out of their sleeves, tossing them away one after the other.

Then, midway through, I stopped.

The second from last tape was in a bright red case, different from the others, and had no printing on it at all. I pulled the cassette out. Written across the label in the middle was a message in black marker pen.

It said, *Help me.*

We didn't speak as I switched on the VCR, slid the tape in and turned the TV on. Blackness. And then, seconds later, the set was filled with a shot of Markham.

He had tears in his eyes.

His brown hair was shorter than in the photo I'd taken from the youth club, and he'd lost the horn-rimmed glasses. Dark eyes like chips of wood gazed out at us; stubble bristled as his hand traced the line of his jaw. He looked in good shape and was dressed well too: a name-brand polo shirt and a pair of jeans. No shoes.

He sniffed and then took in a long breath. His eyes drifted off camera, before coming back again. It was recorded during the day, in the middle of the living room. In the background we could see the kitchen, and a little of the stairs. He ran a hand through his hair, as if he didn't know where to start.

Then he cleared his throat.

'My name is Daniel Markham,' he said, his voice wavering, his eyes watering, his face etched with unease. 'And this is my confession.'

THE DOCTOR

Eleven months ago

Daniel Markham opened the door to his office and stepped inside. It was too warm. The hospital was always either stiflingly hot or freezing cold. Never in between. It was the beginning of November, and the weather had been unseasonably mild for a week, but still the central heating in his part of the building hadn't been adjusted properly. He'd put in two complaints, neither of which had been met with any kind of response. It was the NHS in full working order.

He hung up his coat and went to the windows, opening them as far as they would go. A faint breeze wafted in. Sitting at his desk, he booted up his computer and started going through his unopened mail. At the top of his in-tray was an appointment diary, which his secretary filled in for him at the beginning of each week. Without her, he would be lost. He remembered the faces of his patients, but not always their names and certainly not the times they were expected. The only appointment he *did* remember was the one at

Barton Hill Youth Club on Monday afternoons, where – as part of a drive by the hospital to get consultants out into the field as volunteers – he spent five hours with the parents of kids suffering from cerebral palsy, helping where he could.

Initially, he'd seen the volunteer work as wasted hours. In fact, when the email had first gone round, he'd thought it was a joke. In a hospital system that could barely cope with the ratio of patients to staff as it was, an afternoon field trip seemed like an idea that would only ensure fewer people were seen and more complaints rolled in. But the hospital trust were determined to carry through the commitment they'd made to the community in an expensive PR campaign the previous year, and – after some initial scepticism – Markham had grown to love the time he got to spend at the club. The parents of the kids were so different from the patients he had at the hospital; so positive, despite the heartache they'd had to endure. His patients tended to be the opposite: most of them were antagonistic and cynical and only looked for ways to head further down the spiral.

Throwing away half the mail he'd opened up, he pulled his appointment diary down from the in-tray and turned to 3 November. His days were divided up into hour-long sessions, and the day was full, from 8 a.m. through to 1 p.m., and 2 p.m. through to 6 p.m. First up was a name he definitely didn't recognize: Sykes. Probably a new patient. He turned to his computer, logged into his e-diary and clicked on the entry for 8 a.m. marked 'Sykes'. His medical history came up. Broken arm at nine. Fractured wrist at seventeen. Nondescript doctor's appointments throughout the course of the rest of his life until a fortnight ago when he'd returned five times over the course of a ten-day period complaining of insomnia, anxiety attacks, severe chest pains and problems concentrating at work. Markham scrolled down and clicked on the GP's referral letter. The patient had been given a medical on his last visit to the surgery, and nothing had been found. Physically, he was fine. Markham's two-second diagnosis was depression.

On the desk, his phone started ringing.

He picked up. 'Hello?'

'Mr Sykes is here for you,' his secretary said.

Markham looked at the clock on the wall. It was just before eight.

'Okay. Send him in.'

He moved across to where two sofas were sitting in an L-shape in the corner of the room. They faced a tilting, high-backed leather chair. In between was a coffee table with a series of heavy, and largely tedious, books he'd picked up from a market for a tenner. He wanted the room to seem less like an office in a sprawling, faceless hospital and more like a place to feel at home.

Two knocks at the door.

'Come in.'

Mr Sykes entered. He was in his late thirties and six foot, but looked much shorter. He was stooped, almost curved from the middle of his spine. Brown hair, dark eyes, a couple of days of stubble and a tired expression. Markham studied him: some of it was the lack of sleep, but not all. He carried a kind of sadness with him. 'Mr Sykes?'

He nodded. 'Dr Markham.'

'Please,' Markham said, pointing to the sofas. 'Take a seat.'

Sykes nodded his thanks, and looked around the office, sitting down on the nearest sofa. He perched himself on the edge, legs together at the knees, looking nervous.

'Can I get you something to drink?'

'No, I'm fine, thank you,' Sykes replied, glancing briefly at Markham and away again. He had the look many had on entering the office for the first time: a mix of expectation and terror.

Markham sat in the leather chair. 'So what brings you here today?'

Sykes nodded. Hesitated. 'I, uh . . .' He stopped, looked around the office again. Drummed his fingers on his knees. 'I haven't been feeling right.'

Markham nodded. 'In what way?'

'I don't think I've slept for about six weeks now. Not properly.'

'Has something been bothering you?'

Sykes looked up. 'Yes.'

'What?'

'Lots of things. Lots of different things. I'm worrying so much I'm having anxiety attacks – these great big waves of panic rushing through me.'

'What's been worrying you?'

'I get these chest pains,' Sykes said, his eyes fixed on a space behind Markham. Almost no eye contact so far. 'Physically, they can't find anything wrong, but I can feel something eating away at me from the inside.'

Markham paused. 'Okay. Let's take a couple of steps back. What is it you do?'

Sykes looked up briefly. 'I kind of freelance.'

'Doing what?'

'Dealing with people.'

'You're a manager?'

'No. I observe and then I act.'

Markham frowned. 'Why don't you elaborate?'

'I can't concentrate on my work, on anything in my life. I sit there all day, looking at my computer screen, and all I can see is her face looking back at me.'

'Who are we talking about here?'

Sykes didn't reply. He was staring down into his lap, his fingers on his knees, one of his legs vibrating gently, his shoe tap-tapping against the carpet.

'Mr Sykes?'

No response. Markham leaned forward.

'Who is it you can see looking back?'

Nothing.

'Mr Sykes? Whose face can you see?'

A second later, like a light cutting out, Sykes went completely still. He continued looking down into his lap, the fingers of each hand resting on either knee.

'Mr Sykes?' Markham leaned forward even further, trying to get an angle where he could see Sykes's face more clearly. 'Who can you see?'

Slowly, Sykes started to move: his fingers slid back along his thighs, his legs loosened up and his body seemed to expand, as if filling with air. Suddenly, every inch of his six-foot frame was visible, shoulders broadening, chest filling out, the curve of the stoop fading away. Markham sat back in his seat, aware – without even really understanding why – that Sykes was transforming into someone else. The nervousness was gone. The lack of confidence. The sense of expectation and uncertainty. Finally, Sykes's face tilted upwards, eyes fixed on Markham, a smile worming its way across his face. And, in that moment, Markham realized something: it had all been an act.

'You want to know who I can see, Dr Markham?' he asked, even his voice different now. 'You want to know who I can see every day looking up at me, terrified, from a hole in my floor?' He paused. His eyes flashed; as dark as the entrance to a tomb. 'I can see your wife.'

CHAPTER 57

There was no noise inside the house. On-screen, Markham had stopped talking and was wiping an eye. He'd just gone over the moment he'd first come into contact with Glass.

Healy turned to me. 'Glass kidnapped Markham's *wife*?'

'Now we know why no one can find her.'

We both looked back at Markham. His image was fuzzy, the age of the TV draining colour from his skin. He shifted in his seat as if he couldn't get comfortable.

'So Markham was just a pawn,' Healy said.

'Looks that way.'

'Why? Why would Glass start using Markham?'

I shook my head. 'Maybe we're about to find out.'

We both looked back at the screen again. Markham was still composing himself. 'Glass,' said Healy quietly, as if he'd thought of something. He reached forward and pushed Pause. 'He had a medical history. You heard Markham. Broken arm, anxiety attacks, chest pains. We can trace him.'

'It won't be his.'

'What are you talking about?'

'If Markham had medical records in front of him, they won't have belonged to Glass. He's too careful for that. He doesn't make mistakes.'

We both went quiet and I pressed Play again.

'Everything after that was a lie,' Markham said on-screen. 'But I did it to protect Sue. I couldn't bear the thought of him hurting her. He kept calling me, saying he'd do all these unspeakable things to her – slice her, and stab her, and cut her. In the days after he first came to my office, I tried to fight back. I tried to find him. But he knew what I was doing; he was watching me the whole time. And I couldn't find a trace of him. Nothing. His medical records were a sham. His mobile phone number was untraceable.' He looked around him. 'He doesn't even seem to own this shitty house he makes me live in. And about three or four days after he came to see me that first time, just to prove he was *really* in charge, he called me and made me listen to her begging for her life.'

A long pause. We waited for Markham to continue.

'I was scared of him, and he knew it. He'd play on it. I'd come back to this house and he would have made tiny adjustments to it, swapped my things around, just to show me he'd been inside. He'd leave new toys on the windowsill, or adjust the position of the mannequins, or leave rubber masks attached to their faces. One time, he left Sue's blouse in the middle of the living room, with blood all over it. That was when I really got scared.'

He sniffed. Shifted in his seat. I glanced at Healy and saw him slowly rubbing his fingers and thumb together again. This time it wasn't his craving for nicotine; it was the air of inevitability settling around us. The dread and anticipation that the worst was yet to come. Healy was about to have his heart ripped out.

'So I took three of them,' Markham said, looking up into the camera. Beside me, I felt Healy bristle. 'He told me who he wanted me to take, and I took them. Because the alternative was him killing Sue. I was . . . I just didn't . . .'

Another pause. I turned to look at Healy again. He saw the movement. I could see his eyes flick in my direction and then back to the screen.

'You don't have to watch this,' I said.

'I do.'

'I can watch it and tell you what you need to know.'

'I'm watching it,' he said, teeth gritted.

On-screen, Markham repositioned himself. He wasn't a man used to this kind of thing. Even as his eyes filled with tears there was a strange kind of reticence to him, as if he was frightened by everything he was feeling.

Then he started again: 'I had a lot of guilt left over after Sue and I divorced. The way she went downhill so fast.' A pause. 'I mean, I had her *committed*. Who commits their own *wife*?' He stopped for a second time. 'And then, when she got out, I didn't even contact her. I didn't know what I was supposed to say. I couldn't face her. Couldn't deal with her. And I guess he used that. He played on that. He used all the guilt, and made me think I'd never get the chance to say sorry.'

Healy shook his head. I could smell the sweat on him now.

'So I took Leanne.'

As Markham spoke her name a subtle change passed across Healy's face and I realized something: he hurt too deeply to ever get over what he was about to be told. He could get his vengeance, but it would never repair the hole left behind. All the frustration, all the aggression, all the violence to come – ultimately it meant nothing.

'He must have first picked me out through the youth club,' Markham said. 'He must have been watching that place – watching Leanne and Megan – and seen me there on a Monday. I had a good relationship with both of them. I suppose they trusted me. I mean . . .' He stopped. 'Why wouldn't they?'

I glanced at Healy. He was absolutely still.

'He called Leanne my practice run. I had to make her think I wanted to be with her. Then I had to take her to the woods and give her to him. He told me that if I got found out, if I left anything for anyone to find, he would cut me adrift, and I would never see my wife again.' Markham looked away for a moment. 'So that's what I did. I made Leanne think I liked her. I forced myself into her life. And then, when I had her fooled, I just . . . fed her to him.'

'Healy,' I said.

'It stays on.'

'You can—'

'It stays *on*,' he spat, turning to face me. In the dull light, something shimmered in one of his eyes. And then he fixed his gaze back on the television as Markham got up from his seat. He sniffed, walked past the camera – and everything turned to black.

A second later, it started again.

He moved from behind the camera and headed back to his seat. This time he appeared more composed. 'I got the sense Megan was more important to him than Leanne. I don't know why – that was just what it felt like. He planned everything out for Leanne, but he seemed to be even more meticulous with Megan. Maybe it was just that Leanne was easier to get at. She wasn't very bright and she'd had a disrupted home life. Her mother was having an affair, and her father was never around.'

I glanced at Healy. Nothing.

'Megan was different. She had wealthy parents, and with wealth comes resources. If she disappeared, they'd use that wealth. They'd use all of it if it meant finding her. Leanne, I just got for him. But Megan came with a set of ground rules.'

424

I looked at Healy again. Sweat had soaked through his shirt, under his arms, at his collar. He turned to me, face blank. 'What does he mean by "ground rules"?'

'I think he means the London Conservation Trust,' I said, pushing Pause on the VCR. 'Glass set that up to make himself untraceable. He used bogus newsletters to hide messages in, and the site to give her details of meetings. She thought it was all being sent from Markham – but it wasn't. It was Glass.'

'And Megan didn't think it was a bit weird?'

I shrugged. 'Maybe. But remember, Markham was nearly twenty years older than her. In fact, technically, she wasn't even an adult yet. Glass probably told him to play on that, made Markham tell her that he had a public-facing job and couldn't risk any controversy. Markham must have ended up convincing her that it was safer to use the LCT as cover until she turned eighteen – and then they could tell people about their relationship.'

'What the hell was she thinking?'

'He was the first guy she ever fell in love with. Her friend said she'd never been that way about anyone in her life. She just got swept away by it.'

'They never spoke on the phone?'

'I doubt Glass allowed Markham to communicate with Megan in any other form but the LCT. No other emails. No messaging. No phone calls. Nothing traceable. Only face to face at the youth club and via the website. I mean, what would be the point of going to the trouble of setting up the LCT if they had each other's mobile number?'

Healy shook his head, reached forward and pushed Play.

'It was going okay with Megan,' Markham continued, his voice beginning to wobble. 'I'd managed to convince her that what I felt was genuine, like I had with Leanne. And once she started to believe me, it became easier to fool her about things like the website.' A pause. Another finger brushed his face, this time closer to his eye. 'But then the boy turned up at my door, shouting and threatening me and . . .' He seemed to shrink a little. 'I know it sounds stupid, but I think the things he said to me hurt more than anything anyone's ever said to me in my life. To be called a pervert, a paedophile . . .'

Markham looked down into his lap. Sniffed. Silence descended on-screen. Healy glanced at me. 'Is he talking about the Bryant kid?'

I nodded. 'Charlie, yeah.'

'How did the kid know about Markham?'

I remembered something Kaitlin said to me about Charlie. *He was, like, in love with Megan. Totally in love with her. Sometimes he'd go over the top and creep us all out . . . He'd follow her around.*

'He must have been watching her,' I said. 'He must have gone to tell Markham to stay away from Megan. Charlie was jealous. But by then it was too late. Megan was in love with Markham – or, at least, the idea of him.'

Markham cleared his throat, the sound distorting through the speakers on the TV. 'Maybe he was right about me. Maybe I *was* a pervert.' He cleared his throat a second time. Then, as he spoke again, his voice started to tremor. 'It was an *accident*,' he said quietly. 'It was just an accident. She was supposed to be on the pill.'

Healy looked at me. 'Do you think the Bryant kid knew?'

'That Megan was pregnant? Yeah, he knew. He was the one that warned Kaitlin off telling the police about it, remember. Megan might have told him outright, but it was more likely he found out some other way. Maybe he followed her to a supermarket, or a walk-in clinic, or a pharmacy. Maybe he saw her buying a pregnancy kit.'

The video jumped, crackled, and more lines drifted down the picture. Markham began talking again. 'When he called me the next night, I told him we had a problem. I told him Charlie Bryant knew about Megan and me. I told him about Megan being pregnant as well, thinking that would be the end of the line for me, and for Sue. But he wasn't angry.' He frowned. 'He just laughed. And then said, "Oh, Daniel – that's perfect. Absolutely perfect."'

'Why would he be pleased she was pregnant?' I said, pausing the tape. Healy just shrugged at me. I turned back to the TV. 'It does explain something, though.'

'What?'

'Why Charlie – and his father – were killed.'

'The kid got too close.'

I nodded. We both let that settle, and in the silence I could see Healy's mind ticking over. Eventually he turned back to me: 'Why, though?'

'Why what?'

'Why did he start using Markham? He takes five women before Leanne without the help of Markham. Then he takes three more – Leanne, Megan and Sona – *with* his help. Why?'

'Maybe he wanted to insulate himself.'

'So why didn't he do that from the start?'

I saw where Healy was going. 'Because of Frank White.'

'Exactly. I think Glass was operating just fine on his own until 25 October last year. Five women already in the bag, no one able to pick up his scent. Then things get screwed up at the warehouse, Frank White dies, and suddenly he's back to feeling mortal again. He realizes it only takes one mistake for the whole house of cards to come down. So he pinpoints Markham.'

'Because of his connections to the youth club.'

'Right. Glass spots Megan somewhere – in the street, on a bus, somewhere – and follows her to the youth club. He sees Markham at the club, maybe sees the way Megan looks at him or something, and he realizes he can use Markham to get at Megan, without risking more exposure. And there's an added bonus . . .'

'Susan Markham.'

Healy nodded. 'Glass does a bit of background on Markham and finds out not only that he seems to be in with Megan, but he can be manipulated through his wife.'

I glanced from Healy to the television screen and back again. He was looking at me, no hint of anything in his face now, a mixture of sweat and aftershave coming off him. Maybe this was how he dealt with emotion: bottled it up, pushed it down, until one day he couldn't contain it and ended up doing something he regretted. Like putting his wife in a neck brace. Or arguing with his daughter. Or telling his boss he was going to rip apart the man who'd taken her.

When I started the tape again, it clicked and whirred.

'If you're watching this, he's probably killed me,' Markham said, pausing for a moment. 'I've probably tried to find a way out. I can't take this. I can't see an end. Leanne, Megan, and then we moved on from the youth club; on to Sona . . .' Eye contact with the camera now. 'I know, unless I refuse to do this any more, it's just going to go on and on, and he's going to keep on using me. And although . . .'

He stopped. An eye watered. A part of me felt sorry for him; at the way a good man had been manoeuvred into position against his will. But I couldn't forgive him for taking those women. Because when you faced darkness, sometimes there wasn't a light. Sometimes you had to step in blind

429

and have enough faith, enough fearlessness, to try and find the right way. And the right way for Markham would have been to fight back.

On-screen, he shifted in his seat and he brought out a photograph from under him; from beneath a leg, or out of an unseen pocket. He held it up to the camera.

'This is Sue,' he said. She was pretty: dark, petite, bright eyes. In the photo she looked almost shy; slightly turned away from the camera, a smile on her face. She wore a white blouse and a chain around her neck, a silver heart dangling at her throat. 'Whoever finds this tape, can you tell her something for me? Can you tell her that, although I know I've done some terrible things, and I know I don't deserve forgiveness, I'm just . . .' His voice broke up. 'I'm just so sorry.'

And then he got up, walked to the camera – and everything went black.

Healy didn't move. When I turned to face him, he was still staring at the black screen. After a couple of seconds he stirred, glancing at me, a blur in one of his eyes. Then he looked away.

'We'll find him,' I said.

He didn't reply. Didn't move.

'I promise you – we'll find him.'

CHAPTER 58

Forty minutes later, we were nosing along City Road, heading towards a knot of council houses in King's Cross. In one of them, insulated from the outside world, was the one who'd got away.

Sona was a huge break. A giant rift that should have broken the case the minute she was found. Instead, everything she'd seen, everything she knew, was hidden inside the walls of the safe house in which she was being kept. Her family had watched her disappear, and for a month they'd been waiting for the phone to ring: news that someone had seen her, mentioned her, any scrap, however small. But they'd still be waiting in another month. And they might still be waiting in a year. Because the police weren't going to call them. They were going to squeeze every ounce of recollection out of her in order to get at Dr Glass – and then bury the rest in the ground. It made me sick even thinking about it.

'Her family don't know she's back?'

Healy shook his head. 'No. Just the police.'

'But she didn't just magic herself into police

custody. Someone must have seen her when she came up for air. There must be witnesses. So where are they?'

He glanced sideways at me. 'You been following the news?'

And then it hit me.

I remembered the story I'd seen in passing twice over the past week: once in the café near Newcross Secondary; and once through the windows at the front of Liz's house. *Woman found floating in the Thames.*

'*That* was Sona?'

He nodded.

'But I thought she'd been returned to her family?'

'So does the rest of the world.'

I could feel bile rising in my throat and anger tightening in my muscles. 'It's all a lie?'

'The bit about finding her wasn't. The witnesses aren't either. But everything else is. She didn't ask for anonymity. She didn't ask for anything.'

'So what happened?'

'She washed up in the Thames at seven in the morning. An empty tour boat yanked her out, and one of the tour guides dialled 999. She had mild hypothermia and concussion. Dazed and confused. Didn't say much. Didn't know where she was. No ID, no real idea of where she'd been or what had happened, plus she was pretty messed up.'

'In what way?'

'Bruises. Lots of cuts. Bleeding.'

'What happened after they fished her out?'

'She gets rushed to A&E and the tour guides go off and talk to the media. Next morning, it's playing out in the nationals. That's when Phillips and Hart got wind of it. Luckily for them, half her face was damaged, which made describing her hard. The tour guides told the papers as much as they knew, which wasn't a lot. Next day, the task force leaked a story saying they "believed" she was in her late forties . . .'

Which would have put her out of the age range of any of the women who'd gone missing – including Sona – and dampened any expectation their families might have had. Another hole plugged before it took everything down.

'Couple of days after that, Phillips leaks another story to the media telling them she and her family want to remain anonymous. End of story.'

I looked out into the night, fists clenched, teeth locked together. So many lies, one on top of the other. 'How has everything been contained?'

'What do you mean?'

'I mean, why haven't Professional Standards got wind of this? People talk. You can't tell me everyone on the task force has remained silent.'

'I can – because they have.'

'Nothing has slipped out?'

He shrugged. 'The task forces are small. Trusted. They'll burn the uniform before they give Professional Standards anything to feed on. Cops who investigate other cops are pond life.'

I remembered Phillips's comment to Healy on

the phone earlier: *There's a reason you're not part of this task force, or any other task force for that matter. And it's because you can't be trusted.* 'If it's so water-tight, how do you know so much?'

'After Leanne went missing, one of the guys helped me try to find her. I'd known him a long, long time. He told me some things. I worked the rest out myself.'

I looked at him. In his face I could see the rest: *And I dug around in places I shouldn't, I found out things I wasn't supposed to, and both the task forces know.* That was what Phillips had meant when he said Healy couldn't be trusted. Now the battle wasn't in keeping Healy from telling anyone about what was going on; Healy was too invested in avenging his daughter to be concerned with spilling secrets. The battle was in trying to prevent him from pulling down every pillar they'd raised in their pursuit of Glass and his little black book.

'Does Sona remember why she was in the Thames?'

'No. She hasn't really talked.'

'About what happened?'

'About anything.'

'At all?'

'A little, but not much. He's either totally screwed her up or she genuinely can't remember. Doctors reckon she's got some sort of post-traumatic stress. Maybe mild amnesia too. She needed fourteen stitches in her head.'

'Surely she wants to tell her family she's alive?'

'Phillips, Hart, Davidson, the rest of them – they're playing on her fear. She basically thinks that she can't tell anyone she's alive or Glass will be back for her.'

'This is insane.'

'I told you it would be like this.'

His words from the night before came back to me: *You can come with me, or you can back down. But if you come with me, be prepared for it to get bad.*

'Do we have to worry about her having police protection tonight?'

He shook his head. 'No. We don't maintain a presence there, otherwise it starts to look suspicious. The houses are close together; lots of windows, lots of people. The task force calls her a couple of times a day, and she's got a panic button for emergencies. That's why it's best to go at night. They don't bother her after seven in the evening unless she indicates she's in trouble – and all the neighbours will have their curtains shut, so we won't get any added attention.'

We descended into silence.

Healy turned the radio on, and we both listened to the fallout from a north London derby at the Emirates. About five minutes further on, he hung a right into a short stretch of road with a series of double-storey, grey-brick terraced houses at the far end. They looked like they'd been airlifted in from the Eastern Bloc, then dumped in the centre of the city to decompose. A thin path led through an arch and into a courtyard. There were no doors on the outside of the buildings. The adjacent car park was set in semi-darkness, a solitary street lamp standing sentry, its orange glow flickering on and off. Healy pulled into it and killed the engine.

A second later, my phone started ringing. I'd had it off all day, but had switched it on briefly to check messages as we left Walthamstow. I'd forgotten to turn it back off again. I reached into my pocket and took it out, ready to kill the call.

But it was Jill.

I pressed Answer. 'Hello?'

Silence. A buzz, like interference.

'Jill?'

Then the line went dead. I glanced at Healy. He was looking out of his window to where a group of teenagers had gathered beneath the street light. But he was listening to every word. I tried calling Jill back, but after ten unanswered rings it went to voicemail.

'So what are you going to do?' Healy said, without looking at me.

I flipped my phone shut. 'About what?'

'About her.'

It was obvious he saw this as some kind of weakness in me, as if by expressing mild concern about Jill I'd somehow let my guard down. But I just ignored him, and turned my thoughts back to her. Why call someone if you weren't going to answer? And even if she'd accidentally dialled my number, why not pick up when I rang back?

'We can't afford to waste time.'

'I know that.'

'Where does she live?'

'Acton.'

He rolled his eyes and looked away again, over to where the teenagers had produced a big bottle of cider and a pack of cigarettes. 'Acton's miles away.'

'I *know* that, Healy,' I said sharply.

He made a big show of looking at his watch as if he didn't believe me. I flipped my phone open again and dialled Jill's number, just to piss him off.

The line connected.

I let it ring nine times, then hung up. Next, I dialled directory enquiries and got a landline. They connected me. Again, the line continuously rang for half a minute. But just as I was about to hang up, someone answered.

'Hello?'

'*Jill?*'

'David?'

'Are you okay?'

'Yes, fine. Why?'

'It's just . . . you called me a minute ago and didn't answer.'

A hesitation. 'Did I?'

'I just wanted to make sure you were okay.'

'I'm fine.'

'Are you sure?'

'Yes, I'm good. I just . . .' She faded off.

'Just what?'

'Oh, nothing. I guess I just got spooked again, that's all.'

'About what?'

A pause. 'I don't know. This house, being on my own.'

'What's the matter?'

She didn't reply.

'Jill?'

'It's . . .' She stopped. 'It's just . . .'

'What?'

'I'm sure I just saw someone.'

'What do you mean?'

'The same man from before. The man in the red Ford. The one who was watching my place when you came round that night. I'm sure he keeps passing the house.'

I glanced at Healy. He had turned his head slightly in my direction, shifting closer as he listened to what she was saying. But he made a show of looking at his watch, so he could remind me that our priority was sitting inside a house about five hundred feet away.

'Can you call Aron?'

'No. He's in Paris.'

I remembered him saying he was flying out earlier in the day.

'Okay, listen. I'm going to call a friend of mine and send him around. His name's Ewan Tasker. I'll get him to sit with you until I can get there.'

'Oh, *thank you*, David.'

'Okay. Sit tight.'

I hung up, didn't bother even looking at Healy as he glanced at his watch again, and dialled Tasker's number. He answered on the third ring. I told him what I needed him to do and he agreed immediately to drive around to Jill's. I thanked him, gave him her number just in case, then hung up and got out of the car. Healy looked across at me.

'Well,' I said. 'What are you waiting for?'

CHAPTER 59

The houses in Sona's complex were built into a square, with the front doors facing on to a courtyard. They were two-storey homes, a separate flat on each floor, a stairwell leading to the top-floor flat in each of them. Everything was exactly the same: whitewashed windowsills, blue doors, grey-slate roof.

We moved through the arch and into the courtyard. It was large and overgrown, a huge oak tree spiralling up into the night from the centre. Dull cream street lamps ran in a line, tracing the right angles of the buildings all the way along. Each collection of ten houses had been given a different name: flats 1–20 were Randall; flats 21–40 were Chance. It looked like flats 41–60 were called Wren, but by the time we'd got to numbers 26 and 27, Healy had stopped.

'This is it?'

'Yeah, this is it,' Healy replied, and started moving up the stairwell to the top floor. He looked left and right, and then knocked four times on the door. Paused. Then knocked again. 'Just follow my lead,' he whispered. 'And don't act surprised.'

I frowned at him.

'Just don't act surprised,' he repeated.

A knock on the door, from the inside.

Healy leaned in further, as if he'd been expecting it. 'Charlie, Hotel, Alpha, November, Charlie, Echo. Case number 827-499.'

There was no reply. Healy looked at his watch and back at me, nodding as if this was how things were supposed to go.

'Winter.'

A female voice. So quiet, for a second I wasn't sure if it had come from another house. Healy leaned in again. 'Wintergreen,' he said.

'Spring,' the voice said again.

'Springboard,' Healy replied.

Then everything went quiet again. As we waited, I realized I could hear a TV beyond the door, muffled but audible. Two people were arguing. Healy turned to me, then back to the door. The code confirmed he was part of the task force, even if he wasn't. The responses to her would have been words only known by those intimate to the investigation: the trusted members of the task force Healy had described.

'What do you want?'

Her voice. A little louder now, but still small.

'My name is Detective Sergeant Colm Healy,' he said, adding a softness to his voice that I hadn't heard before. 'I'm part of Operation Gaslight. We haven't met before but I was hoping I might be able to speak to you for a few minutes. We've had some further developments in the case and I'd like to run a couple of things past you.'

I thought I heard something: paper being leafed through.

'You're not one of the names on my list.'

'I know.' He looked at me. There was an expression in his face that suggested this wasn't going according to plan. 'If you come to the window, I will hold up my ID.'

More pages being turned. Then the sound of footsteps. Healy backed away and stepped towards the window, which was adjacent to the door. He held up his warrant card at the glass. The curtain twitched and opened. In the V-shaped gap, we could see a woman, mostly just silhouette, arms on the curtains either side of her. Her eyes moved from the warrant card to Healy, and then to me. The curtain fell back into place. More footsteps.

'Who's he?'

'His name's David Raker. He's a missing persons investigator. He's been trying to trace the whereabouts of Megan Carver.'

'He's not on the list either.'

'Megan Carver was taken by the same man who took you.'

More silence. Even to my ears, even knowing that Healy was basically telling the truth, it sounded suspicious. Two men, neither of whom was on the list of contacts she'd been given by the task force, turning up on her doorstep at ten o'clock at night. Only one with ID. One not even employed by the

Met. If she'd refused to let us in, it wouldn't have been a surprise. Instead there was a noise, like a lock sliding across, and the door opened a fraction on a chain.

In the gap, we could see blonde hair and a sliver of face. An eye. Part of the nose. Some of the cheek. Her eye darted between us and then out into the courtyard.

'Can I see your ID again, please?' she said.

Healy nodded. 'Of course.'

He took out a small black wallet and removed his warrant card, handing it to her through the gap in the door. She took it, disappeared for a moment as she checked it, then gave it back to him. She looked at me. 'And you?'

I got out my wallet, slid out my driver's licence and a business card, and handed it to her. She studied it, then disappeared out of sight. Somewhere in the background I could hear a gentle *tap tap*. About a minute later, she reappeared. Eye flicking between the licence and me. Then, finally, she handed it back and pushed the door closed. The sound of the chain being removed. Healy looked at me once again, this time not saying anything, the same message as earlier etched on his face: *Don't act surprised.*

The door opened.

Framed by the doorway, Sona looked between us. She'd been beautiful. Blonde hair. Blue eyes. A sculpted face that swept through a thin nose and high cheekbones. She was dressed in tracksuit trousers and a vest, her arms exposed. Even as forty approached, she was still slender, the skin on her arms a pale pink, her fingers long and graceful, as unblemished and smooth as a twenty-year-olds. In her file, I remembered reading she was once a catalogue model. It was easy to imagine.

Except, now, imagine was all you could do.

Glass had been halfway through surgery when she'd woken up. Pale blotches covered much of her face, like dye spreading beneath her skin. Both cheeks were entirely bleached. Even whiter lines had formed in the creases in her forehead and in the gentle cleft of her chin, as if something had run across her face and collected there. And it had spread to her neck too, along the ridges of her throat. A scar followed her hairline on the right side of her face, and a second one in the same position on her left. There was bruising too, where the blotches hadn't formed: at the bridge of her nose it was almost black, like the advanced stages of frostbite; and under both eyes purple-blue smears moved down into her cheeks. Her eyes fell on me, chips of blue stone, narrowing slightly as if waiting for me to react to the sight of her. I nodded once, smiled, but didn't break my gaze. She stepped back from the door, glanced at Healy and invited us both in.

Immediately inside was a thin hallway that opened out into a living room, three other rooms leading from it. The first was the kitchen. Plates were piled in the sink, one on top of the other. The next was a bedroom with only a bed and a stand-alone wardrobe. The last was the bathroom. The extractor fan was still on as we came in, condensation on the mirrors and her towel lying in the middle of the floor.

The living room was sparse: two sofas, both of which looked about five years past their sell-by date, and a television on a cardboard box, leads snaking off to a Sky decoder on the floor behind it. There was a small coffee table in the corner. Books were stacked up on it, in two piles: ones that looked as if they'd been read, and ones that looked new. A magazine lay on the floor between one of the sofas and the TV, a crossword puzzle half filled in. There was a laptop as well. It's where the *tap tap* had come from. On the screen I could see she'd done a Google search for my name. The first hit had taken her to the BBC website, where a news report recounted what had happened on my case before Christmas. There was a photo of me leaving a police station, flanked by Liz.

She dropped back on to one of the sofas. Next to her was a remote control. She picked it up and turned off the TV.

We both sat.

'How are you feeling?' Healy asked, smiling again. It was weird seeing him like this. Smiling didn't seem to come easily to him, but he was a convincing Mr Nice Guy.

'Okay,' she said quietly.

She looked between us, waiting for us to react

to her face. When no reaction came, she nodded at a sheet of paper on top of the TV. It was the list of names she'd been referring to. From where I was sitting, it looked like there were only about six. At the top were the words *Operation Gaslight*. At the bottom, in the same handwriting: *These people ONLY.*

'Why aren't you on the list?' she said to Healy.

Healy looked at me, and then back at Sona. He sat forward. 'Okay, truth time. I'm on the task force, but I'm on the outside. Not as far in as I'd like to be.'

A flash of fear in her face.

'It's all right,' he said, holding up a hand. He paused, glanced at me. Another pause, as if unsure whether to commit himself. 'Nine months ago, my daughter was taken – just like you.'

Her expression changed; the embers of the fear fading, replaced by a flicker of surprise. She looked between us but didn't say anything.

'I know the man who took you, took her. I knew it as soon as we got to you. I knew it was the same prick . . .' He stopped. 'Sorry.'

Sona just nodded.

'Anyway, a week ago, David was approached by the family of Megan Carver to look into her disappearance. When that happened – when I found out some of the things he'd discovered – I realized it was time to do something. It was time to find this guy. Because no one else cared about finding my girl. They think she ran away from home

446

because . . .' He paused again, took a sideways glance at me. 'Because we weren't getting on so well as a family.'

I turned to Healy as he was talking, surprised he was being so honest. Maybe he figured Sona had been lied to enough. Everything Markham had fed her. Everything Phillips and Hart were making her believe. Or maybe he saw it as the best way to get her to talk. Problem was, Sona wasn't an ordinary victim, and Healy wasn't an ordinary detective. He was personally invested in her answers, and he needed her much more than she needed him. She was quiet and introspective, driven into her shell by the man who had taken her, and bringing her back out again could take weeks. We had hours.

'So,' he said, picking up the conversation again, 'in order to find him, in order to stop this, I was wondering whether we could go over some of what happened to you.'

He got the reaction I expected: nothing. She looked away, over to the laptop, where the picture of Liz and me still showed.

Healy leaned forward, trying to soften his face. 'Sona?'

'I can't remember,' she said.

He glanced at me. 'Okay.' He readjusted himself, preparing to come at it again. 'Maybe we could start with the man who took you. Daniel Markham. I think you used to call him Mark?'

She flinched a little. But didn't reply.

'Could you tell me about him, do you think?'

Nothing.

'Sona?'

'I can't remember,' she said.

Healy leaned further forward, but this was going nowhere. The secret was to find the chip in her shield that you could slowly open up in order for everything to pour out. Firing a succession of questions at her, or rephrasing the same one, wasn't going to work.

'So, do you remember anything about the day you were taken?' he asked.

She was looking off into space.

'Any detail, however small?'

She shook her head.

'Even if you think it's unimportant?'

Another prolonged silence. Healy paused. Moved in his seat. I could sense he was getting frustrated, but only because we were really short on time. He'd done thousands of interviews. He could pace himself, or he could go in hard and fast, but normally he didn't have to keep an eye on the minute hand. The danger here was that the harder he tried to dig in, the less he'd get out of her, and the more the frustration would build. He shuffled right to the edge of the sofa.

'Sona, we just need to stop this guy.'

She looked down into her lap. We both watched her for a moment, but when she didn't make a move to engage us, Healy glanced at me. I shook my head. *Don't say anything else.* He gave me the look, the one that told me I was overstepping whatever mark he'd made for me in his head. But he was too close to what was happening – he was relying too heavily on her answers – to see why she'd gone back into her shell. In another place, on another case, he may have seen it clearly. But not now.

'You don't have to feel alone,' I said.

She looked up at me. I didn't take my eyes off her, and she didn't take hers off mine. This was the chip in her shield.

'It won't always be like this,' I continued. 'You feel betrayed, I understand that. You feel abandoned, and not just by Daniel Markham – by the police as well. You've been left here, and you've been forgotten about, and all anyone ever seems to want from you are answers.'

Her eyes flicked to Healy, and then back to me. She leaned forward, crossing her arms, almost hugging herself.

'Meanwhile, you can't go to sleep at night without fearing that he's going to come back for you. Because that's what the police have told you.'

Finally I moved closer to her, right to the edge of my seat so that our knees were only inches apart. She glanced down and then back up to me.

'But, Sona, let me tell you something: he doesn't know where you are. He isn't coming back for you. And you're completely and absolutely not alone.'

I moved away from her. She looked at Healy,

and then back to me, but didn't speak. I eyed Healy, telling him not to jump in.

'How do you know he's not coming for me?'

Her voice seemed small after the quiet of what had preceded it. Healy leaned forward again. 'Sorry, I didn't catch that,' he said.

But she was looking at me.

'How do you know he's not coming for me?'

'He doesn't know where you are,' I replied. 'And he's not about to find out.'

She hesitated for a moment, as if the thought of going back would be too painful. Her fingers moved together, sliding around her knee and pulling it into her. An action of protection; subconsciously forming a barrier between us. She glanced off for a second, into the space of the living room. Then her eyes came back to us.

'Okay,' she said quietly. 'I guess we should start with Mark.'

CHAPTER 60

Gradually – very gradually – Sona began to tell us about how she met Markham. She was a receptionist at St John's Hospital, where Markham had worked, and he'd gone up and started talking to her. He told her he hated the name Daniel, and that most people at the hospital just called him Mark. He wouldn't have been trying to conceal his identity – everybody at the youth club already knew his real name – so it was likely that when he told Sona about his name he was, for once, telling her the truth.

He'd probably never looked at her twice before then, even though they'd worked in the same place – but then Glass had discovered her somehow, perhaps after following Markham's movements in and around the hospital, and he'd told Markham to move in on her. Blonde hair, blue eyes. She fitted his twisted fantasy perfectly.

Sona revealed how Markham had been nervous and shy to start with, almost as if he was inexperienced with women. But, in truth, he wasn't shy – he was just being eaten up by the idea of leading another woman into the hands of a psychopath.

'Do you remember the day he attacked you?' Healy asked.

She frowned, looking off, running her hand through her hair.

'Not much of it,' she said quietly. 'He took me for a picnic because it was my birthday. I think maybe he drugged me or something. I started feeling a bit off when we got there. Like a head-ache; a pressure between my eyes.'

'You don't remember where you went?'

Sona shrugged. 'He blindfolded me. But I didn't feel scared. I know it sounds odd him blindfolding me, but it wasn't like that. Or, at least, it never felt like that. He said he wanted to take me some-where as a surprise for my birthday. I trusted him completely. We'd been seeing each other for almost six months.'

Almost six months. That meant Glass had moved Markham on to Sona only days after Megan had been taken.

'What about after the blindfold came off?' Healy asked.

She shook her head. 'No. I mean, I remember snatches of stuff: he laid a blanket out for us, and had brought a picnic basket. And I remember . . .' She paused. A flicker. 'After he attacked me . . . I remember looking up at him, and I remember what he said.'

'What did he say?'

'He said, "I can't do this any more."'

We both nodded, but didn't say anything.

'The next thing I knew, I was waking up in a hole in the ground.'

Sona paused, her eyes fixed off to our right, trying to pull memories out of the darkness. She'd been found three weeks after she'd been taken, and while forensics took urine samples, seventy-two hours was normally the ceiling for IDing anything suspicious. Because of that, the police only speculated on what caused the amnesia. It could have been flunitrazepam, better known as Rohypnol. It would explain the headache and the periods of amnesia. Or it could have been something else. Glass was a surgeon, after all; he would know which drug did what, and how it would protect his plans.

'Going back to the picnic for a second,' Healy said. 'Do you remember anything about your surroundings? It doesn't matter if it seems small or unimportant.'

'Most of it . . . most of it's just a blank.'

'You mentioned a blanket,' I said. 'Were there a lot of trees?'

She looked at me. 'I'm not sure.'

'We think he took you to a place called Hark's Hill Woods. Does that name ring any bells with you? Did Markham ever mention it?'

Silence. Eyes narrowing. Trying to remember.

Finally, she shook her head. 'I'm sorry.'

'It's okay,' I said, holding up a hand. I stopped for a second, to give her time to resettle. 'In your statement, one of the things you did mention was hearing things.'

453

'Yes. Visually, I've got this black wall I can't see past.' She paused. Touched a finger to her face. 'But I can remember *hearing* something.'

'What do you think it was?'

She stopped for a moment.

I leaned forward. 'Sona?'

She looked up at me. 'Nothing I can make any sense out of.'

I looked at Healy and shook my head. *We'll come back to that.* The worst thing we could do was try to force her to remember something. If you tried to force an answer, it either drove them further away or it pressurized them into making something up.

'Can I ask you about him?' I said.

'Mark?'

'No. The man who kept you prisoner.'

She nodded and shifted a little in her seat. I could smell her perfume briefly, and in the bathroom the extractor fan had finally stopped. Complete silence now.

'Did you get a look at him?'

'Never in daylight, but I saw him a couple of times looking down at me from the edge of that hole.'

'What did he look like?'

'Dark hair, dark eyes, kind of . . . ugly, I guess. He had this big forehead, and this horrible smile that looked like it could never . . . I don't know, *form* properly.'

Healy and I glanced at each other. *The Milton Sykes mask.*

'Did he speak to you at all?'

'Yes. But always through this microphone thing. There was always static when he spoke. Feedback. He had a series of speakers hooked up inside the place he kept me, and his voice would always come through those. It was . . .' She paused. 'It was frightening. Why do you think he did that?'

'So he could always communicate,' I said. 'He could talk to you, scare you, tell you whatever he wanted, and he wouldn't even have to be in the same room as you.'

She nodded.

'How did you escape?' Healy asked.

'I woke up,' she said. 'I wasn't meant to. He'd put me under anaesthetic and was . . .' A pause. *Cutting me open.* 'But I woke up.' She peered off behind her for a moment, into the bathroom. 'Some days I look at myself in the mirror and wish I hadn't.'

In the file Healy had given me earlier, it said she had hypopigmentation – a complete loss of skin colour – as a result of a chemical peel that had gone too deep. Phenol and small traces of croton oil had been found in her skin, both of which were used in cosmetic surgery as an exfoliant. Removing the outer layers of skin helped revitalize the face, smoothing out wrinkles in the process. But the peel had burned away too much of Sona's face and gone much too deep, eliminating colouring and freckles. He'd been preparing her skin for treatment for weeks, asking her to apply a liquid moisturizer twice daily. But the end result had gone horribly wrong.

And that bothered me.

Glass may have been a surgeon-for-hire but nothing he'd done so far was amateur. He was meticulous. Exact. Covered his tracks. He would know how far to go when performing a face peel, even if the end results weren't as good as you'd find for five figures at a west London clinic. So why go as deep as he did? And why perform the surgery in the first place? Did he just like cutting women up? Somehow I doubted it. A man like this had a plan. He operated on women because it served some wider purpose.

I watched Sona run a finger across her face, over the bridge of her nose and then along the scar at her hairline. Her nose looked horrific but would recover. The scarring at her ears was a blood red, but would do the same. Her file had called the injuries 'the early stages of rhinoplasty and a rhytidectomy': a nose job and facelift. For the nose job, he'd been cutting from the inside and rasping down the hump. It explained the bruising at the bridge. For the facelift, he'd cut in along her hairline, down past the ear and around the ear lobe to the back. The idea was to separate the skin from the tissue and tighten its appearance. Except he'd never got that far because Sona had woken up. She probably knew how lucky she was. A facelift was the most complicated procedure of them all. Hit a nerve, and the next time you open your eyes it looks like you've had a stroke.

'What happened after you escaped?'

She turned back to me. 'I just ran.'

'Can you describe the place he was keeping you?'

'By that time, my face was . . .' She shook her head. 'It was on fire. And I was scared. I don't think I've ever felt so much pain in my life. One of the doctors at the hospital told me a deep peel like that should be performed under anaesthetic. But I woke up from mine. By the time I found my way out, I didn't feel numb any more. I felt *everything*. I could hardly put one foot in front of the other.'

She looked between us, then took a moment, holding up her hand to apologize. 'All I remember about the place that he kept me was that it looked like a sewer – except there was nothing running through it. It was all dry. Cleaned out. It looked like it might have been adapted somehow, and he'd built a series of rooms inside it, with big glass windows.'

'Rooms?'

'There was a girl in one of them.'

'Did you get a look at her?' Healy asked, shuffling across the sofa towards her.

'No.'

'Was she alive?'

'Yes.'

'Did you see anyone else?'

She shook her head. 'No. No one else.'

Healy leaned back in his seat, his mind ticking over. I picked up the conversation, trying to keep the momentum going. 'So, you were underground?'

'Yes. I escaped through a manhole cover – almost like some kind of service tunnel – into the kitchen of this old house. The walls were all decayed and cracked. Everything was a mess. There was an upstairs, but there was no floor. It was just one big room. The roof had broken too, and there was graffiti on the walls and glass all over the place.'

'Any sign it was lived in at all?'

'No,' she said. 'No way. It had been abandoned a long time ago.'

'Anything else you remember?'

'There were trees overhead – in the space where the roof should have been. They were kind of crawling through the roof and into the house. But apart from that, I don't remember much. I'm sorry, I just got out of there and ran.'

'Ran where?'

'Towards the river.'

'So the house was on the edge of a river?'

'Yes.'

'What did the house look like from the outside?' I asked.

'Concrete. There were trees and vines and stuff all over the roof and the outside walls.'

'What was around it?'

'Not much.' She shook her head, and I could see the emotion was starting to take over. She brushed a finger to her eye. 'I was just running.'

'To the river?'

'Yes. As fast as I could.'

'Anything else close to the river you remember?'

'The river was narrow. Like, *seriously* narrow. More like a canal, I guess. Maybe only six feet across. On the other side there was just a concrete wall: high, with no path in front of it.' She wiped an eye again, but the memories were starting to flow now. 'On my side, there *was* a path, but it was uneven; full of holes and mud. But I didn't take in much after that.'

'Why?'

'He came after me.'

'He chased you?'

'Yes.'

'But he obviously didn't catch you?'

'No.'

'Because you fell into the river?'

She nodded. 'I was barefoot. But that path . . . it was so uneven. So dangerous. I was either going to break my ankle or fall into the water – and I fell into the water.' Sona leaned forward. With her fingers, she parted her hair at the crown of her head. A blood-red line wormed its way across her skull, stitching still visible in it. 'I cracked my head open and must have blacked out for a second before I came to again.'

'What happened then?'

'There was a current in the water. I remember him watching me as the river took me away. He ran after me at first, then when he saw I was going too fast, he stopped. Everything was fuzzy, like I was looking through gauze. I could make out trees and I remember the path finishing after a while, and there just being more concrete and more trees. Oh, and there must have been a slight bend because—' Sona paused and rubbed at the scar on her scalp '—after a while, he disappeared from sight.'

'Anything else?' Healy asked.

Her eyes narrowed, trying to fish for memories.

'It's okay, Sona,' I said, keeping the expectation out of my voice. 'If that's it, if that's all you can remember, that's really good.'

'There was maybe a warehouse,' she continued softly, 'but I just remember the current being really fast, and – as it took me away – the pain starting to seriously kick in. After that, I must have blacked out again.'

'You were found near the Royal Docks, right?'

She nodded. 'They reckon the gown he'd dressed me in blew up and acted as a makeshift buoyancy aid. The current carried me out into the Thames.'

Out from a tributary – which narrowed it down to two possible creeks: Barking or Bow. Both opened out on to the Thames, either side of where she was found. Barking would have made for a simpler investigation: it cut through the city, bisecting Creekmouth and Beckton before roughly following the North Circular through to Ilford. Once it got to Barking itself, it moved in one, relatively straight line north. Bow Creek was different: a two-mile tidal estuary that then fed into the River Lea and became miles and miles and miles of waterways. Her vague description wasn't likely to help: the closer to the Thames you got, the more industry started tracing the path of the water. Eventually *all* it became was the corrugated iron of warehouse walls and brand-new property developments built on the bones of old ones. If the house was abandoned that might help – but the city's river system was a maze. It would take months to walk it all, even if you narrowed down the distance Sona would have travelled given tidal currents.

I turned to Healy. 'Police haven't found the location of the building yet?'

He looked between Sona and me. Shook his head. 'No. They're not close to finding it.' In his face, I could see what he was saying to me: *And that's because this is the most she's talked since she was found.*

When I turned back to Sona, she looked tired. She covered one side of her face with a hand – then her mobile phone started buzzing. It was on the sofa next to her. She looked down at it. 'It's Jamie Hart.'

'You should probably answer it,' I said.

'I don't think that's a good idea,' Healy replied.

I turned to him. 'Why do you think they're calling her? Because they guessed we'd come and find her. They're probably already on their way. It's too late.' I turned back to her. 'It's fine to answer it, Sona.'

She picked up the phone. 'Hello?'

'Sona, it's Jamie Hart.'

We could hear him. She looked back at me. I smiled and nodded for her to continue. 'Hello,' she said quietly.

461

'I just wanted to let you know that we're on our way over.'

I looked at Healy, then back to Sona.

Healy got to his feet and went straight to the window that looked out into the courtyard. Inched the curtains across. Leaned in closer to the glass so he could see along the pathway that led from the main road into the courtyard.

'We're about two minutes out,' Hart said to her.

'Fine.'

'We'll see you in a moment.'

The call ended.

'We need to leave,' Healy said. I glanced at Sona: she was starting to wonder what she'd got herself into now, whether she should have trusted us.

'I just need to ask one more question.'

'*Raker*,' Healy said. 'We need to *go*.'

I held up a hand. 'I know. One question.'

She looked between us.

'You said you couldn't make sense of the things you heard after Markham attacked you, after you blacked out. What did you mean by that?'

Healy was looking at his watch.

She frowned. 'I mean, I heard things. Out-of-place things.'

'Like what?'

Silence.

Then: 'After Mark said "I can't do this any more," everything was black. But . . .' She paused. 'But I swear I could hear something. I swear I could hear whimpering.'

462

CHAPTER 61

As we were jogging down the steps of the house, we saw Hart and Davidson pass the entrance to the complex in an unmarked Ford Focus. They were headed for the car park. 'He'll see my car,' Healy said, panting already.

'He knows we're here,' I said. 'He'll have tracked your phone.'

We darted through the darkened arch linking the courtyard and the road, and then watched as Hart and Davidson emerged from the Focus. They didn't speak, but they were moving with a purpose. They'd picked up our trail faster than I thought.

Hart led the way, Davidson following gingerly. They were an odd pairing; in a different time, they may almost have been comical. It was hard to imagine Davidson ever being slim. Stocky would have been the best he'd been called, but middle age had robbed him of even that. Hart was the polar opposite: gaunt, almost painfully so, like his skeleton was the only part of him. No muscle. No sinew. Just bone.

We backed up and returned to the courtyard. Immediately right, on the opposite side to the safe house, was a long patch of shadow. We moved into it, crouching – and waited. Thirty seconds later they appeared, heading off to their left. We watched them disappear out of view.

And then Healy made a break for it.

I tried to grab him, tried to pull him back, but he was already off, using the darkness as cover. It was a stupid, desperate move. He didn't want to get caught, not now, not by them – but if he'd waited another couple of minutes, we would have been in the clear. I glanced in the direction of Hart and Davidson. Healy had been quiet – but not quiet enough. Gravel scattered. A loose paving slab rocked in its bed. The two detectives came back into view – and saw him.

'Healy!' Davidson shouted.

They both broke into a run, Hart immediately moving faster. I glanced at Healy. His bulk was holding him back. He was built for strength, not pace. He stumbled. Lurched towards one of the walls inside the archway. When he looked back, he could see they were gaining. Could see they'd be on him before he even got to the car. He looked frightened, angry and guilty. Eyes wide. Breath rasping.

He was watching his plan collapse.

I've got to do something.

I stepped out of the darkness, just as Hart was about to pass me. He slowed up, stopping about five feet from where I was standing. Davidson was three or four seconds behind. I held up both hands. 'It's okay.'

Hart glanced at Healy. I looked back over my shoulder and saw him slowing up, then come to a stop. When I turned to Hart again, he was staring at me.

'It's not *okay*, David.'

'Raker?' Healy's voice.

'Take the car and do what you have to do, Healy,' I said, without taking my eyes off Hart. Davidson was alongside him now, but could hardly breathe. He was almost doubled over, hands on hips, his gaze flipping between Healy and me. 'Just do what you have to do.'

Hart's eyes wandered back to Healy, surprise in them.

I looked over my shoulder.

Healy was moving back towards us, his eyes fixed on Hart and Davidson, hands in his pockets. 'Healy, I said take the car and do what you have—'

And then he did something stupid.

He pulled a gun.

It took everyone by surprise. I hadn't glimpsed it on him at all, hadn't even thought to look for one. And yet, in that split second, I wanted to rewind to the moment he'd first picked me up that morning because now it made complete sense. I should have known. Should have seen it. He was a man at the mercy of his demons, a lonely figure hunting with no plan other than revenge. It burned in him. Fed on him. And now he stood facing two of the men he saw as culpable, the weapon out in front of him, his finger drifting across the trigger.

Guns express their owners: they either show your opponent you are in control – or they show him you are completely out of it.

'Back up, Hart,' Healy spat.

Hart took a step back with his hands up in front of him. His eyes drifted between the two of us. 'For fuck's sake, Healy,' Davidson muttered from beside him.

'Healy,' I said gently.

'Shut up.'

'Healy, this isn't the way to—'

'*Shut the fuck up!*' he screamed at me.

Hart nodded at the gun. 'Colm, just calm down.'

'I'm calm,' he said.

'This isn't the way to find Leanne.'

'Which way is the way to find her then?' Healy replied. '*Your* way?' He paused, snorted. 'Phillips already gave me this little talk.'

I watched as Hart raised his hands into the air a bit further. 'I don't know what it feels like to lose a daughter like you have, Colm. I don't. But this isn't the way to do it, I promise you. If you have evidence about the man who took her, then you need to present it in the right way. This . . .' He stopped, looked at the gun. 'This isn't the way to do it.'

Hart glanced at me and I knew what he was saying: *Step up to the plate, David.* He wanted me to stop Healy. He wanted me to grab the gun and put him down. Part of me knew it was the right thing to do. Healy was most of the way down the slippery slope now. Unreliable and dangerous. If it wasn't Hart and Davidson who got in the way, it would be someone else. Sooner or later, someone would get caught in the crossfire.

But I realized, in that moment, I couldn't turn on him.

In a weird way, somewhere deep down, I felt a kinship for him, even as he waved a gun around. He believed he'd been abandoned by the people he worked with, the people he'd spent his life alongside – and I agreed with him. He hated Hart and Davidson and Phillips and all the rest of them because, despite all the cases they'd worked together, all the bodies they'd looked at and the crime scenes they'd stood in, they'd still treated Leanne like just another victim. And some days, he didn't even feel like they'd done that much. By not tying her fully to the other women, they'd just left her as a faceless victim somewhere, anchored to nothing. Part of me understood the sense of injustice he felt because of that. And all of me understood his need to face up to what had happened to the person he'd loved most in the world.

'Colm,' Hart said. 'Just put the gun down and—'

'And *what*?' Healy said, inching towards them, one step at a time. I looked at Hart, who seemed to acknowledge the decision I'd made with another tiny movement of his eyes. 'You're going to find Leanne for me?' Healy continued. 'You're going to admit you were wrong and fit her into your investigation the same as the others? Forget it.

I don't need you now: you, Phillips, your robots back at the station. I've found out more about her in the last day than I found out in nine months working with you.'

'Colm,' Hart said, trying one last time to reel him in.

'Don't call me "Colm". Don't call me anything.'

'We're going to have to come after you.'

'Come after me, don't come after me, it makes no difference to me. But you better be clear on this: I *will* kill the bastard who took my girl. There's not going to be an arrest. There's not going to be an interview. This isn't going to court. There's going to be me putting a bullet in the middle of his face and leaving his body to the fucking flies. And if you want to get in the way, you better make sure your coffin fits, because I *swear* to you: I will kill you too.'

Something moved in the faces of both Hart and Davidson, and we all knew what it was. Healy had just crossed a line, one he didn't have a hope in hell of retreating back across. His career – everything he'd worked for – was over. He was done. An unspoken conversation passed across the space between us, a silent confirmation that this was the end. And then I grabbed Healy's arm and we made a break for the car.

CHAPTER 62

We headed east through empty city streets, rain hammering down, street lights and shopfronts just smudges against the night as Healy carved his way along Commercial Road.

Our homes would be off-limits now. Phillips and Hart had both their task forces on our trails, and they'd have men stationed outside the places we slept. Until this was over – whenever that was, and however it ended – we had to keep ahead of them without being caught. We *had* to find Glass. If we didn't, the next time we saw daylight was going to be when we were doing circuits in a prison yard.

'How much of what Sona told us tonight do the task force already know?'

Healy shrugged. 'Not much. That's the most she's ever talked.'

'She never mentioned anything about the place she was kept?'

'She said that it looked like some sort of sewer tonight. I remember reading that in the statement too. But definitely nothing more. Obviously they know where she ended up, so Phillips and Hart have had teams doing on-foot searches of the rivers.'

'Have they found anything?'

'Do you know how far the water travels north from Bow Creek alone?'

I shook my head.

'Twenty-six miles. All the way up past the M25. She didn't get dragged down from there, obviously, but that's a lot of walking just to be sure.'

'Anything apart from on-foot searches?'

'They pulled blueprints from Thames Water. Checked the network close to both creeks and found nothing matching her description. There are no disused sewers close to any of the water-ways we're talking about.' He looked at me. 'So she wasn't kept in a sewer, if that's what you're thinking. He may have adapted an existing struc-ture, but it wasn't part of the functioning sewer system.'

I nodded and looked out of the window. Rain slid down the glass. Even with the heaters blowing, I could feel the chill of the evening coming off the windows.

'That's good,' I said finally.

'What's good?'

'That no one's figured out where she was taken yet.'

'How the hell is it *good*?'

'Because she was taken from Hark's Hill Woods, and it seems pretty obvious that she was kept there too. Look at all the connections to that place: Glass's obsession with Sykes; the relationship Sykes had with the woods; Sona talking about coming up above ground into that house, and all the trees that were growing around it. Plus, right at the end, she talked about hearing whimpering before Markham attacked her.'

'So?'

'So it was a dog she was hearing. *His* dog.'

'How do you figure that?'

'I went to the Dead Tracks a few days back. While I was there, this mutt emerges from the trees. It's on its last legs. Looks like it's had its fur singed and been badly mistreated.' I paused. It sounded crazy, even though I'd seen it with my own eyes. 'And there was this shaved area on the side of its face where a patch of skin had been grafted on.'

Healy looked at me blankly.

'I think Glass was using it.'

'Using it how?'

'Using it as a lab rat. Seeing if the skin would take.'

'Why?'

'I don't know. But look at what he did to Sona.' I paused, seeing the disbelief in Healy's face. 'You want my best guess? He was planning something big and he didn't want to risk damaging the women.'

He went quiet, and we could both see why: his daughter was one of those women. Rain filled the silence, pounding even harder against the roof of the car, hissing as it exploded against the bodywork.

'So what – we're looking for a messed-up *dog*?'

I shook my head. 'We're looking for the house Sona described. Wherever the house is, the dog is – because that's where Glass is.'

Healy sighed. 'That place is a square mile of nothing but trees. You know how many houses border it?'

'Remember what she said. We're not looking for one that's still being lived in. We're looking for one that's barely standing. A very specific house.'

'Whose?'

I dug around in my pocket and found my notepad. 'Milton Sykes's.'

Healy smirked. 'You're about seventy years late, Raker. They knocked the entire road down during the war and built an industrial estate on top.'

'We're not looking for the house he owned on Forham Avenue,' I said, holding up the pad and placing a finger against one of the entries: *42 Ovlan Road*. 'We're looking for the house he was born in.'

CHAPTER 63

We travelled east down Derry Road, the street I'd parked on before, and turned left at the end, driving between a canyon of abandoned factories and old brick buildings. It looked like an earthquake had passed through it. Either side, roofs had caved in, walls had fallen away and glass lay glinting in overgrown weeds at the base of the buildings.

'This place gives me the creeps,' Healy said.

I studied the buildings, the windows, the doors. So much darkness. In all the time I'd been living and working in London, I'd never seen an area as desolate and abandoned. Healy was right: it was unsettling because it was so out of place.

We turned left again at the end on to what had once been Forham Avenue, the street that eventually lead to Ovlan Road. Except now the whole thing was called Peterson Drive. Nothing remained of the houses that had once occupied the area. The road was bordered by big, metal warehouses on the right and the edges of the woods on the left. The woods were cordoned off by an eight-foot-high wire-mesh fence, broken in parts, but mostly still intact. There were DANGER – KEEP OUT! signs posted along it, every hundred feet or so. At the end, the road opened out into the trading estate I'd seen in the satellite photos.

Healy pulled a U-turn at the entrance to the estate then faced the car back along Peterson Drive. The rain had eased off, but the street lights revealed low-hanging cloud, swollen and dark above us. We both looked at the clock. One-thirty.

'So, where's the house?' Healy said. He leaned forward, eyes on the trees, hands wrapped around the steering wheel. 'In the woods?'

He was half joking. But then he saw my face.

'You think it's *in* the woods?'

'There's no fencing and no warning signs at the south entrance,' I said, nodding at the diamond-shaped DANGER markers. 'Why are there here?'

'Because it's dangerous this side.'

'So maybe the house had a postal address on Ovlan Road, but it wasn't *on* Ovlan Road. Maybe it was inside the boundaries of the woods.'

He shook his head. 'Where the hell did you pluck *that* from?'

'I'm making an assumption here, Healy, okay? Feel free to step in any time you think you might have a better idea.'

Silence settled between us. I'd never met anyone in my life who pissed me off more and had me feeling sorry for him in equal measure.

'The house was all broken,' Healy said quietly. I looked at him and saw what this was: his apology.

'That's what Sona said earlier. The house was all broken.'

I nodded. 'No floors. Trees through the roof, through the windows. Where does that sound like to you?'

Healy glanced at the fencing. 'It sounds like here.'

'It's been a century since Sykes died. About the same since the factories started hitting the buffers. That means at *least* seventy years in which the boundaries of the woods could grow out to this point, uncared for, and untouched. That's enough time for things to disappear. Big things.'

'But they knocked all the houses down after Sykes got the rope.'

'They knocked the houses down along *here*.'

'So, what – they just fenced off the other one and forgot about it?'

'That's what I'm guessing. Back then it was something approaching superstition. These days it's health and safety. The council will want to make sure people don't go in there. A building as old and unstable as that would probably come down in a stiff breeze. People start climbing around, sleeping there, starting fires, it'll end up killing someone. *That's* why they're telling people to keep out.'

'And that's why they put up the wall.'

He meant the concrete wall Sona had described on the other side of the river. I nodded at him. 'I'm betting it was put up the last time this fencing was replaced; to keep out unwanted guests, and as an extra security measure.'

'And on the other side of the wall?'

'Is the river that carried Sona out to the Thames.'

'And on the other side of the river . . .'

'I'm guessing will be the house.'

For a moment there was absolute silence. No distant car noises. No rain falling against the roof. It was as if the woods, and the thought of what lay inside, had sucked every single sound out of the night.

Then my phone started ringing.

It was Ewan Tasker.

'Task. Everything okay at Jill's?'

'I don't know.'

'What do you mean?'

'I mean she isn't there. The house looks like a morgue. No lights on, no answer at the door. I've worn the doorbell out I've rung it so many times.'

'Did you try calling her number?'

'Her mobile's off. The phone in the house just keeps ringing.'

I glanced at Healy. He flicked a look back.

'Did you check for break-ins?'

'Back and front.'

'Nothing?'

'Zero.'

Shit. I looked at Healy again and this time he wasn't even attempting to disguise his interest. He'd shifted in his seat to face me.

'Who was the other guy?' Tasker said.

'What do you mean?'

'The other guy. I'm know I'm old, but I didn't need someone there to hold my hand, Raker. I can babysit with the best of them, I promise you.'

'What are you talking about?'

A confused pause. 'I assumed you sent him.'

'Who?'

'When I turned up at the house, some other guy's already in the back garden. He flashes a warrant card at me. Tells me he'll take care of things.'

'A cop?'

'Yeah. You didn't send him?'

'No. Who was he?'

'I don't know. Didn't tell me his name.' The line drifted. I could hear a car horn in the background. 'Thing is . . .'

'What?'

'I could have sworn to you it looked like he'd just come *out* of the house. Like he'd been inside, taken care of something and then locked up again. He looked shifty. On edge. I let the feeling go, because I thought he was with you.'

Dread thickened and twisted in my chest. 'What did he look like?'

'Medium height, dark hair.'

'Anything else?'

'He had this weird tic.'

'Tic?'

'Kept fiddling with his wedding band.'

And then it hit me like a sledgehammer.

The first time they'd taken me to the station, when Davidson and I had waited in the parking lot as Phillips went to his car to get his mobile phone.

'Was he Scottish?'

'Yeah.'

'Did you see what he was driving?'

'Yeah,' Tasker said. 'A red Ford Mondeo.'

The same car Phillips had.

And the same car that had been watching Jill's house.

CHAPTER 64

We waited for dawn – sleeping in ninety-minute shifts – to help make navigating the woods easier. And at five-thirty, as the clouds started to thin out and the first smudges of daylight stained the sky, we left the car and headed for the fence. About twenty yards down, some of it had begun to rust, the wire mesh dissolving into a flaky brown crust. In the boot of the car, Healy kept a toolbox and had brought a pair of pliers with him. He dropped to his knees at the fence and started to pick away at the mesh, folding it up and creating a hole. After five minutes, he'd created a space big enough for us to get our hands in and peel back.

A minute later, we were inside.

The woods were as thick on the northern edge as they were on the south. Except here there was no path. Between the tree trunks, we could see further in, where a fuzzy grey light had settled in an opening about eighty feet away. I led us across the uneven ground, thick undergrowth against our legs, dew-soaked leaves brushing against our faces. At the opening, the canopy thinned out and the sky was starting to colour.

Healy swatted a low-hanging branch away from his face and stepped in beside me. Ahead it was gloomy: lots of trees trunks side by side, and barely any room to make out what was between them. 'I see what you mean about this place,' he said quietly, and I wasn't sure if he was talking about how thick everything was – or the feeling that pervaded the woods. Just like the first time, the temperature seemed to drop the further in we got, and there was a constant noise in the background: a wind passing through the leaves.

Except, every so often, it sounded like someone speaking.

We carefully moved on in a southerly direction. The foliage was getting thicker and the light was fading, daylight blocked by the canopy and the network of tree trunks and branches. Eventually it got so dense we had to stop and double back. We came around in the same direction but further down, where small arrows of morning light managed to break through from above and angle down.

That was when we hit the wall.

It seemed to appear from nowhere. I'd imagined it being a grey-white colour, laid in the last ten to twenty years. Instead it was almost black, stained with age, mud and moss, and looked at least forty years old. Chunks of it had fallen away. There was a little graffiti, but not much – as if even kids on a dare didn't venture this far in. I placed a hand against it. Dust and a sticky sediment, like sap, clung to the skin of my fingers. I looked up. There were huge fir trees above us and mulched pine cones at our feet.

Crack.

We both turned and looked back in the direction we'd come. Healy glanced at me and then back into the gloom. 'What the hell was that?' he said quietly.

I didn't reply, waiting for it to come again. But it didn't. Instead, a disconcerting hush settled around us, all other noise briefly drifting away, until the only thing I could hear was Healy breathing next to me. *Something* was out of kilter here. I'd been to places where death clung to the walls and the streets and the people left behind. But I'd never been to a place like this. I was no believer in ghosts. But whatever had happened here, whatever lay buried, something of it remained above ground.

Turning, I grabbed the top of the wall and hauled myself up.

At the top, I peered over.

Directly below was the river, just as Sona had described it. Probably slightly more than six feet across, but not much. The current flowed surprisingly fast, sloshing and gurgling as it moved off to the right. On the other side of the water was the rough path she'd fallen into the water from. It looked like it might once have been a wall; maybe a property boundary. Bits of red brick remained embedded in the mud and gravel. Beyond the path, on the other side of the water, huge trees rose out of the earth, like thick fore-arms reaching for the clouds. Then hidden between them, surrounded by nature, was what remained of Ovlan Road. And the house Sona had described.

Four walls. No roof. A dark, empty interior.

Clambering up on to the top of the wall, I waited for Healy to do the same. He was bigger, slower, but seemed to move pretty smoothly. 'Looks like we're going to have to make a leap for it,' I said, turning to him. He didn't seem keen.

I aimed for a patch of grass slightly to the left, and just about hit it. The impact was hard, but not painful. I stood and looked back at Healy. He was sizing it up. A foot either side of the space I'd hit and he'd be landing on brick or stones and breaking an ankle. He glanced at me and then back to the patch he wanted to land on. Then he leapt across the river. As he landed, I heard a hard slapping noise: skin, bones and cartilage impacting against the ground. Mud kicked up, gravel spat away.

'You okay?' I said.

He nodded, moved gingerly. 'I'll survive.'

Now we were closer to the house it looked even bigger and more ominous than before. The opening in its front was a mouth. The windows that remained were eyes. Blackened moss ran from the bricks and was speckled around the entrances, like the house had coughed up its memories. Trees loomed, almost leaning in, as if drawn to the building. And there was a sudden lack of sound again. The river. The rustle of the leaves.

But nothing else.

In my jacket pocket was Healy's torch. I flicked it on and shone it into the darkness of the house. The cone of light swept across the interior. There were two windows upstairs, both long since smashed through, huge branches reaching in from trees lining the rear of the building. Some of the original wooden floors remained, but they'd been chipped and scuffed, broken by falling branches and pieces of masonry. Rubble was scattered everywhere: stone, concrete, wood, tiles.

Further inside it was even colder. And now there was a noise. Very distant, but clearly audible. I turned to Healy. 'You hear that?'

He stepped closer and listened.

A wind passed through the holes in the house, disguising the sound for a moment. Then, as everything settled again, the noise emerged for a second time.

'Something's clicking,' Healy whispered.

Dropping to my haunches, I shone the torchlight towards the centre of the room. Piles of rubble had formed everywhere. To my left was part of the wall that had once divided the kitchen and living room. More rubble. Bricks. Grass coming through a crack in the floor. To my right was what was left of the living room: a fireplace built into the wall; a couple of original floorboards, but mostly just the space beneath them. I got to my feet and walked across to where the floorboards didn't exist any more and shone the torch down. A rat darted across the floor. Lots of dust and debris. Bricks from the walls.

And hidden in the darkness: a manhole cover.

CHAPTER 65

We jumped down into the space below the floorboards. Everything else was decades old, but the manhole looked new. It had been painted black. There was a T-shaped lever built into its middle, sitting in a hollowed-out space. I reached down, wrapped my fingers around the lever and turned it. A squeak. Then it began to move. On the other side the clicking sound continued, neither of us saying anything.

Finally, the lever hit a buffer and there was a gentle clank.

I looked at Healy, nodded, then lifted it out. It was heavy, but relatively easy to move. I shifted it sideways and placed it gently on the floor, among all the debris. Then we turned back to the hole and looked down.

Immediately inside was a speaker, a crackle coming from it like static. Next to that, embedded in the wall, was a small plastic box, about the size of a ten-pound note. There was nothing on it but two LED lights. One red. One green. It was an alarm system. The green light was on, and the clicking was faster now. The light must have changed from red to green the minute I'd removed the manhole cover, and the faster click was the alarm going off somewhere else.

He knows we're coming.

A ladder dropped down into a circle of darkness. I shone the torch into the space. I could see a polished floor below, but not much else. Maybe a cabinet and a door to the right – but the torch was already struggling. The batteries were old, and the beam was starting to fade from using it contin-uously at Markham's house. In fifteen minutes, we'd have a light that couldn't define anything clearly. In twenty minutes, we'd have nothing at all.

I looked at Healy. *Are you okay?* He nodded, but all of a sudden he looked old and ground down. This place; the expectancy of what lay ahead; the confrontations, dead ends and betrayals that had littered his journey: it had all come to a head.

'Healy?' I said softly.

A second's pause, as if he was trying to pull himself out of the funk – and then he did. 'I'm fine,' he replied and, as if to prove it, he shuffled into position at the manhole and started descending the ladder. I put a finger to my lips. *Slowly.* Even as he dropped down through the hole, I could hear the gentle *ching* of his shoes against the metal rungs. When he was about halfway down, I started to wonder if that might not be the point: every surface, every movement, made a sound.

After about ten seconds, all I could see of Healy

was his head. I leaned down and handed him the torch, a fist coming up from the black circle and taking it from me. Then I got into position myself. Below, I could hear him taking the rest of the steps. *Ching ching ching.* Then nothing. He must have reached the bottom. I stopped and peered into the dark. The torch swung left and right, picking out walls, another door and the cabinet I'd glimpsed earlier.

I started down after him. There were thirty-eight rungs in all, and each one felt wet to the touch. Maybe it was dew from Healy's boot. Maybe it was oil. It felt thicker than water, but didn't leave any colour on my skin. Once my feet touched the floor, I wiped my hands on my trousers and looked for Healy. He was off to my right, the torch gripped at shoulder height. He was shining it through a big glass panel in a door in the corner. He tried the door but it was locked. Inside it was mostly dark, but the torch revealed what looked like steel medical storage units, the torch reflecting in their surface as he swung it in all directions. In the centre of the room, drilled into the floor – so dark and so deep we couldn't see the bottom – was a hole.

Healy raised his eyebrows: *That's where he kept Sona.*

Suddenly, a noise exploded around us.

Both of us put our hands to our ears and Healy manoeuvred the torch until he found a second speaker high up on the opposite wall. Then, as quickly as it had started, it stopped. The silence was like a shockwave passing across the room.

Beside me, Healy reached into his jacket and took out his gun.

I followed the circle of light as he moved it around the room. Now he had the torch *and* the gun, and I had nothing. I was completely reliant on him. I didn't like the lack of control, but I liked ceding it to Healy even less. It wasn't that I didn't trust him to watch my back – it was that I didn't trust him to watch his own.

'What *is* this place?' he whispered.

It wasn't part of the sewer network. It wasn't a bomb shelter either – or, at least, wasn't built to house people originally. Which meant it could have been a relic from the factories on the eastern edge: some sort of transportation tunnel. Healy shone the torch towards the manhole again. It looked like a new addition, as if it had been hollowed out and drilled through in order to join the area we were standing in. But everything else looked old. I wondered for a moment how Glass had got equipment down here, and how long it had taken him to do it. And then I thought again about him, how meticulous and patient he was. How, ultimately, the time and logistics wouldn't have mattered. He would have got it done, and – as he'd already proved – he would kill anyone who got in the way.

Healy swung the torch around the room a second time and picked out a thick reinforced door. It looked like a submarine hatch, black and rusting, a hole in the centre where the wheel had once been. It didn't seem to fit the frame, or the frame had been made too big. There were gaps at the bottom and at the right-hand edge, faint light trickling through from the other side. Out of the speaker above it came a constant buzz.

We edged across the room, Healy slightly ahead with the torch and gun up in front of him. His finger was tight in against the trigger. He had the air of a man who'd used one before, and not just in a firing range. Police warrant cards were marked with an endorsement if an officer had the right to carry firearms. Healy's hadn't been. Wherever he'd learned to fire weapons, whatever he'd done with them before, it hadn't been within the boundaries of the law.

At the door, he pulled at the hatch. It stuck, juddered in its frame, then came back at us, squeaking as it swung on its hinges. On the other side was a partially lit corridor, a series of glass panels on the right. The walls were tightly packed red brick and the floors polished concrete. At the end of the corridor, the artificial light stopped and there was a vaguely circular wall of darkness. Above us, wires snaked out of another speaker, static buzzing from it, filling the dead air in the corridor. When we stepped through the hatch, we could see the glass panels were windows.

Just like Sona had described.

There were three of them, looking into three

small rooms, each one about twenty feet square. Everything had been painted white: the brick walls, the ceiling, the concrete floors, the door on the other side. In the first room there was a small table with nothing on it. We edged further along. The second was completely empty.

A noise from up ahead.

Healy shone the torch into the darkness at the end of the corridor. It kinked right at the end, past four unmarked barrels. As we moved forward, towards the third window, the sound of static increased. Healy directed the light upwards. Three feet above us was another speaker, pumping out sound. A constant, unbroken wall of noise like someone had hit a dead TV channel.

We reached the third window.

In the centre of the room was a hospital bed. A white mattress and white bedclothes on top of that, the bedclothes half covering the legs of the woman lying on it. She was semi-conscious and dressed in a pale blue night dress, lying on her side in the foetal position. One of her hands rested on her stomach. After a while, her fingers started moving gently across her midriff, even as she slept. Tracing the roundness of her belly. The swell of her pregnancy. Eventually she shifted position on the mattress, her head tilting in our direction.

It was Megan Carver.

CHAPTER 66

There was no door into the room from the corridor and the glass was a one-way mirror. Reinforced. When I tapped on it, it made almost no sound: just a dull *whup. We need to call the police. We need a medical team.* I took out my phone and flipped it open. There was no signal this far underground. It would only take me a couple of minutes to get up above ground and make the call – but I needed to get to Megan first. I wasn't going to leave her. Not now.

We moved quickly forward, into the gloom of the corridor, torchlight swinging right to left in Healy's hands. When I glanced at him, I could see the desperation building. Sweat was forming on his hairline, even though it was cold in the corridor. His shoulders had tensed. His muscles had hardened. Up ahead, the barrels started to emerge more clearly in the darkness, all four unmarked except for a serial number at their base in Cyrillic. Healy angled the torchlight across them.

Then the torch cut out.

He bashed it against his hand, trying to force new life into the batteries. But they were gone. I got out my phone and flipped it open again. The blue light from the display crawled across the walls and floor, lighting our way for about ten feet. I nodded to his jacket, telling him to remove his mobile. 'One of us needs to move ahead,' I said, keeping my voice low. 'We need to stay six feet apart, then we can light more of the corridor.'

He nodded, discarding the torch on the floor. Then he raised the gun, placed his left hand under the bottom of the grip and put the phone between his teeth. The keypad faced out, the light from the display faintly orange in colour. His face was a mix of nervousness and dread.

We both broke into a jog as we moved around the corner, footsteps echoing, carrying along the corridor like a muffled drumbeat. There were two doors at the end: a heavy one with rivets facing us, and a second submarine-style hatch on the right. When we got to the one on the right, I reached down to the handle. Healy's eyes snapped to a speaker above us and back to me. We both felt it. A chill. A deep sense of unease. Then I gripped the handle tighter and pushed the door the rest of the way.

On the other side was a long, narrow room, running for seventy feet. The stone walls were uneven and the ceiling was low, as little as ten feet in places. It was cold. Under our feet was green linoleum, and above our heads were strip lights. The room was completely empty apart from a hospital bed in the centre. Circling it was a full medical set-up: an ECG, a catheter, an IV tube and saline bag, and electrodes looped around one of the bedposts. There was a metal trolley off to the side, instruments laid out on top: surgeon's scissors, scalpels, a mallet, retractors, forceps. The medical area was absolutely spotless and brightly lit. The rest of the room looked like something from the Middle Ages; a snapshot from the ruins of a medieval castle.

I edged further in and could make out three white doors, partially obscured by the shadows. None of them had handles. Only keyholes. The nearest to me was the one Megan was in. I darted towards it, glancing back over my shoulder at Healy. Except he wasn't there. Back in the corridor, he'd opened the door with the rivets on. In front of him was a wall of solid blackness; a huge dark mouth.

'Healy, wait.'

He just stared at me. He looked dazed, like he suddenly wasn't sure what he was doing. His finger wriggled at the trigger of the gun.

'Don't go in alone.'

His eyes drifted to the black space in front of him and then back to me. He knew I was right. He knew it was better to wait, to go in with support. But he didn't wait. Instead he raised the gun, put the phone between his teeth and stepped through the door. Within a second, he was swallowed up and all that remained was the glow of his phone.

Shit.

I turned back to the room housing Megan. It

was locked. The door moved in its frame when I pressed a hand against it, and had a cheap, hollow kind of feel; like two slabs of wood either side of an empty space.

I retreated a few steps, then glanced back into the darkness Healy had just passed through. I needed to get to him. I needed to back him up. But I needed to get to Megan more. Healy could handle himself. Megan couldn't. She'd been gone six months and now all that separated us was a piece of wood.

I took another step away from the door.

And then I shoulder-charged it.

It cracked away from the frame, swinging full force into the wall. Megan didn't even stir.

'Megan?'

I moved around the bed so I could see her face.

'Megan?'

Nothing. She was heavily sedated, her breathing soft. I put my phone between my teeth, stepped up to the bed and lifted her off. She wasn't heavy, even eight months into her pregnancy. When I brought her in towards me, her head rolled against my chest and I could feel the swell of her belly.

I moved quickly, out into the white room and back into the corridor, pausing for a moment at the door with the rivets. In the darkness, nothing came back. No sound. No light. No movement. I almost called out to Healy, but felt his name stop at my lips as the sound of static rose and fell around me. Deep inside, I knew none of this was right. It was too easy so far. Everything was too easy. But when I looked down at Megan, I let it go, and headed back up the corridor. Past the windows. Through the hatch, to the ladder. Maybe there was an easier way out, maybe there wasn't, but I couldn't afford to take a chance. I had to get her out. I'd have to try and wake her. And then, once she was awake, I had to get her up the ladder to safety.

But the ladder wasn't there.

Looking up, I could see the manhole cover was still open, a circle of blue sky visible, but the ladder had retreated back into the space beneath. It was too far from the floor to reach now. *He raised it.* He hadn't passed us, so the ladder was either remotely operated or he'd been above ground and pulled it up manually from the lip of the hole – which meant there was another exit. It didn't matter now either way. The only option was to go back through the door with the rivets, a thought that filled me with dread. *How the hell am I going to keep her safe when I don't even know what's waiting for me?*

I laid Megan gently down on the floor, pushing her hair away from her face. She felt cool. There was dried blood and snot around her nose, but otherwise she looked okay. A little bigger around the face, but she was carrying most of the baby weight at her front. Looking around, the only light was from the three rooms in the next corridor; everything else was coated in darkness. I needed to wake her before we could find the other exit – because, with her unconscious in my arms, we were both easy targets.

I glanced down at her, trying to figure it out. And this time her eyes were open.

She was looking up at me, wide-eyed, fear etched so clearly and completely in her face, it was like she'd been frozen in ice. She shuffled back across the floor, away from me, her hand covering her stomach, protecting herself and the life she was carrying.

'Megan, it's okay,' I said softly, dropping to my knees.

Her eyes flickered again. She was scared.

'My name's David Raker.' I held up a hand, but stayed where I was. 'Your mum and dad sent me. I'm getting you out of here, okay?'

Her eyes filled with tears.

'But first I need your help. Can you help me, Megan?'

I looked around the room using the light from the phone. Towards the back were a series of six-foot-long metal poles. 'Megan, I'm not going to let anything happen to you. You and your baby are safe. But I need your help. I need to know what you've seen of this place. I need to know how we can get out.'

She didn't say anything.

'Megan?'

Then the static stopped. The silence crashed along the corridor. Five seconds of absolute nothingness. We both looked up to the speaker above the hatch.

And then there was a cry.

'*Noooooooooo! No, no, no, no.*'

Sound suddenly crackled through it, every letter distorting. And my heart sank. It was Healy.

'*You fucking bastard! You fucking piece of shit!*'

He'd found Leanne.

Healy shouted something else, screamed it, but his words were twisted and broken; one long, terrible wail. Then he burst into tears, waves of emotion consuming him. He tried to talk over them. Tried to make sense. But, for a while, nothing came out. Then eventually he just screamed again.

'*Where are you? Where the fuck are you?*'

My heart was beating faster. My mind ticking over. Should I go and find Healy? Should I take Megan with me? Should I take a chance on her staying safe? I could get her to wedge the door shut with the metal poles. But then I'd be hoping I found the surgeon first. It was a risk whatever I decided. Leaving her here would invite him on to her. Take her with me and I didn't know what awaited.

Then I realized something: Healy.

His crying was coming through the speakers, gradually getting louder as if the volume was being turned up.

Or someone was getting closer to him.

'*I'm going to gut him, David.*'

A whisper through the speaker.

Then the feed cut out.

CHAPTER 67

Thirty seconds later we were at the door with the rivets, stepping into the darkness. I'd brought Megan with me, had her hand in mine. I could hear her breathing close to my ear – soft, short, scared – and knew I was taking a risk. But I had to get her and her baby to safety. And I had to get to Healy now too.

We moved inside. I felt a hesitation in her stride and glanced back. She looked terrified. Her eyes widened, glistening in the blue glow from my phone. I squeezed her hand and swung the light around. The room was big. It had ceilings so high the light wouldn't stretch to them. There were no speakers inside this part of the tunnel system, and as we inched further in, the static was replaced by a gentle buzz, like an electrical current. It was freezing cold too. I could feel a breeze at ankle level and chill air against my face and hands.

A breeze. That means an exit.

There was a red-brick wall about fifteen feet to our right, wooden crates stacked up against it. We couldn't see where the room ended on our left. In front of us, a path wound its way through more crates, some broken and empty, some unopened. We must have been going for forty seconds when the buzz got louder. It was definitely an electrical current – and powering something big.

I looked off to the right, the glow of my phone following.

And then it felt like my heart had hit my throat.

Out of the darkness, a series of mannequins appeared, all in a line, all looking straight at us. Some were missing arms. Some legs. All of them were female and completely unclothed, and all were attached to a base by a metal pole.

They were wearing latex masks.

Milton Sykes, over and over and over. Each mask slightly different, a prototype for the next. Adjusted nose. Adjusted cheeks. Bigger chin. Smaller chin. More prominent forehead. Different colouring. Some had torn and didn't hang as well. Some looked completely realistic in the lack of light, only the dummy beneath giving it away. Megan went to scream and then squeezed a hand against her mouth, her breath whistling out of her nose in short bursts.

A noise from our left.

I swivelled and lifted up my phone. The blue light from it dropped off about twenty feet away. I could see the polished concrete floor fade off into the darkness, and some sort of base unit on the edge of the phone's glow. It looked like a plinth. I took a couple of steps forward, pulling Megan along behind me, and the blue light extended across the structure. Another step. Another. It was definitely a plinth.

Then I realized what was lying on top.

A coffin.

It was completely transparent. Reinforced plastic. Every surface, every angle, shone in the light from the phone. Inside it, at the bottom, I could see two blocks – but then realized they weren't blocks. They were feet. I moved the phone up the side of the coffin: feet, legs, hands, arms. It was a woman. Her head was turned to the right, facing out at us, her hair hovering around her face in snaking strands of blonde. She was naked and floating in formalin.

'Fucking hell,' I said quietly, stepping up to the coffin and looking down through the top. Her skin had bleached white, but otherwise she could have been drifting beneath the surface of the waves. Apart from her hair, she was completely still, her body hardened, arms out to either side, legs together, eyes open. She'd been operated on before she died: there was a scar along the side of her face, running past her ear and around to the back. A facelift. The stitches were still in place, but they didn't run all the way down. Level with the top of the ear lobe they stopped, as if the surgeon had abandoned the procedure. Flesh was visible where the stitches didn't continue.

I recognized her as Isabelle Connors.

The first woman to go missing two years before.

I glanced back at Megan. There were tears

running down her face as she looked at the woman in the coffin. I brought her into me, partly to shield her from the sight of the woman looking out, and partly to quieten the sobs she was making.

We moved on.

Out of the dark emerged more shapes, defined and frozen in the glow from the phone. More coffins. More women. All blonde, all posed exactly the same as they lay submerged. When I moved to the next, I could see she'd had the same surgery, except her chin had been cut open too, a piece of silicone visible where the stitches hadn't been closed properly. April Brunel. The second woman to be taken. The coffins were in order.

Then behind me, another noise.

A dull clunk.

I waited for it to repeat, but there was nothing. Just a buzz. I knew then I was right: it was a generator.

The lights came on.

For a second I was disorientated. Then I realized why: the light was purple. Above us, a series of strip lights ran the length of the room, a dull glow travelling along them. It created a watery effect, as if the room's colouring had been turned up a notch on the dial. Every shape in the room suddenly emerged, without being fully defined.

The room wasn't anywhere near as big as it had seemed in the dark, but the ceiling was high – maybe sixty feet – and a half-oval shape, like the mid-section of a railway tunnel. There were crates all over the place, but congregated mostly on my left. Coffins in a row to my right. A big archway behind them, leading into a room full of more mannequins, standing like an army.

On the other side of the room, in the far corner, was a whitewashed wall with photos of the missing women in two rows. Four on the top. Five, including Jill, on the bottom. Each of the women had dotted lines marked on their faces. Surgical marks. Around the pictures was a network of other documents: newspaper cuttings, anatomical drawings, cross-sections of faces, blueprints of buildings. Other photographs. Markham. Frank White. Jamie Hart. Charlie Bryant. My house. My kitchen. My living room. Liz and me standing on the front porch of her house.

Then the lights went out again.

Complete darkness.

Megan moved in even closer to me, her face pressed against my chest, her eyes still closed. I could feel her crying, the movement of her jaw, the soft sound as she tried to dampen the noise. I pressed a hand flat to her head and kept her close, then started inching forward.

Six feet ahead, there was a dull orange glow on the floor.

Healy's phone.

On the very edge of the light, I could see a hand, the gun about a foot from it. As we took another step forward, Healy emerged, lying face down, trails of blood running from his head. Next to him, its muzzle at his chest, was the dog. The patch of skin on its face looked infected. It darted a look at us, eyes turning to pinpricks of light, and then turned and headed off in the other direction.

If the dog is inside here, the exit must be too.

I squeezed Megan to let her know we were going to move again, and then edged forward. When I got to Healy, he was making quiet noises, like air escaping from a balloon. He was still alive – but only just. His blood was smeared across the floor and over the coffin next to him.

The sixth one.

Leanne.

She was looking up through the lid with wide eyes, her skin the colour of snow. In that moment, it was like every ounce of Healy's vengeance had transferred to me. I felt his pain. His burning rage. His need to hit out.

'*Uhhhhhhh . . .*'

As Healy groaned, the generator clunked and purple light erupted right above us again. In my peripheral vision, something moved. A blur, darting right to left. Feet slapping against the floor. *He's trying to confuse me.* I squeezed Megan tighter, looking down at her.

And that was when I saw my hands.

They were fluorescent orange, my fingers, my palms, my wrists, glowing. It was all over the sleeve of my jacket as well. I checked my body and there were marks on my trousers and shoes. Megan's shoulders and her vest were glowing too, where I'd had my arms around her.

I glanced at Healy.

Exactly the same: hands, arms, legs, clothes, shoes, everything illuminated. And suddenly I realized – too late – what was happening. The residue I'd felt on the way down the ladder wasn't dew or oil. The bulbs above me were ultraviolet black light. Virtually no light and no visible effect – until they reacted with fluorescent paint.

And I was covered in it.

'Hello, David.'

I turned. He was standing behind me, all in black, glass shard on a chain at his throat, surgical mask over his mouth and nose. His eyes flared, widening as if trying to draw me in.

'You're easier to see when you're lit up like a Christmas tree.'

And then he stabbed me with a surgeon's knife.

CHAPTER 68

In a split second I pushed Megan to the side and brought my arm up. The knife went into the flesh just above my elbow. The blade wasn't more than two inches, but I felt the pain instantly. It shot up my arm and exploded out across my chest.

I heard footsteps as Megan ran off into the darkness, and I felt a second of relief that she'd got herself away. Glass followed the noise too. By the time he'd realized his mistake, I was on him: one punch to the face; one to the side of the head; one to the chest, next to the heart. We crashed to the floor. The knife pinged off the ground and spun away. He was dazed, but still fighting: hands came up to my throat, surgical gloves clawed at my face, fingers grabbed at my nose and eyes.

I pushed him away and hit him again. All my anger and revulsion channelled into the punch. Something cracked. In the darkness, both of us semi-lit by Healy's phone, his eyes rolled up into his head and I realized I'd broken his nose. Blood slowly soaked through from the inside of the mask.

He lay still. Eyes closed.

Getting up, I searched for Megan in the dull

glow of the black lights. 'Megan?' Silence. I moved towards the shadows at the back of the room, feeling the breeze. 'Megan? It's okay, honey. Everything's okay. I just need to know you're safe.'

Suddenly, everything descended into darkness again and I heard footsteps. I spun on my heel, preparing for Glass's approach – but it didn't arrive. Instead the footsteps circled me. I heard crates tumble and something fall to the floor with a clang. And then a rectangle of creamy light burst open in the space beyond the coffins.

A door.

Glass looked back at me – and then disappeared inside.

I sprinted after him. The corridor looked like it had been some kind of service tunnel. The walls were crumbling, the cement turning to dust. At the end was a stairwell, zigzagging upwards and out of sight. Glass glanced back again from the steps, then started moving up to the surface.

The stairs rose for about thirty feet. At the top, a door had been sealed with a welding torch and a series of boards. To one side, there was daylight coming through a disused air vent. Glass dived inside the vent, clattering against the metal. As I got to the landing area, I headed after him. The vent opened up in a straight line for about forty feet, before angling upwards. When Glass reached the end, he hauled himself up. Feet dangling. Then he was gone. I slowed down five feet from the end and looked up.

Above me, the same LED light alarm system

was in place. The covering for the vent – sitting half over the hole – was a piece of wire mesh. I could see a thick canopy of trees and snatches of blue sky. He wasn't at the lip of the hole. But it didn't mean he wasn't close. If he'd picked up Healy's gun, he would have fired it already. But he might have had another knife – and I wasn't about to fight him from below.

Slowly, quietly, I manoeuvred into position.

Then I gripped the edges at the top of the hole and pulled myself up. The air vent opened into a small brick building with a concrete floor. No roof; trees overhead.

Behind me, stacked against one of the remaining walls were a series of railway sleepers, cobwebs clinging to them. The railway line that had never been laid.

The Dead Tracks.

I searched for a weapon and found a rusting shovel propped against the sleepers, then quickly circled the building. To my left there was a vague path through long grass; to my right, a path that continued for sixty feet before hitting impenetrable woodland.

I headed left.

The canopy was thick and the path quickly became mud and stones. Further along was a length of railway track, cutting across the trail, from one side to the other. I carried on, looking over my shoulder the whole time, the shovel up and primed. Moments later, a wind passed through the woods, the leaves in the trees whispering. A few seconds later it came again, and this time it clearly sounded like a voice. Or maybe I was spooked. I wasn't sure now. I looked around, feeling like someone was watching me.

On my right, I noticed the grass had stopped growing. It had been flattened, ripped away in places. And in the spaces that remained were a series of white posts, spaced equally apart, each one numbered.

An odd sensation shivered through me.

And then I realized why: *he's behind you.*

I turned. His eyes widened above the bloodied mask as he raised the knife at his side. I ducked away from him – but too late. The blade came fast and pierced the skin at the top of my shoulder. I sucked in the pain and rolled away, keeping my grip tight on the shovel.

He came at me a second time, stabbing the knife towards my throat then cutting across in one swift motion. I stepped back but he was keeping me closed up, forcing my arms in against my body as protection, not allowing me to open up an arc for the shovel. The third time he got me in the folds of my top. I heard the tear of fabric, felt the tip of the knife blade come all the way through to my skin. But then, as he was drawing away, I swept the shovel in a half-circle. It thudded against the top of his arm and he slipped on the wet ground, falling to his side. As I went for him again, he raised a forearm, and the shovel clanged against the bone. He screamed out in pain, the noise echoing out through the Dead Tracks. I went again, catching him in the small of his back, and he thumped against the turf like a sack of cement.

Still.

As I edged closer, shovel up, I could see the posts more clearly. There were thirteen of them, all recently driven into the earth. Each one stationed about five feet apart. I stopped, eyes moving from one post to the next, a sickening realization forming. *This is it.* A wind came through the trees towards me. Brief and violent, like the last breath of the thirteen women Milton Sykes had killed a century before.

This is Sykes's burial ground.

Glass had found it. Nurtured it.

I stepped up behind him. The water from the grass had soaked through his medical scrubs. The mask had been pushed up to the top of his head. Long grass covered his features. 'Roll over,' I said to him, teeth gritted. He didn't react. I prodded him with the blade of the shovel. 'Roll over, you piece of shit.'

Nothing.

Forcing the shovel in under him, I flipped his body over. He rolled on to his back. Eyes closed. And suddenly he became someone else.

Someone I knew.

Aron Crane.

But it wasn't the Aron I remembered from the support group. The man who'd sat next to Jill. Even unconscious, he was different: darker and more dangerous. He wasn't the man who'd been concerned about Jill. The man I'd thought I'd bumped into by accident the day before. He wasn't anyone I remembered.

'Aron?'

He moved fast, grabbing my ankle, trying to turn it, trying to twist it the wrong way to force me to the ground. Teeth clenched. Eyes flashing. Adrenalin surging through his system as he saw a last chance to turn the tables. He forced me into a half-turn away from him and was on his feet within a second, grabbing me by the neck and pushing me to the ground. Suddenly I was beneath him, his body on mine, his hands tightening at my throat. As he closed off my air, I started to lose the sensation in my hands: my fingers numbed, my palms, my wrists.

But then his grip loosened.

Not much, but enough.

Nerves fired in my hands. Prickles of sensation drifted into my fingers. And I could feel the shovel again. The wood. The iron. The *weight*.

I gripped it as hard as I could and launched it off the ground towards him. The blade was side-on, the thin width of it leading first. It cracked against his skull, behind his ear, and his fingers sprang from my throat immediately; a bear trap flipping open. His eyes rolled up into his head. He wobbled. Then he slumped sideways and hit the wet ground about an inch from the thirteenth grave.

Above me, the gentle patter of rain started, popping against the canopy, coming down in a fine spray against my face.

Otherwise, the Dead Tracks was silent.

PART V

CHAPTER 69

Police arrived on the northern edge of the woods ten minutes after I called them. I'd dragged Crane's body back to the storage building and tied him up, then found Megan and brought her back up to the surface. We huddled together, away from him, under what remained of the roof. By the time Jamie Hart's head popped up from the air vent, his body covered in a white crime-scene boiler suit, Crane was awake but drowsy. Blood ran from his face, mixing with the rainwater pelting down through the open roof. Hart came over, a uniformed officer flanking him, and told Megan that they were going to take her somewhere safe. She looked at me for some kind of assurance, and when I told her that everything was going to be okay, she whispered a thank you and they led her off and out of sight. A minute after that, I was in handcuffs.

Three hours later, Hart and Davidson were facing me in an interview room. I was tired. I'd barely slept in over thirty hours, and I could feel every minute of it. They'd already taken away what I was wearing as evidence and sent a uniformed officer back to my house to pick up a spare set of clothes. But new clothes and machine coffee didn't help. What my body wanted most was to shut down and recharge.

'How's Healy?' I asked.

Hart had been filling out some paperwork, but he looked up at the mention of the name. He set his pen down, bony fingers tapping out a rhythm on the table. 'Your partner in crime,' he said quietly.

'Is he alive?'

Neither of them said anything for a moment.

Then Hart started to nod. 'Yes, he's alive – but he's in surgery. When he wakes up, he'll probably wish those knife wounds had been a couple of inches to the left.'

A knock on the door.

They both looked up as a uniformed officer let Liz in. She was dressed in a black trouser suit with a cream blouse, her hair against her shoulders. She looked fantastic. She'd come straight from the office: in one hand was a briefcase; in the other a laptop bag. I was pleased to see her – and not just because she was my lawyer.

She looked at me but didn't smile. 'You okay?'

I nodded.

She turned to Hart and Davidson. 'I sincerely hope the tape isn't running.'

Hart shook his head. 'No, we haven't start—'

'Good. Because I want some time to talk to my

client. And that means not here, and not with you two taking notes.' She glanced over her shoulder. 'Is there somewhere my client and I can go where we will have some privacy?'

I could see Davidson twitch. He preferred me the first time they'd brought me in: on my own and lawyer-free. Hart smiled – trying to play the game – but it was wasted on Liz. She just stared at him, and both Hart and Davidson realized in about three seconds that she was the real deal. Hart, a little resigned, leaned back in his chair and then turned to the uniformed officer. 'PC Wright, please show Ms Feeny and Mr Raker to Room C.' He glanced at Liz. 'Just let me know when you're ready.'

She nodded once, then led me out.

I spent an hour going over the case with her. Every detail I could remember. She didn't say much, which only added to the atmosphere between us. I'd never seen her like this. She just typed everything into her laptop, asking me a couple of times to spell names or go back over certain events. This wasn't the Liz I thought I knew.

When we were done she leaned back in her seat and studied me. 'You're in a lot of trouble here.'

I nodded. 'I know.'

'Where's this Healy guy?'

'In a hospital.'

'Is he dead?'

'No.'

She placed her hands on the table. 'Have you got anything to barter with?'

'Maybe.'

'What?'

I told her about the women, how they'd been linked by the task forces – and how the police had kept all the information buried.

'Bloody hell,' she said when I was finished. Her dark eyes were fixed on me, her mind turning things over. She read a couple of lines of whatever she'd written on her laptop, then looked at me again. 'Can I ask you something?'

'Of course.'

She paused. A finger moved to the laptop's screen. 'Why do you do this?'

I frowned. 'It's my job.'

'No, I don't mean that. I mean . . .' She stopped for a second time and pulled her hair away from her face. 'I understand it's your job to find people. I understand that.'

She looked at me, her eyes focused, but didn't say anything. I smiled at her, and she smiled back – but not in the way she normally did.

'What's the matter, Liz?'

Her eyes flicked back to her laptop.

'Liz?'

Finally she looked up. 'You remember the last time we were in a room like this?'

'Sure.'

'Last year, on that case up north. You remember that?'

I held up my hand and showed her my nails. 'I've got the scars here to remind me,' I said, smiling, trying to cut through whatever it was that had settled between us.

'After we were done with that, I thought about what you did, about how far you were prepared to go to finish what you started on that case.' She glanced at me. 'I know you weren't completely honest with me about what went on. I know that. But that's fine. You gave me enough to work with, and we got you off, and that was all that mattered. I kind of filed it away as something that we might need to revisit later on down the line, if anything ever . . . happened between us.'

She traced a finger along her bottom lip.

'But even if you never *did* tell me what happened there, it wouldn't really bother me if it was just a one-off.' She faced me. 'But it's not going to be a one-off.'

'Liz, it's my job. This is what I do. I don't . . .' It was my turn to pause this time. I reached across the desk and took her hand. She pulled it away. 'I find people.'

'You find *screwed-up* people, David. You put yourself on the line, your *body* on the line, and you hope, somehow, you're going to come out the other side still breathing. And I don't care about the lies and the details you leave out. What I care about is *why* you do it.' She stopped and looked at me for a long time. 'Why do you do it?'

'I have other cases.'

'*Do* you?'

'Of course I do.'

'How many since that last one?'

'Four.'

'In ten months?'

'That last one . . .' I looked down at my finger-nails. 'It took a lot out of me. I needed time to recover. But cases like that, cases like this . . .' I smiled. 'They're unusual.'

'But you still take them on.'

'I can't predict how they're going to turn out. If I could do that I wouldn't be finding missing people, I'd be doing the Lottery every week.'

'Yeah, but most people would turn around and walk away when things started going south,' she said. 'Do you think anyone else would have teamed up with Healy, stuck two fingers up at the police and headed right into the lair of a psychopath like Glass?'

'He needed to be stopped.'

'By the police.'

I reached for her, and this time didn't let her wriggle away. 'Sometimes you need to do things because they're right – even if they're not *legally* right.'

She had her head down, facing the table, hair spilling past her ears. I squeezed her hands, trying to get her to look at me. But she didn't. She stayed still. Silent.

'Liz?'

Then she looked up. 'I can't compete with her.'

518

I frowned. 'What are you talking about?'

'Derryn. I can't compete with her, David.'

'What? You don't *have* to compete with—'

'You don't have that mechanism that tells you when enough is enough. You don't know when to stop. You're trying to plug holes in the world because you know what it's like to lose someone, and you think it's your job to stop anyone else suffering the same way. You're doing this for *her*, David. That case up north was for her. And this one is too. You're plugging the hole she left behind by taking on other people's pain. And I can't compete with that.'

I let go of her hands. She looked at me, a tear breaking free, a watery streak of mascara following in its wake. I stared back, unable to articulate. Unable to come back with any argument.

Because I knew, deep down, she might be right.

CHAPTER 70

The interview took two and a half hours. Liz sat beside me the whole time, stopping me if she felt I needed to be redirected away from something harmful. Hart and Davidson came at me hard, like attack dogs, trying to catch me out, trying to lead me into blind alleys and one-way streets. They both played on my relationship with Healy. They tried to make it sound stronger and more purposeful than it was. They used the moment outside the safe house when Healy had pulled a gun to underline their case, Hart making mention of how I'd done nothing to dissuade Healy.

'I told him to put the gun away.'

'Once,' Hart said. 'Half-heartedly. The second time, when you saw what I was telling you to do, you ignored me. Then you ran off into the sunset with him.'

'I felt—'

'You felt a kinship for him, David.'

'No.'

'You believed what he was doing was right.'

'No.' I sighed.

'Then why did you do it?'

I paused, glanced at Liz and then back to them. 'I felt his actions were wrong – but his reasons were right.'

Davidson snorted. 'How do you figure that?'

'I think he was frustrated.'

'With who?'

'With you.'

Silence descended. It was hot in the room, and the only sound now was the whirr of an air-conditioning unit.

'Look at it from his point of view,' I continued. 'You brushed his daughter's disappearance under the carpet with the other seven, but you didn't even have the decency to link her to Glass.'

A tremor passed across the room.

Davidson whitened. Hart crossed his arms and leaned back in his chair. 'What are you talking about, David?'

'You know what I'm talking about.'

No reply. They didn't want anything committed to tape. In their faces, I could see they were trying to figure it out. How I knew. Whether Healy had told me. How he'd found out so much. I had them by the balls and there was no backing out now.

'I get it,' I said. 'Deny all knowledge, maintain the silence. Trouble is, your circle of trust has been breached. You're not the only people who know what *really* happened any more. The rest of the world might think it's a one-in-a-million chance that we stumbled across seven women in that place, but all of us here know different.'

Davidson looked away. Hart maintained eye contact, but his hand was hovering close to the tape recorder, desperate for this to end. I nodded for him to push the button.

He stopped the tape.

Liz leaned forward. 'Okay,' she said. 'Here's the deal: David walks out of here, without charge. You leave him alone. You don't come back for him. Anything to do with his part in this investigation is over. In return, he maintains a dignified silence.'

They looked between us.

Finally, Hart nodded. 'Let me make some calls.'

They left me alone in the interview room with a cup of coffee and a bland ham and cheese sandwich. Liz disappeared to call the office and see what she'd missed out on. She smiled as she left – touching my arm and telling me I'd done brilliantly – but she didn't mention anything we'd talked about earlier. I was too tired, too drained, to figure out if the fissure that had opened between us could ever be pushed back together again. But I was glad, at least, to have got some kind of reaction out of her.

There was no clock in the interview room, but it felt like about fifteen minutes had passed when the door opened again. I turned, expecting to see Liz.

But it was Phillips.

He looked at me, closed the door behind him and walked around to the other side of the table.

I felt like grabbing him by the collar and smashing his face through the wall.

'How are you, David?' he asked, sitting down.

I smirked. 'Oh, just *great.*'

'Can I get you anything else?'

'Yeah,' I said, pushing the coffee cup across the table. 'Another one of those – and an explanation of what the hell you were doing at Jill's.'

He nodded as if he'd expected that straight off the bat. 'She called me.'

'Why would she do that?'

'Because Frank and I went way back. We came up through the ranks together and then I basically got him the job here at the Met. I've known Jill for years.'

'So, what – you just hang around outside her house?'

'She left a weird message on my phone. She didn't say anything – it was just ten seconds of silence – but when I called her back she didn't answer.'

And then it all shifted into focus: the night before, she phoned and didn't answer, and then she'd been odd when I'd called her on the landline. *Because Crane had come for her at home.* The first one had been a distress call. She must have made the same call to Phillips as well. But Crane had found out – and the next time I rang her, Crane had made her tell me everything was fine. Probably with a knife at her throat.

'I didn't like it,' Phillips continued. 'So I went

round there . . .' He glanced behind him, even though the door was closed. 'And I managed to get into her house.' *Just like Ewan Tasker had suspected.* 'But she wasn't there. She was gone.'

I looked at him. 'She called me in a panic one night and said she thought someone had been watching her place. It was you. She saw your car.'

'It was me. It was my car.' He paused. A long-drawn-out breath. 'Frank and I had a kind of . . . arrangement. A promise we made.'

'You'd look out for each other.'

'Right. If either of us . . .' He stopped briefly. 'Look, when I made that promise to Frank, when we made that promise to each other, it was one I never believed I'd have to see through. But now I do. So from time to time, I check in on Jill. I went past her place a couple of times on the way to the station yesterday evening. That night you're talking about, when you went round, I guess I didn't hide well enough. It had been a long day.'

I didn't say anything. Just stared at him.

'You're pissed off,' he said. 'I get it.'

'*Do* you?'

He nodded, trying to defuse the situation. 'Believe it or not, I do.'

'So where's Jill?'

'We don't know.'

'She wasn't in his place in the woods?'

'No. Seven dead women were recovered from there – none of them her.'

'Seven?'

'We found Susan Markham's body in a wall cavity.'

She hadn't been placed with the others. No coffin. No formalin. Which meant he obviously didn't see her as part of his plan. She was just bait to reel Markham in. The other women – even Leanne – were something else. All blonde. All blue-eyed.

All worth keeping.

'Anyway,' Phillips said. 'Jill wasn't there. We tore that place apart.'

'She's not back home?'

'Hasn't been back. Hasn't been anywhere as far as we can tell. Not home, not to work, not with her family.'

Crane knows where she is. 'He won't tell you?'

'He's not said a word. But we found photos of her in his hideout. Pictures of her, her house, her friends. You were in some of them.' His fingers drifted to his wedding band and he leaned back in his chair. 'He took her, I think we both know that.' Finally his eyes moved back to mine. 'Look, David . . .'

I knew what was coming, and I wasn't about to make it easy for him.

'I know you could use what you know against us.'

'You're damn right I could. What you did with those women . . .' He didn't say anything, just looked at me. I felt the anger prickle beneath my skin as I watched him, waiting for him to justify what he'd done. 'It was wrong.'

525

'Agreed.'

'But you did it anyway?'

'By keeping Glass unaware we were on to him, we were within touching distance of the Russians. That doesn't make it right. That doesn't erase those women. But now we have *everything*: murders, drugs, prostitution, people-trafficking, gunrunning, money-laundering. Was it a sacrifice worth making?' He shrugged. 'It depends where you're standing.'

'You had a legal *and* moral obligation to tell their families.'

'Try standing next to the body of a ten-year-old prostitute who has had every hole in her body ripped to shreds. Or at the back of a van that's just brought seventeen women and kids into the country, all of whom have suffocated to death because the van has no ventilation. Or next to the imported guns or the shitty drugs that are killing people, day after day. Things aren't so clear.'

'They look clear.'

He leaned forward. 'Seven women, or seven ten-year-olds?'

'It's not about choosing – it's about doing it all.'

Phillips smiled. 'You're an idealist.'

'Maybe so. But you were wrong.'

Phillips started turning his wedding band again. Then he glanced at his watch. 'We haven't got time for this. We need to find Jill.'

'So find her.'

He eyed me again but didn't speak.

What's going on here?

'Hart tells me we should cut a deal with you,' he said eventually, 'and, given what you know, I think he's right. But what about your new friend Healy?'

'What about him?'

'You willing to help him?'

'Help him how?'

'He's going down, David. Once he's well enough to walk out of that hospital, it'll be in a set of cuffs. Then he'll be up in front of a judge. Then he'll be behind bars. You know what they do to bent coppers on the inside?'

'So?'

'So, we're willing to go easy on Healy in return for a favour.'

'Which is?'

Phillips paused. 'We need you to interview Aron Crane.'

CHAPTER 71

Phillips led Liz and me to a small room with a metal shelf full of electronic equipment and a huge one-way mirror. Through it, I could see Aron Crane seated in the interview room, alone, handcuffed to a metal arch welded into the table. He was staring at the wall, his nose broken and bruises dotted down the side of his face where I'd connected with the shovel. If nothing else, it made me feel good to have hurt him.

Next to the audio equipment an officer sat at a computer, headphones on, a live colour CCTV image on-screen. Also inside the room were Jamie Hart and a uniformed superintendent. I recognized him from the last time I'd been brought in for questioning. He stood and came across to meet us. Shook hands with Liz, but not with me. He introduced himself as Ian Bartholomew. The top cop at the station. He thanked me through gritted teeth for my co-operation, but didn't seem keen on the idea of turning a blind eye to what had happened with Healy and me. It was obviously Hart and Phillips who had persuaded him to go this route. After Bartholomew was done, he seated himself at the back of the room and nodded at Phillips.

'He's only spoken for about a minute since we brought him in,' Phillips said.

The door to the room opened up and a uniformed officer brought a trayful of shop-bought coffees in. I didn't have to put up with machine effluent now they needed my help. I took one, peeled the lid off it and watched Crane. He was absolutely still.

'Play it,' Phillips said to the man at the computer.

The officer clicked a couple of options on the screen, and seconds later a square of CCTV footage appeared. Phillips and Hart in the interview room with Crane.

'You can't stay silent all day,' Hart said.

Crane was looking down. He glanced at Hart, held his eye for a moment and then turned his attention back to the surface of the table. In the corner of the screen was a counter. 01:57:43. One hour, fifty-seven minutes into the interview and he hadn't spoken once.

'You can contact a lawyer any time you want,' Hart added. 'It's your legal right to do that.' Nothing. No response. 'Come on, Aron – where's Jill White?'

Crane sniffed.

'Why don't you tell us about David Raker instead?' Phillips offered.

I turned to Phillips. He didn't meet my eye.

On-screen, Crane finally looked up. 'Why would I do that?'

'He interests you.'

'Does he?'

'In your hideout you had pictures of him on your wall.'

Crane pursed his lips, as if he suddenly realized Phillips was right. 'I'll tell you what,' he said. 'You get Raker in here to talk to me, alone, and you get your confession.'

'You know we can't do that, Aron,' Phillips said.

Crane shrugged. 'Then I guess I don't talk.'

'Why do you want to talk to David Raker?'

Nothing.

'Aron?'

Zero. Crane's head had dropped again, and he was looking down at the table. A couple of seconds later, the video froze. The clip was finished.

'What does he want to talk to you about?' Bartholomew asked.

'I've no idea.' I looked back at Crane. 'But he seemed to think we had some kind of a connection. Something in common.'

'Like what?' Phillips asked.

I shook my head. 'I don't know.'

'This is highly unusual,' Bartholomew said. Next to him, Hart shuffled in his seat, two thin hands together on his lap. 'We're not running a circus here.'

'So I won't talk to him.'

Bartholomew and Phillips looked at one another.

The superintendent got to his feet and came across to me. 'I don't like this, Mr Raker,' he said. 'I don't like any of it.'

'That makes two of us.'

'What could possibly make you so special to him?'

'I don't know,' I said, sipping my coffee and stepping all the way up to the glass. 'But I've got a feeling I'm about to find out.'

CHAPTER 72

A ron Crane looked up as I entered. Behind me, a uniformed officer closed the door. The room was warm and had no windows. No clocks. No daylight. It could have been any time of the day. Crane remained perfectly still, both his hands flat to the table, eyes fixed on me. I sat down. He took a quick sideways glance at the one-way mirror.

'Hello, David,' he said softly.

I studied his face. 'What do you want with me?'

He looked at me, half smiling, but didn't reply.

'If you sit there in silence, I get up and walk out, and I promise you: I don't come back again.'

He started nodding. 'Fair enough.'

'Where's Jill?'

'Why don't we start at the beginning instead?' He ran his tongue along his lips, over a cut on the bottom. Then he used his free hand to hoist up his sleeve, and on the underside of his arm was a scar, almost like a burn mark. 'Isabelle Connors.'

The first woman he killed.

'What about her? She did that to you?'

He looked down at his arm.

'Sweet girl, really,' he said, 'but a nasty temper. A bit . . . *unpredictable*. She didn't like the whole . . .' He used his right hand to wave a couple of fingers in front of his face. 'Came out of her anaesthetic a little quicker than I'd hoped and, before you know it, there's half a bottle of sulphuric acid on my arm.' He stopped. Eyes widened. 'Ouch.'

He touched a finger to the scar. It was mottled and dark pink.

'Lesson I learned? Never buy Sodium Pentothal from Romania. I switched my anaesthetics after that. Got some diethyl ether in from Russia, and that was fine for a while – but eventually I got bored of cleaning up all the puke. It tends to make you feel a bit green around the gills, that stuff.' He paused, studied me. 'Stop me if I'm boring you, David.'

I didn't say anything.

'So it was on to halothane, and that worked well until Sona. Sadly, I once again failed in my job as a part-time anaesthetist. Now you know why they train for seven years.'

He leaned back in his seat as if he was done.

'Are you even a qualified doctor?'

He nodded. 'Five years at medical school, a year of pre-registration, two years of general medical training, a year specializing in plastics. I know how to do a facelift, if that's what you mean. But am I a *qualified* plastic surgeon? No, I'm not.' He rubbed his fingers against his thumb. 'Opportunities arose in my second year of specializing that were more rewarding than following a consultant around and holding a pair of scissors for him.'

'You mean organized crime?'

'You know how much a plastic surgeon makes a year on the NHS?'

I shook my head, all the time trying to work out his play. Trying to figure out the direction he was headed, and the traps he was attempting to set.

'Bottom tier, probably seventy grand. Good ones, eighty or ninety. The best, around the hundred-grand mark. You know how much I made doing that Russian's face?' He meant Akim Gobulev. The Ghost. He tilted his head slightly. 'David?'

'How much?'

He broke out into a smile. 'I thought you'd nodded off for a moment.'

'How much?'

'Two hundred and fifty grand. For *one face*. I made more in seven hours than the top surgeons in the NHS make in a *year*. They're busy doing micro-surgery. Worthy procedures like unfucking a guy's leg after a motorbike accident, or trans-planting muscle. I'm making twice that and putting in half the effort. Taking his jaw back, augmenting his cheekbones, lifting the eyes, tightening his face, thinning out his nose, moving bones, liposucking and cutting and filling. It's complicated, but . . .' He put a finger to his lips and made a *ssshhhhh* gesture. 'He was fucking ugly in the first place, so no one minded that my work looked like shit.'

I stared at him. 'This must feel great.'

'How so?'

'You're just like your hero Milton Sykes now.' I nodded at his hand, chained to the metal arch on the table. 'You can both go down in the history books.'

He laughed. 'True. Only, he didn't bank one and a half million in a single year.'

A smile lingered on his face. One of the nails on his right hand had been torn away. It looked fresh; puffy bruising on the tip of his middle finger. He moved his hand across the table like a spider, the finger out in front.

'It's good to be rich, David,' he said softly.

I ignored him. 'Why the women?'

'We all have certain tastes.'

'Why operate on them?'

He shrugged. Didn't say anything.

'What were you hoping to achieve?'

He glanced at the one-way mirror again and turned back to me, eyes wide. 'I wanted to make an army of lookalikes!' He burst into laughter and leaned back in his seat. Then he stopped, like a light going out. 'No, seriously, I just like cutting up women.'

His words hung in the air, and a silence settled between us. I looked at him. His face was set like concrete. Nothing to read.

'So why didn't you cut up Megan?'

He didn't reply.

'What, you're happy to murder women, but you

draw the line at pregnant teenagers?' A flicker of something in his face. 'I know that's not true.'

He frowned. 'And why's that?'

'The container you left behind at Mile End.'

No response.

'One adult heart. One child's.'

I thought of the cask. The police had found it in Healy's car after getting to the woods. Now it was probably in a forensics lab somewhere.

'This ringing any bells with you?' I asked him.

Again, no reply. His face was blank now.

'Who else was pregnant?' Still nothing. Eventually, when it was obvious he wasn't going to be drawn, I turned to the one-way glass. 'Did any of the other women show signs of having given birth? A C-section? Vaginal trauma?' A pause. A click. Then an echoey response from Phillips: '*No.*' Silence in the interview room again. I looked at Crane. 'Whose hearts were they?'

He watched me, the forefinger and thumb of his left hand brushing together. A thinking gesture. Finally, he shrugged. 'It's not important to this case.'

'Which case?'

'The six women.'

I studied him. 'Do you mean you've killed more?'

He sniffed. 'The six women, they were all just practice runs. I cut them up because it felt good. I *like* cutting people. But I did it in the name of research too.'

'What research?'

536

'I wanted to see how faces could be changed. Think of those women as the first of two canvases. And the second one was the masterpiece.'

'What do you mean?'

He went to speak then stopped himself. Drummed his fingers on the table. 'I just like blondes, David – what can I say?'

'What research?' I said again, fists clenched.

'I guess it's a Marilyn Monroe thing.' He flashed a smile again. 'Or maybe they remind me of my mother.'

'Why would you say that?'

'Isn't that what we're all about?'

'"We're"?'

'Serial killers.' Another smile drifted across his lips. 'Come on, David. You know as well as I do that a serial killer has got to stick to his MO. It's *so important*. Well, the women ticked all the boxes for me. Blonde. Good, strong features. A few flaws – but nothing that couldn't be rectified with a quick . . .' He used his free hand to simulate the slash of a knife. 'They were feminine. Pretty. Slim – but not all skin and bone. I don't like them like that. I like them with a bit of shape. If I wanted skeletons, I'd dig them up.'

'Where did you meet them?'

He looked at me. Still, except for his eyes, which moved across my face. 'I met them around and about. Feisty little Isabelle I met at a workshop I was attending.'

'A medical workshop?'

'No. I was learning how to make masks. Kind of a part-time vocation. After all, I didn't have a day job, and there were only so many Ferraris I could buy with all that dirty money.' His eyes sparkled. 'One of the consultants that I shadowed during my year of specialist training put the idea into my head. Weird little man, he was. He used to order in purpose-made latex masks to put on to dummies, so that we'd always have to look at a face when we were talking about cutting into something. He thought it would be a way of humanizing everything; even mounds of plastic. If you always had to look at a face, you'd always tread more carefully. Except I didn't give a shit about any of that. I just kept looking at the masks and thinking how it would feel to become someone else.'

'So why Sykes?'

'I found him interesting.'

'Because he killed thirteen women?'

'No, because people are still scared of him, even now. You go down to Hark's Hill and mention his name to the old-timers, and they'll fill their pants on the spot. You mention him to the kids that live around there and they might not have heard of him, but they'll know one thing: there's something wrong with that place. I mean, you've been there, David. You've felt it, right?'

I didn't say anything.

He smiled. 'Of course you've felt it. He buried thirteen women in those woods, and no one could find them. And as long as no one found them, that place never lost its power. And all they could do in the end was put up a concrete wall and a fence at one end and let nature take over everywhere else. Try to forget about the bodies, and the house he'd been born in, and the ghosts that wander through that place.' He paused and leaned forward, dropping his voice to a whisper. 'But I didn't forget about them. I *had* to find those bodies.'

'Why?'

'Let's call it a psychological advantage. Find the bodies, and Sykes has no hold over that place any more. He's no longer the daddy.' He paused. Winked. '*I* am.'

'You're fucking nuts.'

'Am I?'

'*Listen* to yourself.'

'I'm listening.' He cupped his free hand to his ear. 'Oh, I think I sound *great*, David. I mean, I'm the man who found Milton Sykes's *victims*. The police should be thanking me. I solved a hundred-year-old mystery.'

'How did you know where they were?'

He leaned forward. Brushed a finger against his broken nose. 'The dog found them.'

'The greyhound?'

'I discovered it wandering around the woods early on. Then it started following me around; bugging me. And then it started digging in that area of the woods day after day after day, and finally it brought back a thigh bone.'

'And you rewarded it so well.'

'I did, didn't I?'

'Cigarette burns, transplanted skin, cutting out one side of its face. Most dog owners just give their pets Pedigree Chum.'

He smiled. 'Some days it annoyed me. Some days I felt sorry for it.'

'I doubt that.'

'It had skin cancer. I took some skin from one of the women's thighs and transplanted it on to the dog. Not very scientific, I'll admit, but what the hell – the girl was already dead.' He shrugged. 'See? Even *I* can be a nice guy.'

Thirty seconds passed. Neither of us spoke; just looked at one another. Eventually he broke the silence.

'Interesting area, Hark's Hill,' he said. 'A whole other world under the surface of the woods, and most people don't even know it's there. Or they've just forgotten. That's where Sykes took Jenny Truman, you know. He convinced her to leave with him, then smuggled her into the tunnels that fed out from the factories.' He stopped. A flash in his eyes. 'It was a ready-made hiding place. That boarded-up door next to the air vent? That leads all the way to the old munitions factory on the other side of the woods. I brought everything down through there. The supplies. The tools. The equipment. And when I was finished, I welded it shut.'

More silence. We looked at each other. He had

the same blank expression on his face again; no hint of emotion, no clue as to what he was thinking. He pushed a strand of dark hair away from his eyes and then sniffed gently, as if inhaling something sweet.

'Why leave the necklaces behind?' I asked.

'Because it was fun.'

'It was what got you caught.'

'Was it?'

'If it hadn't been for the necklaces, no one would have tied the women to each other, *or* to you. You gave yourself away.'

He shrugged. 'I wasn't far off finishing my little project.'

'Meaning what?'

'Meaning the necklaces were a vital component of what I was doing. I liked the idea of leaving something for the police to find. A little calling card. Something to tease them and test them. But it wasn't going to last for ever. One more after Jill, then my research was done.'

'You were just going to walk away?'

He smiled. 'Not exactly.'

'Then what?'

'I hadn't decided yet.'

I studied him. He was running the finger of his free hand along the edge of the table, the skin making a crackling noise as it caught on the chips in the surface.

'How many have you killed?'

He sighed, running his finger along the table in

the opposite direction. 'I don't know, David,' he said, looking up at me. 'How many have you?'

There was a hint of a smile on his face. The coffee had been sitting on the table next to me the entire time, steam curling up from its surface. I took it and sank a few mouthfuls. Then I placed it down and leaned forward, hands flat to the desk.

'Is Aron Crane even your real name?'

He shrugged and sat back. 'Names, numbers, they're not important, David. They don't matter. A name is just a piece of paper. You can give yourself whatever name you want, and it won't make any difference to who you are, or what you do. A name's just a vehicle getting you from one place to another. Another little stage.'

'So Aron Crane was just a stage?'

He nodded, gazing at me, wanting me to look away, as if it would be a victory. But that wasn't going to happen. He wasn't going to win. Not now, not ever.

'Why bring Markham in?'

He sighed. 'I'm sure you know why.'

'You used him after things went wrong at the warehouse in Bow.'

'Correct!' He slammed his unchained right hand down on to the table. Then, suddenly, he was still. Straight-faced. Eyes on mine. 'There were cops undercover in the Russians, and Drayton's operation was getting a little . . . *leaky* too. Sooner or later they were going to move on me. Frank White got in the way, and so did that other stiff, so I killed them and went on my way.'

'As easy as that.'

'Anything's easy when you do enough of it.'

His eyes widened again and then he leaned back in his seat, the handcuffs locking into place.

'Where did you find Markham?'

'He came to my attention when I first started following Megan. I'd been watching her for a while. She seemed . . .' He leaned forward again, whispering. 'She seemed like my type – know what I mean?' He winked. 'I needed to step back after White snuffed it, and Markham seemed to fit the bill. He was friendly with Megan, she trusted him – plus his wife was a fucking nutcase, which meant he had a soft centre.' Eyes narrowed, face straightening. 'People you love tend to be your weakness.'

Something flashed in his eyes, and then it was gone again.

'After Frank White died, there was a lot of coverage about him on the news. I mean, kill a copper and it's the A-bomb dropping, right? Interviews with the people he'd shared an office with, his family, friends – then eventually Jill. The tearful widow. I liked the look of her straight away. She fitted the bill. So I started getting my morning coffee from the same place as her. After a week of giving her the eye, she eventually said hello. After a fortnight, we were chatting. After a month, I had her in the palm of my hand. I can be really quite charming when I want to be.'

'Why not get Markham to bring her to you?'

'I was getting itchy feet watching him do all the fun stuff. Plus, he couldn't keep up with my . . . *appetite*. To be honest, he was a whiney piece of shit. I had to treat him like a child, just to get him to understand all the rules and regulations. Cutting him to pieces did us all a favour, believe me.'

He paused. Made a show of clearing his throat.

'I saw you going into the Carvers' house about a week and a half back. Let's just say, I'd been keeping a close eye on everything to do with Megan. Making sure I was still insulated. As long as the investigation rumbled on, everything was fine.' He nodded sideways at the one-way mirror and then dropped his voice – but loud enough so it would be picked up in the next room. 'They didn't have a clue who I was, David. Not a clue.'

That's why he came to the support group. To keep me close.

'So you were watching me?'

'Basically, yes. When Jill started to trust me, I floated the idea of the support group, so I could actually meet you. But then I realized I needed to know more about you, your skills. So I persuaded her to play on your conscience and get you to look into Frank's death.'

'Why take the risk?'

'It wasn't a risk. Everything you said to her got back to me. Much better than stumbling around blindly trying to work out what you did and did not know. Just that one evening at the support

544

group was enough to get the measure of you. Which is probably just as well. I mean, let's face it, that group is where ambition goes to die.' He winked again and smiled. 'No offence intended, of course, David. I'm sure it's helped you get over seeing your wife lose her hair and her dignity.'

Fire flared in me, shooting up through my throat and into my muscles. I wanted to put my fist through his face. I wanted to feel his bones breaking. But instead I let a tremor pass along my hands and out through my fingers. I met his blank expression. There was no smile on his face now, just a featureless gaze.

'Where's Jill?'

No response. No movement in his face. It was like he could no longer hear me.

'You're not in control any more, Aron. *Where* is she?'

'I broke into your house, David,' he said, as if he still hadn't heard me, continuing in a voice devoid of all emotion. 'When I was in there, I saw some of the pictures of her. Your wife. She was a good-looking woman, Derryn. You know, *before*. Blonde hair. Nice figure. Not bony and boyish. You and me, we have the same taste.'

'We don't have the same anything.'

'*Really?*'

'You're a fucking animal. And if it wasn't the difference between me going to jail or walking away from here, I'd put you in the ground.'

His eyes widened. '*Oooh*, David. Such bravado.'

I didn't reply this time. Didn't take the bait.

'Anyway,' he continued, picking an imaginary hair off the arm of his jumpsuit, 'it is what it is. You play a good grieving widower. It suits you. Women *love* that sort of thing. I bet your lawyer in there gets all wet watching you play the strong, sensitive type.' He took a long, deep breath, looking down at the table. Then he raised his head again and a smile broke out. 'How does it feel to fuck her after years of banging away on the same woman? Is she different?' He licked his lips for effect. 'Is she *tighter*?'

'Let me ask you something,' I said, leaning towards him.

A movement in his eyes. He hadn't got the reaction he'd wanted. But he kept a half-smile on his face; telling me he was still in control. I looked at him. *I think I know why you kept Megan alive now. I think I know who the hearts belong to.*

'Where's your wife buried?'

He leaned back in his chair.

'Because here's my theory, Aron, or Dr Glass, or whatever the fuck your name is. This is your shot at redemption. You're trying to get her back. I think you killed the one person you ever really loved.'

He attempted to force any emotion from his face. But something remained; a light burning away. I'd hit on something.

'Maybe you killed her to satisfy your "appetite". Or maybe you killed her by accident. But now you

546

wish you hadn't, and all these women – the way they look, the way you're cutting them up – they're just replacements for her.' I leaned in even closer. 'Thing is, though, it doesn't matter how many women you kill, how many times you cut them up and try to make them like her, the one you really loved, she's not coming back. Take it from someone who knows.'

His smile shattered. I'd got at him. I'd guessed right.

'Was your wife pregnant when she died?'

He twitched, like he'd been prodded with a taser.

'Were those their hearts I found?'

He laid both hands down on the table in front of me.

'Megan looks exactly like your wife, doesn't she?' I asked him. 'One or two minor adjustments and you have her back. A little younger maybe, but you'll put up with that. *That's* why you went to the trouble of creating the website, inventing the LCT, why you told Markham he could never call her or email her. Because you didn't want to risk this one. Ultimately, Megan was all that mattered.'

He was quiet. Breathing in and out.

'And all the others: they were like the corpses you used to practise on in medical school. Tissue and bones. Mannequins. Nothing more. They were your research. Your little project. You cut into their faces and their noses so that you wouldn't mess up when the time came to do it on the one that *really* mattered. And you finally found her. Megan.

The fact that Markham got Megan pregnant was just terrible luck for them – but for you, it was probably like some kind of a sign. Because in seven weeks' time, not only was the project finally over and Megan all sliced up how you wanted her, not only would you have your wife back, but you'd have your unborn child back too.'

There was nothing in his face now. He'd managed to wipe it clean.

'But here's the thing, Aron: this whole project of yours, it's *insane*. You're a psychopath. I'm sure there's a shrink somewhere that will find you fascinating; the fact you can kill without remorse, yet still retain some sort of positive emotional connection to someone. But to me, you're black and white. There's no mystery. You're just another worthless piece of shit.'

Silence.

I held his gaze for a long time, and then he turned away from me. His left hand, chained to the table, wrapped around the metal ring. The handcuffs jangled against the surface. He seemed to drift off. But seconds later he moved in his seat, the handcuffs jangling for a second time. He released his hand from the ring. Looked at me. Shrugged.

But said nothing.

I got to my feet. His eyes followed me but his body was completely motionless. I walked across the room and buzzed the intercom. The door opened inwards. In the corridor, a uniformed officer was waiting to escort me to the viewing room next door. When I looked back, Crane was staring up at me from under the ridge of his brow, a hint of a smile back on his face. A real one this time. Lips turning up. Eyes widening, like they were trying to suck in all the light in the room.

'We're done,' I said to him.

A sliver of tongue passed along his lips.

'Are we?' he said quietly.

LEGAL RIGHT

The holding cell was small and cold. The white walls looked like they'd been painted recently, but the ceiling – a creamy-beige colour – was peeling all along the middle and in the corners of the room. There was one bunk screwed to the wall and one metal toilet screwed to the floor.

Aron Crane was sitting on the edge of the bed. His clothes had been bagged and taken off somewhere. Now he sat in a dark blue sweater, a pair of black trousers and a pair of black rubber-soled slip-ons. At the door to the cell, a uniformed officer was standing guard. Crane saw part of his head and the white cotton of his shirt when the porthole slid across. Occasionally, other policemen would look in, some in uniform, some in plain clothes.

Everyone wanted to see Dr Glass.

He'd been sitting there for an hour when the door clunked and opened. Two officers were standing in the doorway. One of them was holding a set of handcuffs. They entered and told him to stand, then the one with the handcuffs placed them around his wrists, clicked them into place and led

550

him out. They were taking him back to the room he'd faced Raker in earlier that day.

Raker.

Crane had underestimated him. He thought he could use him, the fact he had sore points. Weaknesses. But Raker was perceptive and clever. He'd used Crane's wife as bait and tried to get inside his head, tried to force Crane to react. But that was okay. Raker might have messed with the project before it was finished, but Crane had plans for him.

Revenge would come.

They turned a corner and moved into the interview room, sitting him down at the table. They chained him to the metal ring, welded to the surface, and then left.

Silence.

They would find out about Phedra eventually. He knew that. If they looked hard enough, they would find what was left of her body. And they would find the body next to it as well. They would realize that the inscription on his chain – PC – were her initials, and that the chain had been hers.

But they would never find out what happened.

Because even he wasn't sure now. He'd moved it around in his head so much, some days he remembered it being an accident and some days he didn't. Some days she was carrying a tray across the decking on the top of their house and stumbled. And some days she was screaming at him, telling him she was two months away from giving birth and she needed him to *care*, and he pushed her. The one thing that was clear was looking over the edge of the roof and seeing her on the grass below him, flat on her back.

Looking up at him as her life ebbed away.

Two plain-clothes policemen entered. One was Hart, the other was Phillips. Hart asked Crane if he was all right. Crane gave no reply. He'd spoken little to them since they'd brought him in; only to tell them he wanted Raker to ask the questions. Now they were going to try again.

'Mr Crane,' Hart said, 'we need to know where Jill White is.'

He studied Hart. *You look like a skeleton.*

'Mr Crane?'

You look like you should be buried in the ground.

'Mr Crane, we really need you to—'

'I want to make a phone call.'

They looked at him. Inside he felt himself smiling. He'd stunned them into silence. Hart glanced at Phillips and back to Crane. 'You want a solicitor now?'

Crane nodded.

'We can appoint you one.'

'I have my own.'

'Okay, we can call him for—'

'No,' Crane said. 'I'll call him.'

They looked at him. Hart leaned forward. Phillips started turning his wedding band, eyes fixed on Crane. 'Why now?' Phillips asked.

'Because it's my legal right.'

'Yeah, but why now?'

'Because it's my legal right.'

More silence. Hart glanced at Phillips, but Phillips was looking at Crane, his head tilted as if trying to work out what made him tick. Crane stared back, the two of them holding each other's gaze. He could tell Phillips had something about him. In many ways he wasn't dissimilar to Raker: they both observed, and watched for the rhythms of conversations – and the things that were out of place. Finally, Phillips stopped turning his wedding band and slowly started to nod.

'Then it looks like you get to call your solicitor,' he said.

CHAPTER 73

It was almost 9 p.m. by the time I got to Derry Road. Police cars were lined up at the entrance to the alley that led through to the Dead Tracks, the entire street cordoned off. The taxi dropped me off at the southern end. I waited while a uniformed officer radioed through to Phillips to tell him I'd arrived. A minute later, he lifted the tape and I ducked under and moved along the pavement, towards the eye of the storm. Windows were open. People were looking down. Sirens were painting the concrete blue. There was the smell of food in the air, drifting out from the houses, and the coolness of imminent rain.

In the middle of the street were two specialist firearms officers. One of them was at the rear of their vehicle, checking a Heckler & Koch MP5 submachine gun, a Glock 17 holstered at his hip. The other was inside the front of the car, on a phone, writing something on a piece of paper he had pressed to the dashboard. Beyond was a Mercedes Sprinter police van. Two officers were stationed outside. Spread around them in a vague semicircle were a series of marked cars. Next to one of them, I could see Phillips and Hart talking to one another, Hart pointing towards the closed rear doors of the police van.

Inside was Aron Crane.

Hart looked up as I approached; Phillips too. Both of them nodded. They didn't want me here, and I didn't want to be here. But when they'd tried to question Crane about where Jill really was, he said he'd show them – as long as I was there. They had a look on their faces I could read as clearly as if it was printed on a billboard: I was tied up in this somehow. But the only thing I knew for sure was that there was something ominous about this whole thing. Something dangerous and sinister.

He'd tracked Jill for months himself, while he forced Markham to lure in Megan and Sona. I imagined he liked the idea of pursuing the wife of the man he'd killed. It massaged his ego. His sense of power. His control. And now, for all the men and the cars and the show of force, there was only one person directing everything: Aron Crane.

Phillips told me he'd be with me shortly, and then both he and Hart turned their backs on me, shielding their conversation. I didn't care. I didn't need to know their strategy to know that everything about this felt wrong.

Around them police officers gathered. Some with dogs. Some with flashlights. The two SFOs fell in next to the rear of the van, eyes taking in the scene. One of them fiddled with the slide on his Glock.

He removed it from its holster, checked it, then returned it. Any moment, the doors were going to be flung open and Crane would be sitting there, looking out. He'd love the chaos he'd created.

Finally, Phillips and Hart finished talking, and Hart wandered off. Phillips had the air of the man in charge. Hart was a career cop. Solid, dependable, bright but not a natural. He'd progressed through the ranks based on decent results and saying the right things. Phillips was different. He could play the game, but he was good at his job too. People would wait for Phillips to give the command.

He came over to me.

'Crane will be handcuffed throughout,' he said, bypassing any sort of greeting. 'Two uniforms up front with flashlights, a couple more at the sides. The firearms officers will be either side of him the whole time – and they'll also have torches.'

He paused as a female officer came and asked him a question about whether he wanted the press pushed back even further. He told her yes, and turned back to me.

'Have you been in?' I asked.

'Yes.'

'Find anything?'

'No. Crane told us the body is about twenty minutes' walk, but wouldn't tell us in which direction.' He stopped, must have seen something in my face. 'We've done a risk assessment and believe we have all the angles covered.'

'It'll be pitch black in there.'

'We wait until morning and Jill might be dead.' He was right, but it didn't make me feel any better. 'A paramedic and two dog-support units will be coming too; one will go out front, another will trail behind us. And that just leaves DCI Hart, myself and you.'

'Are you taking forensics in?'

'No, they'll be on standby. We'll wait to see where he leads us, and then I'll call Davidson.' I looked around me and spotted Davidson talking to a uniform on the other side of the police van. 'We're already taking too many people with us.'

Nearby, one of the SFOs cranked the chamber on his Glock.

'They're a precaution,' Phillips said. 'A man with six women to his name isn't a man worth taking a risk over.'

Six we know about, I thought, and then looked to the alley leading to the woods. 'What about his lawyer?'

'He called him, but he never showed up.'

'How come?'

'Crane wouldn't say.'

I eyed Phillips. 'I don't like this.'

He didn't say anything. But in his eyes I could see what he was thinking: *I don't like it either.* For a moment, something passed between us: a second where we both considered backing out. But then Phillips must have cast his mind back to the risk assessment they'd done at the station, the planning, the officers he was taking in with him, and figured they were as prepared as they could be. Maybe he was right. I certainly hoped he was. But that didn't settle my nerves. Because I knew Crane now. He wouldn't lead us to Jill unless he had a way to skew things in his favour.

'Don't engage him in conversation unless you have to,' Phillips said. 'This is a game to him. We're not playing the game. What we want is to find Jill.'

I nodded. Ultimately, Jill was all that mattered.

'Once we've done that, we call the forensic team and we get the hell out.'

Hart appeared from my left. 'Mr Raker.'

'DCI Hart.'

'We ready?' he said to Phillips.

'Yeah, we're ready.'

'Okay. Let's do it.'

He gestured to one of the uniformed officers to open the rear doors of the van. The two SFOs fell into a position either side, the H&Ks across their chests pointing down at an angle to the floor.

A hush seemed to settle across the scene.

The Mercedes' doors clunked open.

Aron Crane sat just inside the van. His wrists were handcuffed. From our position it was hard to see his face as shadows from the interior cut across him. Then he raised his head and the orange glow from the street lamps and the blue flash of the police sirens bloomed against his skin, and he was frozen for a moment in an eruption of colour. His eyes glinted. He scanned the crowd in front of him, looking for someone. And then, when he stopped, I realized who.

The piece of shit is looking for me.

As he was being helped out of the van, our eyes met. He nodded once and then looked away. The team heading towards the alley fell in around him and started moving. Phillips and Hart walked me towards the group, slipping in behind Crane, with the dog team bringing up the rear. Crane glanced back over his shoulder and pinpointed me immediately. This time a hint of a smile broke out on his face.

And then we headed into the Dead Tracks.

CHAPTER 74

On the other side of the factory beds, everybody stopped. We'd reached the gate. No one had said anything on the way over. We'd walked in silence through the crumbling remains of the buildings and the dumping ground around it. Police torches had swung from left to right, and for brief moments the flashlights had reflected in the windows remaining in the factory shells and in the shards of shattered glass at our feet. But once we were off the concrete and facing the woods, the darkness got thicker and the light shone off into the night and didn't come back again.

We filed through the gate one by one. Crane looked back at me from the other side, and in the glow of a passing flashlight nodded again. Phillips noticed and looked at me, as if some kind of secret message had passed between us. This was all working perfectly for Crane: he was creating conflict between people on the same side, and he hadn't even uttered a word.

Up front, one of the dogs barked. Everyone stopped.

Phillips moved ahead of the pack and joined

the handler. The two of them began talking as the spaniel on the end of the leash looked towards a swathe of black on our right. Behind me, the second dog, a German shepherd, was gazing in the same direction as the spaniel, its nose out in front sniffing the air. Phillips turned around and told one of the uniformed officers to shine his flashlight into the undergrowth. A second later, a patch of thick, tangled bush was illuminated beyond two great big chunks of oak tree. No sign of anything. Just tall grass swaying gently in the breeze, and light drizzle passing across the circle of torchlight.

We moved on.

The woods were incredibly dark. The canopy was fully covering the path now, keeping out any brief glimpse of moonlight and any synthetic glow from the street behind us. All we had were six flashlights – two up front, two at the sides, two attached to guns – passing back and forth across the path and what grew at its edges. *I should have brought one*, I thought. Once again I was relying on other people when the only person I trusted was myself.

A little way down, one of the officers must have seen something reflect back at him. He stopped. About twenty-five feet further along, caught in the light from his torch, I could see the first of the abandoned railway lines, cutting across the trail.

We'd been walking for about ten minutes when the dogs started barking again. Both of them this time. They were facing right, into the woods, noses out, eyes fixed on something. Three of the uniformed officers shone their lights into the under-growth. The trees, leaves, grass and bushes were freeze-framed for a second, rain coming down harder now.

Phillips went up ahead again and chatted to the same handler as before. This time there was no breeze and everyone could hear what they were saying.

'Could it be an animal?' Phillips asked.

'Might be,' came the reply, but the handler didn't sound convinced. The dogs were so highly trained they could smell human blood. They'd been inside collapsed buildings and followed trails to survivors. They could sniff out drugs and guns and explosives. They weren't going to be disturbed by a hedgehog. Everyone was thinking the same, and a couple of them looked to Crane, as if momentarily seeking assurance. He wasn't even turned towards the noise. He just faced ahead, into the darkness.

A couple of the officers carrying torches moved off the path and into the undergrowth as far as they could. Grass fell under their feet and then sprang back up again around them. Beyond the tree trunks, cones of light moved left and right.

'Anything?' Phillips asked from the trail.

'Nothing,' one of them shouted back.

They reappeared about a minute later, dew shining on their trousers and stab vests. Crane looked back at me for a moment and smiled.

'You got something to say?' I asked him.

Everyone glanced at me, then at him. The smile was gone. It had lasted long enough for me to see but no one else. Most of the officers' eyes were back on me now.

'Calm down, Mr Raker,' Hart said from in front of me. 'And you—' pointing at Crane '—keep your bloody eyes on the path.'

About five minutes further on, we hit the clearing I'd found a few days before. The spot where Markham had left Megan for Crane to find. The rain sounded heavier as it fell through the gap in the leaves.

'Pitter patter, pitter patter,' Crane started saying. A few of us looked at him. His head was down, handcuffed wrists together in front of him. 'Pitter patter, *bang*, pitter patter, *bang*.'

Phillips stepped towards him. 'What did you say?'

Crane looked up. 'Sorry?'

'What did you say?'

'Pitter patter, pitter patter. The rain, DCI Phillips. It's coming down hard now. We'd better move on, or we're all going to get soaked.'

Crane scanned the group. Two uniforms up front, torches straying across the path. The two SFOs either side of him. Both dog handlers up ahead now, framed in the flashlights. Two other uniforms either side of us, one standing in the tall grass of the clearing, one on the edge of the woods. The paramedic next to me. Phillips and Hart next to her. Then his eyes fell on Phillips.

Something was up.

In that moment, I knew we should have been turning around and heading back the other way. Crane was a killer and a liar. Trusting him was suicide.

'Wait.'

Everyone looked around at me, including Crane. Phillips was annoyed, but edged a couple of steps back in my direction. 'What is it?'

'This is . . .' I shook my head, glanced at Crane. 'This is wrong.'

Phillips studied me for a moment, saying nothing. But then he turned to Crane. In the expression on his face, I saw that he felt the same as me. But I also saw that he wasn't going to back out. Not now. Not after getting all this signed off. 'Where's Jill?'

'It's not far now.'

'You better not be messing us around here, Crane. If this is all a joke, I'll flush you down the toilet – you understand that, right?'

Crane smiled. 'It's not far now,' he repeated.

We all fell back into position and continued along the path. Under the canopy the rain wasn't as hard. It fell as a mixture of intermittent droplets and drifting drizzle, swirled around in front of us by a gentle breeze that wheezed and groaned. About a hundred yards on, someone's radio crackled, the sound amplified by the oppressive quiet. It was one of the SFOs'. He reached to his belt and adjusted something on his Airwave handset. Except for the rain and the sound of the wind, we were back to complete silence.

Then something cracked in the woods on our left.

Everybody stopped. The dogs were straining on their leashes, noses out again, staring into the dark. 'What can you see?' one of the handlers asked. The spaniel sniffed the air then returned to its original position, primed for whatever had made the noise. Two uniforms moved to the edge of the woods and shone the torch in again. Another one followed about ten seconds later.

I looked along the line. One SFO was facing the opposite way, into the woods on the other side from where the noise had come. The other was watching the uniforms examining the area. We'd bunched together, and I realized Crane was closer to me all of a sudden. So close I could have grabbed him by the throat and stopped this before it got out of hand. To my left, Hart was standing in the grass at the edge of the woods; Phillips a couple of steps behind him, eyes fixed on the dark.

Another crack.

The SFO who was watching the other way glanced over his shoulder. The paramedic looked too, her fluorescent jacket shining in the passing torchlight. One handler moved into the trees, then the other followed. Within twenty seconds, Crane and I were virtually on our own, only the SFOs for company. The rest of them were beyond the treeline, torches flashing back and forth, or were watching on the edges of the forest.

'Do you remember what I said to you, David?' Crane whispered. One of the SFOs' eyes flicked to him. His hands tightened on the barrel of the MP5. The other one saw his partner's movement and did the same. I nodded at them both that it was okay, but they didn't move. They were eyeing Crane with suspicion. 'That we had a connection?'

I didn't reply, but in my head I was trying to figure out what this was about, and why he was trying to engage me in conversation. As the torches passed in semicircles, I could see the officers' silhouettes form and then merge again with the dark. Hart had his mobile phone out, flipping it over inside the palm of his hand. Phillips was next to him.

'I shouldn't have been so cruel about your wife.'

I looked at him. *What are you doing, Crane?*

'Earlier. I shouldn't have said those things about her.'

'Do yourself a favour and shut the fuck up.'

One of the SFOs made a move forward. I glanced at him, then at Crane, then turned back to the woods. The beam from a torch cut out about twenty feet beyond the tree line. A couple of seconds later it flickered back on. One of the uniforms swore, cursing the batteries.

'I'm the same as you, David.'

I looked back at him. His face was blank: no expression, no hint of humour. He just held my gaze. I glanced at the SFO and stepped in closer to Crane.

'I already told you: we're not the same.'

'Sure we are,' he replied, and stopped, smiling. 'You figured me out. My wife. The child she was carrying. I always thought I hid it quite well. But I suppose you must become quite attuned to loss when you spend so much time around it. These cases you take on, they're full of it. And, of course, you have all those memories of your wife inside your home. All the photos. The home movies. Her music collection sitting there in the corner of the living room, untouched.'

'Be careful,' I warned him.

He looked around, eyes scanning the darkness. 'All I'm saying is, I understand. I get you. I lost someone, you lost someone. I kill, you kill.'

I flashed a look at him. 'What?'

A smile wormed its way across his face. 'I know all about that case up north, David. And I'm not talking about the cosy little picture you painted for the police.'

I glanced at the SFOs, then back to him.

'Oh, *come on*,' he said, and made a tut-tut sound. He dropped his voice to a whisper. The SFOs were studying us both now. 'I saw you on the news after what happened up there, just like everybody else. You spend enough time around loss, you pick it up in other people.' He paused. 'You spend enough time around killers, you can do the same.'

'You're insane.'

567

'You're a killer, David. A reluctant one, I'll admit. But a killer nonetheless. I can see it in you. I can read you just like you can read me. So, you and me . . . we're the same.'

Crane winked so only I could see, and backed up a couple of steps, opening himself out to the SFOs again. Above the sound from the woods and the whisper he'd been speaking in, it would have been hard for them to hear anything. But they knew something was up.

'Don't worry,' he continued, winking again, 'your secret's safe with me. But you might want to try and remember what it felt like to, you know . . .' He made a gun sign with one of his hands and pretended to fire it. 'You might want to reacquaint yourself, is all I'm saying.'

I looked at him. *I might want to reacquaint myself with firing a gun.*

'What are you talking about?' I asked again, but he didn't reply, and out of the woods came the search teams. They were finished. Phillips looked over at us, suspicion in his face, and then everybody started to fall back into position. 'Phillips – wait.'

He fixed a stare on me. 'What *now*?'

'We need to go back.'

'Why?'

I glanced at Crane. He was staring at me, his face blank. 'He's got a plan. Some sort of fucked-up plan. I don't know what it is, but someone's going to get hurt.'

Phillips looked between us, then at Hart. Hart was

gazing at me, as if he believed I was the one with the plan. 'What did he say?'

'Something about me needing to fire a gun.'

'What?'

'It's riddles. Just a bunch of . . .' I glanced at Crane again. Nothing in his face now. He'd wiped it clean. 'Look, I know you feel the same: everything about this is off. We're walking into a trap, and until we figure out what it is, I think we need to go back.'

Phillips scanned the group. Everybody was either staring at him or me, and I knew we weren't about to turn around. He may have had the same instincts as me, but this was a challenge to his decision-making. His planning. His position. If he backed down now, he said to everyone here, *I made the wrong choice.*

'We move on,' he said quietly.

'This is a big mistake, Phillips.'

'*Raker,*' he spat back at me, 'you're not in charge here. You have no opinion. You have no choices. You follow *my* orders and *that's it*. Are we clear?'

'This is a mistake.'

'Are we *clear*?'

This was for show now. He didn't deserve a reply. He believed exactly the same as me, felt something was off just as I did, but he was overlooking it to save face. I let my silence hang there, in between us, and then the group started walking again.

Phillips turned to Crane again. 'Where's Jill, you weaselly piece of shite?'

'It's not far now.'

'You said that a quarter of a mile back.'

'I mean it this time.'

The rain started making a chattering sound against the canopy. As we moved across another piece of rusting railway track, the wind picked up too, blowing in from our right. Leaves snapped. Grass swayed. About a minute later, one of the torches flashed past a patch of grass, coiled and twisted around the trunk of a sycamore. Some of it had come loose and was moving, making a gentle sigh like a voice. I watched a few of the team directing their lights towards it, as if they thought they'd heard someone speaking. But it was just this place. The buried secrets. The lost lives.

Then one of the torches passed a shape about sixty feet in front of us.

The light swung back: it was one of the crates from the hideout. Five feet square. Cyrillic printed on the side. It sat on its own in an oval clearing on the right of the trail, where the woods bent away and then came back in further down. We all stopped.

'What's that?' Phillips asked.

'*That*,' Crane replied, 'is Jill.'

CHAPTER 75

Everyone stared at the crate and realized this was it. What we'd come out to the woods for. Then Phillips started to organize things: he told one of the SFOs, one handler, two uniforms with flashlights and the paramedic to follow him over. Hart joined the group as well. The rest of us stayed put.

I glanced at Crane, stepping closer to him in case he tried to make a run for it. I could feel dread worming its way through my chest. *What have you brought us here for, you murdering prick?* He was almost side-on to me now, watching closely, the corners of his mouth turned up in a trace of a smile.

Except he wasn't watching at all.

As I took a step forward, I could see his body was facing forward but his eyes were fixed on the woods to our right. I followed his line of sight. The darkness was thick. The dull glow from the nearest torch had lit the immediate area to the edge of the trees. Beyond that, though, I couldn't see anything. No movement. No sound. Nothing to warrant his attention.

The lull was disturbed by Phillips's voice again. At a distance of sixty feet, and with the rain getting heavier every minute, it was hard to make out his words clearly. But he was going around the group, telling each of them what he wanted from them.

I made sure Crane hadn't moved. His eyes were still watching the woods to his right, so I stepped level with him. He noticed me enter his field of vision. The smile disappeared. He looked like he was trying to decide if he'd given anything away.

'Something you want to share?' I asked him.

His smile returned. 'Just enjoying the show, David.'

He turned back to face what was unfolding in front of him, and we watched as Phillips and his team pulled on forensic gloves. Phillips walked right up to the crate. Placed his fingers around the lid. He nodded once to everyone watching and went to lift it away. It didn't open. He looked from the lid to Crane. Attempted to lift it away again.

Nothing.

Briefly, Crane's eyes flicked right again, then he was back to watching Phillips. He and Hart were examining the crate, trying to work out what was preventing it from opening.

'Constable,' I said to one of the uniforms holding a flashlight. He looked at me. 'Could you shine your torch into the woods over there?'

He frowned. 'Why?'

I glanced at Crane. He was staring at me, his face stoic. 'Just for a second.'

The PC was young, mid twenties. He probably liked the fact I'd come along for the ride because it meant he wasn't bottom of the food chain any more. He shook his head. 'No. I do what DCI Phillips tells me, not you.'

The PC looked back up the trail to the group. Defiant.

The remaining SFO was standing behind me. I turned to him. 'Can you get him to shine the torch into the woods?'

'Why?' he replied.

The PC turned back to face us.

'Because Crane doesn't give a shit about what's happening up there,' I said, nodding to the group at the crate. 'But he can't keep his eyes off the woods.'

They looked from me to Crane, then to the woods. Crane didn't meet their eyes. He was staring up the trail, watching as Phillips, Hart and both uniforms tried to prize the lid of the crate away. A crack sounded, and – beyond the fall of rain – Hart said something. The lid had shifted.

The SFO watched me for a moment, MP5 hanging diagonally across his waist. 'Okay,' he said, and looked at the PC. 'Do what he says.'

Crack.

The lid had come away. Everybody stepped back, leaving Phillips on his own. He placed his hands either side of the lid and lifted it up, dropping it on to the path with a dull *whup*. The group stepped up to the crate and looked inside.

'It's empty!' I heard Hart shout from the crate.

And then the PC shone his light into the woods.

About fifteen feet in was the Hanging Tree, the distinctive T-shaped oak I'd seen in photographs online, and the place Milton Sykes had built a treehouse as a child. Tied to the trunk was Jill. She'd been bound and gagged. Rope had been looped around her throat, pinning her to the bark, a semicircular piece of skin hanging from the top of her face. It took me two or three seconds to realize what it was: her forehead. The flap of skin covered one eye; the other was closed. She had bruises everywhere: her face, her arms, around her collarbone. Her clothes – a pair of jeans and a thin long-sleeve sweater – were soaked through with blood and rainwater, the sweater torn, exposing her stomach. Scrawled across her skin in black ink was *8.5*.

Phillips sprinted towards us, his eyes fixed on Jill, and told me to hold back. I wanted to get to Jill. I wanted to tear her down from the tree and rip Crane apart on the way through. He was fully facing me now, his back to her. Finally I couldn't wait any more: I stepped past him, about three feet from the tree line, unable to take my eyes off the body strapped to the tree.

'What the fuck have you done?' I said.

'I didn't get time to finish her,' he replied in a matter-of-fact voice from behind me, bringing his handcuffed wrists up to the side of his head and scratching a spot next to his eye. 'So we'll call her eight and a half. Would have been good to have had the time to sort out that terrible skin of hers. But while I usually prefer to finish my work, I'll accept this one for what she is.' He paused. His eyes drifted to the woods behind me. 'A marker.'

A second later he dropped to the floor.

Fnip. Fnip.

To my right, the SFO's head exploded into a shower of blood. His gun flipped off to the side, landing with a thud in the grass. *Fnip.* Next to him, the PC went down, a bullet pounding into his chest, close to the heart. I dropped to the floor. Rolled towards the grass at the opposite tree line.

Fuck. It's a set-up.

From behind where I'd been standing two men in balaclavas emerged from the woods, both armed with silence pistols. At the crate, the SFO lifted his MP5. *Fnip.* Another uniform went down, falling against the crate and crushing it beneath him. *Fnip.* Someone else. Maybe Hart. I couldn't tell any more.

The SFO started firing.

It was a thunderous noise, ripping across the woods and echoing away. The two men retreated back into cover, into the trees and bushes. The remaining SFO was left out in the open. One man against the darkness.

I grabbed the MP5 lying on the ground next to the dead SFO and made a break for the other side of the trail, where Jill was now disguised by the night again. *Fnip. Fnip.* Bullets hit the path close to my feet. My body automatically tried to avoid them, and the move unbalanced me: I stumbled forward, hitting the undergrowth hard beyond the tree line. A split second later, another bullet hit a tree about six inches to my left. Bark spat out, dusting me as I tried to move deeper into the darkness.

Fnip. Fnip. Fnip.

Someone cried out. A woman.

The paramedic.

Fnip.

Close to me, the sound of a body hitting the grass. Then the dogs barking. I wasn't sure who was still standing and who was already dead. MP5 gunfire erupted, brief flashes of light illuminating the trail. I could see Crane flat to the floor. Bodies strewn next to him. Torches on the ground – one facing off along the path, one into the side of the woods the men were in.

And right on the edge of its light: a shape.

He was hunkered down behind a tree trunk. Changing magazines. The SFO wouldn't hit him from the crate. He wouldn't even see him.

But I could.

I brought the MP5 up slowly to my shoulder. Stock against my body. Finger around the trigger. I was surrounded by oily darkness, as thick as the inside of a tomb. But as soon as I fired, I would give my position away. I had to get it right.

Aim.

Concentrate.

I thought of my dad teaching me to fire guns. Of him running through the woods behind our farm with me when I was a teenager. Firing a replica Beretta at targets he'd assembled.

Concentrate.

I squeezed the trigger.

The noise was immense. It crackled across the path seconds after the bullet went through the gunman's face. One side to the other. In the periphery of the light, I could see a flash of red. And then he was down. Slumped to his side. Half in the woods, half on the path.

I got to my feet and ran.

Fnip. Fnip.

Bullets hit the space behind me. I clipped a tree with my shoulder, unable to distinguish it as I moved further away from the two torches on the path. Then I hit another and almost knocked myself out. I fell back into the undergrowth.

Quiet.

Nothing now. Just the gentle patter of rain against the canopy. My thoughts were racing: would they hear the gunfire from the road? How long would it take them to get support teams here? It had taken us thirty minutes to walk this far. That probably meant half that at a run. I rolled over. Grass and fallen branches cracked under me.

On the other side of the tree line, about thirty feet away in a diagonal to my right, was another dead PC. His torch was pointing towards him, right up close to his face. It turned his skin red, and the blood at his mouth even redder. Beyond that, further up the trail, was what was left of the crate, just a vague shape against the night. I could see a dead PC lying alongside it. Back the way I'd come, Crane was still down on the floor. He hadn't moved. It meant the last SFO was still alive – or the remaining assassin couldn't be sure. If he knew for certain, Crane would just get up and walk off.

Movement.

Opposite me, across the trail, on the other side of the woods. I squinted into the darkness. Nothing now. Just the tree line and the swathes of black beyond.

But then it came again.

More movement.

Suddenly, gunfire erupted from the direction of the crate, and the whole area lit up. The bodies on the trail. Jill strapped to a tree, further back in the direction I'd come. Crane on the floor of the path. The SFO, MP5 to his shoulder, was firing towards the space I'd seen movement. And the source of the movement: the other assassin, hidden behind a tree, facing in my direction.

We were looking at one another.

And his gun was aimed.

I ducked – late – as two bullets whipped across the trail and hit the tree behind me. They'd missed me by an inch. Through the undergrowth, on my side, I saw him for a second. And then he was gone. The SFO had stopped firing.

The Dead Tracks were black.

No sound but the rain.

I very gently sat up and shifted sideways, moving on my backside, dragging myself through the undergrowth as quickly and as quietly as I could. After about ten feet, my arm hit a tree. I stopped. Lifted the MP5 to my shoulder and aimed it back in the direction of the gunman.

Click.

The SFO was reloading. I was closer to the crate now, could hear the gentle sound of the magazine being fitted back into the gun. A brief moment of silence.

Then more gunfire.

The SFO's bullets hit the tree the man was using as cover. But he was protected. His cover was good.

Except he'd made a mistake.

He was still facing the same position I'd been in before. As soon as the MP5 lit up the woods, he fired twice into the space I'd been. But I wasn't there. Through the sights I could see his balaclava, eyes showing: a moment of hesitation as he realized I was somewhere else. He scanned the woodland, moving left along the edge of the trail. Then surprise as he picked out my position about thirty feet across from him.

Aim. Concentrate.

Hit the target.

I fired.

His head ruptured, blood spattering against the

tree, and his body fell backwards against the floor of the woods. No sound. Through the corner of my eye, I saw the SFO look in my direction and nod. He'd known I was there. He'd tracked my movement from the first time I'd fired. I nodded back. We both realized he'd used me. He'd given me enough light and enough time to take the shot and banked on me hitting the target. I wasn't an expert marksman. With less time to line up the shot I might have missed. But I knew enough to hit two stationary targets, both of which hadn't seen me first. Maybe he knew what I could do. Maybe he'd read what the police had on file about me. Or maybe he'd just taken a chance. Either way it had worked.

Movement to my left. I swivelled.

Crane was up and on his feet, sprinting away.

I headed after him, bending down to pick up the torch lying next to the dead PC's face. The burnt, nauseating stench of gunfire drifted along the trail, and there was the tang of blood in the air, thick and fresh. Crane looked back at me, then veered right, into the woods. I followed. I shone the torch out in front of me and saw him about fifteen feet ahead, my heart thumping in my ears, my hands greased with sweat and rain. He was trying to get some distance between us. Trying to pull away. Trying to lose me and fade into the night. But without a torch, the woods were like a maze.

A second later he fell.

Out of the night, a huge oak tree emerged, springing from the dark like a wall of wood. He clipped it with his shoulder as he went to avoid it. Stumbled. Shifted to his left. As he tried to stop himself from falling, a bramble grasped at his foot, reaching up from the forest floor. He lurched forward and toppled over, hitting the ground hard, the wind thumped out of him, his wrists – locked together – catching under his body. He rolled over, looking up, breath forming in front of his face.

For a moment, he couldn't focus. He stared up in my direction but slightly off to the side. Then he rocked his head from left to right, his eyelids fluttered and he readjusted. His eyes fixed on me. I shone the torch down at him, off to the side of his face, so he could see me as clearly as the darkness of the woods would allow.

'Who were they?' I said.

'Russians.' He coughed then smiled, blood and saliva smeared across his teeth. 'They were scared about what I might be forced to tell the cops. They can get to me in prison. But they can't get to me in a police station. So I made a deal.'

'A deal?'

'The Ghost needs his face doing again. He's paranoid. Thinks the police are closing in on him the whole time.' He paused, ran his tongue across his teeth. 'So I told his people that if he got me out of this, I could delay the police – and I'd do Gobulev's face for free.'

'This was about a *facelift*?'

'No, David,' he said. 'This was about protection. Have you any idea how valuable I am to the police? Have you any idea how much I've *seen*? The Russians were taking out an insurance policy. And anyway, how many plastic surgeons do you think there are in this country willing to work for people like Gobulev?' He paused. 'I'm the star witness. I'm the key. I'm *God*.'

A trickle of blood escaped from his lips and ran down his face. He reached up with his handcuffed wrists and brushed it away. It smeared across the scar on his chin.

'How did they know?' I asked him.

'Let's just say, when I asked for a phone call, I didn't call my lawyer.'

As I stared at Crane, a wind whipped across us, passing through grass and bushes and leaves, as cold as a sheet of ice. A gentle whisper followed in its wake; a far-off noise like a voice repeating itself over and over again.

From the ground, Crane studied me. 'You can feel it.'

'I don't feel anything.'

'But you knew what I was talking about.' In the light from the torch, his eyes widened in delight, flicking back and forth across my face. 'It has a power, this place. All the secrets, the lies, the death, the destruction. It leaves its mark.'

'You're done,' I said quietly.

He shook his head. 'I'm not done yet, David.'

I looked at him, studied him, his eyes flashing

in the subtle glow of the torchlight. I brought the MP5 around and placed it against his head. His eyes crossed for a moment, focusing on the barrel above his eyes. Then he looked back at me.

'We're the same,' he whispered.

My fingers touched the trigger. My left hand squeezed the barrel. The stock cut in against my shoulder. All this misery. All this pain. If I pulled the trigger now, no one would cry for him. No one would miss him. He'd be buried in a cemetery somewhere with no one at his graveside. If I pulled the trigger, no one would mourn him.

'We're the same, David.'

But if I pulled the trigger, he'd be right.

I moved the MP5 away from his face and tossed it into the undergrowth behind me. His expression dissolved. He thought he'd still been in control, even as he looked down the barrel of the gun. He thought we were the same. But we'd never be the same.

Not now. Not ever.

'You were right about me,' I said to him quietly. 'I've killed. But I did it to survive. I did it because the alternative was dying myself. And there hasn't been a day that's gone by – not a single day – I haven't wished I could have done it differently, even though the people I hurt were men just like you: men who feel nothing when they take a life. There's not been a single day when I don't think about what I've done. So you can hunt me, and you can torture me, and you can try to kill me.

And one day, who knows, maybe one of you will succeed.' I reached down, grabbed his collar and pulled him to his feet. 'But don't *ever* say we're the same. Because you'll never understand me. You'll never know who I am. And we'll never be the same.'

And then I led Aron Crane back through the darkness of the Dead Tracks.

CHAPTER 76

Three weeks later, police were still trying to unravel the lie that was Aron Crane's life: his wife, his child, his victims, his reasons. The six women he'd left floating in formalin were there for reference. He could have buried them in the ground like Milton Sykes had, but as he got closer to working on Megan, he needed to be able to refer to the problems he'd encountered during surgery, and the mistakes he'd made along the way.

To start, as had been the case when he was first arrested, he refused to talk. But he did open up a little eventually. Police brought in the best psychologist they could find and he worked some details out of Crane. Small details, like how he pushed his wife Phedra off the decking on the top of his house. Whatever his reasoning, the psychologist failed to illicit any emotion from Crane about the moment he leaned over the railings and looked down at his dead wife, pregnant with his child. Any sign he missed her, or regretted what he'd done. He buried them in the woods, and in all the time people tried chipping away at him, it proved the only chink in his armour. The only way to get him to talk. Crane may have been a wall of silence, but Phedra was the tiny hole that would never seal over.

He pleaded guilty to murdering the six women he preserved in formalin, killing Susan Markham and kidnapping Megan, Jill and Sona, but said virtually nothing during the trial, other than to confirm his name. After four days, the jury found him guilty and he was given seven life sentences, to run concurrently. I watched the news every day during that time, waiting to see an egotistical flash, or hear how he'd smiled at jurors while recounting the horrific things that he'd done. But reporters always described him as subdued, and after a while I realized – without his project, without the opportunity to move from one stage to the next – he had nothing left. When he was even incapable of expressing any regret over what he'd done to his wife and child, it was obvious there were no hidden depths to him. Nothing else to his make-up. With no control and no power, there was no Aron Crane.

After the search of the Dead Tracks was completed, a smaller forensic team went over the burial site Crane had discovered to recover what was left of the thirteen women Milton Sykes had murdered. They found twelve. The thirteenth grave had animal bones in it, but no human remains. Even before an anthropologist had got close to the bodies, I knew what their conclusions would be.

Sykes knew the woods better than anyone: the tiny ravines, the trails, the clearings, the hiding places. He'd lived on its edges all his life. Crane had lucked out by finding the twelve Indian women, but inside those fifty acres, tied to the roots of the place, Jenny Truman would remain hidden. And as long as she lay hidden, maybe there would always be a feel to its paths. A sense that something was trying to get away, to claw its way out of the ground and finally find peace.

The investigation into Russian organized crime continued after Crane was sentenced, and police visited him frequently in prison in the months after, trying to build a case. No one outside the task force knew how much Crane was willing to play ball, or how much he even really knew, but I heard from a couple of people that the prison service had rolled out an unofficial protection detail on the advice of the police – to prevent Crane being got at on the inside – and that they were closer to Akim Gobulev than they'd ever been.

Maybe that was true. But I hoped, most days, the police remembered the sacrifice they'd made to get there. Six dead women, including Leanne. Three more – Megan, Sona and Jill – lucky to be alive. Susan Markham. And then Crane's own wife and child.

Eventually, I went to visit Jill at home. She still had heavy bandaging around the top of her forehead where surgeons had sewn her skin back on to her scalp. But otherwise she looked good. Minimal bruising. Little visible damage. She made some coffee while I stood at the kitchen door listening to her description of the night the man she thought was Aron Crane had come for her.

As we talked, she played with the St Michael pendant at her neck, occasionally glancing at the photographs of her husband looking down at us from the mantelpiece. I saw a lot of myself in her at that moment; having to remind herself over and over that the one person she could rely on, the one person she could trust most in this world, was gone for good. And as I left her house and walked to my car, I realized – after what Crane had done to her – it might be a long time before she gained enough distance to trust again.

Megan was discharged at the same time as Jill. She'd suffered bumps and bruises but the baby was fine. James and Caroline Carver picked her up at the hospital, crying among a scrum of photographers as they walked her back to the car. Soon Megan was crying too. She told them she was sorry for the secrets she'd kept, and sorry for ever believing Daniel Markham. When they got home, the tears stopped for a while as the Carvers told her everything that had happened while she'd been gone. And then they took their pregnant daughter back upstairs to her bedroom and the Carvers – James, Caroline and Megan – spent ten minutes on the edge of her bed, holding each other, while Leigh played on the floor beside them.

Megan gave birth to a baby girl a week early. They called her Faith. She wouldn't ever know her father, and – given everything he had done – maybe that was for the best. But, one day, Megan might tell her of the things she'd had to endure to bring her daughter into the world – and how it was worth every moment of the doubt and fear she'd experienced along the way.

The Healy family finally buried Leanne on 3 November. It was a big Catholic ceremony in a huge church near their home in St Albans. The Irish side of the family flew over from Cork, packing the aisles at the front, and Leanne's friends filled out the middle. I sat at the back next to Phillips, Chief Superintendent Bartholomew and a couple of other members of the task force who had helped Healy, in those first few weeks after her disappearance, to try and find Leanne.

Until the shoot-out at the woods, Healy wouldn't have wanted Phillips there, and Phillips wouldn't have come. But in the bullet Phillips had taken in the leg, and in the wounds Healy had taken in his chest, they had some common ground. As well as that, Phillips had agreed to stand as a character witness for Healy at his review hearing. It was a selfish gesture in many ways, there as a way to prevent Healy from talking publicly about everything the task force had kept suppressed. But Phillips was highly rated and it would look good for Healy to have him there. At the wake afterwards, they talked uncomfortably for a while – Phillips signed off on sick for a month; Healy indefinitely suspended pending a review by the Directorate of Professional Standards – and then Phillips hobbled away on crutches and headed back down to London.

Most of the others who'd been there with us that night weren't so lucky. Jamie Hart had spent his first three days rigged up to life support after a bullet perforated his lung and lodged in his throat. Forty-eight hours later, his wife decided to turn the machine off. Three uniformed officers had also been killed, and the paramedic died on arrival at Whitechapel. The SFO who had provided the cover for me had taken a bullet, but survived, and so had one of the dog handlers. Aron Crane might not have fired the guns, but he was responsible for a bloodbath.

When the sun started falling in the sky, I left the wake and walked back across Verulamium Park to my car. As I started the engine, I looked up and saw Gemma Healy coming across the grass towards my BMW. She was in her late forties, but wore it pretty well: dark hair, a petite frame, tiny creases funnelling out from green eyes, and a strength and assurance in her movements that suggested she'd known pain and handled it better than her husband. For a moment, I thought she was heading to the church. But then she continued towards me and waited while I buzzed the window down.

'Hello,' she said softly. She also had an Irish accent, stronger than her husband's. 'We've never met before, but I know who you are.'

I smiled. 'I'm not sure if that's a good or a bad thing.'

'It's good,' she replied, and managed a smile. 'I just wanted to thank you for what you've done. Away from my husband.' She paused, corrected herself. '*Ex* husband.'

'I don't understand.'

'He needed you. He needed someone strong to rein in his excesses. I don't know what you found in that place, and I don't *want* to know. But I was married to Colm for long enough to know that, in order for you to get him there, in order to contain him, you would have had to have been strong enough to face down his arrogance, his anger and his resentment. And as I can tell you from personal experience, that takes some doing.'

I nodded, not entirely sure how to respond.

'So thank you,' she added quietly.

She went to walk away, and, as she did, I killed the engine. She looked back at me, brow furrowed, eyes moving back and forth across my face.

'Has he ever told you why he did it?'

She knew what I meant. Subconsciously she reached to the spot on her face that he must have struck, and brushed it with a couple of fingers. Then she shook her head.

'It wasn't the affair,' I said, and watched colour

briefly fill her cheeks. 'It was the fact that he thought everyone had turned their backs on him.'

'He still shouldn't have done it.'

'I totally agree.'

'And I can't forgive him.'

I let her know that I understood that too. 'I know why you walked away from him. I even know why you did what you did. But the isolation you felt before you made that decision, that's what he felt in those last few months. That's what he felt when we were looking for your daughter. You hated him. Leanne hated him. He had a case that completely consumed him. But he bottled it up and he pushed it down, and something had to give. I'm not saying it's right, I'm just saying that, if you felt he'd turned his back on you, then I think he might have felt the same.'

She studied me, but didn't say anything.

'I'm sorry,' I said. 'This is none of my business.'

'No,' she said, and held up a hand in front of her. 'It's fine. I just . . . the Colm you're telling me about isn't the Colm I've come to know over the past year.'

I told her that I understood, and started up the car.

Gemma studied me, as if she was about to ask me something, but then turned on her heel and started walking away. After about five paces, she stopped and looked back at me. 'How long does it take?' she asked gently.

I looked at her, her eyes glistening in the half-light of the evening. Healy had asked me the same question two days before, and I wondered why they would both think I had the answer. Perhaps I still carried a sadness around with me, a stain in the fabric of my skin. Or perhaps they saw faint signs of hope, of recovery. A man who had been through the darkness and was standing in the light at the other end.

'You say goodbye to them eventually,' I replied, the sun disappearing beyond a copse of trees behind us. 'But, the truth is . . . you never let them go.'

CHAPTER 77

The sound of the shower woke me at six-thirty. As I slowly stirred, I lay on my back and looked up at the ceiling, steam crawling out through the partially open bathroom door. The bed was empty and the bedroom was cold. I pulled the duvet up and rolled over, studying the photograph of Derryn on my side table. I knew every inch of her face so well: the shape of her eyes, the way her mouth turned up when she smiled, the pattern of her freckles, the curve of her body. Next to the frame was a black coffee, steam rising from inside the mug.

The shower stopped.

I sat up, sipped on the coffee and watched through the gap in the door. The noise of the shower door opening. An arm reaching to the rail for a towel. One side of a body, water droplets running down the skin, tracing the waist and the hips.

Outside, rain spat against the window.

I glanced at the picture of Derryn again and then went to the window. The first pinpricks of day pierced a smear of cloud beyond the houses opposite. I pulled on a pair of boxers and watched one of my neighbours filling his car full of junk. When he was done, his wife came down the drive to him, kissed him, and watched him pull out and disappear along the road.

'Morning.'

I turned. Liz was standing looking at me, a towel around her, her hair darkened by water and sitting against one of her shoulders like a thick tail.

'Morning,' I said, smiling, and held up the coffee. 'Thanks.'

'You're welcome.' She moved around to my side of the bed, then perched herself on the edge. I sat down next to her. 'How are you feeling?' she asked.

I looked at her. She blinked, a little water breaking free from her hairline and running down her cheek.

'I feel good. You?'

She nodded. 'Sorry it's so early.'

'Are you in court today?'

'No,' she said, her eyes moving across my face. 'I'm driving up to Warwick to see Katie again. She's meeting with an investment bank about a graduate programme next week. I'll give her the old mum-to-daughter pep talk and then we'll probably head into Birmingham and go shopping.'

'You excited about seeing her again?'

'Very.'

I remembered the photographs of them I'd seen at Liz's. Katie looked a lot like her mum. She was also beautiful, except with even longer, darker hair.

'I'm sorry.'

I looked at Liz. 'For what?'

595

'For just having to leave like this.'

'You're not just leaving,' I said. 'You're leaving to see your daughter. That's the best kind of excuse.' I took another sip of coffee. 'And in any case, this is a mean cup of coffee to depart on.'

She leaned into me and kissed me. When she moved away again, her eyes were fixed on mine. She looked like she was expecting me to flinch.

'I don't regret what we did,' I said.

'Are you sure?'

More water ran down her face. She placed a hand on my leg, studying me, looking for signs of uncertainty.

'Derryn was a part of my life for fifteen years,' I said, placing my hand on hers. 'She was the first woman I loved, the only thing that ever really mattered to me during the time we were together. If you're asking me if there'll be moments to begin with when I'm a little unsure of myself, or feel like things are maybe moving too fast, then yes, there *will* be moments like that. But if you're asking me if I regret what we did, if I regret spending the night with you, then no. I don't. You've waited for me, and supported me, and comforted me. You've been there for me. I don't regret what I've done.'

Her eyes shimmered a little.

I touched a hand to her face, where a trail of water had worked its way down past her ear, to her neck. 'Like I told you yesterday, you don't have to compete with her.'

'Okay,' she said softly.

'I will always love Derryn,' I said. 'A part of me will always love her, whatever happens.'

She nodded.

'But . . .' I paused and looked into her eyes. 'I'm tired of feeling lonely. I'm tired of being scared of letting go. I'm tired of looking at her in pictures and feeling guilt choking me up when I think about moving on. I feel *guilt*, and yet Derryn never laid any guilt at my door. She would never have expected me to spend my life trying to cling on to every memory I have of her. That wasn't who she was. If she could see the way I'd been for almost two years, sitting alone in this house, feeling terrified about moving on . . . she would never have forgiven me. She would have wanted me to take the next step.'

I ran a hand through Liz's hair and then leaned in and kissed her.

'So, that's exactly what I'm going to do . . .'

Later, as I watched Liz's car disappear into the rain, I thought about what she'd said to me. *You're trying to plug holes in the world because you know what it's like to lose someone, and you think it's your job to stop anyone else suffering the same way.*

She'd been right.

She saw it in me, even before I saw it in myself. She understood that the reason I let Derryn talk me into taking on that first case was because I could see what was happening to her, could see the end coming, and I didn't want anyone else to suffer like I had. The loss. The helplessness. The inevitability. I wanted to help families turn their lives around, to punch through the darkness to the light on the other side.

And then, finally, bring the people that mattered to them back from the dead.

AUTHOR'S NOTE

Anyone even remotely familiar with London geography will know that I've taken some liberties in *The Dead Tracks*. I hope the residents of east London will forgive me for making their home the hunting ground for a notorious Victorian serial killer and a crazed plastic surgeon. Plainly, the woods, and the factories that surround it, don't actually exist.